A Daughter of the Snows

The Fitzroy Edition of the Works of
JACK LONDON
—

THE CRUISE OF THE 'DAZZLER'
THE SON OF THE WOLF
A DAUGHTER OF THE SNOWS
THE PEOPLE OF THE ABYSS

JACK LONDON

A Daughter of the Snows

Edited and introduced by
I. O. EVANS
F. R. G. S.

NEW YORK
ARCHER HOUSE INC.

First published by Archer House Inc. 1963
Printed in Great Britain by
Bristol Typesetting Company Limited
Bristol

INTRODUCTION

In 1897, Jack London left a blind alley job and joined the Klondike Gold Rush in order to earn enough money to get married. He enjoyed some remarkable adventures and, though he failed to bring back any gold, his venture was well worth while. He brought back enough local colour and other first-hand material to make his name as the author of a number of brilliant adventure stories.

Himself a man of action, delighting in fist-fights and hair-breadth escapes, and ready to face cheerfully the most appalling hardships, he was also a man of letters. Largely self-educated, he gave himself not only a wide field of information but a great love of literature—his favourite author was Kipling—and these enabled him to entertain his fellow-prospectors not only by spinning yarns but by lending them copies of such works as *The Origin of Species* and *Paradise Lost*. Unlikely though they may seem, the literary and cultural interests with which he endows his leading characters have a factual basis.

The circumstances in which he developed the political philosophy which inspired his life and which earned him the nickname of ' The Boy Socialist ' are described in the Introduction to his grim account of life in the slums of East London, *The People of the Abyss*.* An old prospector who during a blizzard sought refuge in Jack London's cabin was amazed to find it filled with tobacco-smoke and crowded with passionate men, gesticulating and arguing at the tops of their voices; when he realised what they were arguing about, he said later, he thought he must be delirious—of all improbable subjects, it was Socialism!

His political standpoint enabled Jack London to understand the deep significance of the gold-rush, and to realise its effects not only upon the gold-seekers but upon the hitherto unspoiled natives of the region; this gives body to his narrative, making it more than a mere adventure story with a romantic interest. Like so many of his other works,

*Also included in the Fitzroy Edition.

5

it is coloured by his own philosophy; his aim was not only to interest and enthrall his readers but to make them think.

Socialist though he was, he had no faith in the innate equality of man; his study of evolution had made him believe in the struggle for existence and the survival of the fittest. In the Klondike the struggle was at its most intense and only the very fittest could survive, and Jack London held that these were almost exclusively to be found among the peoples hailing from Western Europe. He was deeply impressed with the exploits of the Norsemen of old, and Du Chaillu's *The Viking Age* was among his most treasured books. Their descendants, of whom he claimed to be one, were to his mind destined to dominate the earth and to rule such 'lesser breeds' as the Amerindians, the Negroes, the Mongolians, and, probably, the Slavs. It will be seen how he puts this belief into the mouth of his heroine, and how it is echoed by his hero.

Though this heroine is probably the weakest character in the book, she is one of the most clearly-drawn of all Jack London's female characters. He was an adept at describing adventurous menfolk; his most convincing women belong to the working class whom he knew so well and esteemed to highly. When he tried to depict women of a higher social status he was apt not to draw from life but simply to use his imagination.

His reading of Nietzsche had convinced London that he was not only a modern Viking but a superman, able to out-fight, out-work and out-drink his contemporaries—and also to out-wench them. Though it was his proud claim that his amours were all above-board, that he had never seduced a confiding girl or wooed any woman by spurious preten-sions of love, he delighted in sheer physical pleasure.

He was in short, a libertine, though a libertine with a conscience. And like many libertines, he had at the back of his mind the ideal of a pure woman who would be above mere amorous adventure.

Yet his ideal woman was no mere virtuous Victorian miss; he sought as his mate an outdoor woman, with a love of adventure which would enable her to join with him in the outdoor exploits in which he revelled. He wanted her, too, to be well-educated and cultured, able to share in his intellectual interests, and with a love of social justice as passionate as his own. Finally, he wanted her to be a competent housewife who would give him a home and a mother who would bear him a son.

It goes without saying that he never found her. His first love was a virtuous, idealistic, and cultured girl, but she had no taste for adventure, and sheer poverty made him give her up. His first wife was well-educated and competent, but he had never really cared deeply for her—he had married her, says his biographer Irving Stone, on a basis of liking and respect and the wish for fine children. Finding that she only gave him two daughters and not the son on which he had set his heart, he forsook her almost at a moment's notice. His second wife was as daring and adventurous as he could wish, but she was utterly incompetent at running a home. And she too failed to give him a son.

In Frona Welse, heroine of *A Daughter of the Snows,* Jack London has immortalised the dream-wife of his imagination, whom he longed for all his life, but whom he failed to find.

I.O.E.

CHAPTER I

'ALL ready, Miss Welse, though I'm sorry we can't spare one of the steamer's boats.'

Frona Welse arose with alacrity and came to the first officer's side.

'We're so busy,' he explained, 'and gold-rushers are such perishable freight, at least—'

'I understand,' she interrupted, 'and I, too, am behaving as though I were perishable. And I am sorry for the trouble I am giving you, but—but—' She turned quickly and pointed to the shore. 'Do you see that big log-house? Between the clump of pines and the river? I was born there.'

'Guess I'd be in a hurry myself,' he muttered, sympathetically, as he piloted her along the crowded deck.

Everybody was in everybody else's way; nor was there one who failed to proclaim it at the top of his lungs. A thousand gold-seekers were clamouring for the immediate landing of their outfits. Each hatchway gaped wide open, and from the lower depths the shrieking donkey-engines were hurrying the misassorted outfits skyward. On either side of the steamer, rows of scows received the flying cargo, and on each of these scows a sweating mob of men charged the descending slings and heaved bales and boxes about in frantic search. Men waved shipping receipts and shouted over the steamer-rails to them. Sometimes two and three identified the same article, and war arose. The 'two-circle' and the 'circle and dot' brands caused endless jangling, while every whipsaw discovered a dozen claimants.

'The purser insists that he is going mad,' the first officer said, as he helped Frona Welse down the gangway to the landing stage, 'and the freight clerks have turned the cargo over to the passengers and quit work. But we're not so unlucky as the *Star of Bethlehem*,' he reassured her, pointing to a steamship at anchor a quarter of a mile away. 'Half of her passengers have pack-horses for Skaguay and White

Pass, and the other half are bound over the Chilcoot. So they've mutinied and everything's at a standstill.'

'Hey, you!' he cried, beckoning to a Whitehall which hovered discreetly on the outer rim of the floating confusion.

A tiny launch, pulling heroically at a huge tow-barge, attempted to pass between; but the boatman shot nervily across her bow, and just as he was clear, unfortunately, caught a crab. This slewed the boat around and brought it to a stop.

'Watch out!' the first officer shouted.

A pair of seventy-foot canoes, loaded with outfits, gold-rushers, and Indians, and under full sail, drove down from the counter direction. One of them veered sharply towards the landing stage, but the other pinched the Whitehall against the barge. The boatman had unshipped his oars in time, but his small craft groaned under the pressure and threatened to collapse. Whereat he came to his feet, and in short, nervous phrases consigned all canoe-men and launch-captains to eternal perdition. A man on the barge leaned over from above and baptised him with crisp and crackling oaths, while the whites and Indians in the canoe laughed derisively.

'Aw, g'wan!' one of them shouted. 'Why don't yeh learn to row?'

The boatman's fist landed on the point of his critic's jaw and dropped him stunned upon the heaped merchandise. Not content with this summary act he proceeded to follow his fist into the other craft. The miner nearest him tugged vigorously at a revolver which had jammed in its shiny leather holster, while his brother argonauts, laughing, waited the outcome. But the canoe was under way again, and the Indian helmsman drove the point of his paddle into the boatman's chest and hurled him backward into the bottom of the Whitehall.

When the flood of oaths and blasphemy was at full tide, and violent assault and quick death seemed most imminent, the first officer had stolen a glance at the girl by his side. He had expected to find a shocked and frightened maiden countenance, and was not at all prepared for the flushed and deeply interested face which met his eyes.

'I am sorry,' he began.

But she broke in, as though annoyed by the interruption, 'No, no; not at all. I am enjoying it every bit. Though I am glad that man's revolver stuck. If it had not—'

'We might have been delayed in getting ashore.' The first officer laughed, and therein displayed his tact.

'That man is a robber,' he went on, indicating the boatman, who had now shoved his oars into the water and was pulling alongside. 'He agreed to charge only twenty dollars for putting you ashore. Said he'd have made it twenty-five had it been a man. He's a pirate, mark me, and he will surely hang some day. Twenty dollars for a half hour's work! Think of it!'

'Easy, sport! Easy!' cautioned the fellow in question, at the same time making an awkward landing and dropping one of his oars over-side. 'You've no call to be flingin' names about,' he added, defiantly, wringing out his shirtsleeve, wet from rescue of the oar.

'You've got good ears, my man,' began the first officer.

'And a quick fist,' the other snapped in.

'And a ready tongue.'

'Need it in my business. No gettin' 'long without it among you sea-sharks. Pirate, am I? And you with a thousand passengers packed like sardines! Charge 'em double first-class passage, feed 'em steerage grub, and bunk 'em worse 'n pigs! Pirate, eh! Me?'

A red-faced man thrust his head over the rail above and began to bellow lustily.

'I want my stock landed! Come up here, Mr Thurston! Now! right away! Fifty cayuses of mine eating their heads off in this dirty kennel of yours, and it'll be a sick time you'll have if you don't hustle them ashore as fast as God'll let you! I'm losing a thousand dollars a day, and I won't stand it! Do you hear? I won't stand it! You've robbed me right and left from the time you cleared dock in Seattle, and by the hinges of hell I won't stand it any more! I'll break this company as sure as my name's Thad Ferguson! D'you hear my spiel? I'm Thad Ferguson, and you can't come and see me any too quick for your health! D'ye hear?'

'Pirate, eh?' the boatman soliloquised. 'Who? Me?'

Mr. Thurston waved his hand appeasingly at the red-faced man, and turned to the girl. 'I'd like to go ashore with you, and as far as the store, but you see how busy we are. Good-bye, and a lucky trip to you. I'll tell off a couple of men at once and break out your baggage. Have it up at the store tomorrow morning, sharp."

She took his hand lightly and stepped aboard. Her weight gave the leaky boat a sudden lurch, and the water hurtled across the bottom boards to her shoe-tops; but she took it coolly enough, settling herself in the stern-sheets and tucking her feet under her.

'Hold on!' the officer cried. 'This will never do, Miss Welse. Come on back, and I'll get one of our boats over as soon as I can."

'I'll see you in—in heaven first,' retorted the boatman, shoving off. 'Let go!' he threatened.

Mr. Thurston gripped tight hold of the gunwale, and as reward for his chivalry had his knuckles rapped sharply by the oar-blade. Then he forgot himself, and Miss Welse also, and swore, and swore fervently.

'I dare say our farewell might have been more dignified,' she called back to him, her laughter rippling across the water.

'Jove!' he muttered, doffing his cap gallantly. 'There is a *woman*!' And a sudden hunger seized him, and a yearning to see himself mirrored always in the grey eyes of Frona Welse. He was not analytical; he did not know why; but he knew that with her he could travel to the end of the earth. He felt a distaste for his profession, and a temptation to throw it all over and strike out for the Klondike whither she was going; then he glanced up the beetling side of the ship, saw the red face of Thad Ferguson, and forgot the dream he had for an instant dreamed.

Splash! A handful of water from his strenuous oar struck her full in the face. 'Hope you don't mind it, miss,' he apologised. 'I'm doin' the best I know how, which ain't much.'

'So it seems,' she answered, good-naturedly.

'Not that I love the sea,' bitterly; 'but I've got to turn a few honest dollars somehow, and this seemed the likeliest way. I oughter 'a ben in Klondike by now, if I'd had any luck at all. Tell you how it was. I lost my outfit on Windy Arm, half way in, after packin' it clean across the Pass—'

Zip! Splash! She shook the water from her eyes, squirming the while as some of it ran down her warm back.

'You'll do,' he encouraged her. 'You're the right stuff for this country. Goin' all the way in?'

She nodded cheerfully.

'Then you'll do. But as I was sayin', after I lost my outfit I hit back for the coast, bein' broke to hustle up another one. That's why I'm chargin' high-pressure rates. And I hope you don't feel sore at what I made you pay. I'm no worse than the rest, miss, sure. I had to dig up a hundred for this old tub, which ain't worth ten down in the States. Same kind of prices everywhere. Over on the Skaguay Trail horseshoe nails is just as good as a quarter any day. A man goes up to the bar and calls for a whisky. Whisky's half a dollar. Well, he drinks his whisky, plunks down two horseshoe nails, and it's O.K. No kick comin' on horseshoe nails. They use 'em to make change.'

'You must be a brave man to venture into the country again after such an experience. Won't you tell me your name? We may meet on the Inside.'

'Who? Me? Oh, I'm Del Bishop, pocket-miner; and if ever we run across each other, remember, I'd give you the last shirt—I mean, remember my last bit of grub is yours.'

'Thank you,' she answered with a sweet smile; for she was a woman who loved the things which rose straight from the heart.

He stopped rowing long enough to fish about in the water around his feet for an old cornbeef can.

'You'd better do some bailin',' he ordered, tossing her the can. 'She's leakin' worse since that squeeze.'

Frona smiled mentally, tucked up her skirts, and bent to the work. At every dip, like great billows heaving along the sky-line, the glacier-fretted mountains rose and fell. Sometimes she rested her back and watched the teeming beach towards which they were heading, and again, the land-locked arm of the sea in which a score or so of great steamships lay at anchor. From each of these, to the shore and back again, flowed a steady stream of scows, launches, canoes, and all sorts of smaller craft. Man, the mighty toiler, reacting upon a hostile environment, she thought, going back in memory to the masters whose wisdom she had shared in lecture-room and midnight study. She was a ripened child of the age, and fairly understood the physical world and the workings thereof. And she had a love for the world, and a deep respect.

For some time Del Bishop had only punctuated the silence with splashes from his oars; but a thought struck him.

'You haven't told me your name,' he suggested, with complacent delicacy.

'My name is Welse,' she answered. 'Frona Welse.'

A great awe manifested itself in his face, and grew to a greater and greater awe. 'You—are—Frona—Welse?' he enunciated slowly. 'Jacob Welse ain't your old man, is he?'

'Yes; I am Jacob Welse's daughter, at your service.'

He puckered his lips in a long low whistle of under-standing and stopped rowing. 'Just you climb back into the stern and take your feet out of that water,' he com-manded. 'And gimme holt that can.'

'Am I not bailing satisfactorily?' she demanded, indig-nantly.

'Yep. You're doin' all right; but, but, you are—are—'

'Just what I was before you knew who I was. Now you go on rowing—that's your share of the work; and I'll take care of mine.'

'Oh, you'll do!' he murmured ecstatically, bending afresh to the oars. 'And Jacob Welse is your old man? I oughter 'a known it, sure!'

When they reached the sand-spit, crowded with hetero-geneous piles of merchandise and buzzing with men, she stopped long enough to shake hands with her ferryman. And though such a proceeding on the part of his feminine patrons was certainly unusual, Del Bishop squared it easily with the fact that she was Jacob Welse's daughter.

'Remember, my last bit of grub is yours,' he reassured her, still holding her hand.

'And your last shirt, too; don't forget.'

14

' Well, you're a—a—a crackerjack!' he exploded with a final squeeze. ' Sure!'

Her short skirt did not block the free movement of her limbs, and she discovered with pleasurable surprise that the quick tripping step of the city pavement had departed from her, and that she was swinging off in the long easy stride which is born of the trail and which comes only after much travail and endeavour. More than one gold-rusher, shooting keen glances at her ankles and grey-gaitered calves, affirmed Del Bishop's judgment. And more than one glanced up at her face, and glanced again; for her gaze was frank, with the frankness of comradeship; and in her eyes there was always a smiling light, just trembling on the verge of dawn; and did the onlooker smile, her eyes smiled also. And the smiling light was protean-mooded,—merry, sympathetic, joyous, quizzical,—the complement of whatsoever kindled it. And sometimes the light spread over all her face, till the smile prefigured by it was realised. But it was always in frank and open comradeship.

And there was much to cause her to smile as she hurried through the crowd, across the sand-spit, and over the flat towards the log-building she had pointed out to Mr. Thurston. Time had rolled back, and locomotion and transportation were once again in the most primitive stages. Men who had never carried more than parcels in all their lives had now become bearers of burdens. They no longer walked upright under the sun, but stooped the body forward and bowed the head to the earth. Every back had become a pack-saddle, and the strap-galls were beginning to form. They staggered beneath the unwonted effort, and legs became drunken with weariness and titubated in divers directions till the sunlight darkened and bearer and burden fell by the way. Other men, exulting secretly, piled their goods on two-wheeled go-carts and pulled out blithely enough, only to stall at the first spot where the great round boulders invaded the trail. Whereat they generalised anew upon the principles of Alaskan travel, discarded the go-cart, or trundled it back to the beach and sold it at fabulous price to the last man landed. Tenderfeet, with ten pounds of Colt's revolvers, cartridges, and hunting-knives belted about them, wandered valiantly up the trail, and crept back

15

softly, shedding revolvers, cartridges, and knives in despairing showers. And so, in gasping and bitter sweat, these sons of Adam suffered for Adam's sin.

Frona felt vaguely disturbed by this great throbbing rush of gold-mad men, and the old scene with its clustering associations seemed blotted out by these toiling aliens. Even the old landmarks appeared strangely unfamiliar. It was the same, yet not the same. Here on the grassy flat, where she had played as a child and shrunk back at the sound of her voice echoing from glacier to glacier, ten thousand men tramped ceaselessly up and down, grinding the tender herbage into the soil and mocking the stony silence. And just up the trail were ten thousand men who had passed by, and over the Chilcoot were ten thousand more. And behind, all down the island-studded Alaskan coast, even to the Horn, were yet ten thousand more, harnessers of wind and steam, hasteners from the ends of the earth. The Dyea River as of old roared turbulently down to the sea; but its ancient banks were gored by the feet of many men, and these men laboured in surging rows at the dripping tow-lines, and the deep-laden boats followed them as they fought their upward way. And the will of man strove with the will of the water, and the men laughed at the old Dyea River and gored its banks deeper for the men who were to follow.

The doorway of the store, through which she had once run out and in, and where she had looked with awe at the unusual sight of a stray trapper or fur-trader, was now packed with a clamorous throng of men. Where of old one letter waiting a claimant was a thing of wonder, she now saw, by peering through the window, the mail heaped up from floor to ceiling. And it was for this mail the men were clamouring so insistently. Before the store, by the scales, was another crowd. An Indian threw his pack upon the scales, the white owner jotted down the weight in a notebook, and another pack was thrown on. Each pack was in the straps, ready for the packer's back and the precarious journey over the Chilcoot. Frona edged in closer. She was interested in freights. She remembered in her day when the solitary prospector or trader had his outfit packed over for six cents—one hundred and twenty dollars a ton.

The tenderfoot who was weighing up consulted his guidebook. 'Eight cents,' he said to the Indian. Whereupon the Indians laughed scornfully and chorused, 'Forty cents!' A pained expression came into his face, and he looked about him anxiously. The sympathetic light in Frona's eyes caught him, and he regarded her with intent blankness. In reality he was busy reducing a three-ton outfit to terms of cash at forty dollars per hundred-weight. 'Twenty-four hundred dollars for thirty miles!' he cried. 'What can I do?'

Frona shrugged her shoulders. 'You'd better pay them the forty cents,' she advised, 'else they will take off their straps.'

The man thanked her, but instead of taking heed went on with his haggling. One of the Indians stepped up and proceeded to unfasten his pack-straps. The tenderfoot wavered, but just as he was about to give in, the packers jumped the price on him to forty-five cents. He smiled after a sickly fashion, and nodded his head in token of surrender. But another Indian joined the group and began whispering excitedly. A cheer went up, and before the man could realise it they had jerked off their straps and departed, spreading the news as they went that freight to Lake Linderman was fifty cents.

Of a sudden, the crowd before the store was perceptibly agitated. Its members whispered excitedly one to another, and all their eyes were focused upon three men approaching from up the trail. The trio were ordinary-looking creatures, ill-clad and even ragged. In a more stable community their apprehension by the village constable and arrest for vagrancy would have been immediate. 'French Louis,' the tenderfeet whispered and passed the word along. 'Owns three Eldorado claims in a block,' the man next to Frona confided to her. 'Worth ten millions at the very least.' French Louis, striding a little in advance of his companions, did not look it. He had parted company with his hat somewhere along the route, and a frayed silk kerchief was wrapped carelessly about his head. And for all his ten millions, he carried his own travelling pack on his broad shoulders. 'And that one, the one with the beard, that's Swiftwater Bill, another of the Eldorado kings.'

'How do you know?' Frona asked, doubtingly.

17

'Know!' the man exclaimed. 'Know! Why his picture has been in all the papers for the last six weeks. See!' He unfolded a newspaper. 'And a pretty good likeness, too. I've looked at it so much I'd know his mug among a thousand.'

'Then who is the third one?' she queried, tacitly accepting him as a fount of authority.

Her informant lifted himself on his toes to see better. 'I don't know,' he confessed sorrowfully, then tapped the shoulder of the man next to him. 'Who is the lean, smooth-faced one? The one with the blue shirt and patch on his knee?'

Just then Frona uttered a glad little cry and darted forward. 'Matt!' she cried. 'Matt McCarthy!'

The man with the patch shook her hand heartily, though he did not know her and distrust was plain in his eyes.

'Oh, you don't remember me!' she chattered. 'And don't you dare say you do! If there weren't so many looking, I'd hug you, you old bear!

'And so Big Bear went home to the Little Bears,' she recited, solemnly. 'And the Little Bears were very hungry. And Big Bear said, "Guess what I have got, my children." And one Little Bear guessed berries, and one Little Bear guessed salmon, and t'other Little Bear guessed porcupine. Then Big Bear laughed "Whoof! Whoof!" and said, "*A Nice Big Fat Man!*"'

As he listened, recollection avowed itself in his face, and, when she had finished, his eyes wrinkled up and he laughed a peculiar, laughable silent laugh.

'Sure, an' it's well I know ye,' he explained; 'but for the life iv me I can't put me finger on ye.'

She pointed into the store and watched him anxiously.

'Now I have ye!' He drew back and looked her up and down, and his expression changed to disappointment. 'It cuddent be. I mistook ye. Ye cud niver a-lived in that shanty,' thrusting a thumb in the direction of the store.

Frona nodded her head vigorously.

'Thin it's yer ownself afther all? The little motherless darlin', with the goold hair I combed the knots out iv many's the time? The little witch that run barefoot an' barelegged over all the place?'

'Yes, yes,' she corroborated, gleefully.

'The little divil that stole the dog-team an' wint over the Pass in the dead o' winter for to see where the world come to an ind on the ither side, just because old Matt McCarthy was afther tellin' her fairy stories?'

'O Matt, dear old Matt! Remember the time I went swimming with the Siwash girls from the Indian camp?'

'An' I dragged ye out by the hair o' yer head?'

'And lost one of your new rubber boots?'

'Ah, an' sure an' I do. And a most shockin' an' immodest affair it was! An' the boots was worth tin dollars over yer father's counter.'

'And then you went away, over the Pass, to the Inside, and we never heard a word of you. Everybody thought you dead.'

'Well I recollect the day. An' ye cried in me arms an' wuddent kiss yer old Matt goodbye. But ye did in the ind,' he exclaimed, triumphantly, 'whin ye saw I was goin' to lave ye for sure. What a wee thing ye were!'

'I was only eight.'

'An' 'tis twelve year agone. Twelve year I've spint on the Inside, with niver a trip out. Ye must be twinty now?'

'And almost as big as you,' Frona affirmed.

'A likely woman ye've grown into, tall, an' shapely an' all that.' He looked her over critically. 'But ye cud 'a' stood a bit more flesh, I'm thinkin'.'

'No, no,' she denied. 'Not at twenty, Matt, not at twenty. Feel my arm, you'll see.' She doubled that member till the biceps knotted.

''Tis muscle,' he admitted, passing his hand admiringly over the swelling bunch; 'just as though ye'd been workin' hard for yer livin'.'

'Oh, I can swing clubs, and box, and fence,' she cried, successively striking the typical postures; 'and swim, and make high dives, chin a bar twenty times, and—and walk on my hands. There!'

'Is that what ye've been doin'? I thought ye wint away for book-larnin',' he commented, dryly.

'But they have new ways of teaching, now, Matt, and they don't turn you out with your head crammed—'

'An' yer legs that spindly they can't carry it all! Well, an' I forgive ye yer muscle.'

'But how about yourself, Matt?' Frona asked. 'How has the world been to you these twelve years?'

'Behold!' He spread his legs apart, threw his head back, and his chest out. 'Ye now behold Mister Matthew McCarthy, a king iv the noble Eldorado Dynasty by the strength iv his own right arm. Me possessions is limitless. I have more dust in wan minute than iver I saw in all me life before. Me intention for makin' this trip to the States is to look up me ancestors. I have a firm belafe that they wance existed. Ye may find nuggets in the Klondike, but niver good whisky. 'Tis likewise me intintion to have wan drink iv the rale stuff before I die. Afther that 'tis me sworn resolve to return to the superveeshion iv me Klondike properties. Indade, and I'm an Eldorado king; an' if ye'll be wantin' the lind iv a tidy bit, it's meself that'll loan it ye.'

'The same old, old Matt, who never grows old,' Frona laughed.

'An' it's yerself is the thrue Welse, for all yer prize-fighter's muscles an' yer philosopher's brains. But let's wander inside on the heels of Louis an' Swiftwater. Andy's still tindin' store, I'm told, an' we'll see if I still linger in the pages iv his mimory.'

'And I, also.' Frona seized him by the hand. It was a bad habit she had of seizing the hands of those she loved. 'It's ten years since I went away.'

The Irishman forged his way through the crowd like a pile-driver, and Frona followed easily in the lee of his bulk. The tenderfeet watched them reverently, for to them they were as Northland divinities. The buzz of conversation rose again.

'Who's the girl?' somebody asked. And just as Frona passed inside the door she caught the opening of the answer: 'Jacob Welse's daughter. Never heard of Jacob Welse? Where have you been keeping yourself?'

CHAPTER II

S H E came out of the wood of glistening birch, and with the first fires of the sun blazoning her unbound hair raced lightly across the dew-dripping meadow. The earth was fat with excessive moisture and soft to her feet, while the dank vegetation slapped against her knees and cast off flashing sprays of liquid diamonds. The flush of the morning was in her cheek, and its fire in her eyes, and she was aglow with youth and love. For she had nursed at the breast of nature —in forfeit of a mother—and she loved the old trees and the creeping green things with a passionate love; and the dim murmur of growing life was a gladness to her ears, and the damp earth-smells were sweet to her nostrils.

Where the upper reach of the meadow vanished in a dark and narrow forest ailse, amid clean-stemmed dandelions and colour-bursting buttercups, she came upon a bunch of great Alaskan violets. Throwing herself at full length, she buried her face in the fragrant coolness, and with her hands drew the purple heads in circling splendour about her own. And she was not ashamed. She had wandered away amid the complexities and smirch and withering heats of the great world, and she had returned, simple, and clean, and wholesome. And she was glad of it, as she lay there, slipping back to the old days, when the universe began and ended at the sky-line, and when she journeyed over the Pass to behold the Abyss.

It was a primitive life, that of her childhood, with few conventions, but such as there were, stern ones. And they might be epitomised, as she had read somewhere in her later years, as ' the faith of food and blanket.' This faith had her father kept, she thought, remembering that his name sounded well on the lips of men. And this was the faith she had learned—the faith she had carried with her across the Abyss and into the world, where men had wandered away from the old truths and made themselves selfish dogmas and casuistries of the subtlest kinds; the faith she had brought back with her, still fresh, and young, and joyous. And it was all so simple, she had contended; why should not their faith be as her faith—*the faith of food and blanket?* The faith of trail and hunting camp? The faith with which strong clean men faced the quick danger and sudden death by field and flood? Why not? The faith of Jacob Welse? Of Matt McCarthy? Of the Indian boys she had played with? Of the Indian girls she had led to Amazonian war? Of the very wolf-dogs straining in the harnesses and running with her across the snow? It was healthy, it was real, it was good, she thought, and she was glad.

The rich notes of a robin saluted her from the birch wood, and opened her ears to the day. A partridge boomed afar in the forest, and a tree-squirrel launched unerringly into space above her head, and went on, from limb to limb and tree to tree, scolding graciously the while. From the hidden river rose the shouts of the toiling adventurers, already parted from sleep and fighting their way towards the Pole.

Frona arose, shook back her hair, and took instinctively the old path between the trees to the camp of Chief George and the Dyea tribesmen. She came upon a boy, breech-clouted and bare, like a copper god. He was gathering wood, and looked at her keenly over his bronze shoulder. She bade him good morning, blithely, in the Dyea tongue; but he shook his head, and laughed insultingly, and paused in his work to hurl shameful words after her. She did not understand, for this was not the old way, and when she passed a great and glowering Sitkan buck she kept her tongue between her teeth. At the fringe of the forest, the camp confronted her. And she was startled. It was not the old camp of a score or more of lodges clustering and hud-dling together in the open as though for company, but a mighty camp. It began at the very forest, and flowed in and out among the scattered tree-clumps on the flat, and spilled over and down to the river bank where the long canoes were lined up ten and twelve deep. It was a gathering of the tribes, like unto none in all the past, and a thousand miles of coast made up the tally. They were all strange Indians, with wives and chattels and dogs. She rubbed shoulders with Juneau and Wrangel men, and was jostled

22

by wild-eyed Sticks from over the Passes, fierce Chilcats, and Queen Charlotte Islanders. And the looks they cast upon her were black and frowning, save—and far worse—where the merrier souls leered patronisingly into her face and chuckled unmentionable things.

She was not frightened by this insolence, but angered; for it hurt her, and embittered the pleasurable home-coming. Yet she quickly grasped the significance of it : the old patriarchal status of her father's time had passed away, and civilisation, in a scorching blast, had swept down upon this people in a day. Glancing under the raised flaps of a tent, she saw haggard-faced bucks squatting in a circle on the floor. By the door a heap of broken bottles advertised the vigils of the night. A white man, low of visage and shrewd, was dealing cards about, and gold and silver coins leaped into heaping bets upon the blanket board. A few steps farther on she heard the cluttering whirl of a wheel of fortune, and saw the Indians, men and women, chancing eagerly their sweat-earned wages for the gaudy prizes of the game. And from tepee and lodge rose the cracked and crazy strains of cheap music-boxes.

An old squaw, peeling a willow pole in the sunshine of an open doorway, raised her head and uttered a shrill cry.

'Hee-Hee! Tenas Hee-Hee!' she muttered as well and as excitedly as her toothless gums would permit.

Frona thrilled at the cry. Tenas Hee-Hee! Little Laughter! Her name of the long gone Indian past! She turned and went over to the old woman.

'And hast thou so soon forgotten, Tenas Hee-Hee?' she mumbled. 'And thine eyes so young and sharp! Not so soon does Neepoosa forget.'

'It is thou, Neepoosa?' Frona cried, her tongue halting from the disuse of years.

'Aye, it is Neepoosa,' the old woman replied, drawing her inside the tent, and despatching a boy, hot-footed, on some errand. They sat down together on the floor, and she patted Frona's hand lovingly, peering, meanwhile, blear-eyed and misty, into her face. 'Aye, it is Neepoosa, grown old quickly after the manner of our women. Neepoosa, who dandled thee in her arms when thou wast a child.

23

Neepoosa, who gave thee thy name, Tenas Hee-Hee. Who fought for thee with Death when thou wast ailing; and gathered growing things from the woods and grasses of the earth and made of them tea, and gave thee to drink. But I mark little change, for I knew thee at once. It was thy very shadow on the ground that made me lift my head. A little change, mayhap. Tall thou art, and like a slender willow in thy grace, and the sun has kissed thy cheeks more lightly of the years; but there is the old hair, flying wild and of the colour of the brown seaweed floating on the tide, and the mouth, quick to laugh and loth to cry. And the eyes are as clear and true as in the days when Neepoosa chid thee for wrong-doing, and thou wouldst not put false words upon thy tongue. Ai! Ai! Not as thou art the other women who come now into the land!'

'And why is a white woman without honour among you?' Frona demanded. 'Your men say evil things to me in the camp, and as I came through the woods, even the boys. Not in the old days, when I played with them, was this shame so.'

'Ai! Ai!' Neepoosa made answer. 'It is so. But do not blame them. Pour not thine anger upon their heads. For it is true it is the fault of thy women who come into the land these days. They can point to no man and say, "That is my man." And it is not good that women should be thus. And they look upon all men, bold-eyed and shameless, and their tongues are unclean, and their hearts bad. Wherefore are thy women without honour among us. As for the boys, they are but boys. And the men; how should they know?'

The tent-flaps were poked aside and an old man came in. He grunted to Frona and sat down. Only a certain eager alertness showed the delight he took in her presence.

'So Tenas Hee-Hee has come back in these bad days,' he vouchsafed in a shrill, quavering voice.

'And why bad days, Muskim?' Frona asked. 'Do not the women wear brighter colours? Are not the bellies fuller with flour and bacon and white man's grub? Do not the young men contrive great wealth what of their pack-straps and paddles? And art thou not remembered with the ancient offerings of meat and fish and blanket? Why bad days, Muskim?'

24

'True,' he replied in his fine, priestly way, a reminiscent flash of the old fire lighting his eyes. 'It is very true. The women wear brighter colours. But they have found favour in the eyes of thy white men, and they look no more upon the young men of their own blood. Wherefore the tribe does not increase, nor do the little children longer clutter the way of our feet. It is so. The bellies are fuller with the white man's grub; but also are they fuller with the white man's bad whisky. Nor could it be otherwise that the young men contrive great wealth; but they sit by night over the cards, and it passes from them, and they speak harsh words one to another, and in anger blows are struck, and there is bad blood between them. As for old Muskim, there are few offerings of meat and fish and blanket. For the young women have turned aside from the old paths, nor do the young men longer honour the old totems and the old gods. So these are bad days, Tenas Hee-Hee, and they behold old Muskim go down in sorrow to the grave.'

'Ai! Ai! It is so!' wailed Neepoosa.

'Because of the madness of thy people have my people become mad,' Muskim continued. 'They come over the salt sea like the waves of the sea, thy people, and they go —ah! who knoweth where?'

'Ai! Who knoweth where?' Neepoosa lamented, rocking slowly back and forth.

'Ever they go towards the frost and cold; and ever do they come, more people, wave upon wave!'

'Ai! Ai! Into the frost and cold! It is a long way, and dark and cold!' She shivered, then laid a sudden hand on Frona's arm. 'And thou goest?'

Frona nodded.

'And Tenas Hee-Hee goeth! Ai! Ai! Ai!'

The tent-flap lifted, and Matt McCarthy peered in. 'It's yerself, Frona, is it? With breakfast waitin' this half-hour on ye, an' old Andy fumin' an' frettin' like the old woman he is. Good mornin' to ye, Neepoosa,' he addressed Frona's companions, 'an' to ye, Muskim, though belike ye've little mimory iv me face.'

The old couple grunted salutation and remained stolidly silent.

'But hurry with ye, girl,' turning back to Frona. 'Me

steamer starts by mid-day, an' it's little I'll see iv ye at
the best. An' likewise there's Andy an' the breakfast pipin'
hot, both iv them.'

CHAPTER III

FRONA waved her hand to Andy and swung out on the trail. Fastened tightly to her back were her camera and a small travelling satchel. In addition, she carried for alpenstock the willow pole of Neepoosa. Her dress was of the mountaineering sort, short-skirted and scant, allowing the greatest play with the least material, and withal grey of colour and modest.

Her outfit, on the backs of a dozen Indians and in charge of Del Bishop, had got under way hours before. The previous day, on her return with Matt McCarthy from the Siwash camp, she had found Del Bishop at the store waiting her. His business was quickly transacted, for the proposition he made was terse and to the point. She was going into the country. He was intending to go in. She would need somebody. If she had not picked any one yet, why he was just the man. He had forgotten to tell her the day he took her ashore that he had been in the country years before and knew all about it. True, he hated the water, and it was mainly a water journey; but he was not afraid of it. He was afraid of nothing. Further, he would fight for her at the drop of the hat. As for pay, when they got to Dawson, a good word from her to Jacob Welse, and a year's outfit would be his. No, no; no grub-stake about it, no strings on him! He would pay for the outfit later on when his sack was dusted. What did she think about it, anyway? And Frona did think about it, for ere she had finished breakfast he was out hustling the packers together.

She found herself making better speed than the majority of her fellows, who were heavily laden and had to rest their packs every few hundred yards. Yet she found herself hard put to keep the pace of a bunch of Scandinavians ahead of her. They were huge strapping blond-haired giants, each striding along with a hundred pounds on his back, and all harnessed to a go-cart which carried fully six hundred more. Their faces were as laughing suns, and

27

the joy of life was in them. The toil seemed child's play and slipped from them lightly. They joked with one another, and with the passers-by, in a meaningless tongue, and their great chests rumbled with cavern-echoing laughs. Men stood aside for them, and looked after them enviously; for they took the rises of the trail on the run, and rattled down the counter slopes, and ground the iron-rimmed wheels harshly over the rocks. Plunging through a dark stretch of woods, they came out upon the river at the ford. A drowned man lay on his back on the sand-bar, staring upward, unblinking, at the sun. A man, in irritated tones, was questioning over and over, ' Where's his pardner? Ain't he got a pardner?' Two more men had thrown off their packs and were coolly taking an inventory of the dead man's possessions. One called aloud the various articles, while the other checked them off on a piece of dirty wrapping-paper. Letters and receipts, wet and pulpy, strewed the sand. A few gold coins were heaped carelessly on a white handkerchief. Other men, crossing back and forth in canoes and skiffs, took no notice.

The Scandinavians glanced at the sight, and their faces sobered for a moment. ' Where's his pardner? Ain't he got a pardner?' the irritated man demanded of them. They shook their heads. They did not understand English. They stepped into the water and splashed onward. Someone called warningly from the opposite bank, whereat they stood still and conferred together. Then they started on again. The two men taking the inventory turned to watch. The current rose nigh to their hips, but it was swift and they staggered, while now and again the cart slipped sideways with the stream. The worst was over, and Frona found herself holding her breath. The water had sunk to the knees of the two foremost men, when a strap snapped on one nearest the cart. His pack swung suddenly to the side, overbalancing him, At the same instant the man next to him slipped, and each jerked the other under. The next two were whipped off their feet, while the cart, turning over, swept from the bottom of the ford into the deep water. The two men who had almost emerged threw themselves backward on the pull-ropes. The effort was heroic, but giants though they were, the task was too great and they were dragged, inch by inch, downward and under.

Their packs held them to the bottom, save him whose strap had broken. This one struck out, not to the shore, but down the stream, striving to keep up with his comrades. A couple of hundred feet below, the rapid dashed over a toothed-reef of rocks, and here, a minute later, they appeared. The cart, still loaded, showed first, smashing a wheel and turning over and over into the next plunge. The men followed in a miserable tangle. They were beaten against the submerged rocks and swept on, all but one. Frona, in a canoe (a dozen canoes were already in pursuit), saw him grip the rock with bleeding fingers. She saw his white face and the agony of the effort; but his hold relaxed and he was jerked away, just as his free comrade, swimming mightily, was reaching for him. Hidden from sight, they took the next plunge, showing for a second, still struggling, at the shallow foot of the rapid.

A canoe picked up the swimming man, but the rest disappeared in a long stretch of swift, deep water. For a quarter of an hour the canoes plied fruitlessly about, then found the dead men gently grounded in an eddy. A towrope was requisitioned from an up-coming boat, and a pair of horses from a pack-train on the bank, and the ghastly jetsam hauled ashore. Frona looked at the five young giants lying in the mud, broken-boned, limp, uncaring. They were still harnessed to the cart, and the poor worthless packs still clung to their backs. The sixth sat in the midst, dry-eyed and stunned. A dozen feet away the steady flood of life flowed by, and Frona melted into it and went on.

The dark spruce-shrouded mountains drew close together in the Dyea Canyon, and the feet of men churned the wet sunless earth into mire and bog-hole. And when they had done this they sought new paths, till there were many paths. And on such a path Frona came upon a man spread carelessly in the mud. He lay on his side, legs apart and one arm buried beneath him, pinned down by a bulky pack. His cheek was pillowed restfully in the ooze, and on his face there was an expression of content. He brightened when he saw her, and his eyes twinkled cheerily.

''Bout time you hove along,' he greeted her. 'Been waitin' an hour on you as it is.'

'That's it,' as Frona bent over him. 'Just unbuckle that strap. The pesky thing! 'Twas just out o' my reach all the time.'

'Are you hurt?' she asked.

He slipped out of his straps, shook himself, and felt the twisted arm. 'Nope. Sound as a dollar, thank you. And no kick to register, either.' He reached over and wiped his muddy hands on a low-bowed spruce. 'Just my luck; but I got a good rest, so what's the good of makin' a beef about it? You see, I tripped on that little root there, and slip! slump! slam! and slush!—there I was, down and out, and the buckle just out o' reach. And there I lay for a blasted hour, everybody hitting the lower path.'

'But why didn't you call out to them?'

'And make 'em climb up the hill to me? Them all tuckered out with their own work? Not on your life! Wasn't serious enough. If any other man 'd make me climb up just because he'd slipped down, I'd take him out o' the mud all right, all right, and punch and punch him back into the mud again. Besides, I knew somebody was bound to come along my way after a while.'

'Oh, you'll do!' she cried, appropriating Del Bishop's phrase. 'You'll do for this country!'

'Yep,' he called back, shouldering his pack and starting off at a lively clip. 'And, anyway, I got a good rest.'

The trail dipped through a precipitous morass to the river's brink. A slender pine-tree spanned the screaming form and bent midway to touch the water. The surge beat upon the taper trunk and gave it a rhythmical swaying motion, while the feet of the packers had worn smooth its wave-washed surface. Eighty feet it stretched in ticklish insecurity. Frona stepped upon it, felt it move beneath her, heard the bellowing of the water, saw the mad rush—and shrank back. She slipped the knot of her shoe-laces and pretended great care in the tying thereof as a bunch of Indians came out of the woods above and down through the mud. Three or four bucks led the way, followed by many squaws, all bending in the head-straps to the heavy packs. Behind came the children burdened according to their years, and in the rear half a dozen dogs, tongues lagging out and dragging forward painfully under their several loads.

The men glanced at her sideways, and one of them said something in an undertone. Frona could not hear, but the snicker which went down the line brought the flush of shame to her brow and told her more forcibly than could the words. Her face was hot, for she sat disgraced in her own sight; but she gave no sign. The leader stood aside, and one by one, and never more than one at a time, they made the perilous passage. At the bend in the middle their weight forced the tree under, and they felt for their footing, up to the ankles in the cold, driving torrent. Even the little children made it without hesitancy, and then the dogs, whining and reluctant but urged on by the man. When the last had crossed over, he turned to Frona.

'Um horse trail,' he said, pointing up the mountain side. 'Much better you take um horse trail. More far; much better.'

But she shook her head and waited till he reached the farther bank; for she felt the call, not only upon her own pride, but upon the pride of her race; and it was a greater demand than her demand, just as the race was greater than she. So she put foot upon the log, and, with the eyes of the alien people upon her, walked down into the foam white swirl.

She came upon a man weeping by the side of the trail. His pack, clumsily strapped, sprawled on the ground. He had taken off a shoe, and one naked foot showed swollen and blistered.

'What is the matter?' she asked, halting before him.

He looked up at her, then down into the depths where the Dyea River cut the gloomy darkness with its living silver. The tears still welled in his eyes, and he sniffed.

'What is the matter?' she repeated. 'Can I be of any help?'

'No,' he replied. 'How can you help? My feet are raw, and my back is nearly broken, and I am all tired out. Can you help any of these things?'

'Well,' judiciously, 'I am sure it might be worse. Think

31

of the men who have just landed on the beach. It will take them ten days or two weeks to back-trip their outfits as far as you have already got yours.'

'But my partners have left me and gone on,' he moaned, a sneaking appeal for pity in his voice. 'And I am all alone, and I don't feel able to move another step. And then think of my wife and babies. I left them down in the States. Oh, if they could only see me now! I can't go back to them, and I can't go on. It's too much for me. I can't stand it, this working like a horse. I was not made to work like a horse. I'll die, I know I will, if I do. Oh, what shall I do? What shall I do?'

'Why did your comrades leave you?'

'Because I was not so strong as they; because I could not pack as much or as long. And they laughed at me and left me.'

'Have you ever roughed it?' Frona asked.

'No.'

'You look well put up and strong. Weigh probably one hundred and sixty-five?'

'One hundred and seventy,' he corrected.

'You don't look as though you had ever been troubled with sickness. Never an invalid?'

'N-no.'

'And your comrades? They are miners?'

'Never mining in their lives. They worked in the same establishment with me. That's what makes it so hard, don't you see! We'd known one another for years! And to go off and leave me just because I couldn't keep up!'

'My friend,' and Frona knew she was speaking for the race, 'you are strong as they. You can work just as hard as they; pack as much. But you are weak of heart. This is no place for the weak of heart. You cannot work like a horse because you will not. Therefore the country has no use for you. The north wants strong men—strong of soul, not body. The body does not count. So go back to the States. We do not want you here. If you come you will die, and what then of your wife and babies? So sell out your outfit and go back. You will be home in three weeks. Good-bye.'

32

She passed through Sheep Camp. Somewhere above, a mighty glacier, under the pent pressure of a subterranean reservoir, had burst asunder and hurled a hundred thousand tons of ice and water down the rocky gorge. The trail was yet slippery with the slime of the flood, and men were rummaging disconsolately in the rubbish of overthrown tents and caches. But here and there they worked with nervous haste, and the stark corpses by the trail-side attested dumbly to their labour. A few hundred yards beyond, the work of the rush went on uninterrupted. Men rested their packs on jutting stones, swapped escapes whilst they regained their breath, then stumbled on to their toil again.

The mid-day sun beat down upon the stone 'Scales.' The forest had given up the struggle, and the dizzying heat recoiled from the unclothed rock. On either hand rose the ice-marred ribs of earth, naked and strenuous in their nakedness. Above towered storm-beaten Chilcoot. Up its gaunt and ragged front crawled a slender string of men. But it was an endless string. It came out of the last fringe of dwarfed shrub below, drew a black line across a dazzling stretch of ice, and filed past Frona where she ate her lunch by the way. And it went on, up the pitch of the steep, growing fainter, and smaller, till it squirmed and twisted like a column of ants and vanished over the crest of the pass.

Even as she looked, Chilcoot was wrapped in rolling mist and whirling cloud, and a storm of sleet and wind roared down upon the toiling pigmies. The light was swept out of the day, and a deep gloom prevailed; but Frona knew that somewhere up there, clinging and climbing and immortally striving, the long line of ants still twisted towards the sky. And she thrilled at the thought, strong with man's ancient love of mastery, and stepped into the line which came out of the storm behind and disappeared into the storm before.

She blew through the gap of the pass in a whirlwind of vapour, with hand and foot clambered down the volcanic ruin of Chilcoot's mighty father, and stood on the bleak edge of the lake which filled the pit of the crater. The lake was angry and white-capped, and, though a hundred caches were waiting ferriage, no boats were plying back and forth. A rickety skeleton of sticks, in a shell of greased canvas, lay upon the rocks. Frona sought out the owner, a bright-faced young fellow, with sharp black eyes and a salient jaw. Yes, he was the ferryman, but he had quit work for the day. Water too rough for freighting. He charged twenty-five dollars for passengers, but he was not taking passengers today. Had he not said it was too rough? That was why.

'But you will take me, surely?' she asked.

He shook his head and gazed out over the lake. 'At the far end it's rougher than you see it here. Even the big wooden boats won't tackle it. The last that tried, with a gang of packers aboard, was blown over on the west shore. We could see them plainly. And as there's no trail around from there, they'll have to camp it out till the blow is over.'

'But they're better off than I am. My camp outfit is at Happy Camp, and I can't very well stay here.' Frona smiled winsomely, but there was no appeal in the smile; no feminine helplessness throwing itself on the strength and chivalry of the male. 'Do reconsider and take me across.'

'No.'

'I'll give you fifty.'

'No, I say.'

'But I'm not afraid, you know.'

The young fellow's eyes flashed angrily. He turned upon her suddenly, but on second thought did not utter the words forming on his lips. She realised the unintentional slur she had cast, and was about to explain. But on second thought she, too, remained silent; for she read him, and knew that it was perhaps the only way for her to gain her point. They stood there, bodies inclined to the storm in the manner of seamen on sloped decks, unyieldingly looking into each other's eyes. His hair was plastered in wet ringlets on his forehead, while hers, in longer wisps, beat furiously about her face.

'Come on, then!' He flung the boat into the water with an angry jerk, and tossed the oars aboard. 'Climb in! I'll take you, but not for your fifty dollars. You pay the regulation price, and that's all.'

A gust of the gale caught the light shell and swept it

34

broadside for a score of feet. The spray drove inboard in a continuous stinging shower, and Frona at once fell to work with the bailing-can.

'I hope we're blown ashore,' he shouted, stooping forward to the oars. 'It would be embarrassing—for you.' He looked up savagely into her face.

'No,' she modified; 'but it would be very miserable for both of us—a night without tent, blankets, or fire. Besides, we're not going to blow ashore.'

She stepped out on the slippery rocks and helped him heave up the canvas craft and tilt the water out. On either side uprose bare wet walls of rock. A heavy sleet was falling steadily, through which a few streaming caches showed in the gathering darkness.

'You'd better hurry up,' he advised, thanking her for the assistance and relaunching the boat. 'Two miles of stiff trail from here to Happy Camp. No wood until you get there, so you'd best hustle along. Good-bye.'

Frona reached out and took his hand, and said, 'You are a brave man.'

'Oh, I don't know.' He returned the grip with usury and looked his admiration.

A dozen tents held grimly to their pegs on the extreme edge of the timber line at Happy Camp. Frona, weary with the day, went from tent to tent. Her wet skirts clung heavily to her tired limbs, while the wind buffeted her brutally about. Once, through a canvas wall, she heard a man apostrophising gorgeously, and felt sure that it was Del Bishop. But a peep into the interior told a different tale; so she wandered fruitlessly on till she reached the last tent in the camp. She untied the flap and looked in. A spluttering candle showed the one occupant, a man, down on his knees and blowing lustily into the fire-box of a smoky Yukon stove.

CHAPTER IV

S H E cast off the lower flap-fastenings and entered. The man still blew into the stove, unaware of his company. Frona coughed, and he raised a pair of smoke-reddened eyes to hers.

'Certainly,' he said, casually enough. 'Fasten the flaps and make yourself comfortable.' And thereat returned to his borean task.

'Hospitable, to say the least,' she commented to herself, obeying his command and coming up to the stove.

A heap of dwarfed spruce, gnarled and wet and cut to proper stove-length, lay to one side. Frona knew it well, creeping and crawling and twisting itself among the rocks of the shallow alluvial deposit, unlike its arboreal proto-type, rarely lifting its head more than a foot from the earth. She looked into the oven, found it empty, and filled it with the wet wood. The man arose to his feet, coughing from the smoke which had been driven into his lungs, and nodding approval.

When he had recovered his breath, 'Sit down and dry your skirts. I'll get supper.'

He put a coffee-pot on the front lid of the stove, emptied the bucket into it, and went out of the tent after more water. As his back disappeared, Frona dived for her satchel, and when he returned a moment later he found her with a dry skirt on and wringing the wet one out. While he fished about in the grub box for dishes and eating utensils, she stretched a spare bit of rope between the tent-poles and hung the skirt on it to dry. The dishes were dirty, and, as he bent over and washed them, she turned her back and deftly changed her stockings. Her childhood had taught her the value of well-cared feet for the trail. She put her wet shoes on a pile of wood at the back of the stove, substi-tuting for them a pair of soft and dainty house-moccasins of Indian make. The fire had now grown strong, and she was content to let her under-garments dry on her body.

During all this time neither had spoken a word. Not

only had the man remained silent, but he went about his work in so preoccupied a way that it seemed to Frona that he turned a deaf ear to the words of explanation she would have liked to utter. His whole bearing conveyed the impression that it was the most ordinary thing under the sun for a young woman to come in out of the storm and night and partake of his hospitality. In one way, she liked this; but in so far as she did not comprehend it, she was troubled. She had a perception of a something being taken for granted which she did not understand. Once or twice she moistened her lips to speak, but he appeared so oblivious of her presence that she withheld.

After opening a can of corned beef with the axe, he fried half a dozen thick slices of bacon, set the frying-pan back, and boiled the coffee. From the grub-box he resurrected the half of a cold heavy flap-jack. He looked at it dubiously, and shot a quick glance at her. Then he threw the sodden thing out of doors and dumped the contents of a sea-biscuit bag upon a camp cloth. The sea-biscuit had been crumbled into chips and fragments and generously soaked by the rain till it had become a mushy, pulpy mass of dirty white.

'It's all I have in the way of bread,' he muttered; 'but sit down and we will make the best of it.'

'One moment—' And before he could protest, Frona had poured the sea-biscuit into the frying-pan on top of the grease and bacon. To this she added a couple of cups of water and stirred briskly over the fire. When it had sobbed and sighed with the heat for some few minutes, she sliced up the corned beef and mixed it in with the rest. And by the time she had seasoned it heavily with salt and black pepper, a savoury steam was rising from the concoction.

'Must say it's pretty good stuff,' he said, balancing his plate on his knee and sampling the mess avidiously. 'What do you happen to call it?'

'Slumgullion,' she responded curtly, and thereafter the meal went on in silence.

Frona helped him to the coffee, studying him intently the while. And not only was it not an unpleasant face, she decided, but it was strong. Strong, she amended, potentially rather than actually. A student, she added, for she had seen

37

many students' eyes and knew the lasting impress of the midnight oil long continued; and his eyes bore the impress. Brown eyes, she concluded, and handsome as the male's should be handsome; but she noted with surprise, when she refilled his plate with slumgullion, that they were not at all brown in the ordinary sense, but hazel-brown. In the daylight, she felt certain, and in times of best health, they would seem grey, and almost blue-grey. She knew it well; her one girl chum and dearest friend had had such an eye.

His hair was chestnut-brown, glinting in the candlelight to gold, and the hint of waviness in it explained the perceptible droop to his tawny moustache. For the rest, his face was clean-shaven and cut on a good masculine pattern. At first she found fault with the more than slight cheek-hollows under the cheekbones, but when she measured his well-knit, slenderly muscular figure, with its deep chest and heavy shoulders, she discovered that she preferred the hollows; at least they did not imply lack of nutrition. The body gave the lie to that; while they themselves denied the vice of over-feeding. Height, five feet, nine, she summed up from out of her gymnasium experience; and age anywhere between twenty-five and thirty, though nearer the former most likely.

'Haven't many blankets,' he said abruptly, pausing to drain his cup and set it over on the grub-box. 'I don't expect my Indians back from Lake Linderman till morning, and the beggars have packed over everything except a few sacks of flour and the bare camp outfit. However, I've a couple of heavy ulsters which will serve just as well.'

He turned his back, as though he did not expect a reply, and untied a rubber-covered roll of blankets. Then he drew the two ulsters from a clothes-bag and threw them down on the bedding.

'Vaudeville artist, I suppose?'

He asked the question seemingly without interest, as though to keep the conversation going, and, in fact, as if he knew the stereotyped answer beforehand. But to Frona the question was like a blow in the face. She remembered Neepoosa's philippic against the white women who

38

were coming into the land, and realised the falseness of her position and the way in which he looked upon her.

But he went on before she could speak. 'Last night I had two vaudeville queens, and three the night before. Only there was more bedding then. It's unfortunate, isn't it, the aptitude they display in getting lost from their outfits? Yet somehow I have failed to find any lost outfits so far. And they are all queens, it seems. No under-studies or minor turns about them—no, no. And I presume you are a queen, too?'

The too-ready blood sprayed her cheek, and this made her angrier than did he; for whereas she was sure of the steady grip she had on herself, her flushed face betokened a confusion which did not really possess her.

'No,' she answered, coolly; 'I am not a vaudeville artist.'

He tossed several sacks of flour to one side of the stove, without replying, and made of them the foundation of a bed; and with the remaining sacks he duplicated the operation on the opposite side of the stove.

'But you are some kind of an artist, then,' he insisted when he had finished, with an open contempt on the 'artist'.

'Unfortunately, I am not any kind of an artist at all.'

He dropped the blanket he was folding and straightened his back. Hitherto he had no more than glanced at her; but now he scrutinised her carefully, every inch of her, from head to heel and back again, the cut of her garments and the very way she did her hair. And he took his time about it.

'Oh! I beg pardon,' was his verdict, followed by another stare. 'Then you are a very foolish woman, dreaming of fortune and shutting your eyes to the dangers of the pilgrimage. It is only meet that two kinds of women come into this country. Those who by virtue of wifehood and daughterhood are respectable, and those who are not respectable. Vaudeville stars and artists, they call themselves for the sake of decency; and out of courtesy we countenance it. Yes, yes, I know. But remember, the women who come over the trail must be one or the other. There is no middle course, and those who attempt it are bound to fail. So you are a very, very foolish girl, and you had better turn back while there is yet a chance. If you will view it in the light of a loan from a stranger, I will advance your passage back to the States, and start an Indian over the trail with you tomorrow for Dyea."

Once or twice Frona had attempted to interrupt him, but he had waved her imperatively to silence with his hand.

'I thank you,' she began; but he broke in—

'Oh, not at all, not at all.'

'I thank you,' she repeated; 'but it happens that—a—that you are mistaken. I have just come over the trail from Dyea and expect to meet my outfit already in camp here at Happy Camp. They started hours ahead of me, and I can't understand how I passed them—yes I do, too! A boat was blown over to the west shore of Crater Lake this afternoon, and they must have been in it. That is where I missed them and came on. As for my turning back, I appreciate your motive for suggesting it, but my father is in Dawson, and I have not seen him for three years. Also, I have come through from Dyea this day, and am tired, and I would like to get some rest. So, if you still extend your hospitality, I'll go to bed.'

'Impossible!' He kicked the blankets to one side, sat down on the flour sacks, and directed a blank look upon her.

'Are—are there any women in the other tents?' she asked hesitatingly. 'I did not see any, but I may have overlooked.'

'A man and his wife were, but they pulled stakes this morning. No; there are no other women except—except two or three in a tent, which—er—which will not do for you.'

'Do you think I am afraid of their hospitality?' she demanded hotly. 'As you said, they are women.'

'But I said it would not do,' he answered, absently, staring at the straining canvas and listening to the roar of the storm. 'A man would die in the open on a night like this.

'And the other tents are crowded to the walls,' he mused. 'I happen to know. They have stored all their caches inside because of the water, and they haven't room to turn around. Besides, a dozen other strangers are storm-bound with them. Two or three asked to spread their beds in here tonight if they couldn't pinch room elsewhere. Evidently they have; but that does not argue that there is any surplus space left. And anyway—'

He broke off helplessly. The inevitableness of the situation was growing.

'Can I make Deep Lake tonight?' Frona asked, forgetting herself to sympathise with him, then becoming conscious of what she was doing and bursting into laughter.

'But you couldn't ford the river in the dark.' He frowned at her levity. 'And there are no camps between.'

'Are *you* afraid?' she asked with just the shadow of a sneer.

'Not for myself.'

'Well, then, I think I'll go to bed.'

'I might sit up and keep the fire going,' he suggested after a pause.

'Fiddlesticks?' she cried. 'As though your foolish little code were saved in the least! We are not in civilisation. This is the trail to the Pole. Go to bed.'

He elevated his shoulders in token of surrender. 'Agreed. What shall I do then?'

'Help me make my bed, of course. Sacks laid crosswise! Thank you, sir, but I have bones and muscles that rebel. Here— Pull them around this way.'

Under her direction he laid the sacks lengthwise in a double row. This left an uncomfortable hollow with lumpy sack-corners down the middle; but she smote them flat with the side of the axe, and in the same manner lessened the slope to the walls of the hollow. Then she made a triple longitudinal fold in a blanket and spread it along the bottom of the long depression.

'Hum!' he soliloquised. 'Now I see why I slept so badly. Here goes!' And he speedily flung his own sacks into shape.

'It is plain you are unused to the trail,' she informed him, spreading the topmost blanket and sitting down.

'Perhaps so,' he made answer. 'But what do you know about this trail life?' he growled a little later.

'Enough to conform,' she rejoined equivocally, pulling

out the dried wood from the oven and replacing it with wet.

'Listen to it! How it storms!' he explained. 'It's growing worse, if worse be possible.'

The tent reeled under the blows of the wind, the canvas booming hollowly at every shock, while the sleet and rain rattled overhead like skirmish-fire grown into a battle. In the lulls they could hear the water streaming off at the side-walls with the noise of small cataracts. He reached up curiously and touched the wet roof. A burst of water followed instantly at the point of contact and coursed down upon the grub-box.

'You mustn't do that!' Frona cried, springing to her feet. She put her finger on the spot, and, pressing tightly against the canvas, ran it down to the side-wall. The leak at once stopped. 'You mustn't do it, you know,' she reproved.

'Jove!' was his reply. 'And you came through from Dyea today! Aren't you stiff?'

'Quite a bit,' she confessed, candidly, 'and sleepy.'

'Good night,' she called to him several minutes later, stretching her body luxuriously in the warm blankets. And a quarter of an hour after that, 'Oh, I say! Are you awake?'

'Yes,' his voice came muffled across the stove. 'What is it?'

'Have you the shavings cut?'

'Shavings?' he queried, sleepily. 'What shavings?'

'For the fire in the morning, of course. So get up and cut them.'

He obeyed without a word; but ere he was done she had ceased to hear him.

The ubiquitous bacon was abroad on the air when she opened her eyes. Day had broken, and with it the storm. The wet sun was shining cheerily over the drenched landscape and in at the wide-spread flaps. Already work had begun, and groups of men were filing past under their packs. Frona turned over on her side. Breakfast was cooked. Her host had just put the bacon and fried potatoes in the oven, and was engaged in propping the door ajar with two sticks of firewood.

'Good morning,' she greeted.

42

'And good morning to you,' he responded, rising to his feet and picking up the water-bucket. 'I don't hope that you slept well, for I know you did.'

Frona laughed.

'I'm going out after some water,' he vouchsafed. 'And when I return I shall expect you ready for breakfast.'

After breakfast, basking herself in the sun, Frona descried a familiar bunch of men rounding the trail of the glacier in the direction of Crater Lake. She clapped her hands.

'There comes my outfit, and Del Bishop as shamefaced as can be, I'm sure, at his failure to connect.' Turning to the man, and at the same time slinging camera and satchel over her shoulder, 'So I must say good-bye, not forgetting to thank you for your kindness.'

'Oh, not at all, not at all. Pray don't mention it. I'd do the same for any—'

'Vaudeville artist!'

He looked his reproach, but went on, 'I don't know your name, nor do I wish to know it.'

'Well, I shall not be so harsh, for I do know your name, MISTER VANCE CORLISS! I saw it on the shipping tags, of course,' she explained. 'And I want you to come and see me when you get to Dawson. My name is Frona Welse. Good-bye.'

'Your father is not Jacob Welse?' he called after her as she ran lightly down towards the trail.

She turned her head and nodded.

But Del Bishop was not shamefaced, nor even worried. 'Trust a Welse to land on their feet on a soft spot,' he had consoled himself as he dropped off to sleep the night before. But he was angry—'madder 'n hops,' in his own vernacular.

'Good mornin',' he saluted. 'And it's plain by your face you had a comfortable night of it, and no thanks to me.'

'You weren't worried, were you?' she asked.

'Worried? About a Welse? Who? Me? Not on your life. I was too busy tellin' Crater Lake what I thought of it. I don't like the water. I told you so. And it's always playin' me scurvy—not that I'm afraid of it, though.'

43

'Hey, you Pete!' turning to the Indians. 'Hit 'er up! Got to make Linderman by noon!'

'Frona Welse?' Vance Corliss was repeating to himself.

The whole thing seemed a dream, and he reassured himself by turning and looking after her retreating form. Del Bishop and the Indians were already out of sight behind a wall of rock. Frona was just rounding the base. The sun was full upon her, and she stood out radiantly against the black shadow of the wall beyond. She waved her alpenstock, and as he doffed his cap, rounded the brink and disappeared.

CHAPTER V

THE position occupied by Jacob Welse was certainly an anomalous one. He was a giant trader in a country without commerce, a ripened product of the nineteenth century flourishing in a society as primitive as that of the Mediterranean vandals. A captain of industry and a splendid monopolist, he dominated the most independent aggregate of men ever drawn together from the ends of the earth. An economic missionary, a commercial St Paul, he preached the doctrines of expediency and force. Believing in the natural rights of man, a child himself of democracy, he bent all men to his absolutism. Government of Jacob Welse, for Jacob Welse and the people, by Jacob Welse, was his unwritten gospel. Single-handed he had carved out his dominion till he gripped the domain of a dozen Roman provinces. At his ukase the population ebbed and flowed over a hundred thousand miles of territory, and cities sprang up or disappeared at his bidding.

Yet he was a common man. The air of the world first smote his lungs on the open prairie by the River Platte, the blue sky over head, and beneath, the green grass of the earth pressing against his tender nakedness. On the horses his eyes first opened, still saddled and gazing in mild wonder on the miracle; for his trapper father had but turned aside from the trail that the wife might have quiet and the birth be accomplished. An hour or so and the two, which were now three, were in the saddle and overhauling their trapper comrades. The party had not been delayed; no time lost. In the morning his mother cooked the breakfast over the camp-fire, and capped it with a fifty-mile ride into the next sun-down.

The trapper father had come of the sturdy Welsh stock which trickled into early Ohio out of the jostling East, and the mother was a nomadic daughter of the Irish emigrant settlers of Ontario. From both sides came the Wanderlust of the blood, the fever to be moving, to be pushing on to the edge of things. In the first year of his life, ere he had learned

45

the way of his legs, Jacob Welse had wandered a-horse through a thousand miles of wilderness, and wintered in a hunting-lodge on the head-waters of the Red River of the North. His first foot-gear was moccasins, his first taffy the tallow from a moose. His first generalisations were that the world was composed of great wastes and white vastnesses, and populated with Indians and white hunters like his father. A town was a cluster of deer-skin lodges; a trading-post a seat of civilisation; and a factor God Almighty Himself. Rivers and lakes existed chiefly for man's use in travelling. Viewed in this light, the mountains puzzled him; but he placed them away in his classification of the Inexplicable and did not worry. Men died, sometimes. But their meat was not good to eat, and their hides worthless—perhaps because they did not grow fur. Pelts were valuable, and with a few bales a man might purchase the earth. Animals were made for men to catch and skin. He did not know what men were made for, unless, perhaps, for the factor.

As he grew older he modified these concepts, but the process was a continual source of naïve apprehension and wonderment. It was not until he became a man and had wandered through half the cities of the States that this expression of childish wonder passed out of his eyes and left them wholly keen and alert. At his boy's first contact with the cities, while he revised his synthesis of things, he also generalised afresh. People who lived in cities were effeminate. They did not carry the points of the compass in their heads, and they got lost easily. That was why they elected to stay in the cities. Because they might catch cold and because they were afraid of the dark, they slept under shelter and locked their doors at night. The women were soft and pretty, but they could not lift a snowshoe far in a day's journey. Everybody talked too much. That was why they lied and were unable to work greatly with their hands. Finally, there was a new human force called 'bluff'. A man who made a bluff must be dead sure of it, or else be prepared to back it up. Bluff was a very good thing—when exercised with discretion.

Later, though living his life mainly in the woods and mountains, he came to know that the cities were not all bad; that a man might live in a city and still be a man.

Accustomed to do battle with natural forces, he was attracted by the commercial battle with social forces. The masters of marts and exchanges dazzled but did not blind him, and he studied them, and strove to grasp the secrets of their strength. And further, in token that some good did come out of Nazareth, in the full tide of manhood he took to himself a city-bred woman. But he still yearned for the edge of things, and the leaven in his blood worked till they went away, and above the Dyea Beach, on the rim of the forest, built the big log trading-post. And here, in the mellow of time, he got a proper focus on things and unified the phenomena of society precisely as he had already unified the phenomena of nature. There was naught in one which could not be expressed in terms of the other. The same principles underlay both; the same truths were manifest of both. Competition was the secret of creation. Battle was the law and the way of progress. The world was made for the strong, and only the strong inherited it, and through it all there ran an eternal equity. To be honest was to be strong. To sin was to weaken. To bluff an honest man was to be dishonest. To bluff a bluffer was to smite with the steel of justice. The primitive strength was in the arm; the modern strength in the brain. Though it had shifted ground, the struggle was the same old struggle. As of old time, men still fought for the mastery of the earth and the delights thereof. But the sword had given way to the ledger; the mail-clad baron to the soft-garbed industrial lord, and the centre of imperial political power to the seat of commercial exchanges. The modern will had destroyed the ancient brute. The stubborn earth yielded only to force. Brain was greater than body. The man with the brain could best conquer things primitive.

He did not have much education as education goes. To the three R's his mother taught him by camp-fire and candle-light, he had added a somewhat miscellaneous book-knowledge; but he was not burdened with what he had gathered. Yet he read the facts of life understandingly, and the sobriety which comes of the soil was his, and the clear earth-vision.

And so it came about that Jacob Welse crossed over the Chilcoot in an early day, and disappeared into the vast unknown. A year later he emerged at the Russian Missions clustered about the mouth of the Yukon on Bering Sea. He had journeyed down a river three thousand miles long, he had seen things, and dreamed a great dream. But he held his tongue and went to work, and one day the defiant whistle of a crazy stern-wheel tub saluted the midnight sun on the dank river-stretch by Fort o' Yukon. It was a magnificent adventure. How he achieved it only Jacob Welse can tell; but with the impossible to begin with, plus the impossible, he added steamer to steamer and heaped enterprise upon enterprise. Along many a thousand miles of river and tributary he built trading-posts and warehouses. He forced the white man's axe into the hands of the aborigines, and in every village and between the villages rose the cords of four-foot firewood for his boilers. On an island in Bering Sea, where the river and the ocean meet, he established a great distributing station, and on the North Pacific he put big ocean steamships; while in his offices in Seattle and San Francisco it took clerks by the score to keep the order and system of his business.

Men drifted into the land. Hitherto famine had driven them out, but Jacob Welse was there now, and his grub-stores; so they wintered in the frost and groped in the frozen muck for gold. He encouraged them, grub-staked them, carried them on the books of the company. His steamers dragged them up the Koyokuk in the old days of Arctic City. Wherever pay was struck he built a warehouse and a store. The town followed. He explored; he speculated; he developed. Tireless, indomitable, with the steel-glitter in his dark eyes, he was everywhere at once, doing all things. In the opening up of a new river he was in the van; and at the tail end also, hurrying forward the grub. On the Outside he fought trade-combinations; made alliances with the corporations of the earth, and forced discriminating tariffs from the great carriers. On the Inside he sold flour, and blankets, and tobacco; built saw-mills, staked town-sites, and sought properties in copper, iron, and coal; and that the miners should be well-equipped, ransacked the lands of the Arctic even as far as Siberia for native-made snowshoes, muclucs, and parkas.

He bore the country on his shoulders; saw to its needs;

did its work. Every ounce of its dust passed through his hands; every postcard and letter of credit. He did its banking and exchange; carried and distributed its mails. He frowned upon competition; frightened out predatory capital; bluffed militant syndicates, and when they would not, backed his bluff and broke them. And for all, yet found time and place to remember his motherless girl, and to love her, and to fit her for the position he had made.

CHAPTER VI

'So I think, captain, you will agree that we must exaggerate the seriousness of the situation.' Jacob Welse helped his visitor into his fur great-coat and went on. 'Not that it is not serious, but that it may not become more serious. Both you and I have handled famines before. We must frighten them, and frighten them now, before it is too late. Take five thousand men out of Dawson and there will be grub to last. Let those five thousand carry their tale of famine to Dyea and Skaguay, and they will prevent five thousand more coming in over the ice.'

'Quite right! And you may count on the hearty co-operation of the police, Mr. Welse.' The speaker, a strong-faced grizzled man, heavy-set and of military bearing, pulled up his collar and rested his hand on the door-knob. 'I see already, thanks to you, the newcomers are beginning to sell their outfits and buy dogs. Lord! won't there be a stampede out over the ice as soon as the river closes down! And each that sells a thousand pounds of grub and goes lessens the proposition by one empty stomach and fills another that remains. When does the *Laura* start?'

'This morning, with three hundred grubless men aboard. Would that they were three thousand!'

'Amen to that! And by the way, when does your daughter arrive?'

''Most any day, now.' Jacob Welse's eyes warmed. 'And I want you to dinner when she does, and bring along a bunch of your young bucks from the Barracks. I don't know all their names, but just the same extend the invitation as though from me personally. I haven't cultivated the social side much—no time, but see to it that the girl enjoys herself. Fresh from the States and London, and she's liable to feel lonesome. You understand.'

Jacob Welse closed the door, tilted his chair back, and cocked his feet on the guard-rail of the stove. For one half-minute a girlish vision wavered in the shimmering air above the stove, then merged into a woman of fair Saxon type.

The door opened. 'Mr Welse, Mr Foster sent me to find out if he is to go on filling signed warehouse orders?'

'Certainly, Mr Smith. But tell him to scale them down by half. If a man holds an order for a thousand pounds, give him five hundred.'

He lighted a cigar and tilted back again in his chair.

'Captain McGregor wants to see you, sir.'

'Send him in.'

Captain McGregor strode in and remained standing before his employer. The rough hand of the New World had been laid upon the Scotsman from his boyhood; but sterling honesty was written in every line of his bitter-seamed face, while a prognathous jaw proclaimed to the onlooker that honesty was the best policy—for the onlooker at any rate, should he wish to do business with the owner of the jaw. This warning was backed up by the nose, side-twisted and broken, and by a long scar which ran up the forehead and disappeared in the grey-grizzled hair.

'We throw off the lines in an hour, sir; so I've come for the last word.'

'Good.' Jacob Welse whirled his chair about. 'Captain McGregor.'

'Aye.'

'I had other work cut out for you this winter; but I have changed my mind and chosen you to go down with the *Laura*. Can you guess why?'

Captain McGregor swayed his weight from one leg to the other, and a shrewd chuckle of a smile wrinkled the corners of his eyes. 'Going to be trouble,' he grunted.

'And I couldn't have picked a better man. Mr Bally will give you detailed instructions as you go aboard. But let me say this: If we can't scare enough men out of the country, there'll be need for every pound of grub at Fort Yukon. Understand?'

'Aye.'

'So no extravagance. You are taking three hundred men down with you. The chances are that twice as many more will go down as soon as the river freezes. You'll have a thousand to feed through the winter. Put them on rations—working rations—and see that they work. Cordwood, six dollars per cord, and piled on the bank where steamers can make a landing. No work, no rations. Understand?'

'Aye.'

'A thousand men can get ugly, if they are idle. They can get ugly anyway. Watch out they don't rush the caches. If they do—do your duty.'

The other nodded grimly. His hands gripped unconsciously, while the scar on his forehead took on a livid hue.

'There are five steamers in the ice. Make them safe against the spring break-up. But first transfer all their cargoes to one big cache. You can defend it better, and make the cache impregnable. Send a messenger down to Fort Burr, asking Mr Carter for three of his men. He doesn't need them. Nothing much is doing at Circle City. Step in on the way down and take half of Mr Burdwell's men. You'll need them. There'll be gun-fighters in plenty to deal with. Be stiff. Keep things in check from the start. Remember, the man who shoots first comes off with the whole hide. And keep a constant eye on the grub.'

'And on the forty-five-nineties,' Captain McGregor rumbled back as he passed out the door.

'John Melton—Mr Melton, sir. Can he see you?'

'See here, Welse, what's this mean?' John Melton followed wrathfully on the heels of the clerk, and he almost walked over him as he flourished a paper before the head of the company. 'Read that! What's it stand for?'

Jacob Welse glanced over it and looked up coolly. 'One thousand pounds of grub.'

'That's what I say, but that fellow you've got in the warehouse says no—five hundred's all it's good for.'

'He spoke the truth.'

'But—'

'It stands for one thousand pounds, but in the warehouse it is only good for five hundred.'

'That your signature?' thrusting the receipt again into the other's line of vision.

'Yes.'

'Then what are you going to do about it?'

52

'Give you five hundred. What are you going to do about it?'

'Refuse to take it.'

'Very good. There is no further discussion.'

'Yes there is. I propose to have no further dealings with you. I'm rich enough to freight my own stuff in over the Passes, and I will next year. Our business stops right now and for all time.'

'I cannot object to that. You have three hundred thousand dollars in dust deposited with me. Go to Mr Atsheler and draw it at once.'

The man fumed impotently up and down. 'Can't I get that other five hundred? Great god, man! I've paid for it! You don't intend me to starve?'

'Look here, Melton.' Jacob Welse paused to knock the ash from his cigar. 'At this very moment what are you working for? What are you trying to get?'

'A thousand pounds of grub.'

'For your own stomach?'

The Bonanza king nodded his head.

'Just so.' The lines showed more sharply on Jacob Welse's forehead. 'You are working for your own stomach. I am working for the stomachs of twenty thousand.'

'But you filled Tim McReady's thousand pounds yesterday all right.'

'The scale-down did not go into effect until today.'

'But why am I the one to get it in the neck hard?'

'Why didn't you come yesterday, and Tim McReady today?'

Melton's face went blank, and Jacob Welse answered his own question with shrugging shoulders.

'That's the way it stands, Melton. No favouritism. If you hold me responsible for Tim McReady, I shall hold you responsible for not coming yesterday. Better we both throw it upon Providence. You went through the Forty Mile Famine. You are a white man. A Bonanza property, or a block of Bonanza properties, does not entitle you to a pound more than the oldest penniless "sour-dough" or the newest baby born. Trust me. As long as I have a pound of grub you shall not starve. Stiffen up. Shake hands. Get a smile on your face and make the best of it.'

53

Still savage of spirit, though rapidly toning down, the king shook hands and flung out of the room. Before the door could close on his heels, a loose-jointed Yankee shambled in, thrust a moccasined foot to the side and hooked a chair under him, and sat down.

'Say,' he opened up, confidentially, 'people's gittin' scairt over the grub proposition, I guess some.'

'Hello, Dave. That you?'

'S'pose so. But ez I was sayin', there'll be a lively stampede fer the Outside soon as the river freezes.'

'Think so?'

'Unh huh.'

'Then I'm glad to hear it. It's what the country needs. Going to join them?'

'Not in a thousand years.' Dave Harney threw his head back with smug complacency. 'Freighted my truck up to the mine yesterday. Wa'n't a bit too soon about it, either. But say . . . Suthin' happened to the sugar. Had it all on the last sled, an' jest where the trail turns off the Klondike into Bonanza, what does that sled do but break through the ice! I never seen the beat of it—the last sled of all, an' all the sugar! So I jest thought I'd drop in today an' git a hundred pounds or so. White or brown, I ain't pertickler.'

Jacob Welse shook his head and smiled, but Harney hitched his chair closer.

'The clerk of yourn said he didn't know, an' ez there wa'n't no call to pester him, I said I'd jest drop round an' see you. I don't care what it's wuth. Make it a hundred even; that'll do me handy.

'Say,' he went on easily, noting the decidedly negative poise of the other's head. 'I've got a tolerable sweet tooth, I have. Recollect the taffy I made over on Preacher Creek that time? I declare! how time does fly! That was all of six years ago if it's a day. More'n that, surely. Seven, by the Jimcracky! But ez I was sayin', I'd ruther do without my plug of "Star" than sugar. An' about that sugar? Got my dogs outside. Better go round to the warehouse an' git it, eh? Pretty good idea.'

But he saw the 'No' shaping on Jacob Welse's lips and hurried on before it could be uttered.

'Now, I don't want to hog it. Wouldn't do that fer the world. So if yer short, I can put up with seventy-five—' (he studied the other's face), 'an' I might do with fifty. I 'preciate your position, an' I ain't low-down critter enough to pester—'

'What's the good of spilling words, Dave? We haven't a pound of sugar to spare—'

'Ez I was sayin', I ain't no hog; an' seein' 's it's you, Welse, I'll make to scrimp along on twenty-five—'

'Not an ounce!'

'Not the least leetle mite? Well, well, don't git het up. We'll jest fergit I ast you fer any, an' I'll drop round some likelier time. So long. Say!' He threw his jaw to one side and seemed to stiffen the muscles of his ear as he listened intently. 'That's the *Laura's* whistle. She's startin' soon. Goin' to see her off? Come along.'

Jacob Welse pulled on his bearskin coat and mittens, and they passed through the outer offices into the main store. So large was it, that the ten-score purchasers before the counters made no apparent crowd. Many were serious-faced, and more than one looked darkly at the head of the company as he passed. The clerks were selling everything except grub, and it was grub that was in demand. 'Holding it for a rise. Famine prices,' a red-whiskered miner sneered. Jacob Welse heard it but took no notice. He expected to hear it many times and more unpleasantly ere the scare was over.

On the sidewalk he stopped to glance over the public bulletins posted against the side of the building. Dogs lost, found, and for sale occupied some space, but the rest was devoted to notices of sales of outfits. The timid were already growing frightened. Outfits of five hundred pounds were offering at a dollar a pound, without flour; others, with flour, at a dollar and a half. Jacob Welse saw Melton talking with an anxious-faced newcomer, and the satisfaction displayed by the Bonanza king told that he had succeeded in filling his winter's cache.

'Why don't you smell out the sugar, Dave?' Jacob Welse asked, pointing to the bulletins.

Dave Harney looked his reproach. 'Mebbe you think I ain't ben smellin'. I've clean wore my dogs out chasin'

55

round from Klondike City to the Hospital. Can't git yer fingers on it fer love or money.'

They walked down the block-long sidewalk, past the warehouse doors and the long teams of waiting huskies curled up in wolfish comfort in the snow. It was for this snow, the first permanent one of the fall, that the miners up-creek had waited to begin their freighting.

'Curious, ain't it?' Dave hazarded suggestively, as they crossed the main street to the river bank. 'Mighty curious —me ownin' two five-hundred-foot Eldorado claims an' a fraction, wuth five millions if I'm wuth a cent, an' no sweetenin' fer my coffee or mush! Why, gosh-dang-it! this country kin go to blazes! I'll sell out! I'll quit it cold! I'll—I'll—go back to the States!'

'Oh, no, you won't,' Jacob Welse answered. 'I've heard you talk before. You put in a year up Stewart River on straight meat, if I haven't forgotten. And you ate salmon-belly and dogs up the Tanana, to say nothing of going through two famines; and you haven't turned your back on the country yet. And you never will. And you'll die here as sure as that's the *Laura's* spring being hauled aboard. And I look forward confidently to the day when I shall ship you out in a lead-lined box and burden the San Francisco end with the trouble of winding up your estate. You are a fixture, and you know it.'

As he talked he constantly acknowledged greetings from the passers-by. Those who knew him were mainly old-timers and he knew them all by name, though there was scarcely a newcomer to whom his face was not familiar.

'I'll jest bet I'll be in Paris in 1900,' the Eldorado king protested feebly.

But Jacob Welse did not hear. There was a jangling of gongs as McGregor saluted him from the pilot-house and the *Laura* slipped out from the bank. The men on the shore filled the air with good-luck farewells and last advice, but the three hundred grubless ones, turning their backs on the golden dream, were moody and dispirited, and made small response. The *Laura* backed out through a channel cut in the shore-ice, swung about in the current, and with a final blast put on full steam ahead.

The crowd thinned away and went about its business,

56

leaving Jacob Welse the centre of a group of a dozen or so. The talk was of the famine, but it was the talk of men. Even Dave Harney forgot to curse the country for its sugar shortage, and waxed facetious over the newcomers— *chechaquos*, he called them, having recourse to the Siwash tongue. In the midst of his remarks his quick eye lighted on a black speck floating down with the mush-ice of the river. 'Jest look at that!' he cried. 'A Peterborough canoe runnin' the ice!'

Twisting and turning, now paddling, now shoving clear of the floating cakes, the two men in the canoe worked in to the rim-ice, along the edge of which they drifted, waiting for an opening. Opposite the channel cut out by the steamer, they drove their paddles deep and darted into the calm dead water. The waiting group received them with open arms, helping them up the bank and carrying their shell after them. In its bottom were two leather mail-pouches, a couple of blankets, coffee-pot and frying-pan, and a scant grub-sack. As for the men, so frosted were they, and so numb with the cold, that they could hardly stand. Dave Harney proposed whisky, and was for haling them away at once; but one delayed long enough to shake stiff hands with Jacob Welse.

'She's coming,' he announced. 'Passed her boat an hour back. It ought to be round the bend any minute. I've got despatches for you, but I'll see you later. Got to get something into me first.' Turning to go with Harney, he stopped suddenly and pointed up stream. 'There she is now. Just coming out past the bluff.'

'Run along, boys, an' git yer whisky,' Harney admonished him and his mate. 'Tell 'm it's on me, double dose, an' jest excuse me not drinkin' with you, fer I'm goin' to stay.'

The Klondike was throwing a thick flow of ice, partly mush and partly solid, and swept the boat out towards the middle of the Yukon. They could see the struggle plainly from the bank—four men standing up and poling a way through the jarring cakes. A Yukon stove aboard was sending up a trailing pillar of blue smoke, and, as the boat drew closer, they could see a woman in the stern working the long steering-sweep. At sight of this there was a snap and

57

sparkle in Jacob Welse's eyes. It was the first omen, and it was good, he thought. She was still a Welse; a struggler and a fighter. The years of her culture had not weakened her. Though tasting of the fruits of the first remove from the soil, she was not afraid of the soil; she could return to it gleefully and naturally.

So he mused till the boat drove in, ice-rimmed and battered, against the edge of the rim-ice. The one white man aboard sprang out, painter in hand, to slow it down and work into the channel. But the rim-ice was formed of the night, and the front of it shelved off with him into the current. The nose of the boat sheered out under the pressure of a heavy cake, so that he came up at the stern. The woman's arm flashed over the side to his collar, and at the same instant, sharp and authoritative, her voice rang out to the Indian oarsmen to back water. Still holding the man's head above water, she threw her body against the sweep and guided the boat stern-foremost into the opening. A few more strokes and it grounded at the foot of the bank. She passed the collar of the chattering man to Dave Harney, who dragged him out and started him off on the trail of the mail-carriers.

Frona stood up, her cheeks glowing from the quick work. Jacob Welse hesitated. Though he stood within reach of the gunwale, a gulf of three years was between. The womanhood of twenty, added unto the girl of seventeen, made a sum more prodigious than he had imagined. He did not know whether to bear-hug the radiant young creature or to take her hand and help her ashore. But there was no apparent hitch, for she leaped beside him and was into his arms. Those above looked away to a man till the two came up the bank hand in hand.

'Gentlemen, my daughter.' There was a great pride in his face.

Frona embraced them all with a comrade smile, and each man felt that for an instant her eyes had looked straight into his.

CHAPTER VII

THAT Vance Corliss wanted to see more of the girl he had divided blankets with, goes with the saying. He had not been wise enough to lug a camera into the country, but nonetheless, by a yet subtler process, a sun-picture had been recorded somewhere on his cerebral tissues. In the flash of an instant it had been done. A wave message of light and colour, a molecular agitation and integration, a certain minute though definite corrugation in a brain recess —and there it was, a picture complete! The blazing sunlight on the beetling black; a slender grey form, radiant, starting forward to the vision from the marge where light and darkness met; a fresh young morning smile wreathed in a flame of burning gold.

It was a picture he looked at often, and the more he looked the greater was his desire to see Frona Welse again. This event he anticipated with a thrill, with the exultancy over change which is common of all life. She was something new, a fresh type, a woman unrelated to all women he had met. Out of the fascinating unknown a pair of hazel eyes smiled into his, and a hand, soft of touch and strong of grip, beckoned him. And there was an allurement about it which was as the allurement of sin.

Not that Vance Corliss was anybody's fool, nor that his had been an anchorite's existence; but that his upbringing, rather, had given his life a certain puritanical bent. Awakening intelligence and broader knowledge had weakened the early influence of an austere mother, but had not wholly eradicated it. It was there, deep down, very shadowy, but still a part of him. He could not get away from it. It distorted, ever so slightly, his concepts of things. It gave a squint to his perceptions, and very often, when the sex feminine was concerned, determined his classifications. He prided himself on his largeness when he granted that there were three kinds of women. His mother had only admitted two. But he had outgrown her. It was incontestable that there were three kinds—the good, the bad, and

59

the partly good and partly bad. That the last usually went bad, he believed firmly. In its very nature such a condition could not be permanent. It was the intermediary stage, marking the passage from high to low, from best to worst.

All of which might have been true, even as he saw it; but with definitions for premises, conclusions cannot fail to be dogmatic. What was *good* and *bad*? There it was. That was where his mother whispered with dead lips to him. Nor alone his mother, but divers conventional generations, even back to the sturdy ancestor who first uplifted from the soil and looked down. For Vance Corliss was many times removed from the red earth, and, though he did not know it, there was a clamour within him for a return lest he perish.

Not that he pigeon-holed Frona according to his inherited definitions. He refused to classify her at all. He did not dare. He preferred to pass judgment later, when he had gathered more data. And there was the allurement, the gathering of the data; the great critical point where purity reaches dreamy hands towards pitch and refuses to call it pitch—till defiled. No; Vance Corliss was not a cad. And since purity is merely a relative term, he was not pure. That there was no pitch under his nails was not because he had manicured diligently, but because it had not been his luck to run across any pitch. He was not good because he chose to be, because evil was repellent; but because he had not had opportunity to become evil. But from this, on the other hand, it is not to be argued that he would have gone bad had he had a chance.

He was a product of the sheltered life. All his days had been lived in a sanitary dwelling; the plumbing was excellent. The air he had breathed had been mostly ozone artificially manufactured. He had been sun-bathed in balmy weather, and brought in out of the wet when it rained. And when he reached the age of choice he had been too fully occupied to deviate from the straight path, along which his mother had taught him to creep and toddle, and along which he now proceeded to walk upright, without thought of what lay on either side.

Vitality cannot be used over again. If it be expended on one thing, there is none left for the other thing. And so with Vance Corliss. Scholarly lucubrations and healthy exercises during his college days had consumed all the energy his normal digestion extracted from a wholesome omnivorous diet. When he did discover a bit of surplus energy, he worked it off in the society of his mother and of the conventional minds and prim teas she surrounded herself with. Result : A very nice young man, of whom no maid's mother need ever be intrepidation; a very strong young man, whose substance had not been wasted in riotous living; a very learned young man, with a Freiberg mining engineer's diploma and a B.A. sheepskin from Yale; and, lastly, a very self-centred, self-possessed young man.

Now his greatest virtue lay in this : he had not become hardened in the mould baked by his several forbears and into which he had been pressed by his mother's hands. Some atavism had been at work in the making of him, and he had reverted to that ancestor who sturdily uplifted. But so far this portion of his heritage had lain dormant. He had simply remained adjusted to a stable environment. There had been no call upon the adaptability which was his. But whensoever the call came, being so constituted, it was manifest that he should adapt, should adjust himself to the unwonted pressure of new conditions. The maxim of the rolling stone may be all true; but notwithstanding, in the scheme of life, the inability to become fixed is an excellence *par excellence*. Though he did not know it, this inability was Vance Corliss's most splendid possession.

But to return. He looked forward with great sober glee to meeting Frona Welse, and in the meanwhile consulted often the sun-picture he carried of her. Though he went over the Pass and down the lakes and river with a push of money behind him (London syndicates are never niggardly in such matters), Frona beat him into Dawson by a fortnight. While on his part money in the end overcame obstacles, on hers the name of Welse was a talisman greater than treasure. After his arrival, a couple of weeks were consumed in buying a cabin, presenting his letters of introduction, and settling down. But all things come in the fulness of time, and so, one night after the river closed, he pointed his moccasins in the direction of Jacob Welse's house. Mrs Schoville, the Gold Commissioner's wife, gave him the honour of her company.

Corliss wanted to rub his eyes. Steam-heating apparatus in the Klondike! But the next instant he had passed out of the hall through the heavy portières and stood inside the drawing-room. And it *was* a drawing-room. His moose-hide moccasins sank luxuriantly into the deep carpet, and his eyes were caught by a Turner sunrise on the opposite wall. And there were other paintings and things in bronze. Two Dutch fireplaces were roaring full with huge back-logs of spruce. There was a piano; and somebody was singing. Frona sprang from the stool and came forward, greeting him with both hands. He had thought his sun-picture perfect, but this fire-picture, this young creature with the flush and warmth of ringing life, quite eclipsed it. It was a whirling moment, as he held her two hands in his, one of those moments when an incomprehensible orgasm quickens the blood and dizzies the brain. Though the first syllables came to him faintly, Mrs Schoville's voice brought him back to himself.

'Oh!' she cried. 'You know him!'

And Frona answered, 'Yes, we met on the Dyea Trail; and those who meet on the Dyea Trail can never forget.'

'How romantic!'

The Gold Commissioner's wife clapped her hands. Though fat and forty, and phlegmatic of temperament, between exclamations and hand-clappings her waking existence was mostly explosive. Her husband secretly averred that did God Himself deign to meet her face to face, she would smite together her chubby hands and cry out, 'How romantic!'

'How did it happen?' she continued. 'He didn't rescue you over a cliff, or that sort of thing, did he? Do say that he did! And you never said a word about it, Mr Corliss. Do tell me. I'm just dying to know!'

'Oh, nothing like that,' he hastened to answer. 'Nothing much. I, that is we—'

62

He felt a sinking as Frona interrupted. There was no telling what this remarkable girl might say.

'He gave me of his hospitality, that was all,' she said. 'And I can vouch for his fried potatoes; while for his coffee, it is excellent—when one is very hungry.'

'Ingrate!' he managed to articulate, and thereby to gain a smile, ere he was introduced to a cleanly built lieutenant of the Mounted Police, who stood by the fireplace discussing the grub proposition with a dapper little man very much out of place in a white shirt and stiff collar.

Thanks to the particular niche in society into which he happened to be born, Corliss drifted about easily from group to group, and was much envied therefore by Del Bishop, who sat stiffly in the first chair he had dropped into, and who was waiting patiently for the first person to take leave that he might know how to compass the manoeuvre. In his mind's eye he had figured most of it out, knew just how many steps required to carry him to the door, was certain he would have to say good-bye to Frona, but did not know whether or not he was supposed to shake hands all around. He had just dropped in to see Frona and say 'Howdee,' as he expressed it, and had unwittingly found himself in company.

Corliss, having terminated a buzz with a Miss Mortimer on the decadence of the French symbolists, encountered Del Bishop. But the pocket-miner remembered him at once from the one glimpse he had caught of Corliss standing by his tent-door in Happy Camp. Was almighty obliged to him for his night's hospitality to Miss Frona, seein' as he'd ben side-tracked down the line; that any kindness to her was a kindness to him; and that he'd remember it, by God, as long as he had a corner of a blanket to pull over him. Hoped it hadn't put him out. Miss Frona'd said that bedding was scarce, but it wasn't a cold night (more blowy than crisp), so he reckoned there couldn't 'a' ben much shiverin'. All of which struck Corliss as perilous, and he broke away at the first opportunity, leaving the pocket-miner yearning for the door.

But Dave Harney, who had not come by mistake, avoided gluing himself to the first chair. Being an Eldorado king, he had felt it incumbent to assume the position in society to which his numerous millions entitled him; and though unused all his days to social amenities other than the outhanging latch-string and the general pot, he had succeeded to his own satisfaction as a knight of the carpet. Quick to take a cue, he circulated with an aplomb which his striking garments and long shambling gait only heightened, and talked choppy and disconnected fragments with whomsoever he ran up against. The Miss Mortimer, who spoke Parisian French, took him aback with her symbolists; but he evened matters up with a goodly measure of the bastard lingo of the Canadian *voyageurs,* and left her gasping and meditating over a proposition to sell him twenty-five pounds of sugar, white or brown. But she was not unduly favoured, for with everybody he adroitly turned the conversation to grub, and then led up to the eternal proposition. 'Sugar or bust,' he would conclude gaily each time and wander on to the next.

But he put the capstone on his social success by asking Frona to sing the touching ditty, 'I Left My Happy Home for You'. This was something beyond her, though she had him hum over the opening bars so that she could furnish the accompaniment. His voice was more strenuous than sweet, and Del Bishop, discovering himself at last, joined in raucously on the choruses. This made him feel so much better that he disconnected himself from the chair, and when he finally got home he kicked up his sleepy tent-mate to tell him about the high time he'd had over at the Welse's. Mrs Schoville tittered and thought it all so unique, and she thought it so unique several times more when the lieutenant of Mounted Police and a couple of compatriots roared 'Rule Britannia' and 'God Save the Queen' and the Americans responded with 'My Country, 'Tis of Thee', and 'John Brown'. Then big Alec Beaubien, the Circle City king, demanded the 'Marseillaise', and the company broke up chanting 'Die Wacht am Rhein' to the frosty night.

'Don't come on these nights,' Frona whispered to Corliss at parting. 'We haven't spoken three words, and I know we shall be good friends. Did Dave Harney succeed in getting any sugar out of you?'

They mingled their laughter, and Corliss went home under the aurora borealis, striving to reduce his impressions to some kind of order.

CHAPTER VIII

'AND why should I not be proud of my race?'

Frona's cheeks were flushed and her eyes sparkling. They had both been harking back to childhood, and she had been telling Corliss of her mother, whom she faintly remembered. Fair and flaxen-haired, typically Saxon, was the likeness she had drawn, filled out largely with knowledge gained from her father and from old Andy of the Dyea Post. The discussion had then turned upon the race in general, and Frona had said things in the heat of enthusiasm which affected the more conservative mind of Corliss as dangerous and not solidly based on fact. He deemed himself too large for race egotism and insular prejudice, and had seen fit to laugh at her immature convictions.

'It's a common characteristic of all peoples,' he proceeded, 'to consider themselves superior races—a naïve, natural egoism, very healthy and very good, but none the less manifestly untrue. The Jews conceived themselves to be God's chosen people, and they still so conceive themselves—'

'And because of it they have left a deep mark down the page of history,' she interrupted.

'But time has not proved the stability of their conceptions. And you must also view the other side. A superior people must look upon all others as inferior peoples. This comes home to you. To be a Roman were greater than to be a king, and when the Romans rubbed against your savage ancestors in the German forests, they elevated their brows and said, "An inferior people, barbarians."'

'But we are here, now. We are, and the Romans are not. The test is time. So far we have stood the test; the signs are favourable that we shall continue to stand it. We *are* the best fitted!'

'Egotism.'

'But wait. Put it to the test.'

As she spoke her hand flew out impulsively to his. At

the touch his heart pulsed upward, there was a rush of blood and a tightening across the temples. Ridiculous, but delightful, he thought. At this rate he could argue with her the night through.

'The test,' she repeated, withdrawing her hand without embarrassment. 'We are a race of doers and fighters, of globe-encirclers and zone-conquerors. We toil and struggle, and stand by the toil and struggle no matter how hopeless it may be. While we are persistent and resistant, we are so made that we fit ourselves to the most diverse conditions. Will the Indian, the Negro, or the Mongol ever conquer the Teuton? Surely not! The Indian has persistence without variability; if he does not modify he dies, if he does try to modify he dies anyway. The Negro has adaptability, but he is servile and must be led. As for the Chinese they are permanent. All that the other races are not, the Anglo-Saxon, or Teuton if you please, is. All that the other races have not, the Teuton has. What race is to rise up and overwhelm us?'

'Ah, you forget the Slav,' Corliss suggested slyly.

'The Slav!' Her face fell. 'True, the Slav! The only stripling in this world of young men and greybeards! But he is still in the future, and in the future the decision rests. In the meantime we prepare. It may be we shall have such a start that we shall prevent him growing. You know, because he was better skilled in chemistry, knew how to manufacture gunpowder, that the Spaniard destroyed the Aztec. May not we, who are possessing ourselves of the world and its resources, and gathering to ourselves all its knowledge, may not we nip the Slav ere he grows a thatch to his lip?'

Vance Corliss shook his head non-committally, and laughed.

'Oh! I know I become absurd and grow overwarm!' she exclaimed. 'But after all, one reason that we are the salt of the earth is because we have the courage to say so.'

'And I am sure your warmth spreads,' he responded. 'See, I'm beginning to glow myself. We are not God's, but Nature's chosen people, we Angles, and Saxons, and Normans, and Vikings, and the earth is our heritage. Let us arise and go forth!'

67

'Now you are laughing at me, and, besides, we have already gone forth. Why have you fared into the north, if not to lay hands on the race legacy?'

She turned her head at the sound of approaching footsteps, and cried for greeting, 'I appeal to you, Captain Alexander! I summon you to bear witness!'

The captain of police smiled in his sternly mirthful fashion as he shook hands with Frona and Corliss. 'Bear witness?' he questioned. 'Ah, yes!

'"Bear witness, O my comrades, what a hard-bit gang were we,—
    The servants of the sweep-head, but the masters of the sea!"'

He quoted the verse with a savage solemnity exulting through his deep voice. This, and the appositeness of it, quite carried Frona away, and she had both his hands in hers on the instant. Corliss was aware of an inward wince at the action. It was uncomfortable. He did not like to see her so promiscuous with those warm, strong hands of hers. Did she so favour all men who delighted her by word or deed? He did not mind her fingers closing round his, but somehow it seemed wanton when shared with the next comer. By the time he had thought thus far, Frona had explained the topic under discussion, and Captain Alexander was testifying.

'I don't know much about your Slav and other kin, except that they are good workers and strong; but I do know that the white man is the greatest and best breed in the world. Take the Indian, for instance. The white man comes along and beats him at all his games, outworks him, out-roughs him, out-fishes him, out-hunts him. As far back as their myths go, the Alaskan Indians have packed on their backs. But the gold-rushers, as soon as they had learned the tricks of the trade, packed greater loads and packed them farther than did the Indians. Why, last May, the Queen's birthday, we had sports on the river. In the one, two, three, four, and five men canoe races we beat the Indians right and left. Yet they had been born to the paddle, and most of us had never seen a canoe until man-grown.'

'But why is it?' Corliss queried.

'I do not know why. I only know that it is. I simply bear

68

witness. I do know that we do what they cannot do, and what they can do, we do better.'

Frona nodded her head triumphantly at Corliss. 'Come, acknowledge your defeat, so that we may go in to dinner. Defeat for the time being, at least. The concrete facts of paddles and pack-straps quite overcome your dogmatics. Ah, I thought so. More time? All the time in the world. But let us go in. We'll see what my father thinks of it—and Mr Kellar. A symposium on Anglo-Saxon supremacy!'

Frost and enervation are mutually repellent. The Northland gives a keenness and zest to the blood which cannot be obtained in warmer climes. Naturally so, then, the friendship which sprang up between Corliss and Frona was anything but languid. They met often under her father's roof-tree, and went to many places together. Each found a pleasurable attraction in the other, and a satisfaction which the things they were not in accord with could not mar. Frona liked the man because he was a man. In her wildest flights she could never imagine linking herself with any man, no matter how exalted spiritually, who was not a man physically. It was a delight to her and a joy to look upon the strong males of her kind, with bodies comely in the sight of God and muscles swelling with the promise of deeds and work. Man, to her, was pre-eminently a fighter. She believed in natural selection and in sexual selection, and was certain that if man had thereby become possessed of faculties and functions they were for him to use and could but tend to his good. And likewise with instincts. If she felt drawn to any person or thing, it was good for her to be so drawn, good for herself. If she felt impelled to joy in a well-built frame and well-shaped muscle, why should she restrain? Why should she not love the body, and without shame? The history of the race, and of all races, sealed her choice with approval. Down all time, the weak and effeminate males had vanished from the world-stage. Only the strong could inherit the earth. She had been born of the strong, and chose to cast her lot with the strong.

Yet of all creatures she was the last to be deaf and blind to the things of the spirit. But the things of the spirit she demanded should be likewise strong. No halting, no stut-

69

tered utterance, tremulous waiting, minor wailing! The mind and the soul must be as quick and definite and certain as the body. Nor was the spirit made alone for immortal dreaming. Like the flesh, it must strive and toil. It must be workaday as well as idle day. She could understand a weakling singing sweetly and even greatly, and in so far she could love him for his sweetness and greatness; but her love would have fuller measure were he strong of body as well. She believed she was just. She gave the flesh its due and the spirit its due; but she had, over and above, her own choice, her own individual ideal. She liked to see the two go hand in hand. Prophecy and dyspepsia did not affect her as a felicitous admixture. A splendid savage and a weak-kneed poet! She could admire the one for his brawn and the other for his song; but she would prefer that they had been made one in the beginning.

As to Vance Corliss. First, and most necessary of all, there was that physiological affinity between them that made the touch of his hand a pleasure to her. Though souls may rush together, if body cannot endure body, happiness is reared on sand and the structure will be ever unstable and tottery. Next, Corliss had the physical potency of the hero without the grossness of the brute. His muscular development was more qualitative than quantitative, and it is the qualitative development which gives rise to beauty of form. A giant need not be proportioned in the mould; nor a thew be symmetrical to be massive.

And finally—none the less necessary but still finally—Vance Corliss was neither spiritually dead nor decadent. He affected her as fresh and wholesome and strong, as reared above the soil but not scorning the soil. Of course, none of this she reasoned out otherwise than by subconscious processes. Her conclusions were feelings, not thoughts.

Though they quarrelled and disagreed on innumerable things, deep down, underlying all, there was a permanent unity. She liked him for a certain stern soberness that was his, and for his saving grace of humour. Seriousness and banter were not incompatible. She liked him for his gallantry, made to work with and not for display. She liked the spirit of his offer at Happy Camp, when he proposed giving her an Indian guide and passage-money back to the

United States. He could *do* as well as talk. She liked him for his outlook, for his innate liberality, which she felt to be there, somehow, no matter that often he was narrow of expression. She liked him for his mind. Though somewhat academic, somewhat tainted with latter-day scholasticism, it was still a mind which permitted him to be classed with the 'Intellectuals'. He was capable of divorcing sentiment and emotion from reason. Granted that he included all the factors, he could not go wrong. And here was where she found chief fault with him—his narrowness which precluded all the factors; his narrowness which gave the lie to the breadth she knew was really his. But she was aware that it was not an irremediable defect, and that the new life he was leading was very apt to rectify it. He was filled with culture; what he needed was a few more of life's facts.

And she liked him for himself, which is quite different from liking the parts which went to compose him. For it is no miracle for two things, added together, to produce not only the sum of themselves, but a third thing which is not to be found in either of them. So with him. She liked him for himself, for that something which refused to stand out as a part, or a sum or parts; for that something which is the corner-stone of Faith and which has ever baffled Philosophy and Science. And further, to like, with Frona Welse, did not mean to love.

First, and above all, Vance Corliss was drawn to Frona Welse because of the clamour within him for a return to the soil. In him the elements were so mixed that it was impossible for women many times removed to find favour in his eyes. Such he had met constantly, but not one had ever drawn from him a superfluous heart-beat. Though there had been in him a growing instinctive knowledge of lack of unity—the lack of unity which must precede, always, the love of man and woman—not one of the daughters of Eve he had met had flashed irresistibly in to fill the void. Elective affinity, sexual affinity, or whatsoever the intangible essence known as love is, had never been manifest. When he met Frona it had at once sprung, full-fledged, into existence. But he quite misunderstood it, took it for a mere attraction towards the new and unaccustomed.

71

Many men, possessed of birth and breeding, have yielded to this clamour for return. And giving the apparent lie to their own sanity and moral stability, many such men have married peasant girls or bar-maids. And those to whom evil apportioned itself have been prone to distrust the impulse they obeyed, forgetting that nature makes or mars the individual for the sake, always, of the type. For in every such case of return, the impulse was sound—only that time and space interfered, and propinquity determined whether the object of choice should be bar-maid or peasant girl.

Happily for Vance Corliss, time and space were propitious, and in Frona he found the culture he could not do without, and the clean sharp tang of the earth he needed. In so far as her education and culture went, she was an astonishment. He had met the scientifically smattered young woman before, but Frona had something more than smattering. Further, she gave new life to old facts, and her interpretations of common things were coherent and vigorous and new. Though his acquired conservatism was alarmed and cried danger, he could not remain cold to the charm of her philosophising, while her scholarly attainments were fully redeemed by her enthusiasm. Though he could not agree with much that she passionately held, he yet recognised that the passion of sincerity and enthusiasm was good.

But her chief fault, in his eyes, was her unconventionality. Woman was something so inexpressively sacred to him, that he could not bear to see any good woman venturing where the footing was precarious. Whatever good woman thus ventured, overstepping the metes and bounds of sex and status, he deemed did so of wantonness. And wantonness of such order was akin to—well, he could not say it when thinking of Frona, though she hurt him often by her unwise acts. However, he only felt such hurts when away from her. When with her, looking into her eyes which always looked back, or at greeting and parting pressing her hand which always pressed honestly, it seemed certain that there was in her nothing but goodness and truth.

And then he liked her in many different ways for many

different things. For her impulses, and for her passions which were always elevated. And already, from breathing the Northland air, he had come to like her for that comradeship which at first had shocked him. There were other acquired likings, her lack of prudishness, for instance, which he awoke one day to find that he had previously confounded with lack of modesty. And it was only the day before that day that he drifted, before he thought, into a discussion with her of 'Camille'. She had seen Bernhardt, and dwelt lovingly on the recollection. He went home afterwards, a dull pain gnawing at his heart, striving to reconcile Frona with the ideal impressed upon him by his mother that innocence was another term for ignorance. Notwithstanding by the following day he had worked it out and loosened another finger of the maternal grip.

He liked the flame of her hair in the sunshine, the glint of its gold by the firelight, and the waywardness of it and the glory. He liked her neat-shod feet and the grey-gaitered calves—alas, now hidden in long-skirted Dawson. He liked her for the strength of her slenderness; and to walk with her, swinging her step and stride to his, or merely to watch her come across a room or down the street, was a delight. Life and the joy of life romped through her blood, abstemiously filling out and rounding off each shapely muscle and soft curve. And he liked it all. Especially he liked the swell of her forearm, which rose firm and strong and tantalising and sought shelter all too quickly under the loose-flowing sleeve.

The co-ordination of physical with spiritual beauty is very strong in normal men, and so it was with Vance Corliss. That he liked the one was no reason that he failed to appreciate the other. He liked Frona for both, and for herself as well. And to like, with him, though he did not know it, was to love.

CHAPTER IX

VANCE CORLISS proceeded at a fair rate to adapt himself to the Northland life, and he found that many adjustments came easy. While his own tongue was alien to the brimstone of the Lord, he became quite used to strong language on the part of other men, even in the most genial conversation. Carthey, a little Texan who went to work for him for a while, opened or closed every second sentence, on an average, with the mild expletive, 'By damn!' It was also his invariable way of expressing surprise, disappointment, consternation, or all the rest of the tribe of sudden emotions. By pitch and stress and intonation, the protean oath was made to perform every function of ordinary speech. At first it was a constant source of irritation and disgust to Corliss, but ere long he grew not only to tolerate it, but to like it, and to wait for it eagerly. Once, Carthey's wheel-dog lost an ear in a hasty contention with a dog of the Hudson Bay, and when the young fellow bent over the animal and discovered the loss, the blended endearment and pathos of the 'by damn' which fell from his lips was a revelation to Corliss. All was not evil out of Nazareth, he concluded sagely, and, like Jacob Welse of old, revised his philosophy of life accordingly.

Again, there were two sides to the social life of Dawson. Up at the Barracks, at the Welse's, and a few other places, all men of standing were welcomed and made comfortable by the womenkind of like standing. There were teas, and dinners, and dances and socials for charity, and the usual run of things; all of which, however, failed to wholly satisfy the men. Down in the town there was a totally different though equally popular other side. As the country was too young for club-life, the masculine portion of the community expressed its masculinity by herding together in the saloons —the ministers and missionaries being the only exceptions to this mode of expression. Business appointments and deals were made and consummated in the saloons, enterprises projected, shop talked, the latest news discussed, and a general good fellowship maintained. There all life rubbed shoulders, and kings and dog-drivers, old-timers and *chechaquos,* met on a common level. And it so happened, probably because saw-mills and house-space were scarce, that the saloons accommodated the gambling tables, and the polished dance-house floors. And here, because he needs must bend to custom, Corliss's adaptation went on rapidly. And as Carthey, who appreciated him, soliloquised, ' The best of it is he likes it damn well, by damn !'

But any adjustment must have its painful periods, and while Corliss's general change went on smoothly, in the particular case of Frona it was different. She had a code of her own, quite unlike that of the community, and perhaps believed woman might do things at which even the saloon-inhabiting males would be shocked. And because of this, she and Corliss had their first disagreeable disagreement.

Frona loved to run with the dogs through the biting frost, cheeks tingling, blood bounding, body thrust forward, and limbs rising and falling ceaselessly to the pace. And one November day, with the first cold snap on and the spirit thermometer frigidly marking sixty-five below, she got out the sled, harnessed her team of huskies, and flew down the river trail. As soon as she cleared the town she was off and running. And in such manner, running and riding by turns, she swept through the Indian village below the bluffs, made an eight-mile circle up Moosehide Creek and back, crossed the river on the ice, and several hours later came flying up the west bank of the Yukon opposite the town. She was aiming to tap and return by the trail for the wood-sleds which crossed thereabout, but a mile away from it she ran into the soft snow and brought the winded dogs to a walk.

Along the rim of the river and under the frown of the overhanging cliffs, she directed the path she was breaking. Here and there she made detours to avoid the out-jutting talus, and at other times followed the ice in against the precipitous walls and hugged them closely around the abrupt bends. And so, at the head of her huskies, she came suddenly upon a woman sitting in the snow and gazing across the river at smoke-canopied Dawson. She had been crying, and this was sufficient to prevent Frona's scrutiny from wandering farther. A tear, turned to a globule of ice, rested on her cheek, and her eyes were dim and moist; there was an expression of hopeless, fathomless woe.

'Oh!' Frona cried, stopping the dogs and coming up to her. 'You are hurt? Can I help you?' she queried, though the stranger shook her head. 'But you mustn't sit there. It is nearly seventy below, and you'll freeze in a few minutes. Your cheeks are bitten already.' She rubbed the afflicted parts vigorously with a mitten of snow, and then look down on the warm returning glow.

'I beg pardon.' The woman rose somewhat stiffly to her feet. 'And I thank you, but I am perfectly warm, you see' (settling the fur cape more closely about her with a snuggling movement), 'and I had just sat down for the moment.'

Frona noted that she was very beautiful, and her woman's eye roved over and took in the splendid furs, the make of the gown, and the bead-work of the moccasins which peeped from beneath. And in view of all this, and of the fact that the face was unfamiliar, she felt an instinctive desire to shrink back.

'And I haven't hurt myself,' the woman went on. 'Just a mood, that was all, looking out over the dreary endless white.'

'Yes,' Frona replied, mastering herself; 'I can understand. There must be much of sadness in such a landscape, only it never comes that way to me. The sombreness and the sternness of it appeal to me, but not the sadness.'

'And that is because the lines of our lives have been laid in different places,' the other ventured, reflectively. 'It is not what the landscape is, but what we are. If we were not, the landscape would remain, but without human significance. That is what we invest it with.

'"Truth is within ourselves; it takes no rise
From outward things, whate'er you may believe."'

Frona's eyes brightened, and she went on to complete the passage:

76

'" There is an inmost centre in us all,
     Where truth abides in fulness ; and around,"

' And—and—how does it go? I have forgotten.'

'" Wall upon wall, the gross flesh hems it in— "'

The woman ceased abruptly, her voice trilling off into silvery laughter with a certain bitter reckless ring to it which made Frona inwardly shiver. She moved as though to go back to her dogs, but the woman's hand went out in a familiar gesture—twin to Frona's own—which went at once to Frona's heart.

' Stay a moment,' she said, with an undertone of pleading in the words, ' and talk with me. It is long since I have met a woman '—she paused while her tongue wandered for the word—' who could quote *Paracelsus*. You are—I know you, you see,—you are Jacob Welse's daughter, Frona Welse, I believe.'

Frona nodded her identity, hesitated, and looked at the woman with secret intentness. She was conscious of a great and pardonable curiosity, of a frank out-reaching for fuller knowledge. This creature, so like, so different; old as the oldest race, and young as the last rose-tinted babe; flung far as the farthermost fires of men, and eternal as humanity itself—where were they unlike, this woman and she? Her five senses told her not; by every law of life they were not; only, only by the fast-drawn lines of social caste and social wisdom were they not the same. So she thought, even as for one searching moment she studied the other's face. And in the situation she found an uplifting awfulness, such as comes when the veil is thrust aside and one gazes on the mysteriousness of Deity. She remembered : ' Her feet take hold of hell; her house is the way to the grave, going down to the chamber of death,' and in the same instant strong upon her was the vision of the familiar gesture with which the woman's hand had gone out in mute appeal, and she looked aside, out over the dreary endless white, and for her, too, the day became filled with sadness.

She gave an involuntary, half-nervous shiver, though she said, naturally enough, ' Come, let us walk on and get the

77

blood moving again. I had no idea it was so cold till I stood still.' She turned to the dogs : ' Mush-on ! King ! You Sandy ! Mush !' And back again to the woman, ' I am quite chilled, and as for you, you must be— '

' Quite warm, of course. You have been running and your clothes are wet against you, while I have kept up the needful circulation and no more. I saw you when you leaped off the sled below the hospital and vanished down the river like a Diana of the snows. How I envied you ! You must enjoy it.'

' Oh, I do,' Frona answered, simply. ' I was raised with the dogs.'

' It savours of the Greek.'

Frona did not reply, and they walked on in silence. Yet Frona wished, though she dared not dare, that she could give her tongue free rein, and from out of the other's bitter knowledge, for her own soul's sake and sanity, draw the pregnant human generalisations which she must possess. And over her welled a wave of pity and distress; and she felt a discomfort, for she knew not what to say or how to voice her heart. And when the other's speech broke forth, she hailed it with a great relief.

' Tell me,' the woman demanded, half-eagerly, half-masterly, ' tell me about yourself. You are new to the Inside. Where were you before you came in? Tell me.'

So the difficulty was solved, in a way, and Frona talked on about herself, with a successfully feigned girlhood innocence, as though she did not appreciate the other or understand her ill-concealed yearning for that which she might not have, but which was Frona's.

' There is the trail you are trying to connect with.' They had rounded the last of the cliffs, and Frona's companion pointed ahead to where the walls receded and wrinkled to a gorge, out of which the sleds drew the firewood across the river to town. ' I shall leave you there,' she concluded.

' But are you not going back to Dawson?' Frona queried. ' It is growing late, and you had better not linger.'

' No ... I ...'

Her painful hesitancy brought Frona to a realisation of her own thoughtlessness. But she had made the step, and she knew she could not retrace it.

'We will go back together,' she said, bravely. And in candid all-knowledge of the other, 'I do not mind.'

Then it was that the blood surged into the woman's cold face, and her hand went out to the girl in the old, old way.

'No, no, I beg of you,' she stammered. 'I beg of you . . . I . . . I prefer to continue my walk a little farther. See! Someone is coming now!'

By this time they had reached the wood-trail and Frona's face was flaming as the other's had flamed. A light sled, dogs a-lope and swinging down out of the gorge, was just upon them. A man was running with the team, and he waved his hand to the two women.

'Vance!' Frona exclaimed, as he threw his lead-dogs in the snow and brought the sled to a halt. 'What are you doing over here? Is the syndicate bent upon cornering the firewood also?'

'No. We're not so bad as that.' His face was full of smiling happiness at the meeting as he shook hands with her. 'But Carthey is leaving me—going prospecting somewhere around the North Pole, I believe—and I came across to look up Del Bishop, if he'll serve.'

He turned his head to glance expectantly at her companion, and she saw the smile go out of his face and anger come in. Frona was helplessly aware that she had no grip over the situation, and, though a rebellion at the cruelty and injustice of it was smouldering somewhere deep down, she could only watch the swift culmination of the little tragedy. The woman met his gaze with a half-shrinking, as from an impending blow, and with a softness of expression which entreated pity. But he regarded her long and coldly, then deliberately turned his back. As he did this, Frona noted her face go tired and grey, and the hardness and recklessness of her laughter were there painted in harsh tones, and a bitter devil rose up and lurked in her eyes. It was evident that the same bitter devil rushed hotly to her tongue. But it chanced just then that she glanced at Frona, and all expression was brushed from her face save the infinite tiredness. She smiled wistfully at the girl and without a word turned and went down the trail.

And without a word Frona sprang upon her sled and was

off. The way was wide, and Corliss swung in his dogs abreast of hers. The smouldering rebellion flared up, and she seemed to gather to herself some of the woman's recklessness.

'You brute!'

The words left her mouth, sharp, clear-cut, breaking the silence like the lash of a whip. The unexpectedness of it, and the savagery, took Corliss aback. He did not know what to do or say.

'Oh, you coward! You coward!'

'Frona! Listen to me—'

But she cut him off. 'No. Do not speak. You can have nothing to say. You have behaved abominably. I am disappointed in you. It is horrible! horrible!'

'Yes, it was horrible—horrible that she should walk with you, have speech with you, be seen with you.'

'"Not until the sun excludes you, do I exclude you,"' she flung back at him.

'But there is a fitness of things—'

'Fitness!' She turned upon him and loosed her wrath. 'If she is unfit, are you fit? May you cast the first stone with that smugly sanctimonious air of yours?'

'You shall not talk to me in this fashion. I'll not have it.'

He clutched at her sled, and even in the midst of her anger she noticed it with a little thrill of pleasure.

'Shall not? You coward!'

He reached out as though to lay hands upon her, and she raised her coiled whip to strike. But to his credit he never flinched; his white face calmly waited to receive the blow. Then she deflected the stroke, and the long lash hissed out and fell among the dogs. Swinging the whip briskly, she rose to her knees on the sled and called frantically to the animals. Hers was the better team, and she shot rapidly away from Corliss. She wished to get away, not so much from him as from herself, and she encouraged the huskies into wilder and wilder speed. She took the steep river-bank in full career and dashed like a whirlwind through the town and home. Never in her life had she been in such a condition; never had she experienced such terrible anger. And not only was she already ashamed, but she was frightened and afraid of herself.

CHAPTER X

The next morning Corliss was knocked out of a late bed by Bash, one of Jacob Welse's Indians. He was the bearer of a brief little note from Frona, which contained a request for the mining engineer to come and see her at his first opportunity. That was all that was said, and he pondered over it deeply. What did she wish to say to him? She was still such an unknown quantity—and never so much as now in the light of the day before—that he could not guess. Did she desire to give him his dismissal on a definite, well-understood basis? To take advantage of her sex and further humiliate him? To tell him what she thought of him in coolly considered, cold-measured terms? Or was she penitently striving to make amends for the unmerited harshness she had dealt him? There was neither contrition nor anger in the note, no clew, nothing save a formally worded desire to see him.

So it was in a rather unsettled and curious frame of mind that he walked in upon her as the last hour of the morning drew to a close. He was neither on his dignity nor off, his attitude being strictly non-committal against the moment she should disclose hers. But without beating about the bush, in that way of hers which he had come already to admire, she at once showed her colours and came frankly forward to him. The first glimpse of her face told him, the first feel of her hand, before she had said a word, told him that all was well.

'I am glad you have come,' she began. 'I could not be at peace with myself until I had seen you and told you how sorry I am for yesterday, and how deeply ashamed I—'

'There, there. It's not so bad as all that.' They were still standing, and he took a step nearer to her. 'I assure you I can appreciate your side of it; and though, looking at it theoretically, it was the highest conduct, demanding the fullest meed of praise, still, in all frankness, there is much to—to—'

' Yes.'

' Much to deplore in it from the social standpoint. And unhappily, we cannot leave the social standpoint out of our reckoning. But so far as I may speak for myself, you have done nothing to feel sorry for or be ashamed of.'

' It is kind of you,' she cried, graciously. ' Only it is not true, and you know it is not true. You know that you acted for the best; you know that I hurt you, insulted you; you know that I behaved like a fish-wife, and you do know that I disgusted you—'

' No, no!' He raised his hand as though to ward from her the blows she dealt herself.

' But yes, yes. And I have all reason in the world to be ashamed. I can only say this in defence: the woman had affected me deeply—so deeply that I was close to weeping. Then you came on the scene—you know what you did— and the sorrow for her bred an indignation against you, and—well, I worked myself into a nervous condition such as I had never experienced in my life. It was hysteria, I suppose. Anyway, I was not myself.'

' We were neither of us ourselves.'

' Now you are untrue. I did wrong, but you were your-self, as much so then as now. But do be seated. Here we stand as though you were ready to run away at first sign of another outbreak."

' Surely you are not so terrible!' he laughed, adroitly pulling his chair into position so that the light fell upon her face.

' Rather, you are not such a coward. I must have been terrible yesterday. I—I almost struck you. And you were certainly brave when the whip hung over you. Why, you did not even attempt to raise a hand and shield yourself.'

' I notice the dogs your whip falls among come neverthe-less to lick your hand and to be petted.'

' Ergo?' she queried, audaciously.

' Ergo, it all depends,' he equivocated.

' And, notwithstanding, I am forgiven?'

' As I hope to be forgiven.'

' Then I am glad—only, you have done nothing to be forgiven for. You acted according to your light, and I to mine, though it must be acknowledged that mine casts the broader flare. Ah! I have it,' clapping her hands in delight, 'I was not angry with you yesterday; nor did I behave rudely to you, or even threaten you. It was utterly impersonal, the whole of it. You simply stood for society, for the type which aroused my indignation and anger; and, as its representative, you bore the brunt of it. Don't you see?'

'I see, and cleverly put; only, while you escape the charge of maltreating me yesterday, you throw yourself open to it today. You make me out all that is narrow-minded and mean and despicable, which is very unjust. Only a few minutes past I said that your way of looking at it, theoretically considered, was irreproachable. But not so when we include society.'

'But you misunderstand me, Vance. Listen.' Her hand went out to his, and he was content to listen. 'I have always upheld that what is is well. I grant the wisdom of the prevailing social judgment in this matter. Though I deplore it, I grant it; for the human is so made. But I grant it socially only. I, as an individual, choose to regard such things differently. And as between individuals so minded, why should it not be so regarded? Don't you see? Now I find you guilty. As between you and me, yesterday, on the river, you did not so regard it. You behaved as narrow-mindedly as would have the society you represent.'

'Then you would preach two doctrines?' he retaliated. 'One for the elect and one for the herd? You would be a democrat in theory and an aristocrat in practice? In fact, the whole stand you are making is nothing more or less than Jesuitical.'

'I suppose with the next breath you will be contending that all men are born free and equal, with a bundle of natural rights thrown in? You are going to have Del Bishop work for you; by what equal free-born right will he work for you, or you suffer him to work?'

'No,' he denied. 'I should have to modify somewhat the questions of equality and rights.'

'And if you modify, you are lost!' she exulted. 'For you can only modify in the direction of my position, which is neither so Jesuitical nor so harsh as you have defined it. But don't let us get lost in dialectics. I want to see what I can see, so tell me about this woman.'

'Not a very tasteful topic,' Corliss objected.

'But I seek knowledge.'

'Nor can it be wholesome knowledge.'

Frona tapped her foot impatiently, and studied him.

'She is beautiful, very beautiful,' she suggested. 'Do you not think so?'

'As beautiful as hell.'

'But still beautiful,' she insisted.

'Yes, if you will have it so. And she is as cruel, and hard, and hopeless as she is beautiful.'

'Yet I came upon her, alone, by the trail, her face softened, and tears in her eyes. And I believe, with a woman's ken, that I saw a side of her to which you are blind. And so strongly did I see it, that when you appeared my mind was blank to all save the solitary wail, *Oh the pity of it! The pity of it!* And she is a woman, even as I, and I doubt not that we are very much alike. Why, she even quoted Browning—'

'And last week,' he cut her short, 'in a single sitting, she gambled away thirty thousand of Jack Dorsey's dust— Dorsey, with two mortgages already on his dump! They found him in the snow next morning, with one chamber empty in his revolver.'

Frona made no reply, but, walking over to the candle, deliberately thrust her finger into the flame. Then she held it up to Corliss that he might see the outraged skin, red and angry.

'And so I point the parable. The fire is very good, but I misuse it, and I am punished.'

'You forget,' he objected. 'The fire works in blind obedience to natural law. Lucile is a free agent. That which she has chosen to do, that she has done.'

'Nay, it is you who forget, for just as surely Dorsey was a free agent. But you said Lucile. Is that her name? I wish I knew her better.'

Corliss winced. 'Don't! You hurt me when you say such things.'

'And why, pray?'

'Because—because—'

'Yes?'

'Because I honour woman highly. Frona, you have

always made a stand for frankness, and I can now advantage by it. It hurts me because of the honour in which I hold you, because I cannot bear to see taint approach you. Why, when I saw you and that woman together on the trail, I—you cannot understand what I suffered.'

'Taint?' There was a tightening about her lips which he did not notice, and a just perceptible lustre of victory lighted her eyes.

'Yes, taint—contamination,' he reiterated. 'There are some things which it were not well for a good woman to understand. One cannot dabble with mud and remain spotless.'

'That opens the field wide.' She clasped and unclasped her hands gleefully. 'You have said that her name was Lucile; you display a knowledge of her; you have given me facts about her; you doubtless retain many which you dare not give; in short, if one cannot dabble and remain spotless, how about you?'

'But I am—'

'A man, of course. Very good. Because you are a man, you may court contamination. Because I am a woman, I may not. Contamination contaminates, does it not? Then you, what do you here with me? Out upon you!'

Corliss threw up his hands laughingly. 'I give in. You are too much for me with your formal logic. I can only fall back on the higher logic, which you will not recognise.'

'Which is—'

'Strength. What man wills for woman, that will he have.'

'I take you, then, on your own ground,' she rushed on. 'What of Lucile? What man has willed that he has had. So you, and all men, have willed since the beginning of time. So poor Dorsey willed. You cannot answer, so let me speak something that occurs to me concerning that higher logic you call strength. I have met it before. I recognised it in you, yesterday, on the sleds.'

'In me?'

'In you, when you reached out and clutched at me. You could not down the primitive passion, and, for that matter, you did not know it was uppermost. But the expression on your face, I imagine, was very like that of a woman-

85

stealing cave-man. Another instant, and I am sure you would have laid violent hands upon me.'

'Then I ask your pardon. I did not dream—'

'There you go, spoiling it all! I—I quite liked you for it. Don't you remember, I, too, was a cave-woman, brandishing the whip over your head?

'But I am not done with you yet, Sir Doubleface, even if you have dropped out of the battle.' Her eyes were sparkling mischievously, and the wee laughter-creases were forming on her cheek. 'I purpose to unmask you.'

'As clay in the hands of the potter,' he responded, meekly.

'Then you must remember several things. At first, when I was very humble and apologetic, you made it easier for me by saying that you could only condemn my conduct on the ground of being socially unwise. Remember?'

Corliss nodded.

'Then, just after you branded me as Jesuitical, I turned the conversation to Lucile, saying that I wished to see what I could see.'

Again he nodded.

'And just as I expected, I saw. For in only a few minutes you began to talk about taint, and contamination, and dabbling in mud—and all in relation to me. There are your two propositions, sir. You may only stand on one, and I feel sure that you stand on the last one. Yes, I am right. You do. And you were insincere, confess, when you found my conduct unwise only from the social point of view. I like sincerity.'

'Yes,' he began, 'I was unwittingly insincere. But I did not know it until further analysis, with your help, put me straight. Say what you will, Frona, my conception of woman is such that she should not court defilement.'

'But cannot we be as gods, knowing good and evil?'

'But we are not gods?' he shook his head, sadly.

'Only the men are?'

'That is new-womanish talk,' he frowned. 'Equal rights, the ballot, and all that.'

'Oh! Don't!' she protested. 'You won't understand me; you can't. I am no woman's rights' creature; and I stand, not for the new woman, but for the new womanhood.

86

Because I am sincere; because I desire to be natural, and honest, and true; and because I am consistent with myself, you choose to misunderstand it all and to lay wrong strictures upon me. I do try to be consistent, and I think I fairly succeed; but you can see neither rhyme nor reason in my consistency. Perhaps it is because you are unused to consitent, natural women; because, more likely, you are only familiar with the hot-house breeds—pretty, helpless, well-rounded, stall-fatted little things, blissfully innocent and criminally ignorant. They are not natural or strong; nor can they mother the natural and strong.'

She stopped abruptly. They heard somebody enter the hall, and a heavy, soft-moccasined tread approaching.

'We are friends,' she added hurriedly, and Corliss answered with his eyes.

'Ain't intrudin', am I?' Dave Harney grinned broad insinuation and looked about ponderously before coming up to shake hands.

'Not at all,' Corliss answered. 'We've bored each other till we were pining for someone to come along. If you hadn't, we would soon have been quarrelling, wouldn't we, Miss Welse?'

'I don't think he states the situation fairly,' she smiled back. 'In fact, we had already begun to quarrel.'

'You do look a mite flustered,' Harney criticised, dropping his loose-jointed frame all over the pillows of the lounging couch.

'How's the famine?' Corliss asked. 'Any public relief started yet?'

'Won't need any public relief. Miss Frona's old man was too forehanded fer 'em. Scairt the daylights out of the critters, I do b'lieve. Three thousand went out over the ice hittin' the high places, an' half ez many again went down to the caches, and the market's loosened some considerable. Jest what Welse figgered on, everybody speculated on a rise and held all the grub they could lay hand to. That helped scare the shorts, and away they stampeded fer Salt Water, the whole caboodle, atakin' all the dogs with 'em. Say!' he sat up solemnly, 'corner dogs! They'll rise suthin' unheard on in the spring when freightin' gits brisk I've corralled a hundred a'ready, an' I figger to
87

clear a hundred dollars clean on every hide of 'em.'

'Think so?'

'Think so! I guess yes. Between we three, confidential, I'm startin' a couple of lads down into the Lower Country next week to buy up five hundred of the best huskies they kin spot. Think so! I've limbered my jints too long in the land to git caught nappin'.'

Frona burst out laughing. 'But you got pinched on the sugar, Dave.'

'Oh, I dunno,' he responded, complacently. 'Which reminds me. I've got a noospaper, an' only four weeks old, the *Seattle Post-Intelligencer*.'

'Has the United States and Spain—'

'Not so fast, not so fast!' The long Yankee waved his arms for silence, cutting off Frona's question which was following fast on that of Corliss.

'But have you read it?' they both demanded.

'Unh huh, every line, advertisements an' all.'

'Then do tell me,' Frona began. 'Has—'

'Now you keep quiet, Miss Frona, till I tell you about it reg'lar. That noospaper cost me fifty dollars—caught the man comin' in round the bend above Klondike City, an' bought it on the spot. The dummy could a'got a hundred fer it, easy, if he'd held on till he made town—'

'But what does it say? Has—'

'Ez I was sayin', that noospaper cost me fifty dollars. It's the only one that come in. Everybody's jest dyin' to hear the noos. So I invited a select number of 'em to come here to yer parlours tonight, Miss Frona, ez the only likely place, an' they kin read it out loud, by shifts, ez long ez they want or till they're tired—that is, if you'll let 'em have the use of the place.'

'Why, of course, they are welcome. And you are very kind to—'

He waved her praise away. 'Jest ez I kalkilated. Now it so happens, ez you said, that I was pinched on sugar. So every mother's son and daughter that gits a squint at that paper tonight got to pony up five cups of sugar. Savve? Five cups—big cups, white, or brown, or cube—an' I'll take their I.O.U's, an' send a boy round to their shacks the day followin' to collect.'

Frona's face went blank at the telling, then the laughter came back into it. 'Won't it be jolly? I'll do it if it raises a scandal. Tonight, Dave? Sure tonight?'

'Sure. An' you git a complimentary, you know, fer the loan of yer parlour.'

'But papa must pay his five cups. You must insist upon it, Dave.'

Dave's eyes twinkled appreciatively. 'I'll git it back on him, you bet!'

'And I'll make him come,' she promised, 'at the tail of Dave Harney's chariot.'

'Sugar cart,' Dave suggested. 'An' tomorrow night I'll take the paper down to the Opery House. Won't be fresh, then, so they kin git in cheap; a cup'll be about the right thing, I reckon.' He sat up and cracked his huge knuckles boastfully. 'I ain't ben a-burnin' daylight sence navigation closed; an' if they set up all night they won't be up early enough in the mornin' to git ahead of Dave Harney—even on a sugar proposition.'

CHAPTER XI

O V E R in the corner Vance Corliss leaned against the piano, deep in conversation with Colonel Trethaway. The latter, keen and sharp and wiry, for all his white hair and sixty-odd years, was as young in appearance as a man of thirty. A veteran mining engineer, with a record which put him at the head of his profession, he represented as large American interests as Corliss did British. Not only had a cordial friendship sprung up between them, but in a business way they had already been of large assistance to each other. And it was well that they should stand together—a pair who held in grip and could direct at will the potent capital which two nations had contributed to the development of the land under the Pole.

The crowded room was thick with tobacco smoke. A hundred men or so, garbed in furs and warm-coloured wools, lined the walls and looked on. But the mumble of their general conversation destroyed the spectacular feature of the scene and gave to it the geniality of common comradeship.

For all its *bizarre* appearance, it was very like the living-room of the home when the members of the household come together after the work of the day. Kerosene lamps and tallow candles glimmered feebly in the murky atmosphere, while large stoves roared their red-hot and white-hot cheer.

On the floor a score of couples pulsed rhythmically to the swinging waltz-time music. Starched shirts and frock coats were not. The men wore their wolf and beaver-skin caps, with the gay-tasselled ear-flaps flying free, while on their feet were the moose-skin moccasins and walrus-hide muclucs of the north. Here and there a woman was in moccasins, though the majority danced in frail ballroom slippers of silk and satin. At one end of the hall a great open doorway gave glimpse of another large room where the crowd was even denser. From this room, in the lulls in the music, came the pop of corks and the clink of glasses, and as an undertone the steady click and clatter of chips and roulette balls.

The small door at the rear opened, and a woman, befurred and muffled, came in on a wave of frost. The cold rushed in with her to the warmth, taking form in a misty cloud which hung close to the floor, hiding the feet of the dancers, and writhing and twisting until vanquished by the heat.

'A veritable frost queen, my Lucile,' Colonel Trethaway addressed her.

She tossed her head and laughed, and, as she removed her capes and street-moccasins, chatted with him gaily. But of Corliss, though he stood within a yard of her, she took no notice. Half a dozen dancing men were waiting patiently at a little distance till she should have done with the colonel. The piano and violin played the opening bars of a schottische, and she turned to go; but a sudden impulse made Corliss step up to her. It was wholly unpremeditated; he had not dreamed of doing it.

'I am very sorry,' he said.

Her eyes flashed angrily as she turned upon him.

'I mean it,' he repeated, holding out his hand. 'I am very sorry. I was a brute and a coward. Will you forgive me?'

She hesitated, and, with the wisdom bought of experience, searched him for the ulterior motive. Then her face softened, and she took his hand. A warm mist dimmed her eyes.

'Thank you,' she said.

But the waiting men had grown impatient, and she was whirled away in the arms of a handsome young fellow, conspicuous in a cap of yellow Siberian wolf-skin. Corliss came back to his companion, feeling unaccountably good, and marvelling at what he had done.

'It's a damned shame.' The colonel's eye still followed Lucile, and Vance understood. 'Corliss, I've lived my three-score, and lived them well, and do you know, woman is a greater mystery than ever. Look at them, look at them all!' He embraced the whole scene with his eyes. 'Butter-flies, bits of light and song and laughter, dancing, dancing down the last tail-reach of hell. Not only Lucile, but the rest of them. Look at May, there, with the brow of a Madonna and the tongue of a gutter-devil. And Myrtle—for all the world one of Gainsborough's old English beauties stepped down from the canvas to riot out the century in Dawson's dance-halls. And Laura, there, wouldn't she make a mother? Can't you see the child in the curve of her arm against her breast? They're the best of the boiling, I know —a new country always gathers the best—but there's something wrong, Corliss, something wrong. The heats of life have passed with me, and my vision is truer, surer. It seems a new Christ must arise and preach a new salvation—economic or sociologic—in these latter days, it matters not, so long as it is preached. The world has need of it.'

The room was wont to be swept by sudden tides, and notably between the dances, when the revellers ebbed through the great doorway to where corks popped and glasses tinkled. Colonel Trethaway and Corliss followed out on the next ebb to the bar, where fifty men and women were lined up. They found themselves next to Lucile and the fellow in the yellow wolf-skin cap. He was undeniably handsome, and his looks were enhanced by a warm overplus of blood in the cheeks and a certain mellow fire in the eyes. He was not technically drunk, for he had himself in perfect physical control; but his was the soul-exhilaration which comes of the juice of the grape. His voice was raised the least bit and joyous, and his tongue made quick and witty—just in the unstable condition when vices and virtues are prone to extravagant expression.

As he raised his glass, the man next to him accidentally jostled his arm. He shook the wine from his sleeve and spoke his mind. It was not a nice word, but one customarily calculated to rouse the fighting blood. And the other man's blood roused, for his fist landed under the wolf-skin cap with force sufficient to drive its owner back against Corliss. The insulted man followed up his attack swiftly. The women slipped away, leaving a free field for the men, some of whom were for crowding in, and some for giving room and fair play.

The wolk-skin cap did not put up a fight or try to meet the wrath he had invoked, but, with his hands shielding his face, strove to retreat. The crowd called upon him to stand up and fight. He nerved himself to the attempt, but weakened as the man closed in on him, and dodged away.

'Let him alone. He deserves it,' the colonel called to Vance as he showed signs of interfering. 'He won't fight. If he did, I think I could almost forgive him.'

'But I can't see him pummelled,' Vance objected. 'If he would only stand up, it wouldn't seem so brutal.'

The blood was streaming from his nose and from a slight cut over one eye, when Corliss sprang between. He attempted to hold the two men apart, but pressing too hard against the truculent individual, overbalanced him and threw him to the floor. Every man has friends in a bar-room fight, and before Vance knew what was taking place he was staggered by a blow from a chum of the man he had downed. Del Bishop, who had edged in, let drive promptly at the man who had attacked his employer, and the fight became general. The crowd took sides on the moment and went at it.

Colonel Trethaway forgot that the heats of life had passed, and swinging a three-legged stool, danced nimbly into the fray. A couple of mounted police, on liberty, joined him, and with half a dozen others safeguarded the man with the wolf-skin cap.

Fierce though it was, and noisy, it was purely a local disturbance. At the far end of the bar, the bar-keepers still dispensed drinks, and in the next room the music was on and the dancers afoot. The gamblers continued their play, and at only the near tables did they evince any interest in the affair.

'Knock'm down an' drag'm out!' Del Bishop grinned, as he fought for a brief space shoulder to shoulder with Corliss.

Corliss grinned back, met the rush of a stalwart dog-driver with a clinch, and came down on top of him among the stamping feet. He was drawn close, and felt the fellow's teeth sinking into his ear. Like a flash, he surveyed his whole future and saw himself going one-eared through life, and in the same flash, as though inspired, his thumbs flew to the man's eyes and pressed heavily on the balls. Men fell over him and trampled upon him, but it all seemed very dim and far away. He only knew, as he pressed with his thumbs

93

that the man's teeth wavered reluctantly. He added a little pressure (a little more, and the man would have been eyeless), and the teeth slackened and slipped their grip.

After that, as he crawled out of the fringe of the *mélée* and came to his feet by the side of the bar, all distaste for fighting left him. He had found that he was very much like other men after all, and the imminent loss of part of his anatomy had scraped off twenty years of culture. Gambling without stakes is an insipid amusement, and Corliss discovered, likewise, that the warm blood which rises from hygienic gymnasium work is something quite different from that which pounds hotly along when thew matches thew and flesh impacts on flesh and the stake is life and limb. As he dragged himself to his feet by means of the bar-rail, he saw a man in a squirrel-skin *parka* lift a beer-mug to hurl at Trethaway, a couple of paces off. And the fingers, which were more used to test-tubes and water colours, doubled into a hard fist which smote the mug-thrower cleanly on the point of the jaw. The man merely dropped the glass and himself on the floor. Vance was dazed for the moment, then he realised that he had knocked the man unconscious—the first in his life—and a pang of delight thrilled through him.

Colonel Trethaway thanked him with a look, and shouted, 'Get on the outside! Work to the door, Corliss! Work to the door!'

Quite a struggle took place before the storm-doors could be thrown open; but the colonel, still attached to the three-legged stool, effectually dissipated the opposition, and the Opera House disgorged its turbulent contents into the street. This accomplished, hostilities ceased, after the manner of such fights, and the crowd scattered. The two policemen went back to keep order, accompanied by the rest of the allies, while Corliss and the colonel, followed by the Wolf-skin Cap and Del Bishop, proceeded up the street.

'Blood and sweat! Blood and sweat!' Colonel Trethaway exulted. 'Talk about putting the vim into one! Why, I'm twenty years younger if I'm a day! Corliss, your hand. I congratulate you, I do, I heartily do. Candidly, I didn't think it was in you. You're a surprise, sir, a surprise!'

'And a surprise to myself,' Corliss answered. The reaction

94

had set in, and he was feeling sick and faint. 'And you, also, are a surprise. The way you handled that stool— '

'Yes, now! I flatter myself I did fairly well with it. Did you see— well, look at that!' He held up the weapon in question, still tightly clutched, and joined in the laugh against himself.

'Whom have I to thank, gentlemen?'

They had come to a pause at the corner, and the man they had rescued was holding out his hand.

'My name is St Vincent,' he went on, 'and— '

'What name?' Del Bishop queried with sudden interest.

'St Vincent, Gregory St Vincent— '

Bishop's fist shot out, and Gregory St Vincent pitched heavily into the snow. The colonel instinctively raised the stool, then helped Corliss to hold the pocket-miner back.

'Are you crazy, man?' Vance demanded.

'The skunk! I wish I'd hit 'm harder!' was the response. Then, 'Oh, that's all right. Let go o' me. I won't hit 'm again. Let go o' me, I'm going home. Good night.'

As they helped St Vincent to his feet, Vance could have sworn he heard the colonel giggling. And he confessed to it later, as he explained, 'It was so curious and unexpected.' But he made amends by taking it upon himself to see St Vincent home.

'But why did you hit him?' Corliss asked, unavailingly, for the fourth time after he had got into his cabin.

'The mean, crawlin' skunk!' the pocket-miner gritted in his blankets. 'What'd you stop me for, anyway? I wish I'd hit 'm twice as hard!'

CHAPTER XII

'Mr. Harney, please to meet you. Dave, I believe, Dave Harney?' Dave Harney nodded, and Gregory St Vincent turned to Frona. 'You see, Miss Welse, the world is none so large. Mr. Harney and I are not strangers after all.'

The Eldorado king studied the other's face until a glimmering intelligence came to him. 'Hold on!' he cried, as St Vincent started to speak, 'I got my finger on you. You were smooth-faced then. Let's see—'86 fall of '87, summer of '88,—yep, that's when. Summer of '88 I come floatin' a raft out of Stewart River, loaded down with quarters of moose an' strainin' to make the Lower Country 'fore they went bad. Yep, an' down the Yukon you come, in a Linderman boat. An' I was holdin' strong ez it was Wednesday, an' my pardner ez it was Friday, an' you put us straight—Sunday, I b'lieve it was. Yep, Sunday. I declare! Nine years ago! And we swapped moose-steaks fer flour an' bakin' soda, an'—an'—an' sugar! By the Jimcracky! I'm glad to see you!'

He shoved out his hand and they shook again.

'Come an' see me,' he invited, as he moved away. 'I've a right tidy little shack up on the hill, and another on Eldorado. Latch-string's always out. Come an' see me, an' stay ez long ez you've a mind to. Sorry to quit you cold, but I got to traipse down to the Opery House and collect my taxes—sugar. Miss Frona'll tell you.'

'You are a surprise, Mr St Vincent.' Frona switched back to the point of interest, after briefly relating Harney's saccharine difficulties. 'The country must indeed have been a wilderness nine years ago, and to think that you went through it at that early day! Do tell me about it.'

Gregory St Vincent shrugged his shoulders. 'There is very little to tell. It was an ugly failure, filled with many things that are not nice, and containing nothing of which to be proud.'

'But do tell me. I enjoy such things. They seem closer

96

and truer to life than the ordinary everyday happenings. A failure, as you call it, implies something attempted. What did you attempt?'

He noted her frank interest with satisfaction. 'Well, if you will, I can tell you in few words all there is to tell. I took the mad idea into my head of breaking a new path around the world, and in the interest of science and journalism, particularly journalism, I proposed going through Alaska, crossing the Bering Straits on the ice, and journeying to Europe by way of Northern Siberia. It was a splendid undertaking, most of it being virgin ground, only I failed. I crossed the Straits in good order, but came to grief in Eastern Siberia—all because of Tamerlane is the excuse I have grown accustomed to making.'

'A Ulysses!' Mrs. Schoville clapped her hands and joined them. 'A modern Ulysses! How romantic!'

'But not an Othello,' Frona replied. 'His tongue is a sluggard. He leaves one at the most interesting point with an enigmatical reference to a man of a bygone age. You take an unfair advantage of us, Mr St Vincent, and we shall be unhappy until you show how Tamerlane brought your journey to an untimely end.'

He laughed, and with an effort put aside his reluctance to speak of his travels. 'When Tamerlane swept with fire and sword over Eastern Asia, states were disrupted, cities overthrown, and tribes scattered like star-dust. In fact, a vast people was hurled broadcast over the land. Fleeing before the mad lust of the conquerors, these refugees swung far into Siberia, circling to the north and east and fringing the rim of the polar basin with a spray of Mongol tribes— am I not tiring you?'

'No, no!' Mrs Schoville exclaimed. 'It is fascinating! Your method of narration is so vivid! It reminds me of—of—'

'Of Macaulay,' St Vincent laughed, good-naturedly. 'You know I am a journalist, and he has strongly influenced my style. But I promise you I shall tone down. However, to return, had it not been for these Mongol tribes, I should not have been halted in my travels. Instead of being forced to marry a greasy princess, and to become proficient in interclannish warfare and reindeer-stealing, I should have travelled easily and peaceably to St Petersburg.

'Oh, these heroes! Are they not exasperating, Frona? But what about the reindeer-stealing and the greasy princesses?'

The Gold Commissioner's wife beamed upon him, and glancing for permission to Frona, he went on.

'The coast people were Eskimo stock, merry-natured and happy, and inoffensive. They called themselves the Oukilion, or the Sea Men. I bought dogs and food from them, and they treated me splendidly. But they were subject to the Chow Chuen, or interior people, who were known as the Deer Men. The Chow Chuen were a savage, indomitable breed, with all the fierceness of the untamed Mongol, plus double his viciousness. As soon as I left the coast they fell upon me, confiscated my goods, and made me a slave.'

'But were there no Russians?' Mrs Schoville asked.

'Russians? Among the Chow Chuen?' He laughed his amusement. 'Geographically, they are within the White Tsar's domain; but politically, no. I doubt if they ever heard of him. Remember, the interior of North-Eastern Siberia is hidden in the polar gloom, a *terra incognita,* where few men have gone and none has returned.'

'But you—'

'I chance to be the exception. Why I was spared, I do not know. It just so happened. At first I was vilely treated, beaten by the women and children, clothed in vermin infested mangy furs, and fed on refuse. They were utterly heartless. How I managed to survive is beyond me; but I know that often and often, at first, I meditated suicide. The only thing that saved me during that period from taking my own life was the fact that I quickly became too stupefied and bestial, what of my suffering and degradation. Half-frozen, half-starved, under-going untold misery and hardship, beaten many and many a time into insensibility, I became the sheerest animal.

'On looking back much of it seems a dream. There are gaps which my memory cannot fill. I have vague recollections of being lashed to a sled and dragged from camp to camp and tribe to tribe. Carted about for exhibition purposes, I suppose, much as we do lions and elephants and wild men. How far I so journeyed up and down that bleak

98

region I cannot guess, though it must have been several thousand miles. I do know that when consciousness returned to me and I really became myself again, I was fully a thousand miles to the west of the point where I was captured.

'It was springtime, and from out of a forgotten past it seemed I suddenly opened my eyes. A reindeer thong was about my waist and made fast to the tail-end of a sled. This thong I clutched with both hands like an organ-grinder's monkey; for the flesh of my body was raw and in great sores from where the thong had cut in.

'A low cunning came to me and I made myself agree-able and servile. That night I danced and sang, and did my best to amuse them, for I was resolved to incur no more of the maltreatment which had plunged me into darkness. Now the Deer Men traded with the Sea Men, and the Sea Men with the whites, especially the whalers. So later I discovered a deck of cards in the possession of one of the women, and I proceeded to mystify the Chow Chuen with a few commonplace tricks. Likewise, with fitting solemnity, I perpetrated upon them the little I knew of parlour legerdemain. Result : I was appreciated at once, and was better fed and better clothed.

'To make a long story short, I gradually became a man of importance. First the old people and the women came to me for advice, and later the chiefs. My slight but rough and ready knowledge of medicine and surgery stood me in good stead, and I became indispensable. From a slave, I worked myself to a seat among the head men, and in war and peace, so soon as I had learned their ways, was an un-challenged authority. Reindeer was their medium of ex-change, their unit of value as it were, and we were almost constantly engaged in cattle forays among the adjacent clans, or in protecting our own herds from their inroads. I improved upon their methods, taught them better strategy and tactics, and put a snap and go into their operations which no neighbour tribe could withstand.

'But still, though I became a power, I was no nearer my freedom. It was laughable, for I had over-reached my-self and made myself too valuable. They cherished me with exceeding kindness, but they were jealously careful. I could go and come and command without restraint, but when the trading parties went down to the coast I was not permitted to accompany them. That was the one restriction placed upon my movements.

'Also, it is very tottery in the high places, and when I began altering their political structures I came to grief again. In the process of binding together twenty or more of the neighbouring tribes in order to settle rival claims, I was given the over-lordship of the federation. But Old Pi-Une was the greatest of the under-chiefs—a king in a way—and in relinquishing his claim to the supreme leadership he refused to forego all the honours. The least that could be done to appease him was for me to marry his daughter Ilswunga. Nay, he demanded it. I offered to abandon the federation, but he would not hear of it. And—'

'And?' Mrs Schoville murmured ecstatically.

'And I married Ilswunga, which is the Chow Chuen name for Wild Deer. Poor Ilswunga! Like Swinburne's Iseult of Brittany, and I Tristram! The last I saw of her she was playing solitaire in the Mission of Irkutsky and stubbornly refusing to take a bath.'

'Oh, mercy! It's ten o'clock!' Mrs. Schoville suddenly cried, her husband having at last caught her eye from across the room. 'I'm so sorry I can't hear the rest, Mr St Vincent, how you escaped and all that. But you must come and see me. I am just dying to hear!'

'And I took you for a tenderfoot, a *chechaquo*," Frona said meekly, as St Vincent tied his ear-flaps and turned up his collar preparatory to leaving.

'I dislike posing,' he answered, matching her meekness. 'It smacks of insincerity; it really is untrue. And it is so easy to slip into it. Look at the old-timers—'sour-doughs' as they proudly call themselves. Just because they have been in the country a few years, they let themselves grow wild and woolly and glorify in it. They may not know it, but it is a pose. In so far as they cultivate salient peculiarities, they cultivate falseness to themselves and live lies.'

'I hardly think you are wholly just,' Frona said, in defence of her chosen heroes. 'I do like what you say about the matter in general, and I detest posing, but the majority of the old-timers would be peculiar in any country, under any circumstances. That peculiarity is their own; it is their mode of expression. And it is, I am sure, just what makes them go into new countries. The normal man, of course, stays at home.'

'Oh, I quite agree with you, Miss Welse,' he temporised easily. 'I did not intend it so sweepingly. I meant to brand that sprinkling among them who are *poseurs*. In the main, as you say, they are honest, and sincere, and natural.'

'Then we have no quarrel. But, Mr St Vincent, before you go, would you care to come tomorrow evening? We are getting up theatricals for Christmas. I know you can help us greatly, and I think it will not be altogether unenjoyable to you. All the younger people are interested— the officials, officers of police, mining engineers, gentlemen rovers, and so forth, to say nothing of the nice women. You are bound to like them.'

'I am sure I shall,' as he took her hand. 'Tomorrow, did you say?'

'Tomorrow evening. Good night.'

A brave man, she told herself as she went back from the door, and a splendid type of the race.

CHAPTER XIII

GREGORY ST VINCENT swiftly became an important factor in the social life of Dawson. As a representative of the Amalgamated Press Association, he had brought with him the best credentials a powerful influence could obtain, and over and beyond, he was well qualified socially by his letters of introduction. It developed in a quiet way that he was a wanderer and explorer of no small parts, and that he had seen life and strife pretty well all over the earth's crust. And withal, he was so mild and modest about it, that nobody, not even among the men, was irritated by his achievements. Incidentally, he ran across numerous old acquaintances. Jacob Welse he had met at St Michael's in the fall of '88, just prior to his crossing Bering Straits on the ice. A month or so later, Father Barnum (who had come up from the Lower River to take charge of the hospital) had met him a couple of hundred miles on his way north of St Michael's. Captain Alexander, of the Police, had rubbed shoulders with him in the British Legation at Peking. And Bettles, another old-timer of standing, had met him at Fort o' Yukon nine years before.

So Dawson, ever prone to look askance at the casual comer, received him with open arms. Especially was he a favourite with the women. As a promoter of pleasures and an organiser of amusements he took the lead, and it quickly came to pass that no function was complete without him. Not only did he come to help in the theatricals, but insensibly, and as a matter of course, he took charge. Frona, as her friends charged, was suffering from a stroke of Ibsen, so they hit upon the 'Doll's House', and she was cast for Nora. Corliss, who was responsible, by the way, for the theatricals, having first suggested them, was to take Torvald's part; but his interest seemed to have died out, or at any rate he begged off on the plea of business rush. So St Vincent, without friction, took Torvald's lines. Corliss did manage to attend one rehearsal. It might have been that he had come tired from forty miles with the dogs, and it might have been that Torvald was obliged to put his arm about Nora at divers times and to toy playfully with her ear; but, one way or the other, Corliss never attended again.

Busy he certainly was, and when not away on trail he was closeted almost continually with Jacob Welse and Colonel Trethaway. That it was a deal of magnitude was evidenced by the fact that Welse's mining interests involved alone mounted to several millions. Corliss was primarily a worker and doer, and on discovering that his thorough theoretical knowledge lacked practical experience, he felt put upon his mettle and worked the harder. He even marvelled at the silliness of the men who had burdened him with such responsibilities, simply because of his pull, and he told Trethaway as much. But the colonel, while recognising his shortcomings, liked him for his candour, and admired him for his effort and for the quickness with which he came to grasp things actual.

Del Bishop, who had refused to play any hand but his own, had gone to work for Corliss because by so doing he was enabled to play his own hand better. He was practically unfettered, while the opportunities to further himself were greatly increased. Equipped with the best of outfits and a magnificent dog-team, his task was mainly to run the various creeks and keep his eyes and ears open. A pocket-miner, first, last, and always, he was privately on the constant lookout for pockets, which occupation did not interfere in the least with the duty he owed his employer. And as the days went by he stored his mind with miscellaneous data concerning the nature of the various placer deposits and the lay of the land, against the summer when the thawed surface and the running water would permit him to follow a trace from creek-bed to side-slope and source.

Corliss was a good employer, paid well, and considered it his right to work men as he worked himself. Those who took service with him either strengthened their own manhood and remained, or quit and said harsh things about him. Jacob Welse noted this trait with appreciation, and he sounded the mining engineer's praises continually. Frona heard and was gratified, for she liked the things her father liked; and she was more gratified because the man was

Corliss. But in his rush of business she saw less of him than formerly, while St Vincent came to occupy a greater and growing portion of her time. His healthful, optimistic spirit pleased her, while he corresponded well to her idealised natural man and favourite racial type. Her first doubt—that if what he said was true—had passed away. All the evidence had gone counter. Men who at first questioned the truth of his wonderful adventures gave in after hearing him talk. Those to any extent conversant with the parts of the world he made mention of, could not but acknowledge that he knew what he talked about. Young Soley, representing Bannock's News Syndicate, and Holmes of the *Fairweather,* recollected his return to the world in '91, and the sensation created thereby. And Sid Winslow, Pacific Coast journalist, had made his acquaintance at the Wanderers' Club shortly after he landed from the United States revenue cutter which had brought him down from the north. Further, as Frona well saw, he bore the ear-marks of his experiences; they showed their handiwork in his whole outlook on life. Then the primitive was strong in him, and his was a passionate race pride which fully matched hers. In the absence of Corliss they were much together, went out frequently with the dogs, and grew to know each other thoroughly.

All of which was not pleasant to Corliss, especially when the brief intervals he could devote to her were usually intruded upon by the correspondent. Naturally, Corliss was not drawn to him, and other men, who knew or had heard of the Opera House occurrence, only accepted him after a tentative fashion. Trethaway had the indiscretion, once or twice, to speak slightingly of him, but so fiercely was he defended by his admirers that the colonel developed the good taste to thenceforward keep his tongue between his teeth. Once, Corliss, listening to an extravagant panegyric bursting from the lips of Mrs Schoville, permitted himself the luxury of an incredulous smile; but the quick wave of colour in Frona's face, and the gathering of the brows, warned him.

At another time he was unwise enough and angry enough to refer to the Opera House broil. He was carried away, and what he might have said of that night's happening would have redounded neither to St Vincent's credit nor to his own, had not Frona innocently put a seal upon his lips ere he had properly begun.

'Yes,' she said. 'Mr St Vincent told me about it. He met you for the first time that night, I believe. You all fought loyally on his side—you and Colonel Trethaway. He spoke his admiration unreservedly and, to tell the truth, with enthusiasm.'

Corliss made a gesture of depreciation.

'No! no! From what he said you must have behaved splendidly. And I was most pleased to hear. It must be great to give the brute the rein now and again, and healthy, too. Great for us who have wandered from the natural and softened to sickly ripeness. Just to shake off artificiality and rage up and down! and yet, the inmost mentor, serene and passionless, viewing all and saying : " This is my other self. Behold! I, who am now powerless, am the power behind and ruleth still! This other self, mine ancient, violent, elder self, rages blindly as the beast, but 'tis I, sitting apart, who discern the merit of the cause and bid him rage or bid him cease !" Oh, to be a man !'

Corliss could not help a humouring smile, which put Frona upon defence at once.

'Tell me, Vance, how did it feel? Have I not described it rightly? Were the symptoms yours? Did you not hold aloof and watch yourself play the brute?'

He remembered the momentary daze which came when he stunned the man with his fist, and nodded.

'And pride?' she demanded, inexorably. 'Or shame?'

'A—a little of both, and more of the first than the second,' he confessed. 'At the time I suppose I was madly exultant; then afterwards came the shame, and I tossed awake half the night.'

'And finally?'

'Pride, I guess. I couldn't help it, couldn't down it. I awoke in the morning feeling as though I had won my spurs. In a subconscious way I was inordinately proud of myself, and time and again, mentally, I caught myself throwing chests. Then came the shame again, and I tried to reason back my self-respect. And last of all, pride. The fight was fair and open. It was none of my seeking. I was forced into it by the best of motives. I am not sorry, and I would repeat it if necessary.'

'And rightly so.' Frona's eyes were sparkling. 'And how did Mr St Vincent acquit himself?'

'He? . . . Oh, I suppose all right, creditably. I was too busy watching my other self to take notice.'

'But he saw you.'

'Most likely so. I acknowledge my negligence. I should have done better, the chances are, had I thought it would have been of interest to you—pardon me, just my bungling wit. The truth is, I was too much of a greenhorn to hold my own and spare glances on my neighbours.'

So Corliss went away, glad that he had not spoken, and keenly appreciating St Vincent's craft whereby he had so adroitly forestalled adverse comment by telling the story in his own modest, self-effacing way.

Two men and a woman! The most potent trinity of factors in the creating of human pathos and tragedy! As ever in the history of man, since the first father dropped down from his arboreal home and walked upright, so at Dawson. Necessarily, there were minor factors, not least among which was Del Bishop, who, in his aggressive way, stepped in and accelerated things. This came about in a trail-camp on the way to Miller Creek, where Corliss was bent on gathering in a large number of low-grade claims which could only be worked profitably on a large scale.

'I'll not be wastin' candles when I make a strike, savve!' the pocket-miner remarked savagely to the coffee, which he was settling with a chunk of ice. 'Not on your life, I guess rather not!'

'Kerosene?' Corliss queried, running a piece of bacon-rind round the frying-pan and pouring in the batter.

'Kerosene, hell! You won't see my trail for smoke when I get a gait on for God's country, my wad in my poke and the sunshine in my eyes. Say! How'd a good juicy tenderloin strike you just now, green onions, fried potatoes, and fixin's on the side? S'help me, that's the first proposition I'll hump myself up against. Then a general whoop-la! for a week—Seattle or 'Frisco, I don't care a rap which, and then—'

'Out of money and after a job.'

'Not on your family tree!' Bishop roared. 'Cache my sack before I go on the tear, sure pop, and then, afterwards, Southern California. Many's the day I've had my eye on a peach of a fruit farm down there—forty thousand'll buy it. No more workin' for grub-stakes and the like. Figured it out long ago—hired men to work the ranch, a manager to run it, and me ownin' the game and livin' off the percentage. A stable with always a couple of bronchos handy; handy to slap the packs and saddles on and be off and away whenever the fever for chasin' pockets came over me. Great pocket country down there, to the east and along the desert.'

'And no house on the ranch?'

'Cert! With sweet peas growin' up the sides, and in back a patch for vegetables—string-beans and spinach and radishes, cucumbers and 'sparagrass, turnips, carrots, cabbage, and such. And a woman inside to draw me back when I get to runnin' loco after the pockets. Say, you know all about minin'. Did you ever go snoozin' round after pockets? No? Then just steer clear. They're worse than whisky, horses, or cards. Women, when they come afterwards, ain't in it. Whenever you get a hankerin' after pockets, go right off and get married. It's the only thing'll save you; and even then, mebbe, it won't. I ought 'a' done it years ago. I might 'a' made something of myself if I had. Jerusalem! the jobs I've jumped and the good things chucked in my time, just because of pockets! Say, Corliss, you want to get married, you do, and right off. I'm tellin' you straight. Take warnin' from me and don't stay single any longer than God'll let you, sure!

Corliss laughed.

'Sure. I mean it. I'm older'n you, and know what I'm talking. Now there's a bit of a thing down in Dawson I'd like to see you get your hands on. You was made for each other, both of you.'

Corliss was past the stage when he would have treated Bishop's meddling as an impertinence. The trail, which turns men into the same blankets and makes them brothers, was the great leveller of distinctions, as he had come to learn. So he flopped a flapjack and held his tongue.

'Why don't you waltz in and win?' Del demanded, insistently. 'Don't you cotton to her? I know you do, or you wouldn't come back to cabin, after bein' with her, a-walkin'-like on air. Better waltz in while you got a chance. Why, there was Emmy, a tidy bit of flesh as women go, and we took to each other on the jump. But I kept a-chasin' pockets and chasin' pockets, and delayin'. And then a big black lumberman, a Kanuck, began sidlin' up to her, and I made up my mind to speak—only I went off after one more pocket, just one more, and when I got back she was Mrs Somebody Else.

'So take warnin'. There's that writer-guy, that skunk I poked outside the Opera House. He's walkin' right in and gettin' thick; and here's you, just like me, a-racin' round all creation and lettin' matrimony slide. Mark my words, Corliss! Some fine frost you'll come slippin' into camp and find 'em housekeepin'. Sure! With nothin' left for you in life but pocketing!'

The picture was so unpleasant that Corliss turned surly and ordered him to shut up.

'Who? Me?' Del asked so aggrievedly that Corliss laughed.

'What would you do, then?' he asked.

'Me? In all kindness I'll tell you. As soon as you get back you go and see her. Make dates with her ahead till you got to put 'em on paper to remember 'em all. Get a cinch on her spare time ahead so as to shut the other fellow out. Don't get down in the dirt to her—she's not that kind —but don't be too high and mighty, neither. Just so-so— savve? And then, some time when you see she's feelin' good, and smilin' at you in that way of hers, why up and call her hand. Of course I can't say what the show-down'll be. That's for you to find out. But don't hold off too long about it. Better married early than never. And if that writer-guy shoves in, poke him in the breadbasket—hard! That'll settle him plenty. Better still, take him off to one side and talk to him. Tell'm you're a bad man, and that you staked that claim before he was dry behind the ears, and that if he comes nosin' around tryin' to file on it you'll beat his head off.'

Bishop got up, stretched, and went outside to feed the

dogs. 'Don't forget to beat his head off,' he called back.
'And if you're squeamish about it, just call on me. I won't
keep 'm waitin' long.'

CHAPTER XIV

———

'A H , the salt water, Miss Welse, the strong salt water and the big waves and the heavy boats for smooth or rough—that I know. But the fresh water, and the little canoes, egg-shells, fairy bubbles; a big breath, a sigh, a heart-pulse too much, and pouf ! over you go; not so, that I do not know.' Baron Courbertin smiled self-commiseratingly and went on. 'But it is delightful, magnificent. I have watched and envied. Some day I shall learn.'

'It is not so difficult,' St Vincent interposed. 'Is it, Miss Welse? Just a sure and delicate poise of mind and body—'

'Like the tight-rope dancer?'

'Oh, you are incorrigible,' Frona laughed. 'I feel certain that you know as much about canoes as we.'

'And you know?—a woman?' Cosmopolitan as the Frenchman was, the independence and ability for doing of the Yankee women were a perpetual wonder to him. 'How?'

'When I was a very little girl, at Dyea, among the Indians. But next spring, after the river breaks, we'll give you your first lessons, Mr St Vincent and I. So you see, you will return to civilisation with accomplishments. And you will surely love it.'

'Under such charming tutorship,' he murmured, gallantly. 'But you, Mr St Vincent, do you think I shall be so successful that I may come to love it? Do you love it?— you, who stand always in the background, sparing of speech, inscrutable, as though able but unwilling to speak from out the eternal wisdom of a vast experience.' The baron turned quickly to Frona. 'We are old friends, did I not tell you? So I may, what you Americans call, *josh* with him. Is it not so, Mr St Vincent?'

Gregory nodded, and Frona said, 'I am sure you met at the ends of the earth somewhere.'

'Yokohama,' St Vincent cut in shortly; 'eleven years ago, in cherry-blossom time. But Baron Courbertin does me an injustice, which stings, unhappily, because it is not true. I am afraid, when I get started, that I talk too much about myself.'

'A martyr to your friends,' Frona conciliated. 'And such a teller of good tales that your friends cannot forbear imposing upon you.'

'Then tell us a canoe story,' the baron begged. 'A good one! A—what you Yankees call—*a hair-raiser!*'

They drew up to Mrs Schoville's fat wood-burning stove, and St Vincent told of the great whirlpool in the Box Canyon, of the terrible corkscrew in the mane of the White Horse Rapids, and of his cowardly comrade, who, walking around, had left him to go through alone—nine years before when the Yukon was virgin.

Half an hour later Mrs Schoville bustled in, with Corliss in her wake.

'That hill! The last of my breath!' she gasped, pulling off her mittens. 'Never saw such luck!' she declared none the less vehemently the next moment. 'This play will never come off! I never shall be Mrs Linden! How can I? Krogstad's gone on a stampede to Indian River, and no one knows when he'll be back! Krogstad.' (to Corliss) 'is Mr Maybrick, you know. And Mrs Alexander has the neuralgia and can't stir out. So there's no rehearsal today, that's flat!' She attitudinised dramatically : '" *Yes, in my first terror! But a day has passed, and in that day I have seen incredible things in this house! Helmer must know everything! There must be an end to this unhappy secret! O Krogstad, you need me, and I—I need you,*" and you are over on the Indian River making sour-dough bread, and I shall never see you more!'

They clapped their applause.

'My only reward for venturing out and keeping you all waiting was my meeting with this ridiculous fellow.' She shoved Corliss forward. 'Oh! you have not met! Baron Courbertin, Mr Corliss. If you strike it rich, baron, I advise you to sell to Mr Corliss. He has the money-bags of Crœsus, and will buy anything so long as the title is good. And if you don't strike, sell anyway. He's a professional philanthropist, you know.

'But would you believe it!' (addressing the general

group) 'this ridiculous fellow kindly offered to see me up the hill and gossip along the way—gossip! though he refused point-blank to come in and watch the rehearsal. But when he found there wasn't to be any, he changed about like a weather-vane. So here he is, claiming to have been away to Miller Creek; but between ourselves there is no telling what dark deeds—'

'Dark deeds! Look!' Frona broke in, pointing to the tip of an amber mouth-piece which projected from Vance's outside breast-pocket. 'A pipe! My congratulations.'

She held out her hand and he shook good-humouredly.

'All Del's fault,' he laughed. 'When I go before the great white throne, it is he who shall stand forth and be responsible for that particular sin.'

'An improvement, nevertheless,' she argued. 'All that is wanting is a good round swear-word now and again.'

'Oh, I assure you I am not unlearned,' he retorted. 'No man can drive dogs else. I can swear from hell to breakfast, by damn, and back again, if you will permit me, to the last link of perdition. By the bones of Pharaoh and the blood of Judas, for instance, are fairly efficacious with a string of huskies; but the best of my dog-driving nomenclature, more's the pity, women cannot stand. I promise you, however, in spite of hell and high water—'

'Oh! Oh!' Mrs Schoville screamed, thrusting her fingers into her ears.

'Madame,' Baron Courbertin spoke up gravely, 'it is a fact, a lamentable fact, that the dogs of the north are responsible for more men's souls than all other causes put together. Is it not so? I leave it to the gentlemen.'

Both Corliss and St Vincent solemnly agreed, and proceeded to detonate the lady by swapping heart-rending and apposite dog tales.

St Vincent and the baron remained behind to take lunch with the Gold Commissioner's wife, leaving Frona and Corliss to go down the hill together. Silently consenting, as though to prolong the descent, they swerved to the right, cutting transversely the myriad foot-paths and sled roads which led down into the town. It was a mid-December day, clear and cold; and the hesitant high-noon sun, having laboriously dragged its pale orb up from behind the southern land-rim, balked at the great climb to the zenith, and began its shamefaced slide back beneath the earth. Its oblique rays refracted from the floating frost particles till the air was filled with glittering jewel-dust—resplendent, blazing, flashing light and fire, but cold as outer space.

They passed down through the scintillant, magical sheen, their moccasins rhythmically crunching the snow and their breaths wreathing mysteriously from their lips in sprayed opalescence. Neither spoke, nor cared to speak, so wonderful was it all. At their feet, under the great vault of heaven, a speck in the midst of the white vastness, huddled the golden city—puny and sordid, feebly protesting against immensity, man's challenge to the infinite!

Calls of men and cries of encouragement came sharply to them from close at hand, and they halted. There was an eager yelping, a scratching of feet, and a string of ice-rimed wolf-dogs, with hot-lolling tongues and dripping jaws, pulled up the slope and turned into the path ahead of them. On the sled, a long and narrow box of rough-sawed spruce told the nature of the freight. Two dog-drivers, a woman walking blindly, and a black-robed priest, made up the funeral cortège. A few paces farther on the dogs were again put against the steep, and with whine and shout and clatter the unheeding clay was hauled on and upward to its ice-hewn hillside chamber.

'A zone-conqueror,' Frona broke voice.

Corliss found his thought following hers, and answered, 'These battlers of frost and fighters of hunger! I can understand how the dominant races have come down out of the north to empire. Strong to venture, strong to endure, with infinite faith and infinite patience, is it to be wondered at?'

Frona glanced at him in eloquent silence.

'"We smote with our swords,"' he chanted; '"to me it was a joy like having my bright bride by me on the couch." "I have marched with my bloody sword, and the raven has followed me. Furiously we fought; the fire passed over the dwellings of men; we slept in the blood of those who kept the gates."'

113

'But do you feel it, Vance?' she cried, her hand flashing out and resting on his arm.

'I begin to feel, I think. The north has taught me, is teaching me. The old things come back with new significance. Yet I do not know. It seems a tremendous egotism, a magnificent dream.'

'But you are not a negro or a Mongol, nor are you descended from the negro or Mongol.'

'Yes,' he considered, 'I am my father's son, and the line goes back to the sea-kings who never slept under the smoky rafters of a roof or drained the ale-horn by inhabited hearth. There must be a reason for the dead-status of the black, a reason for the Teuton spreading over the earth as no other race has ever spread. There must be something in race heredity, else I would not leap at the summons.'

'A great race, Vance. Half of the earth its heritage, and all of the sea! And in threescore generations it has achieved it all—think of it! threescore generations!—and today it reaches out wider-armed than ever. The smiter and the destroyer among nations! the builder and the law-giver! Oh, Vance, my love is passionate, but God will forgive, for it is good. A great race, greatly conceived; and if to perish, greatly to perish! Don't you remember:

' "*Trembles Yggdrasil's ash yet standing; groans that ancient tree, and the Jötun Loki is loosed. The shadows groan on the ways of Hel, until the fire of Surt has consumed the tree. Hrym steers from the east, the waters rise, the mundane snake is coiled in jötun-rage. The worm beats the water, and the eagle screams; the pale of beak tears carcases; the ship Naglfar is loosed. Surt from the south comes with flickering flame; shines from his sword the Val-god's sun."*'

Swaying there like a furred Valkyrie above the final carnage of men and gods, she touched his imagination, and the blood surged exultingly along unknown channels, thrilling and uplifting.

' "*The stony hills are dashed together, the giantesses totter; men tread the path of Hel, and heaven is cloven. The sun darkens, earth in ocean sinks, fall from heaven the bright stars, fire's breath assails the all-nourishing tree, towering fire plays against heaven itself."*'

114

Outlined against the blazing air, her brows and lashes white with frost, the jewel-dust striking and flashing against hair and face, and the south-sun lighting her with a great redness, the man saw her as the genius of the race. The traditions of the blood laid hold of him, and he felt strangely at one with the white-skinned, yellow-haired giants of the younger world. And as he looked upon her the mighty past rose before him, and the caverns of his being resounded with the shock and tumult of forgotten battles. With bellowing of storm-winds and crash of smoking North Sea waves, he saw the sharp-beaked fighting galleys, and the sea-flung Northmen, great-muscled, deep-chested, sprung from the elements, men of sword and sweep, marauders and scourgers of the warm southlands! The din of twenty centuries of battle was roaring in his ears, and the clamour for return to type strong upon him. He seized her hands passionately.

"Be the bright bride by me, Frona! Be the bright bride by me on the couch!'

She started and looked down at him, questioningly. Then the import of it reached her and she involuntarily drew back. The sun shot a last failing flicker across the earth and vanished. The fire went out of the air, and the day darkened. Far above, the hearse-dogs howled mournfully.

'No,' he interrupted, as words formed on her lips. 'Do not speak. I know my answer, your answer . . . now . . . I was a fool . . . Come, let us go down.'

It was not until they had left the mountain behind them, crossed the flat, and come out on the river by the saw-mill, that the bustle and scurry of human life made it seem possible for them to speak. Corliss had walked with his eyes moodily bent to the ground; and Frona, with head erect and looking everywhere, stealing an occasional glance to his face. Where the road rose over the log run-way of the mill the footing was slippery, and catching at her to save her from falling, their eyes met.

'I—I am grieved,' she hesitated. And then, in unconscious self-defence, ' It was so . . . I had not expected it— just then.'

'Else you would have prevented?' he asked, bitterly.

'Yes. I think I should have. I did not wish to give you pain—'

'Then you expected it, some time?'

'And feared it. But I had hoped . . . I . . . Vance, I did not come into the Klondike to get married. I liked you at the beginning, and I have liked you more and more—never so much as today—but—'

'But you had never looked upon me in the light of a possible husband—that is what you are trying to say.'

As he spoke, he looked at her sidewise, and sharply; and when her eyes met his with the same old frankness, the thought of losing her maddened him.

'But I have,' she answered at once. 'I have looked upon you in that light, but somehow it was not convincing. Why, I do not know. There was so much I found to like in you, so much—'

He tried to stop her with a dissenting gesture, but she went on.

'So much to admire. There was all the warmth of friendship, and closer friendship—a growing *camaraderie,* in fact; but nothing more. Though I did not wish more, I should have welcomed it had it come.'

'As one welcomes the unwelcome guest.'

'Why won't you help me, Vance, instead of making it harder? It is hard on you, surely, but do you imagine that I am enjoying it? I feel because of your pain, and, further, I know when I refuse a dear friend for a lover the dear friend goes from me. I do not part with friends lightly.'

'I see; doubly bankrupt; friend and lover both. But they are easily replaced. I fancy I was half lost before I spoke. Had I remained silent, it would have been the same anyway. Time softens; new associations, new thoughts and faces; men with marvellous adventures—'

She stopped him abruptly.

'It is useless, Vance, no matter what you may say. I shall not quarrel with you. I can understand how you feel—'

'If I am quarrelsome, then I had better leave you.' He halted suddenly, and she stood beside him. 'Here comes Dave Harney. He will see you home. It's only a step.'

'You are doing neither yourself nor me kindness.' She

116

spoke with final firmness. 'I decline to consider this the end. We are too close to it to understand it fairly. You must come and see me when we are both calmer. I refuse to be treated in this fashion. It is childish of you.' She shot a hasty glance at the approaching Eldorado king. 'I do not think I deserve it at your hands. I refuse to lose you as a friend. And I insist that you come and see me, that things remain on the old footing.'

He shook his head.

'Hello!' Dave Harney touched his cap and slowed down loose-jointedly. 'Sorry you didn't take my tip? Dogs gone up a dollar a pound since yesterday, and still a-whoopin'. Good afternoon, Miss Frona, and Mr Corliss. Goin' my way?'

'Miss Welse is.' Corliss touched the visor of his cap and half-turned on his heel.

'Where're you off to?' Dave demanded.

'Got an appointment,' he lied.

'Remember,' Frona called to him, 'you must come and see me.'

'Too busy, I'm afraid, just now. Good-bye. So long, Dave.'

'Jemimy!' Dave remarked, staring after him; 'but he's a hustler. Always busy—with big things, too. Wonder why he didn't go in for dogs?'

CHAPTER XV

B U T Corliss did go back to see her, and before the day was out. A little bitter self-communion had not taken long to show him his childishness. The sting of loss was hard enough, but the thought, now they could do nothing to each other, that her last impressions of him should be bad, hurt almost as much, and in a way, even more. And further, putting all to the side, he was really ashamed. He had thought that he could have taken such a disappointment more manfully, especially since in advance he had not been at all sure of his footing.

So he called upon her, walked with her up to the Barracks, and on the way, with her help, managed to soften the awkwardness which the morning had left between them. He talked reasonably and meekly, which she countenanced, and would have apologised roundly had she not prevented him.

'Not the slightest bit of blame attaches to you,' she said. 'Had I been in your place, I should probably have done the same and behaved much more outrageously. For you were outrageous, you know.'

'But had you been in my place, and I in yours,' he answered, with a weak attempt at humour, 'there would have been no need.'

She smiled, glad that he was feeling less strongly about it.

'But, unhappily, our social wisdom does not permit such a reversal,' he added, more with a desire to be saying something.

'Ah!' she laughed. 'There's where my Jesuitism comes in. I can rise above our social wisdom.'

'You don't mean to say—that—?'

'There, shocked as usual!' No, I could not be so crude as to speak outright, but I might *finesse,* as you whist-players say. Accomplish the same end, only with greater delicacy. After all, a distinction without a difference.'

'Could you?' he asked.

'I know I could—if the occasion demanded. I am not one to let what I might deem life-happiness slip from me without a struggle. That' (judicially) 'occurs only in books and among sentimentalists. As my father always says, I belong to the strugglers and fighters. That which appeared to me great and sacred, that would I battle for, though I brought heaven tumbling about my ears.'

'You have made me very happy, Vance,' she said at parting by the Barrack gates. 'And things shall go along in the same old way. And mind, not a bit less of you than formerly, but, rather, much more.'

But Corliss, after several perfunctory visits, forgot the way which led to Jacob Welse's home, and applied himself savagely to his work. He even had the hypocrisy, at times, to felicitate himself upon his escape, and to draw bleak fireside pictures of the dismal future which would have been had he and Frona incompatibly mated. But this was only at times. As a rule, the thought of her made him hungry, in a way akin to physical hunger; and the one thing he found to overcome it was hard work and plenty of it. But even then, what of trail and creek, and camp and survey, he could only get away from her in his waking hours. In his sleep he was ignobly conquered, and Del Bishop, who was with him much, studied his restlessness and gave a ready ear to his mumbled words.

The pocket-miner put two and two together and made a correct induction from the different little things which came under his notice. But this did not require any great astuteness. The simple fact that he no longer called on Frona was sufficient evidence of an unprospering suit. But Del went a step farther, and drew the corollary that St Vincent was the cause of it all. Several times he had seen the correspondent with Frona, going one place and another, and was duly incensed thereat.

'I'll fix 'm yet!' he muttered in camp one evening, over on Gold Bottom.

'Whom?' Corliss queried.

'Who? That newspaper man, that's who!'

'What for?'

'Aw—general principles. Why'n't you let me paste 'm that night at the Opera House?'

Corliss laughed at the recollection. 'Why did you strike him, Del?'

'General principles,' Del snapped back, and shut up.

But Del Bishop, for all his punitive spirit, did not neglect the main chance, and on the return trip, when they came to the forks of Eldorado and Bonanza, he called a halt.

'Say, Corliss,' he began at once, 'd'you know what a hunch is?' His employer nodded his comprehension. 'Well, I've got one. I ain't never asked favours of you before, but this once I want you to lay over here till tomorrow. Seems to me my fruit ranch is 'most in sight. I can damn near smell the oranges a-ripenin'.'

'Certainly,' Corliss agreed. 'But better still, I'll run on down to Dawson, and you can come in when you've finished hunching.'

'Say!' Del objected. 'I said it was a hunch; and I want to ring you in on it, savve? You're all right, and you've learned a hell of a lot out of books. You're a regular high-roller when it comes to the laboratory, and all that; but it takes yours truly to get down and read the face of nature without spectacles. Now I've got a theory——'

Corliss threw up his hands in affected dismay, and the pocket-miner began to grow angry.

'That's right! Laugh! But it's built right up on your own pet theory of erosion and changed river-beds. And I didn't pocket among the Mexicans two years for nothin'. Where d'you s'pose this Eldorado gold came from?—rough, and no signs of washin'? Eh? There's where you need your spectacles. Books have made you short-sighted. But never mind how. 'Tisn't exactly pockets, neither, but I know what I'm speiling about. I ain't been keepin' tab on traces for my health. I can tell you mining sharps more about the lay of Eldorado Creek in one minute than you could figure out in a month of Sundays. But never mind, no offence. You lay over with me till tomorrow, and you can buy a ranch 'long-side of mine, sure.'

'Well, all right. I can rest up and look over my notes while you're hunting your ancient river-bed.'

'Didn't I tell you it was a hunch?' Del reproachfully demanded.

'And haven't I agreed to stop over? What more do you want?'

'To give you a fruit ranch, that's what! Just to go with me, and nose round a bit, that's all.'

'I do not want any of your impossible fruit ranches. I'm tired and worried; can't you leave me alone? I think I am more than fair when I humour you to the extent of stopping over. You may waste your time nosing around, but I shall stay in camp. Understand?'

'Burn my body, but you're grateful! By the Jumpin' Methuselah, I'll quit my job in two minutes if you don't fire me. Me a-layin' 'wake nights and workin' up my theory, and calculatin' on lettin' you in, and you a-snorin' and Frona-this and Frona-that—'

'That'll do! Stop it!'

'The hell it will! If I didn't know more about gold-mining that you do about courtin'—'

Corliss sprang at him, but Del dodged to one side and put up his fists. Then he ducked a wild right and left swing and side-stepped his way into firmer footing on the hard trail.

'Hold on a moment,' he cried, as Corliss made to come at him again. 'Just a second. If I lick you, will you come up the hillside with me?'

'Yes.'

'And if I don't you can fire me. That's fair. Come on.'

Vance had no show whatever, as Del well knew, who played with him, feinting, attacking, retreating, dazzling, and disappearing every now and again out of his field of vision in a most exasperating way. As Vance speedily discovered, he possessed very little correlation between mind and body, and the next thing he discovered was that he was lying in the snow and slowly coming back to his senses.

'How—how did you do it?' he stammered to the pocket-miner, who had his head on his knee and was rubbing his forehead with snow.

'Oh, you'll do!' Del laughed, helping him limply to his feet. 'You're the right stuff. I'll show you some time. You've got lots to learn yet what you won't find in books. But not now. We've got to wade in and make camp, then you're comin' up the hill with me.'

'Hee! hee!' he chuckled later, as they fitted the pipe of the Yukon stove. 'Slow sighted and short. Couldn't follow me, eh? But I'll show you some time, oh, I'll show you all right, all right!'

'Grab an axe an' come on,' he commanded when the camp was completed.

He led the way up Eldorado, borrowed a pick, shovel, and pan at a cabin, and headed up among the benches near the mouth of French Creek. Vance, though feeling somewhat sore, was laughing at himself by this time, and enjoying the situation. He exaggerated the humility with which he walked at the heel of his conqueror, while the extravagant servility which marked his obedience to his hired man made that individual grin.

'You'll do. You've got the makin's in you!' Del threw down the tools and scanned the run of the snow-surface carefully. 'Here, take the axe, shinny up the hill, and lug me down some *skookum* dry wood.'

By the time Corliss returned with the last load of wood, the pocket-miner had cleared away the snow and moss in divers spots, and formed, in general design, a rude cross.

'Cuttin' her both ways,' he explained. 'Mebbe I'll hit her here, or over there, or up above; but if there's anything in the hunch, this is the place. Bed-rock dips in above, and it's deep there and most likely richer, but too much work. This is the rim of the bench. Can't be more'n a couple of feet down. All we want is indications; afterwards we can tap in from the side.'

As he talked, he started fires here and there on the uncovered spaces. 'But look here, Corliss, I want you to mind this ain't pocketin'. This is just plain ordinary 'prentice work; but pocketin''—he straightened up his back and spoke reverently—'but pocketin' is the deepest science and the finest art. Delicate to a hair's breadth, hand and eye true and steady as steel. When you've got to burn your pan blue-black twice a day, and out of a shovelful of gravel wash down to the one wee speck of flour gold—why, that's washin', that's what it is. Tell you what, I'd sooner follow a pocket than eat.'

'And you would sooner fight than do either.'

Bishop stopped to consider. He weighed himself with

care equal to that of retaining the one wee speck of flour gold. 'No, I wouldn't, neither. I'd take pocketin' in mine every time. It's as bad as dope, Corliss, sure. If it once gets a-hold of you, you're a goner. You'll never shake it. Look at me! And talk about pipe-dreams; they can't burn a candle 'longside of it.'

He walked over and kicked one of the fires apart. Then he lifted the pick, and the steel point drove in and stopped with a metallic clang, as though brought up by solid cement.

'Ain't thawed two inches,' he muttered, stooping down and groping with his fingers in the wet muck. The blades of last year's grass had been burned away, but he managed to gather up and tear away a handful of the roots.

'Hell!'

'What's the matter?' Corliss asked.

'Hell!' he repeated in a passionless way, knocking the dirt-covered roots against the pan.

Corliss went over and stooped to closer inspection. 'Hold on!' he cried, picking up two or three grimy bits of dirt and rubbing them with his fingers. A bright yellow flashed forth.

'Hell!' the pocket-miner reiterated tonelessly. 'First rattle out the box. Begins at the grass roots and goes all the way down.'

Head turned to the side and up, eyes closed, nostrils distended and quivering, he rose suddenly to his feet and sniffed the air. Corliss looked up wonderingly.

'Huh!' the pocket-miner grunted. Then he drew a deep breath. 'Can't you smell them oranges?'

CHAPTER XVI

THE stampede to French Hill was on by the beginning of Christmas week. Corliss and Bishop had been in no hurry to record, for they looked the ground over carefully before blazing their stakes, and let a few close friends into the secret.—Harney, Welse, Trethaway, a Dutch *chechaquo* who had forfeited both feet to the frost, a couple of the mounted police, an old pal with whom Del had prospected through the Black Hills Country, the washerwoman at the Forks, and last, and notably, Lucile. Corliss was responsible for her getting in on the lay, and he drove and marked her stakes himself, though it fell to the colonel to deliver the invitation to her to come and be rich.

In accordance with the custom of the country, those thus benefited offered to sign over half-interests to the two discoverers. Corliss would not tolerate the proposition. Del was similarly minded, though swayed by no ethical reasons. He had enough as it stood. 'Got my fruit ranch paid for, double the size I was calculatin' on,' he explained; 'and if I had any more, I wouldn't know what to do with it, sure.'

After the strike, Corliss took it upon himself as a matter of course to look about for another man; but when he brought a keen-eyed Californian into camp, Del was duly wroth.

'Not on your life,' he stormed.

'But you are rich now,' Vance answered, 'and have no need to work.'

'Rich, hell!' the pocket-miner rejoined. 'Accordin' to covenant, you can't fire me; and I'm goin' to hold the job down as long as my sweet will 'll let me. Savve?'

On Friday morning, early, all interested parties appeared before the Gold Commissioner to record their claims. The news went abroad immediately. In five minutes the first stampeders were hitting the trail. At the end of half an hour the town was afoot. To prevent mistakes on their property—jumping, moving of stakes, and mutilation of notices—Vance and Del, after promptly recording, started to return. But with the government seal attached to their holdings, they took it leisurely, the stampeders sliding past them in a steady stream. Midway, Del chanced to look behind. St Vincent was in sight, footing it at a lively pace, the regulation stampeding pack on his shoulders. The trail made a sharp bend at that place, and with the exception of the three of them no one was in sight.

'Don't speak to me. Don't recognise me,' Del cautioned sharply, as he spoke buttoning his nose-strap across his face, which served quite to hide his identity. 'There's a water-hole over there. Get down on your belly and make a blind at gettin' a drink. Then go on by your lonely to the claims; I've business of my own to handle. And for the love of your mother don't say a word to me or to the skunk. Don't let 'm see your face.'

Corliss obeyed wonderingly, stepping aside from the beaten path, lying down in the snow, and dipping into the water-hole with an empty condensed milk-can. Bishop bent on one knee and stooped as though fastening his moccasin. Just as St Vincent came up with him he finished tying the knot, and started forward with the feverish haste of a man trying to make up for lost time.

'I say, hold on, my man,' the correspondent called out to him.

Bishop shot a hurried glance at him and pressed on. St Vincent broke into a run till they were side by side again.

'Is this the way—'

'To the benches of French Hill?' Del snapped him short. 'Betcher life. That's the way I'm headin'. So long.'

He ploughed forward at a tremendous rate, and the correspondent, half-running, swung in behind with the evident intention of taking the pace. Corliss, still in the dark, lifted his head and watched them go; but when he saw the pocket-miner swerve abruptly to the right and take the trail up Adams Creek, the light dawned upon him and he laughed softly to himself.

Late that night Del arrived in camp on Eldorado exhausted but jubilant.

'Didn't do a thing to him,' he cried before he was half inside the tent-flaps. 'Gimme a bite to eat' (grabbing at

125

the tea-pot and running a hot flood down his throat)—
'cookin'-fat, slush, old moccasins, candle-ends, anything!'

Then he collapsed upon the blankets and fell to rubbing his stiff leg-muscles while Corliss fried bacon and
dished up the beans.

'What about 'm?' he exulted between mouthfuls. 'Well,
you can stack your chips that he didn't get in on the
French Hill benches. *How far is it, my man?*' (in the well-
mimicked, patronising tones of St Vincent). '*How far is it?*'
with the patronage left out. '*How far to French Hill?*'
weakly. '*How far do you think it is?*' very weakly, with a
tremolo which hinted of repressed tears. '*How far—*'

The pocket-miner burst into roars of laughter, which
were choked by a misdirected flood of tea, and which left
him coughing and speechless.

'Where'd I leave 'm?' when he had recovered. 'Over on
the divide to Indian River, winded, plum-beaten, done for.
Just about able to crawl into the nearest camp, and that's
about all? I've covered fifty stiff miles myself, so here's for
bed. Good night. Don't call me in the mornin'.'

He turned into the blankets all-standing, and as he dozed
off Vance could hear him muttering, '*How far is it, my
man? I say, how far is it?*'

Regarding Lucile, Corliss was disappointed. 'I confess I
cannot understand her,' he said to Colonel Trethaway. 'I
thought her bench claim would make her independent
of the Opera House.'

'You can't get a dump out in a day,' the colonel interposed.

'But you can mortgage the dirt in the ground when it
prospects as hers does. Yet I took that into consideration,
and offered to advance her a few thousand, non-interest
bearing, and she declined. Said she didn't need it—in fact,
was really grateful; thanked me, and said that any time I
was short to come and see her.'

Trethaway smiled and played with his watch-chain.
'What would you? Life, even here, certainly means more
to you and me than a bit of grub, a piece of blanket, and
a Yukon stove. She is as gregarious as the rest of us, and
probably a little more so. Suppose you cut her off from the

Opera House—what then? May he go up to the Barracks and consort with the captain's lady, make social calls on Mrs Schoville, or chum with Frona? Don't you see? Will you escort her, in daylight, down the public street?'

'Will you?' Vance demanded.

'Aye,' the colonel replied, unhesitatingly, 'and with pleasure.'

'And so will I; but—' He paused and gazed gloomily into the fire. 'But see how she is going on with St Vincent. As thick as thieves they are, and always together.'

'Puzzles me,' Trethaway admitted. 'I can grasp St Vincent's side of it. Many irons in the fire, and Lucile owns a bench claim on the second tier of French Hill. Mark me, Corliss, we can tell infallibly the day that Frona consents to go to his bed and board—if she ever does consent.'

'And that will be?'

'The day St Vincent breaks with Lucile.'

Corliss pondered, and the colonel went on.

'But I can't grasp Lucile's side of it. What she can see in St Vincent—'

'Her taste is no worse than—than that of the rest of the women,' Vance broke in hotly. 'I am sure that—'

'Frona could not display poor taste, eh?'

Corliss turned on his heel and walked out, and left Colonel Trethaway smiling grimly.

Vance Corliss never knew how many people, directly and indirectly, had his cause at heart that Christmas week. Two men strove in particular, one for him and one for the sake of Frona. Pete Whipple, an old-timer in the land, possessed an Eldorado claim directly beneath French Hill, also a woman of the country for a wife—a swarthy *breed*, not over pretty, whose Indian mother had mated with a Russian fur-trader some thirty years before at Kutlik on the Great Delta. Bishop went down one Sunday morning to yarn away an hour or so with Whipple, but found the wife alone in the cabin. She talked a bastard English gibberish which was an anguish to hear, so the pocket-miner resolved to smoke a pipe and depart without rudeness. But he got her tongue wagging, and to such an extent that he stopped and smoked many pipes, and whenever she lagged, urged her on again. He grunted and chuckled and swore in undertones while he listened, punctuating her narrative regularly with *hells!* which adequately expressed the many shades of interest he felt.

In the midst of it, the woman fished an ancient leather-bound volume, all scarred and marred, from the bottom of a dilapidated chest, and thereafter it lay on the table between them. Though it remained unopened, she constantly referred to it by look and gesture, and each time she did so a greedy light blazed in Bishop's eyes. At the end, when she could say no more and had repeated herself from two to half a dozen times, he pulled out his sack. Mrs. Whipple set up the gold scales and placed the weights, which he counterbalanced with a hundred dollar's worth of dust. Then he departed up the hill to the tent, hugging the purchase closely, and broke in on Corliss, who sat in the blankets mending moccasins.

'I'll fix 'm yet,' Del remarked casually, at the same time patting the book and throwing it down on the bed.

Corliss looked up inquiringly and opened it. The paper was yellow with age and rotten from the weather-wear of trail, while the text was printed in Russian. 'I didn't know you were a Russian scholar, Del,' he quizzed. 'But I can't read a line of it.'

'Neither can I, more's the pity; nor does Whipple's woman savve the lingo. I got it from her. But her old man—he was full Russian, you know—he used to read it aloud to her. But she knows what she knows and what her old man knew, and so do I.'

'And what do the three of you know?'

'Oh, that's tellin',' Bishop answered, coyly. 'But you wait and watch my smoke, and when you see it risin', you'll know too.'

Matt McCarthy came in over the ice Christmas week, summed up the situation so far as Frona and St Vincent were concerned, and did not like it. Dave Harney furnished him with full information, to which he added that obtained from Lucile, with whom he was on good terms. Perhaps it was because he received the full benefit of the sum of their prejudice; but no matter how, he at any rate answered roll-call with those who looked upon the correspondent with disfavour. It was impossible for them to tell why they did not approve of the man, but somehow St Vincent was never much of a success with men. This, in turn, might have been due to the fact that he shone so resplendently with women as to cast his fellows in eclipse; for otherwise, in his intercourse with men, he was all that a man could wish. There was nothing domineering or over-riding about him, while he manifested a good fellowship at least equal to their own.

Yet, having withheld his judgment after listening to Lucile and Harvey, Matt McCarthy speedily reached a verdict upon spending an hour with St Vincent at Jacob Welse's—and this in face of the fact that what Lucile had said had been invalidated by Matt's learning of her intimacy with the man in question. Strong of friendship, quick of heart and hand, Matt did not let the grass grow under his feet. ''Tis I'll be takin' a social fling meself, as befits a mimber iv the noble Eldorado Dynasty,' he explained, and went up the hill to a whist party in Dave Harney's cabin. To himself he added, 'An' belike, if Satan takes his eye off his own, I'll put it to that young cub iv his.'

But more than once during the evening he discovered himself challenging his own judgment. Probe as he would with his innocent wit, Matt found himself baffled. St Vincent certainly rang true. Simple, light-hearted, unaffected, joking and being joked in all good-nature, thoroughly democratic, Matt failed to catch the faintest echo of insincerity.

'May the dogs walk on me grave,' he communed with himself while studying a hand which suffered from a plethora of trumps. 'Is it the years are tellin' puttin' the frost in me veins and chillin' the blood? A likely lad, an' is it for me to misjudge because his is a takin' way with the ladies? Just because the swate creatures smile on the lad an' flutter warm at the sight iv him? Bright eyes and brave men! 'Tis the way they have iv lovin' valour. They're shuddered an' shocked at the cruel an' bloody dades iv war, yet who so quick do they lose their hearts to as the brave butcher-bye iv a sodger? Why not? The lad's done brave things, and the girls give him the warm soft smile. Small reason, that, for me to be callin' him the devil's own cub. Out upon ye, Matt McCarthy, for a crusty old sour-dough, with vitals frozen an' summer gone from yer heart! 'Tis an ossification ye've become! But bide a wee, Matt, bide a wee,' he supplemented. 'Wait till ye've felt the fale iv his flesh.'

The opportunity came shortly, when St Vincent, with Frona opposite, swept in the full thirteen tricks.

'A rampse!' Matt cried. 'Vincent, me lad, a rampse! Yer hand on it, me brave!'

It was a stout grip, neither warm nor clammy, but Matt shook his head dubiously. 'What's the good iv botherin'?' he muttered to himself as he shuffled the cards for the next deal. 'Ye old fool! Find out first how Frona darlin' stands, an' if it's pat she is, thin 'tis time for doin'.'

'Oh, McCarthy's all hunky,' Dave Harney assured them later on, coming to the rescue of St Vincent, who was getting the rough side of the Irishman's wit. The evening was over and the company was putting on its wraps and mittens. 'Didn't tell you 'bout his visit to the cathedral, did he, when he was on the Outside? Well, it was suthin' like this, ez he was explainin' it to me. He went to the cathedral durin' service, an' took in the priests and choir-boys in their surplices—*parkas,* he called 'em—an' watched the burnin' of the holy incense. " An' do you know, Dave," he sez to me, " they got in an' made a smudge, and there wa'n't a darned mosquito in sight." '

'True, ivery word iv it.' Matt unblushingly fathered Harney's yarn. 'An' did ye niver hear tell iv the time Dave an' me got drunk on condensed milk?'

'Oh! Horrors!' cried Mrs. Schoville. 'But how? Do tell us.'

''Twas durin' the time iv the candle famine at Forty Mile. Cold snap on, an' Dave slides into me shack to pass the time o' day, and glues his eyes on me case iv condensed milk. "How'd ye like a sip iv Moran's good whisky?" he sez, eyin' the case iv milk the while. I confiss me mouth went wet at the naked thought iv it. "But what's the use iv likin'?" sez I, "with me sack bulgin' with emptiness." "Candles worth tin dollars the dozen," sez he, "a dollar apiece. Will ye give six cans iv milk for a bottle iv the old stuff?" "How'll ye do it?" sez I. "Trust me," sez he. "Give me the cans. 'Tis cold out iv doors, an' I've a pair iv candle-moulds."

'An' it's the sacred truth I'm tellin' ye all, an' if ye run across Bill Moran he'll back me word; for what does Dave Harney do but lug off me six cans, freeze the milk into his candle-moulds, an' trade them in to Bill Moran for a bottle iv tangle-foot!'

As soon as he could be heard through the laughter, Harney raised his voice. 'It's true, as McCarthy tells, but he's only told you the half. Can't you guess the rest, Matt?'

Matt shook his head.

'Bein' short on milk myself, an' not over much sugar, I doctored three of your cans with water, which went to make the candles. An' by the bye, I had milk in my coffee for a month to come.'

'It's on me, Dave,' McCarthy admitted. ''Tis only that yer me host, or I'd be shockin' the ladies with yer nortorious disgraces. But I'll lave ye live this time, Dave. Come, spare the partin' guests; we must be movin'.'

'No ye don't, ye young laddy-buck,' he interposed, as St Vincent started to take Frona down the hill. ''Tis her foster-daddy sees her home this night.'

McCarthy laughed in his silent way and offered his arm to Frona, while St Vincent joined in the laugh against himself, dropped back, and joined Miss Mortimer and Baron Courbertin.

'What's this I'm hearin' about you an' Vincent?' Matt bluntly asked as soon as they had drawn apart from the others.

He looked at her with his keen grey eyes, but she returned the look quite as keenly.

'How should I know what you have been hearing?' she countered.

'Whin the talk goes round iv a maid an' a man, the one pretty an' the other not unhandsome, both young an' neither married, does it 'token aught but the one thing?'

'Yes?'

'An' the one thing the greatest thing in all the world.'

'Well?' Frona was the least bit angry, and did not feel inclined to help him.

'Marriage, iv course,' he blurted out. ''Tis said it looks that way with the pair of ye.'

'But is it said that it *is* that way?'

'Isn't the looks iv it enough?' he demanded.

'No; and you are old enough to know better. Mr St Vincent and I—we enjoy each other as friends, that is all. But suppose it is as you say, what of it?'

'Well,' McCarthy deliberated, 'there's other talk goes round. 'Tis said Vincent is over-thick with a jade down in the town—Lucile, they speak iv her.'

'All of which signifies?'

She waited, and McCarthy watched her dumbly.

'I know Lucile, and I like her,' Frona continued, filling the gap of his silence, and ostentatiously manoeuvring to help him on. 'Do you know her? Don't you like her?'

Matt started to speak, cleared his throat, and halted. At last, in desperation, he blurted out, 'For two cents, Frona, I'd lay ye acrost me knee.'

She laughed. 'You don't dare. I'm not running barelegged at Dyea.'

'Now don't be tasin',' he blarneyed.

'I'm not teasing. Don't you like her?—Lucile?'

'An' what iv it?' he challenged, brazenly.

'Just what I asked—what of it?'

'Thin I'll tell ye in plain words from a man old enough to be yer father. 'Tis undacent, damnably undacent for a man to kape company with a good young girl—'

'Thank you,' she laughed, dropping a courtesy. Then she added, half in bitterness, 'There have been others who—'

'Name me the man!' he cried hotly.

'There, there, go on. You were saying?'

'That it's a crying shame for a man to kape company with—with you, an' at the same time be chake by jowl with a woman iv her stamp.'

'And why?'

'To come drippin' from the muck to dirty yer claneness! An' ye can ask why?'

'But wait, Matt, wait a moment. Granting your premises—'

132

'Little I know iv primises,' he growled. ''Tis facts I'm dalin' with.'

Frona bit her lip. 'Never mind. Have it as you will; but let me go on and I will deal with facts, too. When did you last see Lucile?'

'An' why are ye askin'?' he demanded, suspiciously.

'Never mind why. The fact.'

'Well, thin, the fore part iv last night, an' much good may it do ye.'

'And danced with her?'

'A rollickin' Virginia reel, an' not sayin' a word iv a quadrille or so. 'Tis at square dances I excel meself.'

Frona walked on in a simulated brown study, no sound going up from the twain save the complaint of the snow from under their moccasins.

'Well, thin?' he questioned, uneasily.

'An' what iv it?' he insisted after another silence.

'Oh, nothing,' she answered. 'I was just wondering which was the muckiest, Mr St Vincent or you—or myself, with whom you have both been cheek by jowl.'

Now, McCarthy, was unversed in the virtues of social wisdom, and, though he felt somehow the error of her position, he could not put it into definite thought; so he steered wisely, if weakly, out of danger.

'It's gettin' mad ye are with yer old Matt,' he insinuated, 'who has yer own good at heart, an' because iv it makes a fool iv himself.'

'No, I'm not.'

'But ye are.'

'There!' leaning swiftly to him and kissing him. 'How could I remember the Dyea days and be angry?'

'Ah, Frona darlin', well may ye say it. I'm the dust iv the dirt under yer feet, an' ye may walk on me—anything save get mad. I cud die for ye, swing for ye, to make ye happy. I cud kill the man that gave ye sorrow, were it but a thimbleful, an' go plump into hell with a smile on me face an' joy in me heart.'

They had halted before her door, and she pressed his arm gratefully. 'I am not angry, Matt. But with the exception of my father you are the only person I would have permitted to talk to me about this—this affair in the way you have. And though I like you, Matt, love you better than ever, I shall nevertheless be very angry if you mention it again. You have no right. It is something that concerns me alone. And it is wrong of you—'

'To prevint ye walkin' blind into danger?'

'If you wish to put it that way, yes.'

He growled deep down in his throat.

'What is it you are saying?' she asked.

'That ye may shut me mouth, but that ye can't bind me arm.'

'But you mustn't, Matt, dear, you mustn't.'

Again he answered with a subterranean murmur.

'And I want you to promise me, now, that you will not interfere in my life that way, by word or deed.'

'I'll not promise.'

'But you must.'

'I'll not. Further, it's gettin' cold on the stoop, an' ye'll be frostin' yer toes, the pink little toes I fished splinters out iv at Dyea. So it's in with ye, Frona girl, an' good night.'

He thrust her inside and departed. When he reached the corner he stopped suddenly and regarded his shadow on the snow. 'Matt McCarthy, yer a damned fool! Who iver heard iv a Welse not knowin' their own mind? As though ye'd niver had dalin's with the stiff-necked breed, ye calamitous son iv misfortune!'

Then he went his way, still growling deeply, and at every growl the curious wolf-dog at his heels bristled and bared its fangs.

CHAPTER XVII

'TIRED?'

Jacob Welse put both hands on Frona's shoulders, and his eyes spoke the love his stiff tongue could not compass. The tree and the excitement and the pleasure were over with, a score or so of children had gone home frostily happy across the snow, the last guest had departed, and Christmas Eve and Christmas Day were blending into one.

She returned his fondness with glad-eyed interest, and they dropped into huge comfortable chairs on either side the fireplace, in which the back-log was falling to ruddy ruin.

'And this time next year?' He put the question seemingly to the glowing log, and, as if in ominous foreshadow, it flared brightly and crumbled away in a burst of sparks.

'It is marvellous,' he went on, dismissing the future in an effort to shake himself into a wholesomer frame of mind. 'It has been one long continuous miracle, the last few months, since you have been with me. We have seen very little of each other, you know, since your childhood, and when I think upon it soberly it is hard to realise that you are really mine, sprung from me, bone of my bone and flesh of my flesh. As the tangle-haired wild young creature of Dyea—a healthy, little, natural animal and nothing more— it required no imagination to accept you as one of the breed of Welse. But as Frona, the woman, as you were tonight, as you are now as I look at you, as you have been since you came down the Yukon, it is hard . . . I cannot realise . . . I . . .' He faltered and threw up his hands help-lessly. 'I almost wish that I had given you no education, that I had kept you with me, faring with me, adventuring with me, achieving with me, and failing with me. I would have known you, now, as we sit by the fire. As it is, I do not. To that which I did know there has been added, some-how (what shall I call it?), a subtlety, complexity,—favour-ite words of yours—which is beyond me.

'No.' He waved the speech abruptly from her lips. She came over and knelt at his feet, resting her head on his knee and clasping his hand in firm sympathy. 'No, that is not true. Those are not the words. I cannot find them. I fail to say what I feel. Let me try again. Underneath all you do carry the stamp of the breed. I knew I risked the loss of that when I sent you away, but I had faith in the persistence of the blood and I took the chance; doubted and feared when you were gone; waited and prayed dumbly, and hoped oftentimes hopelessly; and then the day dawned, the day of days! When they said your boat was coming, death rose and walked on the one hand of me, and on the other life everlasting. *Made or marred; made or marred*— the words rang through my brain till they maddened me. Would the Welse remain the Welse? Would the blood persist? Would the young shoot rise straight and tall and strong, green with sap and fresh and vigorous? Or would it droop limp and lifeless, withered by the heats of the world other than the little simple, natural Dyea world?

'It was the day of days, and yet it was a lingering, watching, waiting tragedy. You know I had lived the years lonely, fought the lone fight, and you away, the only kin. If it had failed . . . But your boat shot from the bluffs into the open, and I was half-afraid to look. Men have never called me coward, but I was nearer the coward then than ever and all before. Aye, that moment I had faced death easier. And it was foolish, absurd. How could I know whether it was for good or ill when you drifted a distant speck on the river? Still, I looked, and the miracle began, for I did know. You stood at the steering-sweep. You were a Welse. It seems so little; in truth it meant so much. It was not to be expected of a mere woman, but of a Welse, yes. And when Bishop went over the side, and you gripped the situation as imperatively as the sweep, and your voice rang out, and the Siwashes bent their backs to your will— then was it the day of days.'

'I tried always, and remembered,' Frona whispered. She crept up softly till her arm was about his neck and her head against his breast. He rested one arm lightly on her body, and poured her bright hair again and again from his hand in glistening waves.

'As I said, the stamp of the breed was unmarred, but there was yet a difference. There is a difference. I have

136

watched it, studied it, tried to make it out. I have sat at table, proud by the side of you, but dwarfed. When you talked of little things I was large enough to follow; when of big things, too small. I knew you, had my hand on you, when *presto!* and you were away, gone—I was lost. He is a fool who knows not his own ignorance; I was wise enough to know mine. Art, poetry, music—what do I know of them? And they were the great things, are the great things to you, mean more to you than the little things I may comprehend. And I had hoped, blindly, foolishly, that we might be one in the spirit as well as the one flesh. It has been bitter, but I have faced it, and understand. But to see my own red blood get away from me, elude me, rise above me! It stuns. God! I have heard you read from your Browning—no, no; do not speak—and watched the play of your face, the uplift and the passion of it, and all the while the words droning in upon me, meaningless, musical, maddening. And Mrs Schoville sitting there, nursing an expression of idiotic ecstasy, and understanding no more than I. I could have strangled her.

'Why, I have stolen away, at night, with your Browning, and locked myself in like a thief in fear. The text was senseless. I have beaten my head with my fist like a wild man, to try and knock some comprehension into it. For my life had worked itself out along one set groove, deep and narrow. I was in the rut. I had done those things which came to my hand and done them well; but the time was past; I could not turn my hand anew. I, who am strong and dominant, who have played large with destiny, who could buy body and soul a thousand painters and versifiers, was baffled by a few paltry cents' worth of printed paper!'

He spilled her hair for a moment's silence.

'To come back. I had attempted the impossible, gambled against the inevitable. I had sent you from me to get that which I had not, dreaming that we would still be one. As though two could be added to two and still remain two. So, to sum up, the breed still holds, but you have learned an alien tongue. When you speak it I am deaf. And bitterest of all, I know that the new tongue is the greater. I do not know why I have said all this, made my confession of weakness—'

E*   137

'Oh, father mine, greatest of men!' She raised her head and laughed into his eyes, the while brushing back the thick iron-grey hair which thatched the dome of his forehead. 'You, who have wrestled more mightily, done greater things than these painters and versifiers. You who know so well the law of change. Might not the same plaint fall from your father's lips were he to sit now beside you and look upon your work and you?'

'Yes, yes. I have said that I understand. Do not let us discuss it . . . a moment's weakness. My father was a great man.'

'And so mine.'

'A struggler to the end of his days. He fought the great long fight—'

'And so mine.'

'And died fighting.'

'And so shall mine. So shall we all, we Welses.'

He shook her playfully, in token of returning spirits. 'But I intend to sell out—mines, Company, everything—and study Browning.'

'Still the fight. You can't discount the blood, father.'

'Why were you not a boy?' he demanded, abruptly. 'You would have been a splendid one. As it is, a woman, made to be the delight of some man, you must pass from me—tomorrow, next day, this time next year, who knows how soon? Ah! now I know the direction my thought has been trending. Just as I know you do, so do I recognise the inevitableness of it and the justness. But the man, Frona, the man?'

'Don't,' she demurred. 'Tell me of your father's fight, the last fight, the great lone fight at Treasure City. Ten to one it was, and well fought. Tell me.'

'No, Frona. Do you realise that for the first time in our lives we talk together seriously, as father and daughter—for the first time? You have had no mother to advise; no father, for I trusted the blood, and wisely, and let you go. But there comes a time when the mother's counsel is needed, and you, you who never knew one?'

Frona yielded, in instant recognition, and waiting, snuggled more closely to him.

'This man, St Vincent—how is it between you?'

'I . . . I do not know. How do you mean?'

'Remember always, Frona, that you have free choice, yours is the last word. Still, I would like to understand. I could . . . perhaps . . . I might be able to suggest. But nothing more. Still, a suggestion . . .'

There was something inexpressibly sacred about it, yet she found herself tongue-tied. Instead of the one definite thing to say, a muddle of ideas fluttered in her brain. After all, could he understand? Was there not a difference which prevented him from comprehending the motives which, for her, were impelling? For all her harking back to the primitive and stout defence of its sanity and truth, did his native philosophy give him the same code which she drew from her acquired philosophy? Then she stood aside and regarded herself and the queries she put, and drew apart from them, for they breathed of treason.

'There is nothing between us, father,' she spoke up resolutely. 'Mr St Vincent has said nothing, nothing. We are good friends, we like each other, we are very good friends. I think that is all.'

'But you like each other; you like him. Is it in the way a woman must like a man before she can honestly share her life with him, lose herself in him? Do you feel with Ruth, so that when the time comes you can say, "Thy people are my people, and thy God my God"?'

'No-o. It may be; but I cannot, dare not face it, say it or not say it, think it or not think it—now. It is the great affirmation. When it comes it must come no one may know how or why, in a great white flash, like a revelation, hiding nothing, revealing everything in dazzling, blinding truth. At least I so imagine.'

Jacob Welse nodded his head with the slow meditation of one who understands, yet stops to ponder and weigh again.

'But why have you asked, father? Why has Mr St Vincent been raised? I have been friends with other men.'

'But I have not felt about other men as I do of St Vincent. We may be truthful, you and I, and forgive the pain we give each other. My opinion counts for no more than another's. Fallibility is the commonest of curses. Nor can I explain why I feel as I do—I suppose much in the way you expect to when your great white flash sears your eyes. But, in a word, I do not like St Vincent.'

'A very common judgment of him among the men,' Frona interposed, driven irresistibly to the defensive.

'Such consensus of opinion only makes my position stronger,' he returned, but not disputatively. 'Yet I must remember that I look upon him as men look. His popularity with women must proceed from the fact that women look differently than men just as women do differ physically and spiritually from men. It is deep, too deep for me to explain. I but follow my nature and try to be just.'

'But have you nothing more definite?' she asked, groping for better comprehension of his attitude. 'Can you not put into some sort of coherence some one certain thing of the things you feel?'

'I hardly dare. Intuitions can rarely be expressed in terms of thought. But let me try. We Welses have never known a coward. And where cowardice is, nothing can endure. It is like building on sand, or like a vile disease which rots and rots and we know not when it may break forth.'

'But it seems to me that Mr St Vincent is the last man in the world with whom cowardice may be associated. I cannot conceive of him in that light.'

The distress in her face hurt him. 'I know nothing against St Vincent. There is no evidence to show that he is anything but what he appears. Still, I cannot help feeling it, in my fallible human way. Yet there is one thing I have heard, a sordid pot-house brawl in the Opera House. Mind you, Frona, I say nothing against the brawl or the place, —men are men—but it is said that he did not act as a man ought that night.'

'But as you say, father, men are men. We would like to have them other than they are, for the world surely would be better; but we must take them as they are. Lucile—'

'No, no; you misunderstand. I did not refer to her, but to the fight. He did not . . . he was cowardly.'

'But as you say, it is *said*. He told me about it, not long afterwards, and I do not think he would have dared had there been anything—'

'But I do not make it as a charge,' Jacob Welse hastily

broke in. 'Merely hearsay, and the prejudice of the men would be sufficient to account for the tale. And it has no bearing, anyway. I should not have brought it up, for I have known good men funk in my time—buck fever, as it were. And now let us dismiss it all from our minds. I merely wished to suggest, and I suppose I have bungled. But understand this, Frona,' turning her face up to his, 'understand above all things and in spite of them, first, last, and always, that you are my daughter, and that I believe your life is sacredly yours, not mine, yours to deal with and to make or mar. Your life is yours to live, and in so far that I influence it you will not have lived your life, nor would your life have been yours. Nor would you have been a Welse, for there was never a Welse yet who suffered dictation. They died first, or went away to pioneer on the edge of things.

'Why, if you thought the dance house the proper or natural medium for self-expression, I might be sad, but tomorrow I would sanction your going down to the Opera House. It would be unwise to stop you, and, further, it is not our way. The Welses have ever stood by, in many a lost cause and forlorn hope, knee to knee and shoulder to shoulder. Conventions are worthless for such as we. They are for the swine who without them would wallow deeper. The weak must obey or be crushed; not so with the strong. The mass is nothing; the individual everything; and it is the individual, always, that rules the mass and gives the law. A fig for what the world says! If the Welse should procreate a bastard line this day, it would be the way of the Welse, and you would be a daughter of the Welse, and in the face of hell and heaven, of God himself, we would stand together, we of the one blood, Frona, you and I.'

'You are larger than I,' she whispered, kissing his forehead, and the caress of her lips seemed to him the soft impact of a leaf falling through the still autumn air.

And as the heat of the room ebbed away, he told of her foremother and of his, and of the sturdy Welse who fought the great lone fight, and died, fighting at Treasure City.

CHAPTER XVIII

T H E 'Doll's House' was a success. Mrs Schoville ecstasised over it in terms so immeasurable, so unqualifiable, that Jacob Welse, standing near, bent a glittering gaze upon her plump white throat and unconsciously clutched and closed his hand on an invisible windpipe. Dave Harney proclaimed its excellence effusively, though he questioned the soundness of Nora's philosophy and swore by his Puritan gods that Torvald was the longest-eared jack in two hemispheres. Even Miss Mortimer, antagonistic as she was to the whole school, conceded that the players had redeemed it; while Matt McCarthy announced that he didn't blame Nora darlin' the least bit, though he told the Gold Commisioner privately that a song or so and a skirt dance wouldn't have hurt the performance.

'Iv course the Nora girl was right,' he insisted to Harney, both of whom were walking on the heels of Frona and St Vincent. 'I'd be seein'—'

'Rubber—'

'Rubber yer gran'mother!' Matt wrathfully exclaimed.

'Ez I was sayin',' Harney continued, imperturbably, 'rubber boots is goin' to go sky-high 'bout the time of wash-up. Three ounces the pair, an' you kin put your chips on that for a high card. You kin gather 'em in now for an ounce a pair and clear two on the deal. A cinch, Matt, a dead open an' shut.'

'The devil take you an' yer cinches! It's Nora darlin' I have in me mind the while.'

They bade good-bye to Frona and St Vincent and went off disputing under the stars in the direction of the Opera House.

Gregory St Vincent heaved an audible sigh. 'At last.'

'At last what?' Frona asked, incuriously.

'At last the first opportunity for me to tell you how well you did. You carried off the final scene wonderfully; so well that it seemed you were really passing out of my life forever.'

'What a misfortune!'

'It was terrible.'

'No.'

'But, yes. I took the whole condition upon myself. You were not Nora, you were Frona; nor I Torvald, but Gregory. When you made your exit, capped and jacketed and travelling-bag in hand, it seemed I could not possibly stay and finish my lines. And when the door slammed and you were gone, the only thing that saved me was the curtain. It brought me to myself, or else I would have rushed after you in the face of the audience.'

'It is strange how a simulated part may react upon one,' Frona speculated.

'Or rather?' St Vincent suggested.

Frona made no answer, and they walked on without speech. She was still under the spell of the evening, and the exaltation which had come to her as Nora had not yet departed. Besides, she read between the lines of St Vincent's conversation, and was oppressed by the timidity which comes over woman when she faces man on the verge of the greater intimacy.

It was a clear, cold night, not over-cold—not more than forty below—and the land was bathed in a soft, diffused flood of light which found its source not in the stars, nor yet in the moon, which was somewhere over on the other side of the world. From the south-east to the north-west a pale-greenish glow fringed the rim of the heavens, and it was from this the dim radiance was exhaled.

Suddenly, like the ray of a searchlight, a band of white light ploughed overhead. Night turned to ghostly day on the instant, then blacker night descended. But to the south-east a noiseless commotion was apparent. The glowing greenish gauze was in a ferment, bubbling, uprearing, downfalling, and tentatively thrusting huge bodiless hands into the upper ether. Once more a cyclopean rocket twisted its fiery way across the sky, from horizon to zenith, and on, and on, in tremendous flight, to horizon again. But the span could not hold, and in its wake the black night brooded. And yet again, broader, stronger, deeper, lavishly spilling streamers to right and left, it flaunted the midmost zenith with its gorgeous flare, and passed on and down to the further edge of the world. Heaven was bridged at last, and the bridge endured!

At this flaming triumph the silence of earth was broken, and ten thousand wolf-dogs, in long-drawn unisoned howls, sobbed their dismay and grief. Frona shivered, and St Vincent passed his arm about her waist. The woman in her was aware of the touch of man, and of a slight tingling thrill of vague delight; but she made no resistance. And as the wolf-dogs mourned at her feet and the aurora wantoned overhead, she felt herself drawn against him closely.

'Need I tell my story?' he whispered.

She drooped her head in tired content on his shoulder, and together they watched the burning vault wherein the stars dimmed and vanished. Ebbing, flowing, pulsing to some tremendous rhythm, the prism colours hurled themselves in luminous deluge across the firmament. Then the canopy of heaven became a mighty loom, wherein imperial purple and deep sea-green blended, wove, and interwove, with blazing woof and flashing warp, till the most delicate of tulles, fluorescent and bewildering, was daintily and airily shaken in the face of the astonished night.

Without warning the span was sundered by an arrogant arm of black. The arch dissolved in blushing confusion. Chasms of blackness yawned, grew, and rushed together. Broken masses of strayed colour and fading fire stole timidly towards the sky-line. Then the dome of night towered imponderable, immense, and the stars came back one by one, and the wolf-dogs mourned anew.

'I can offer you so little, dear,' the man said with a slightly perceptible bitterness. 'The precarious fortunes of a gipsy wanderer.'

And the woman, placing his hand and pressing it against her heart, said, as a great woman had said before her, 'A tent and a crust of bread with you, Richard.'

CHAPTER XIX

HOW-HA was only an Indian woman, bred of a long line of fish-eating, meat-rending carnivora, and her ethics were as crude and simple as her blood. But long contact with the whites had given her an insight into their way of looking at things, and though she grunted contemptuously in her secret soul, she none the less understood their way perfectly. Ten years previous she had cooked for Jacob Welse, and served him in one fashion or another ever since; and when on a dreary January morning she opened the front door in response to the deep-tongued knocker, even her stolid presence was shaken as she recognised the visitor. Not that the average man or woman would have so recognised. But How-ha's faculties of observing and remembering details had been developed in a hard school where death dealt his blow to the lax and life saluted the vigilant.

How-ha looked up and down the woman who stood before her. Through the heavy veil she could barely distinguish the flash of the eyes, while the hood of the *parka* effectually concealed the hair, and the *parka* proper the particular outlines of the body. But How-ha paused and looked again. There was something familiar in the vague general outline. She quested back to the shrouded head again, and knew the unmistakable poise. Then How-ha's eyes went blear as she traversed the simple windings of her own brain, inspecting the bare shelves taciturnly stored with the impressions of a meagre life. No disorder; no confused mingling of records; no devious and interminable impress of complex emotions, tangled theories, and bewildering abstractions—nothing but simple facts, neatly classified and conveniently collated. Unerringly from the stores of the past she picked and chose and put together in the instant present, till obscurity dropped from the woman before her, and she knew her, word and deed and look and history.

'Much better you go 'way quickety-quick,' How-ha informed her.

'Miss Welse. I wish to see her.'

The strange woman spoke in firm, even tones which betokened the will behind, but which failed to move How-ha.

'Much better you go,' she repeated, stolidly.

'Here, take this to Frona Welse, and—ah! would you!' (thrusting her knee between the door and jamb) 'and leave the door open.'

How-ha scowled, but took the note; for she could not shake off the grip of the ten years of servitude to the superior race.

May I see you?

LUCILE.

So the note ran. Frona glanced up expectantly at the Indian woman.

'Um kick toes outside,' How-ha explained. 'Me tell um go 'way quickety-quick? Eh? You t'ink yes? Um no good. Um—'

'No. Take her,'—Frona was thinking quickly—'no; bring her up here.'

'Much better—'

'Go!'

How-ha grunted, and yielded up the obedience she could not withhold; though, as she went down the stairs to the door, in a tenebrous, glimmering way she wondered that the accident of white skin or swart made master or servant as the case might be.

In the one sweep of vision, Lucile took in Frona smiling with extended hand in the foreground, the dainty dressing-table, the simple finery, the thousand girlish evidences; and with the sweet wholesomeness of it pervading her nostrils, her own girlhood rose up and smote her. Then she turned a bleak eye and cold ear on outward things.

'I am glad you came,' Frona was saying. 'I have so wanted to see you again, and—but do get that heavy *parka* off, please. How thick it is, and what splendid fur and workmanship!'

'Yes, from Siberia.' A present from St Vincent, Lucile felt like adding, but said instead, 'The Siberians have not yet learned to scamp their work, you know.'

146

She sank down into the low-seated rocker with a native grace which could not escape the beauty-loving eye of the girl, and with proud-poised head and silent tongue listened to Frona as the minutes ticked away, and observed with impersonal amusement Frona's painful toil at making conversation.

'What has she come for?' Frona asked herself, as she talked on furs and weather and indifferent things.

'If you do not say something, Lucile, I shall get nervous, soon,' she ventured at last in desperation. 'Has anything happened?'

Lucile went over to the mirror and picked up, from among the trinkets beneath, a tiny open-work miniature of Frona. 'This is you? How old were you?'

'Sixteen.'

'A sylph, but a cold northern one.'

'The blood warms late with us,' Frona reproved; 'but is—'

'None the less warm for that,' Lucile laughed. 'And how old are you now?'

'Twenty.'

'Twenty,' Lucile repeated, slowly. 'Twenty,' and resumed her seat. 'You are twenty. And I am twenty-four.'

'So little difference as that!'

'But *our* blood warms early.' Lucile voiced her reproach across the unfathomable gulf which four years could not plumb.

Frona could hardly hide her vexation. Lucile went over and looked at the miniature again and returned.

'What do you think of love?' she asked abruptly, her face softening unheralded into a smile.

'Love?' the girl quavered.

'Yes, love. What do you know about it? What do you think of it?'

A flood of definitions, glowing and rosy, sped to her tongue, but Frona swept them aside and answered, 'Love is immolation.'

'Very good—sacrifice. And, now, does it pay?'

'Yes, it pays. Of course it pays. Who can doubt it?'
Lucile's eyes twinkled amusedly.

'Why do you smile?' Frona asked.

'Look at me, Frona.' Lucile stood up and her face blazed. 'I am twenty-four. Not altogether a fright; not altogether a dunce. I have a heart, I have good red blood and warm. And I have loved. I do not remember the pay. I know only that I have paid.'

'And in the paying were paid,' Frona took up warmly. 'The price was the reward. If love be fallible, yet you have loved; you have done, you have served. What more would you?'

'The whelpage love,' Lucile sneered.

'Oh! You are unfair.'

'I do you justice,' Lucile insisted firmly. 'You would tell me that you know; that you have gone unveiled and seen clear-eyed; that without placing more than lips to the brim you have divined the taste of the dregs, and that the taste is good. Bah! The whelpage love! And, oh, Frona, I know; you are full womanly and broad, and lend no ear to little things, but '—she tapped a slender finger to forehead—'it is all here. It is a heady brew, and you have smelled the fumes overmuch. But drain the dregs, turn down the glass, and say that it is good. No, God forbid!' she cried passionately. 'There are good loves. You should find no masquerade, but one fair and shining.'

Frona was up to her old trick—their common one—and her hand slid down Lucile's arm till hand clasped in hand. 'You say things which I feel are wrong, yet may not answer. I can, but how dare I? I dare not put mere thoughts against your facts. I, who have lived so little, cannot in theory give the lie to you who have lived so much— '

' "For he who lives more lives than one, more lives than one must die." '

From out of her pain, Lucile spoke the words of her pain, and Frona, throwing arms about her, sobbed on her breast in understanding. As for Lucile, the slight nervous ingathering of the brows above her eyes smoothed out, and she pressed the kiss of motherhood, lightly and secretly on the other's hair. For a space—then the brows ingathered, the lips drew firm, and she put Frona from her.

'You are going to marry Gregory St Vincent?'

Frona was startled. It was only a fortnight old, and not

148

a word had been breathed. 'How do you know?'

'You have answered.' Lucile watched Frona's open face and the bold running advertisement, and felt as the skilled fencer who fronts a tyro, weak of wrist, each opening naked to his hand. 'How do I know?' She laughed harshly. 'When a man leaves one's arms suddenly, lips wet with last kisses and mouth areek with last lies!'

'And?'

'Forgets the way back to those arms.'

'So?' The blood of the Welse pounded up, and like a hot sun dried the mists from her eyes and left them flashing. 'Then that is why you came. I could have guessed it had I given second thought to Dawson's gossip.'

'It is not too late.' Lucile's lip curled. 'And it is your way.'

'And I am mindful. What is it? Do you intend telling me what he has done, what he has been to you? Let me say that it is useless. He is a man, as you and I are women.'

'No,' Lucile lied, swallowing her astonishment. 'I had not thought that any action of his would affect you. I knew you were too great for that. But—have you considered me?'

Frona caught her breath for a moment. Then she straightened out her arms to hold the man in challenge to the arms of Lucile.

'Your father over again!' Lucile exclaimed. 'Oh, you impossible Welses!'

'But he is not worthy of you, Frona Welse,' she continued; 'of me, yes. He is not a nice man, a great man, nor a good. His love cannot match with yours. Bah! He does not possess love; passion, of one sort and another, is the best he may lay claim to. That you do not want. It is all, at the best, he can give you. And you, pray what may you give him? Yourself? A prodigious waste! But your father's yellow— '

'Don't go on, or I shall refuse to listen. It is wrong of you.' So Frona made her cease, and then, with bold inconsistency, 'And what may the woman Lucile give him?'

'Some few wild moments,' was the prompt response; 'a burning burst of happiness, and the regrets of hell—

which latter he deserves, as do I. So the balance is maintained, and all is well.'

'But—but—'

'For there is a devil in him,' she held on, 'a most alluring devil, which delights me, on my soul it does, and which, pray God, Frona, you may never know. For you have no devil; mine matches his and mates. I am free to confess that the whole thing is only an attraction. There is nothing permanent about him, nor about me. And there's the beauty, the balance is preserved.'

Frona lay back in her chair and lazily regarded her visitor. Lucile waited for her to speak. It was very quiet.

'Well?' Lucile at last demanded, in a low, curious tone, at the same time rising to slip into her *parka*.

'Nothing, I was only waiting.'

'I am done.'

'Then let me say that I do not understand you,' Frona summed up, coldly. 'I cannot somehow just catch your motive. There is a flat ring to what you have said. However, of this I am sure : for some unaccountable reason you have been untrue to yourself today. Do not ask me, for, as I said before, I do not know where or how; yet I am none the less convinced. This I do know, you are not the Lucile I met by the wood trail across the river. That was the true Lucile, little though I saw of her. The woman who is here today is a strange woman. I do not know her. Sometimes it has seemed she was Lucile, but rarely. This woman has lied, lied to me, and lied to me about herself. As to what she said of the man, at the worst that is merely an opinion. It may be she has lied about him likewise. The chance is large that she has. What do you think about it?'

'That you are a very clever girl, Frona. That you speak sometimes more truly than you know, and that at others you are blinder than you dream.'

'There is something I could love in you, but you have hidden it away so that I cannot find it.'

Lucile's lips trembled on the verge of speech. But she settled her *parka* about her and turned to go.

Frona saw her to the door herself, and How-ha pondered over the white who made the law and was greater than the law.

When the door had closed, Lucile spat into the street. 'Faugh! St Vincent! I have defiled my mouth with your name!' And she spat again.

'Come in.'

At the summons Matt McCarthy pulled the latch-string, pushed the door open, and closed it carefully behind him.

'Oh, it is you!' St Vincent regarded his visitor with dark abstraction, then, recollecting himself, held out his hand. 'Why, hello, Matt, old man. My mind was a thousand miles away when you entered. Take a stool and make yourself comfortable. There's the tobacco by your hand. Take a try at it and give us your verdict.'

'An' well may his mind be a thousand miles away,' Matt assured himself; for in the dark he had passed a woman on the trail who looked suspiciously like Lucile. But aloud, 'Sure, an' it's day-dreamin' ye mane. An' small wondher.'

'How's that?' the correspondent asked, cheerily.

'By the same token that I met Lucile down the trail a piece, an' the heels iv her moccasins pointing to yer shack. It's a bitter tongue the jade slings on occasion,' Matt chuckled.

'That's the worst of it.' St Vincent met him frankly. 'A man looks sidewise at them for a passing moment, and they demand that the moment be eternal.'

'Off with the old love's a stiff proposition, eh?'

'I should say so. And you understand. It's easy to see, Matt, you've had some experience in your time.'

'In me time? I'll have ye know I'm not too old to still enjoy a bit iv a fling.'

'Certainly, certainly. One can read it in your eyes. The warm heart and the roving eye, Matt!' He slapped his visitor on the shoulder with a hearty laugh.

'An' I've none the best iv ye, Vincent. 'Tis a wicked lad ye are, with a takin' way with the ladies—as plain as the nose on yer face. Manny's the idle kiss ye've given, an' manny's the heart ye've broke. But, Vincent, bye, did ye iver know the rale thing?'

'How do you mean?'

151

'The rale thing, the rale thing—that is—well, have ye been iver a father?'

St Vincent shook his head.

'And niver have I. But have ye felt the love iv a father, thin?'

'I hardly know. I don't think so.'

'Well, I have. An' it's the rale thing, I'll tell ye. If iver a man suckled a child, I did, or the next door to it. A girl child at that, an' she's woman grown, now, an' if the thing is possible, I love her more than her own blood-father. Bad luck, exciptin' her, there was niver but one woman I loved, an' that woman had mated beforetime. Not a soul did I brathe a word to, trust me, nor even herself. But she died, God's love be with her.'

His chin went down upon his chest and he quested back to a flaxen-haired Saxon woman, strayed like a bit of sunshine into the log store by the Dyea River. He looked up suddenly, and caught St Vincent's stare bent blankly to the floor as he mused on other things.

'A truce to foolishness, Vincent.'

The correspondent returned to himself with an effort and found the Irishman's small blue eyes boring into him.

'Are ye a brave man, Vincent?'

For a second's space they searched each other's souls. And in that space Matt could have sworn he saw the faintest possible flicker or flutter in the man's eyes.

He brought his fist down on the table with a triumphant crash. 'By God, yer not!'

The correspondent pulled the tobacco jug over to him and rolled a cigarette. He rolled it carefully, the delicate rice paper crisping in his hand without a tremor; but all the while a red tide mounting up from beneath the collar of his shirt, deepening in the hollows of the cheeks and thinning against the cheekbones above, creeping, spreading, till all his face was aflame.

''Tis good. An' likely it saves me fingers a dirty job. Vincent, man, the girl child which is woman grown slapes in Dawson this night. God help us, you an' me, but we'll niver hit again the pillow as clane an' pure as she! Vincent, a word to the wise: ye'll niver lay holy hand or otherwise upon her.'

The devil, which Lucile had proclaimed, began to quicken—a fuming, fretting, irrational devil.

'I do not like ye. I kape me raysons to meself. It is sufficient. But take this to heart, an' take it well: should ye be mad enough to make her yer wife, iv that damned day ye'll never see the inding, nor lay eye upon the bridal bed. Why, man, I cud bate ye to death with me two fists if need be. But it's to be hoped I'll do a nater job. Rest aisy. I promise ye.'

'You Irish pig!'

So the devil burst forth, and all unaware, for McCarthy found himself eye-high with the muzzle of a Colt's revolver.

'Is it loaded?' he asked. 'I belave ye. But why are ye lingerin'? Lift the hammer, will ye?'

The correspondent's trigger-finger moved and there was a warning click.

'Now pull it. Pull it, I say. As though ye cud, with that flutter to yer eye.'

St Vincent attempted to turn his head aside.

'Look at me, man!' McCarthy commanded. 'Kape yer eyes on me when ye do it.'

Unwillingly the sideward movement was arrested, and his eyes returned and met the Irishman's.

'Now!'

St Vincent ground his teeth and pulled the trigger—at least he thought he did, as men think they do things in dreams. He willed the deed, flashed the order forth; but the flutter of his soul stopped it.

''Tis paralysed, is it, that shaky little finger?' Matt grinned into the face of the tortured man. 'Now turn it aside, so, an' drop it, gently . . . gently . . . gently.' His voice crooned away in soothing diminuendo.

When the trigger was safely down, St Vincent let the revolver fall from his hand, and with a slight audible sigh sank nervelessly upon a stool. He tried to straighten himself, but instead dropped down upon the table and buried his face in his palsied hands. Matt drew on his mittens, looking down upon him pityingly the while, and went out, closing the door softly behind him.

CHAPTER XX

WHERE nature shows the rough hand, the sons of men are apt to respond with kindred roughness. The amenities of life spring up only in mellow lands, where the sun is warm and the earth fat. The damp and soggy climate of Britain drives men to strong drink; the rosy Orient lures to the dream splendours of the lotus. The big-bodied, white-skinned northern dweller, rude and ferocious, bellows his anger uncouthly and drives a gross fist into the face of his foe. The supple south-sojourner, silken of smile and lazy of gesture, waits, and does his work from behind, when no man looketh, gracefully and without offence. Their ends are one; the difference lies in their ways, and therein the climate, and the cumulative effect thereof, is the determining factor. Both are sinners, as men born of women have ever been; but the one does his sin openly, in the clear sight of God; the other—as though God could not see— veils his iniquity with shimmering fancies, hiding it like it were some splendid mystery.

These be the ways of men, each as the sun shines upon him and the wind blows against him, according to his kind, and the seed of his father, and the milk of his mother. Each is the resultant of many forces which go to make a pressure mightier than he, and which moulds him in the predestined shape. But, with sound legs under him, he may run away, and meet with a new pressure. He may continue running, each new pressure prodding him as he goes, until he dies, and his final form will be that predestined of the many pressures. An exchange of cradle-babes, and the base-born slave may wear the purple imperially, and the royal infant beg an alms as wheedlingly or cringe to the lash as abjectly as his meanest subject. A Chesterfield, with an empty belly, chancing upon good fare, will gorge as faithfully as the swine in the next sty. And an Epicurus, in the dirt-igloo of the Eskimos, will wax eloquent over the whale oil and walrus blubber, or die.

Thus, in the young Northland, frosty and grim and

menacing, men stripped off the sloth of the south and gave battle greatly. And they stripped likewise much of the veneer of civilisation—all of its follies, most of its foibles, and perhaps a few of its virtues. Maybe so; but they reserved the great traditions and at least lived frankly, laughed honestly, and looked one another in the eyes.

And so it is not well for women, born south of fifty-three and reared gently, to knock loosely about the Northland, unless they be great of heart. They may be soft and tender and sensitive, possessed of eyes which have not lost the lustre and the wonder, and of ears used only to sweet sounds; but if their philosophy is sane and stable, large enough to understand and to forgive, they will come to no harm and attain comprehension. If not, they will see things and hear things which hurt, and they will suffer greatly, and lose faith in man—which is the greatest evil that may happen them. Such should be sedulously cherished, and it were well to depute this to their men-folk, the nearer of kin the better. In line, it were good policy to seek out a cabin on the hill overlooking Dawson, or—best of all— across the Yukon on the western bank. Let them not move abroad unheralded and unaccompanied; and the hillside back of the cabin may be recommended as a fit field for stretching muscles and breathing deeply, a place where their ears may remain undefiled by the harsh words of men who strive to the utmost.

Vance Corliss wiped the last in dish and filed it away on the shelf, lighted his pipe, and rolled over on his back on the bunk to contemplate the moss-chinked roof of his French Hill cabin. This French Hill cabin stood on the last dip of the hill into Eldorado Creek, close to the main-travelled trail; and its one window blinked cheerily of nights at those who journeyed late.

The door was kicked open, and Del Bishop staggered in with a load of firewood. His breath had so settled on his face in a white rime that he could not speak. Such a condition was ever a hardship with the man, so he thrust his face forthwith into the quivering heat above the stove. In a trice the frost was started and the thawed streamlets dancing madly on the white-hot surface beneath. Then the ice began to fall from his beard in chunks, rattling on the lid-tops and simmering spitefully till spurted upward in clouds of steam.

'And so you witness an actual phenomenon, illustrative of the three forms of matter,' Vance laughed, mimicking the monotonous tones of the demonstrator; 'solid, liquid, and vapour. In another moment you will have the gas.'

'Th—th—that's all very well,' Bishop spluttered, wrestling with an obstructing piece of ice until it was wrenched from his upper lip and slammed stoveward with a bang.

'How cold do you make it, Del? Fifty?'

'Fifty?' the pocket-miner demanded with unutterable scorn, wiping his face. 'Quicksilver's been solid for hours, and it's been gittin' colder an' colder ever since. Fifty? I'll bet my new mittens against your old moccasins that it ain't a notch below seventy.'

'Think so?'

'D'ye want to bet?'

Vance nodded laughingly.

'Centigrade or Fahrenheit?' Bishop asked, suddenly suspicious.

'Oh, well, if you want my old moccasins so badly,' Vance rejoined, feigning to be hurt by the other's lack of faith, 'why, you can have them without betting.'

Del snorted and flung himself down on the opposite bunk. 'Think yer funny, don't you?' No answer forthcoming, he deemed the retort conclusive, rolled over, and fell to studying the moss chinks.

Fifteen minutes of this diversion sufficed. 'Play you a rubber of crib before bed,' he challenged across to the other bunk.

'I'll go you.' Corliss got up, stretched, and moved the kerosene lamp from the shelf to the table. 'Think it will hold out?' he asked, surveying the oil-level through the cheap glass.

Bishop threw down the crib-board and cards, and measured the contents of the lamp with his eye. 'Forgot to fill it, didn't I? Too late now. Do it tomorrow. It'll last the rubber out, sure.'

Corliss took up the cards, but paused in the shuffling.

'We've a big trip before us, Del, about a month from now, the middle of March as near as I can plan it—up the Stewart River to McQuestion; up McQuestion and back again down the Mayo; then across country to Mazy May, winding up at Henderson Creek—'

'On the Indian River?'

'No, Corliss replied, as he dealt the hands; 'just below where the Stewart taps the Yukon. And then back to Dawson before the ice breaks.'

The pocket-miner's eyes sparkled. 'Keep us hustlin'; but, say, it's a trip, isn't it! Hunch?'

'I've received word from the Parker outfit on the Mayo, and McPherson isn't asleep on Henderson—you don't know him. They're keeping quiet, and of course one can't tell, but . . .'

Bishop nodded his head sagely, while Corliss turned the trump he had cut. A sure vision of a 'twenty-four' hand was dazzling him, when there was a sound of voices without and the door shook to a heavy knock.

'Come in!' he bawled. 'An' don't make such a row about it! Look at that '—to Corliss, at the same time facing his hand—'fifteen-eight, fifteen-sixteen, and eight are twenty-four. Just my luck!'

Corliss started swiftly to his feet. Bishop jerked his head about. Two women and a man had staggered clumsily in through the door, and were standing just inside, momentarily blinded by the light.

'By all the Prophets! Cornell!' The pocket-miner wrung the man's hand and led him forward. 'You recollect Cornell, Corliss? Jake Cornell, Thirty-Seven and a Half Eldorado.'

'How could I forget?' the engineer acknowledged warmly, shaking his hand. 'That was a miserable night you put us up last fall, about as miserable as the moose-steak was good that you gave us for breakfast.'

Jake Cornell, hirsute and cadaverous of aspect, nodded his head with emphasis and deposited a corpulent demijohn on the table. Again he nodded his head, and glared wildly about him. The stove caught his eye and he strode over to it, lifted a lid, and spat out a mouthful of amber-coloured juice. Another stride and he was back.

157

''Course I recollect the night,' he rumbled, the ice clattering from his hairy jaws. 'And I'm danged glad to see you, that's a fact.' He seemed suddenly to remember himself, and added a little sheepishly, 'The fact is, we're all danged glad to see you, ain't we, girls?' He twisted his head about and nodded his companions up. 'Blanche, my dear, Mr Corliss—hem—it gives me . . . hem . . . it gives me pleasure to make you acquainted. Cariboo Blanche, sir, Cariboo Blanche.'

'Pleased to meet you.' Cariboo Blanche put out a frank hand and looked him over keenly. She was a fair-featured, blondish woman, originally not unpleasing of appearance, but now with lines all deepened and hardened as on the faces of men who have endured much weather-beat.

Congratulating himself upon his social proficiency, Jake Cornell cleared his throat and marshalled the second woman to the front. 'Mr Corliss, the Virgin; I make you both acquainted. Hem !' in response to the query in Vance's eyes—'Yes, the Virgin. That's all, just the Virgin.'

She smiled and bowed, but did not shake hands. 'A toff' was her secret comment upon the engineer; and from her limited experience she had been led to understand that it was not good form among 'toffs' to shake hands.

Corliss fumbled his hand, then bowed, and looked at her curiously. She was a pretty, low-browed creature; darkly pretty, with a well-favoured body, and for all that the type was mean, he could not escape the charm of her over-brimming vitality. She seemed bursting with it, and every quick, spontaneous movement appeared to spring from every excess of red blood and superabundant energy.

'Pretty healthy proposition, ain't she?' Jake Cornell demanded, following his host's gaze with approval.

'None o' your gammon, Jake,' the Virgin snapped back, with lip curled contemptuously for Vance's especial benefit. 'I fancy it'd be more in keeping if you'd look to pore Blanche, there.'

'Fact is, we're plum ding dong played out,' Jake said. 'An' Blanche went through the ice just down the trail, and her feet's like to freezin'.'

Blanche smiled as Corliss piloted her to a stool by the fire, and her stern mouth gave no indication of the pain

158

she was suffering. He turned away when the Virgin addressed herself to removing the wet footgear, while Bishop went rummaging for socks and moccasins.

'Didn't go in more'n to the ankles,' Cornell explained confidentially; 'but that's plenty a night like this.'

Corliss agreed with a nod of the head.

'Spotted your light, and—hem—and so we come. Don't mind, do you?'

'Why, certainly not—'

'No intrudin'?'

Corliss reassured him by laying hand on his shoulder and cordially pressing him to a seat. Blanche sighed luxuriously. Her wet stockings were stretched up and already steaming, and her feet basking in the capacious warmth of Bishop's Siwash socks. Vance shoved the tobacco canister across, but Cornell pulled out a handful of cigars and passed them around.

'Uncommon bad piece of trail just this side of the turn,' he remarked stentoriously, at the same time flinging an eloquent glance at the demijohn. 'Ice rotten from the springs and no sign till you're into it.' Turning to the woman by the stove, 'How're you feeling, Blanche?'

'Tony,' she responded, stretching her body lazily and redisposing her feet; 'though my legs ain't as limber as when we pulled out.'

Looking to his host for consent, Cornell tilted the demijohn over his arm and partly filled the four tin mugs and an empty jelly glass.

'Wot's the matter with a toddy?' the Virgin broke in; 'or a punch?'

'Got any lime juice?' she demanded of Corliss. 'You 'ave? Jolly!' She directed her dark eyes towards Del. ''Ere, you cookie! Trot out your mixing-pan and sling the kettle for 'ot water. Come on! All hands! Jake's treat, and I'll show you 'ow! Any sugar, Mr Corliss? And nutmeg? Cinnamon, then? O.K. It'll do. Lively now, cookie!'

'Ain't she a peach?' Cornell confided to Vance, watching her with mellow eyes as she stirred the steaming brew.

But the Virgin directed her attentions to the engineer. 'Don't mind 'im, sir,' she advised. ''E's more'n arf-gorn a'ready, a-'itting the jug every blessed stop.'

'Now, my dear—' Jake protested.

'Don't you my-dear me,' she sniffed. 'I don't like you.'

'Why?'

'Cos . . .' She ladled the punch carefully into the mugs and meditated. 'Cos you chew tobacco. Cos your whiskery. Wot I take to is smooth-faced young chaps.'

'Don't take any stock in her nonsense,' the Fraction King warned. 'She just does it a-purpose to get me mad.'

'Now then!' she commanded, sharply. 'Step up to your licker! 'Ere's 'ow!'

'What'll it be?' cried Blanche from the stove.

The elevated mugs wavered and halted.

'The Queen, Gawd bless 'er!' the Virgin toasted promptly.

'And Bill!' Del Bishop interrupted.

Again the mugs wavered.

'Bill 'oo?' the Virgin asked, suspiciously.

'McKinley.'

She favoured him with a smile. 'Thank you, cookie, you're a trump. Now! 'Ere's a go, gents! Take it standing. The Queen, Gawd bless 'er, and Bill McKinley!'

'Bottoms up!' thundered Jake Cornell, and the mugs smote the table with clanging rims.

Vance Corliss discovered himself amused and interested. According to Frona, he mused ironically,—this was learning life, was adding to his sum of human generalisations. The phrase was hers, and he rolled it over a couple of times. Then, again, her engagement with St Vincent crept into his thought, and he charmed the Virgin by asking her to sing. But she was coy, and only after Bishop had rendered the several score stanzas of 'Flying Cloud!' did she comply. Her voice, in a weakly way, probably registered an octave and a half; below that point it underwent strange metamorphoses, while on the upper levels it was devious and rickety. Nevertheless she sang 'Take Back Your Gold' with touching effect, which brought a fiery moisture into the eyes of the Fraction King, who listened greedily, for the time being experiencing unwonted ethical yearnings.

The applause was generous, followed immediately by Bishop, who toasted the singer as the 'Enchantress of Bow Bells,' to the reverberating 'bottoms up!' of Jake Cornell.

Two hours later Frona Welse rapped. It was a sharp, insistent rap, penetrating the din within and bringing Corliss to the door.

She gave a glad little cry when she saw who it was. 'Oh! it is you, Vance! I didn't know you lived here.'

He shook hands and blocked the doorway with his body. Behind him the Virgin was laughing and Jake Cornell roaring:

> 'Oh, cable this message along the track:
> The Prod's out West, but he's coming back;
> Put plenty of veal for one on the rack,
>   Trolla lala, la la la, la la!'

'What is it?' Vance questioned. 'Anything up?'

'I think you might ask me in.' There was a hint of reproach in Frona's voice, and of haste. 'I blundered through the ice, and my feet are freezing.'

'O Gawd!' in the exuberant tones of the Virgin, came whirling over Vance's shoulder, and the voices of Blanche and Bishop joining in a laugh against Cornell, and that worthy's vociferous protestations. It seemed to him that all the blood of his body had rushed into his face. 'But you can't come in, Frona. Don't you hear them?'

'But I must,' she insisted. 'My feet are freezing.'

With a gesture of resignation he stepped aside and closed the door after her. Coming suddenly in from the darkness, she hesitated a moment, but in that moment recovered her sight and took in the scene. The air was thick with tobacco smoke, and the odour of it, in the close room, was sickening to one fresh from the pure outside. On the table a column of steam was ascending from the big mixing-pan. The Virgin, fleeing before Cornell, was defending herself with a long mustard-spoon. Evading him and watching her chance, she continually daubed his nose and cheeks with the yellow smear. Blanche had twisted about from the stove to see the fun, and Del Bishop, with a mug at rest half-way to his lips, was applauding the successive strokes. The faces of all were flushed.

Vance leaned nervelessly against the door. The whole situation seemed so unthinkably impossible. An insane desire to laugh came over him, which resolved itself into a coughing fit. But Frona, realising her own pressing need by the growing absence of sensation in her feet, stepped forward.

'Hello, Del!' she called.

The mirth froze on his face at the familiar sound, and he slowly and unwillingly turned his head to meet her. She had slipped the hood of her *parka* back, and her face outlined against the dark fur, rosy with the cold and bright, was like a shaft of the sun shot into the murk of a boozing-ken. They all knew her, for who did not know Jacob Welse's daughter? The Virgin dropped the mustard-spoon with a startled shriek, while Cornell, passing a dazed hand across his yellow markings and consummating the general smear, collapsed on the nearest stool. Cariboo Blanche alone retained her self-possession, and laughed softly.

Bishop managed to articulate 'Hello!' but was unable to stave off the silence which settled down.

Frona waited a second, then said, 'Good evening, all.'

'This way.' Vance had recovered himself, and seated her by the stove opposite Blanche. 'Better get your things off quickly, and be careful of the heat. I'll see what I can find for you.'

'Some cold water, please,' she asked. 'It will take the frost out. Del will get it.'

'I hope it is not serious?'

'No.' She shook her head and smiled up to him, at the same time working away at her ice-coated moccasins. 'There hasn't been time for more than surface-freezing. At the worst the skin will peel off.'

An unearthly silence brooded in the cabin, broken only by Bishop filling a basin from the water-bucket, and by Corliss seeking out his smallest and daintiest house-moccasins and his warmest socks.

Frona, rubbing her feet vigorously, paused and looked up. 'Don't let me chill the festivities just because I'm cold,' she laughed. 'Please go on.'

Jake Cornell straightened up and cleared his throat inanely, and the Virgin looked over-dignified; but Blanche came over and took the towel out of Frona's hands.

'I wet my feet in the same place,' she said, kneeling down and bringing a glow to the frosted feet.

'I suppose you can manage some sort of a fit with them. Here!' Vance tossed over the house-moccasins and woollen wrappings, which the two women, with low laughs and confidential undertones, proceeded to utilise.

'But what in the world were you doing on trail, alone, at this time of night?' Vance asked. In his heart he was marvelling at the coolness and pluck with which she was carrying off the situation.

'I know beforehand that you will censure me,' she replied, helping Blanche arrange the wet gear over the fire. 'I was at Mrs Stanton's; but first, you must know, Miss Mortimer and I are staying at the Pently's for a week. Now, to start fresh again. I intended to leave Mrs Stanton's before dark; but her baby got into the kerosene, her husband had gone down to Dawson, and—well, we weren't sure of the baby up to half an hour ago. She wouldn't hear of me returning alone; but there was nothing to fear; only I had not expected soft ice in such a snap.'

'How'd you fix the kid?' Del asked, intent on keeping the talk going now that it had started.

'Chewing tobacco.' And when the laughter had subsided, she went on: 'There wasn't any mustard, and it was the best I could think of. Besides, Matt McCarthy saved my life with it once, down at Dyea, when I had the croup. But you were singing when I came,' she suggested. 'Do go on.'

Jake Cornell hawed prodigiously. 'And I got done.'

'Then you, Del. Sing 'Flying Cloud' as you used to coming down the river.'

'Oh, 'e 'as!' said the Virgin.

'Then you sing. I am sure you do.'

She smiled into the Virgin's eyes, and that lady delivered herself of a coster ballad with more art than she was aware. The chill of Frona's advent was quickly dissipated, and song and toast and merriment went round again. Nor was Frona above touching lips to the jelly glass in fellowship; and she contributed her quota by singing 'Annie Laurie' and 'Ben Bolt'. Also, but privily, she watched the drink saturating the besotted souls of Cornell and the Virgin. It was an experience, and she was glad of it, though sorry in a way for Corliss, who played the host lamely.

But he had little need of pity. 'Any other woman—' he

163

said to himself a score of times, looking at Frona and trying to picture numerous women he had known by his mother's tea-pot, knocking at the door and coming in as Frona had done. Then, again, it was only yesterday that it would have hurt him, Blanche's rubbing her feet; but now he gloried in Frona's permitting it, and his heart went out in a more kindly way to Blanche. Perhaps it was the elevation of the liquor, but he seemed to discover new virtues in her rugged face.

Frona had put on her dried moccasins and risen to her feet, and was listening patiently to Jake Cornell, who hiccoughed a last incoherent toast.

'To the—hic—man,' he rumbled, cavernously, 'the man —hic—that made—that made—'

'The blessed country,' volunteered the Virgin.

'True, my dear—hic. To the man that made the blessed country. To—hic—to Jacob Welse!'

'And a rider!' Blanche cried. 'To Jacob Welse's daughter!'

'Aye! Standing! And bottoms up!'

'Oh! she's a jolly good fellow!' Del led off, the drink ruddying his cheek.

'I'd like to shake hands with you, just once,' Blanche said in a low voice, while the rest were chorusing.

Frona slipped her mitten, which she had already put on, and the pressure was firm between them.

'No,' she said to Corliss, who had put on his cap and was tying the ear-flaps. 'Blanche tells me the Pently's are only half a mile from here. The trail is straight. I'll not hear of any one accompanying me.

'No!' This time she spoke so authoritatively that he tossed his cap into the bunk. 'Good night, all!' she called, sweeping the roisterers with a smile.

But Corliss saw her to the door and stepped outside. She glanced up to him. Her hood was pulled only partly up, and her face shone alluringly under the starlight.

'I—Frona . . . I wish—'

'Don't be alarmed,' she whispered. 'I'll not tell on you, Vance.'

He saw the mocking glint in her eyes, but tried to go on.

'I wish to explain just how—'

'No need. I understand. But at the same time I must confess I do not particularly admire your taste—'

'Frona!' The evident pain in his voice reached her.

'Oh, you big foolish!' she laughed. 'Don't I know? Didn't Blanche tell me she wet her feet?'

Corliss bowed his head. 'Truly, Frona, you are the most consistent woman I ever met. Furthermore,' with a straightening of his form and a dominant assertion in his voice, 'this is not the last.'

She tried to stop him, but he continued. 'I feel, I know that things will turn out differently. To fling your own words back at you, all the factors have not been taken into consideration. As for St Vincent . . . I'll have you yet. For that matter, now could not be too soon!'

He flashed out hungry arms to her, but she read quicker than he moved, and, laughing, eluded him and ran lightly down the trail.

'Come back, Frona! Come back!' he called. 'I am sorry.'

'No, you're not,' came the answer. 'And I'd be sorry if you were. Good night.'

He watched her merge into the shadows, then entered the cabin. He had utterly forgotten the scene within, and at the first glance it startled him. Cariboo Blanche was crying softly to herself. Her eyes were luminous and moist, and, as he looked, a lone tear stole down her cheek. Bishop's face had gone serious. The Virgin had sprawled head and shoulders on the table, amid overturned mugs and dripping lees, and Cornell was titubating over her, hiccoughing, and repeating vacuously, 'You're all right, my dear. You're all right.'

But the Virgin was inconsolable. 'O Gawd! W'en I think on wot is, an' was . . . an' no fault of mine. No fault of mine, I tell you!' she shrieked with quick fierceness. ''Ow was I born, I ask? Wot was my old man? A drunk, a chronic. An' my old woman! Talk of Whitechapel! 'Oo guv a cent for me, or 'ow I was dragged up? 'Oo cared a rap, I say? 'Oo cared a rap?'

A sudden revulsion came over Corliss. 'Hold your tongue!' he ordered.

The Virgin raised her head, her loosened hair streaming

about her like a Fury's. 'Wot is she?' she sneered. 'Sweet-'eart?'

Corliss whirled upon her savagely, face white and voice shaking with passion.

The Virgin cowered down and instinctively threw up her hands to protect her face. 'Don't 'it me, sir!' she whined. 'Don't 'it me!'

He was frightened at himself, and waited till he could gather control. 'Now,' he said, calmly, 'get into your things and go. All of you. Clear out. Vamose.'

'You're no man, you ain't,' the Virgin snarled, discovering that physical assault was not imminent.

But Corliss herded her particularly to the door, and gave no heed.

'A-turning ladies out!' she sniffed, with a stumble over the threshold.

'No offence,' Jake Cornell muttered, pacifically; 'no offence.'

'Good night. Sorry,' Corliss said to Blanche, with the shadow of a forgiving smile, as she passed out.

'You're a toff! That's wot you are, a bloomin' toff!' the Virgin howled back as he shut the door.

He looked blankly at Del Bishop and surveyed the sodden confusion on the table. Then he walked over and threw himself down on his bunk. Bishop leaned an elbow on the table and pulled at his wheezy pipe. The lamp smoked, flickered, and went out; but still he remained, filling his pipe again and again and striking endless matches.

'Del! Are you awake?' Corliss called at last.

Del grunted.

'I was a cur to turn them out into the snow. I am ashamed.'

'Sure,' was the affirmation.

A long silence followed. Del knocked the ashes out and raised up.

''Sleep?' he called.

There was no reply, and he walked to the bunk softly and pulled the blankets over the engineer.

166

CHAPTER XXI

'Y E S; what does it all mean?' Corliss stretched lazily, and cocked up his feet on the table. He was not especially interested, but Colonel Trethaway persisted in talking seriously.

'That's it! The very thing—the old and ever young demand which man slaps into the face of the universe.' The colonel searched among the scraps in his note-book.

'See,' holding up a soiled slip of typed paper, 'I copied this out years ago. Listen. "What a monstrous spectre is this man, this disease of the agglutinated dust, lifting alternate feet or lying drugged with slumber; killing, feeding, growing, bringing forth small copies of himself; grown up with hair like grass, fitted with eyes that glitter in his face; a thing to set children screaming. Poor soul, here for so little, cast among so many hardships, filled with desires so incommensurate and so inconsistent; savagely surrounded, savagely descended, irremediably condemned to prey upon his fellow-lives. Infinitely childish, often admirably valiant, often touchingly kind; sitting down to debate of right or wrong and the attributes of the deity; rising up to battle for an egg or die for an idea!"

'And all to what end?' he demanded, hotly, throwing down the paper, 'this disease of the agglutinated dust?'

Corliss yawned in reply. He had been on trail all day and was yearning for between-blankets.

'Here am I, Colonel Trethaway, modestly along in years, fairly well preserved, a place in the community, a comfortable bank account, no need to ever exert myself again, yet enduring life bleakly and working ridiculously with a zest worthy of a man half my years. And to what end? I can only eat so much, smoke so much, sleep so much, and this tail-dump of earth men call Alaska is the worst of all possible places in the matter of grub, tobacco, and blankets.'

'But it is the living strenuously which holds you,' Corliss interjected.

'Frona's philosophy,' the colonel sneered.

'And my philosophy, and yours.'

'And of the agglutinated dust—'

'Which is quickened with a passion you do not take into account—the passion of duty, of race, of God!'

'And the compensation?' Trethaway demanded.

'Each breath you draw. The Mayfly lives an hour.'

'I don't see it.'

'Blood and sweat! Blood and sweat! You cried that after the rough and tumble in the Opera House, and every word of it was receipt in full.'

'Frona's philosophy.'

'And yours and mine.'

The colonel threw up his shoulders, and after a pause confessed. 'You see, try as I will, I can't make a pessimist out of myself. We are all compensated, and I more fully than most men. What end? I asked, and the answer forthcame: Since the ultimate end is beyond us, then the immediate. More compensation, here and now!'

'Quite hedonistic.'

'And rational. I shall look to it at once. I can buy grub and blankets for a score; I can eat and sleep for only one; ergo, why not for two?'

Corliss took his feet down and sat up. 'In other words?'

'I shall get married, and—give the community a shock. Communities like shocks. That's one of their compensations for being agglutinative.'

'I can't think of but one woman,' Corliss essayed tentatively, putting out his hand.

Trethaway shook it slowly. 'It is she.'

Corliss let go, and misgiving shot into his face. 'But St Vincent?'

'Is your problem, not mine.'

'Then Lucile—?'

'Certainly not. She played a quixotic little game of her own and botched it beautifully.'

'I—I do not understand.' Corliss brushed his brows in a dazed sort of way.

Trethaway parted his lips in a superior smile. 'It is not necessary that you should. The question is, Will you stand up with me?'

'Surely. But what a confoundedly long way around you took. It is not your usual method.'

'Nor was it with her,' the colonel declared, twisting his moustache proudly.

A captain of the North-West Mounted Police, by virtue of his magisterial office, may perform marriages in time of stress as well as execute exemplary justice. So Captain Alexander received a call from Colonel Trethaway, and after he left jotted down an engagement for the next morning. Then the impending groom went to see Frona. Lucile did not make the request, he hastened to explain, but—well, the fact was she did not know any women, and, furthermore, he (the colonel) knew whom Lucile would like to ask, did she dare. So he did it upon his own responsibility. And coming as a surprise, he knew it would be a great joy to her.

Frona was taken aback by the suddenness of it. Only the other day, it was, that Lucile had made a plea to her for St Vincent, and now it was Colonel Trethaway! True, there had been a false quantity somewhere, but now it seemed doubly false. Could it be, after all, that Lucile was mercenary? These thoughts crowded upon her swiftly, with the colonel anxiously watching her face the while. She knew she must answer quickly, yet was distracted by an involuntary admiration for his bravery. So she followed, perforce, the lead of her heart, and consented.

Yet the whole thing was rather strained when the four of them came together, next day, in Captain Alexander's private office. There was a gloomy chill about it. Lucile seemed ready to cry, and showed a repressed perturbation quite unexpected of her; while, try as she would, Frona could not call upon her usual sympathy to drive away the coldness which obtruded intangibly between them. This, in turn, had a consequent effect on Vance, and gave a certain distance to his manner which forced him out of touch even with the colonel.

Colonel Trethaway seemed to have thrown twenty years off his erect shoulders, and the discrepancy in the match which Frona had felt vanished as she looked at him. 'He has lived the years well,' she thought, and prompted mysteriously, almost with vague apprehension, she turned her eyes to Corliss. But if the groom had thrown off twenty years, Vance was not a whit behind. Since their last meeting he had sacrificed his brown moustache to the frost, and his smooth face, smitten with health and vigour, looked uncommonly boyish; and yet, withal, the naked upper lip advertised a stiffness and resolution hitherto concealed. Furthermore, his features portrayed a growth, and his eyes, which had been softly firm, were now firm with the added harshness or hardness which is bred of coping with things and coping quickly—the stamp of executiveness which is pressed upon men who do, and upon all men who do, whether they drive dogs, buck the sea, or dictate the policies of empires.

When the simple ceremony was over, Frona kissed Lucile; but Lucile felt that there was a subtle something wanting, and her eyes filled with unshed tears. Trethaway, who had felt the aloofness from the start, caught an opportunity with Frona while Captain Alexander and Corliss were being pleasant to Mrs Trethaway.

'What's the matter, Frona?' the colonel demanded bluntly. 'I hope you did not come under protest. I am sorry, not for you, because lack of frankness deserves nothing, but for Lucile. It is not fair to her.'

'There has been a lack of frankness throughout.' Her voice trembled. 'I tried my best—I thought I could do better—but I cannot feign what I do not feel. I am sorry, but I . . . I am disappointed. No, I cannot explain, and to you least of all.'

'Let's be above-board, Frona. St Vincent's concerned?' She nodded.

'And I can put my hand right on the spot. First place,' he looked to the side and saw Lucile stealing an anxious glance to him—'first place, only the other day she gave you a song about St Vincent. Second place, and therefore, you think her heart's not in this present proposition, that she doesn't care a rap for me; in short, that she's marrying me for reinstatement and spoils. Isn't that it?'

'And isn't it enough? Oh, I am disappointed, Colonel Trethaway, grievously, in her, in you, in myself.'

'Don't be a fool! I like you too well to see you make

170

yourself one. The play's been too quick, that is all. Your eye lost it. Listen. We've kept it quiet, but she's in with the elect on French Hill. Her claim's prospected the richest of the outfit. Present indication half a million at least. In her own name, no strings attached. Couldn't she take that and go anywhere in the world and reinstate herself? And for that matter, you might presume that I am marrying her for spoils. Frona, she cares for me, and in your ear, she's too good for me. My hope is that the future will make up. But never mind that—haven't got the time now.

'You consider her affection sudden, eh? Let me tell you we've been growing into each other from the time I came into the country, and with our eyes open. St Vincent? Pshaw! I knew it all the time. She got it into her head that the whole of him wasn't worth a little finger of you, and she tried to break things up. You'll never know how she worked with him. I told her she didn't know the Welse, and she said so, too, after. So there it is; take it or leave it.'

'But what do you think about St Vincent?'

'What I think is neither here nor there; but I'll tell you honestly that I back her judgment. But that's not the point. What are you going to do about it? about her? now?'

She did not answer, but went back to the waiting group. Lucile saw her coming and watched her face.

'He's been telling you—?'

'That I am a fool,' Frona answered. 'And I think I am.' And with a smile, 'I take it on faith that I am, anyway. I—I can't reason it out just now, but . . .'

Captain Alexander discovered a prenuptial joke just about then, and led the way over to the stove to crack it upon the colonel, and Vance went along to see fair play.

'It's the first time,' Lucile was saying, 'and it means more to me, so much more, than to . . . most women. I am afraid. It is a terrible thing for me to do. But I do love him, I do!' And when the joke had been duly digested and they came back, she was sobbing, 'Dear, dear Frona.'

It was just the moment, better than he could have chosen; and capped and mittened, without knocking, Jacob Welse came in.

'The uninvited guest,' was his greeting. 'Is it all over? So?' And he swallowed Lucile up in his huge bearskin.

171

'Colonel, your hand, and your pardon for my intruding, and your regrets for not giving me the word. Come, out with them! Hello, Corliss! Captain Alexander, a good day.'

'What have I done?' Frona wailed, received the bear-hug, and managed to press his hand till it almost hurt.

'Had to back the game,' he whispered; and this time his hand did hurt.

'Now, colonel, I don't know what your plans are, and I don't care. Call them off. I've got a little spread down to the house, and the only honest case of champagne this side of Circle. Of course, you're coming, Corliss, and—' His eye roved past Captain Alexander with hardly a pause.

'Of course,' came the answer like a flash, though the Chief Magistrate of the North-West had had time to canvass the possible results of such unofficial action. 'Got a hack?'

Jacob Welse laughed and held up a moccasined foot.

'Walking be—chucked!' The captain started impulsively towards the door. 'I'll have the sleds up before you're ready. Three of them, and bells galore!'

So Trethaway's forecast was correct, and Dawson vindicated its agglutinativeness by rubbing its eyes when three sleds, with three scarlet-tunicked policemen swinging the whips, tore down its main street; and it rubbed its eyes again when it saw the occupants thereof.

'We shall live quietly,' Lucile told Frona. 'The Klondike is not all the world, and the best is yet to come.'

But Jacob Welse said otherwise. 'We've got to make this thing go,' he said to Captain Alexander, and Captain Alexander said that he was unaccustomed to backing out.

Mrs Schoville emitted preliminary thunders, marshalled the other women, and became chronically seismic and unsafe.

Lucile went nowhere save to Frona's. But Jacob Welse, who rarely went anywhere, was often to be found by Colonel Trethaway's fireside, and not only was he to be found there, but he usually brought somebody along. 'Anything on hand this evening?' he was wont to say on casual meeting. 'No? Then come along with me.' Sometimes he said it with lamb-like innocence, sometimes with a challenge brooding under his bushy brows, and rarely did he fail to get his man. These men had wives, and thus were the germs of dissolution sown in the ranks of the opposition.

Then, again, at Colonel Trethaway's there was something to be found besides weak tea and small talk; and the correspondents, engineers, and gentlemen rovers kept the trail well packed in that direction, though it was the Kings, to a man, who first broke the way. So the Trethaway cabin became the centre of things, and, backed commercially, financially, and officially, it could not fail to succeed socially.

The only bad effect of all this was to make the lives of Mrs Schoville and divers others of her sex more monotonous, and to cause them to lose faith in certain hoary and inconsequent maxims. Furthermore, Captain Alexander, as highest official, was a power in the land, and Jacob Welse was the Company, and there was a superstition extant concerning the unwisdom of being on indifferent terms with the Company. And the time was not long till probably a bare half-dozen remained in outer cold, and they were considered a warped lot, anyway.

CHAPTER XXII

Q UITE an exodus took place in Dawson in the spring. Men, because they had made stakes, and other men, because they had made none, bought up the available dogs and rushed out for Dyea over the last ice. Incidentally, it was discovered that Dave Harney possessed most of these dogs.

'Going out?' Jacob Welse asked him on a day when the meridian sun for the first time felt faintly warm to the naked skin.

'Well, I calkilate not. I'm clearin' three dollars a pair on the moccasins I cornered, to say nothing but saw wood on the boots. Say, Welse, not that my nose is out of joint, but you jest cinched me everlastin' on sugar, didn't you?'

Jacob Welse smiled.

'And by the Jimcracky I'm squared! Got any rubber boots?'

'No; went out of stock early in the winter.'

Dave snickered slowly. 'And I'm the pertickler party that hocus-pocused 'em.'

'Not you. I gave special orders to the clerks. They weren't sold in lots.'

'No more they wa'n't. One man to the pair and one pair to the man, and a couple of hundred of them; but it was my dust they chucked into the scales an' nobody else's. Drink? Don't mind. Easy! Put up your sack. Call it rebate, for I kin afford it . . . Goin' out? Not this year, I guess. Wash-up's comin'.'

A strike on Henderson the middle of April, which promised to be sensational, drew St Vincent to Stewart River. And a little later, Jacob Welse, interested on Gallagher Gulch and with an eye riveted on the copper mines of White River, went up into the same district, and with him went Frona, for it was more vacation than business. In the meantime, Corliss and Bishop, who had been on trail for a month or more running over the Mayo and McQuestion Country, rounded up on the left fork of

Henderson, where a block of claims waited to be surveyed.

But by May, spring was so far advanced that travel on the creeks became perilous, and on the last of the thawing ice the miners travelled down to the bunch of islands below the mouth of the Stewart, where they went into temporary quarters or crowded the hospitality of those who possessed cabins. Corliss and Bishop located on Split-up Island (so called through the habit parties from the Outside had of dividing there and going several ways), where Tommy McPherson was comfortably situated. A couple of days later, Jacob Welse and Frona arrived from a hazardous trip out of White River, and pitched tent on the high ground at the upper end of Split-up. A few *chechaquos,* the first of the spring rush, strung in exhausted and went into camp against the breaking of the river. Also, there were still men going out who, barred by the rotten ice, came ashore to build poling-boats and await the break-up or to negotiate with the residents for canoes. Notably among these was the Baron Courbertin.

'Ah! Excruciating! Magnificent! Is it not?'

So Frona first ran across him on the following day. 'What?' she asked, giving him her hand.

'You! You!' doffing his cap. 'It is a delight!'

'I am sure—' she began.

'No! No!' He shook his curly mop warmly. 'It is not you. See!' He turned to a Peterborough, for which McPherson had just mulcted him of thrice its value. 'The canoe! Is it not—not—what you Yankees call—a bute?'

'Oh, the canoe,' she repeated, with a falling inflection of chagrin.

'No! No! Pardon!' He stamped angrily upon the ground. 'It is not so. It is not you. It is not the canoe. It is—ah! I have it now! It is your promise. One day, do you not remember, at Madame Schoville's, we talked of the canoe, and of my ignorance, which was sad, and you promised, you said—'

'I would give you your first lesson?'

'And is it not delightful? Listen! Do you not hear? The rippling—ah! the rippling!—deep down at the heart of things! Soon will the water run free. Here is the canoe! Here we meet! The first lesson! Delightful! Delightful!'

The next island below Split-up was known as Roubeau's Island, and was separated from the former by a narrow back-channel. Here, when the bottom had about dropped out of the trail, and with the dogs swimming as often as not, arrived St Vincent—the last man to travel the winter trail. He went into the cabin of John Borg, a taciturn, gloomy individual, prone to segregate himself from his kind. It was the mischance of St Vincent's life that of all cabins he chose Borg's for an abiding-place against the break-up.

'All right,' the man said, when questioned by him. 'Throw your blankets into the corner. Bella'll clear the litter out of the spare bunk.'

Not till evening did he speak again, and then, 'You're big enough to do your own cooking. When the woman's done with the stove you can fire away.'

The woman, or Bella, was a comely Indian girl, young, and the prettiest St Vincent had run across. Instead of the customary greased swarthiness of the race, her skin was clear and of a light-bronze tone, and her features less harsh, more felicitously curved, than those common to the blood.

After supper, Borg, both elbows on table and huge mis-shapen hands supporting chin and jaws, sat puffing stinking Siwash tobacco and staring straight before him. It would have seemed ruminative, the stare, had his eyes been softer or had he blinked; as it was, his face was set and trance-like.

'Have you been in the country long?' St Vincent asked, endeavouring to make conversation.

Borg turned his sullen-black eyes upon him, and seemed to look into him and through him and beyond him, and, still regarding him, to have forgotten all about him. It was as though he pondered some great and weighty matter —probably his sins, the correspondent mused nervously, rolling himself a cigarette. When the yellow cube had dis-sipated itself in curling fragrance, and he was deliberating about rolling a second, Borg suddenly spoke.

'Fifteen years,' he said, and returned to his tremendous cogitation.

Thereat, and for half an hour thereafter, St Vincent,

fascinated, studied his inscrutable countenance. To begin with, it was a massive head, abnormal and top-heavy, and its only excuse for being was the huge bull-throat which supported it. It had been cast in a mould of elemental generousness, and everything about it partook of the asymmetrical crudeness of the elemental. The hair, rank of growth, thick and unkempt, matted itself here and there into curious splotches of grey; and again, grinning at age, twisted itself into curling locks of lustreless black—locks of unusual thickness, like crooked fingers, heavy and solid. The shaggy whiskers, almost bare in places, and in others massing into bunchgrass-like clumps, were plentifully splashed with grey. They rioted monstrously over his face and fell raggedly to his chest, but failed to hide the great hollowed cheeks or the twisted mouth. The latter was thin-lipped and cruel, but cruel only in a passionless sort of way. But the forehead was the anomaly—the anomaly required to complete the irregularity of the face. For it was a perfect forehead, full and broad, and rising superbly strong to its high dome. It was as the seat and bulwark of some vast intelligence; omniscience might have brooded there.

Bella, washing the dishes and placing them away on the shelf behind Borg's back, dropped a heavy tin cup. The cabin was very still, and the sharp rattle came without warning. On the instant, with a brute roar, the chair was overturned and Borg was on his feet, eyes blazing and face convulsed. Bella gave an inarticulate, animal-like cry of fear and cowered at his feet. St Vincent felt his hair bristling, and an uncanny chill, like a jet of cold air, played up and down his spine. Then Borg righted the chair and sank back into his old position, chin on hands and brooding ponderously. Not a word was spoken, and Bella went on unconcernedly with the dishes, while St Vincent rolled a shaky cigarette and wondered if it had been a dream.

Jacob Welse laughed when the correspondent told him. 'Just his way,' he said; 'for his ways are like his looks—unusual. He's an unsociable beast. Been in the country more years than he can number acquaintances. Truth to say, I don't think he has a friend in all Alaska, not even among the Indians, and he's chummed thick with them off and on. " Johnny Sorehead," they call him, but it might as well be " Johnny Break-um-head," for he's got a quick temper and a rough hand. Temper! Some little misunderstanding popped up between him and the agent at Arctic City. He was in the right, too—agent's mistake—but he tabooed the Company on the spot and lived on straight meat for a year. Then I happened to run across him at Tanana Station, and after due explanations he consented to buy from us again.'

' Got the girl from up the head-waters of the White,' Bill Brown told St Vincent. ' Welse thinks he's pioneering in that direction, but Borg could give him cards and spades on it and then win out. He's been over the ground years ago. Yes, strange sort of a chap. Wouldn't hanker to be bunk-mates with him.'

But St Vincent did not mind the eccentricities of the man, for he spent most of his time on Split-up Island with Frona and the Baron. One day, however, and innocently, he ran foul of him. Two Swedes, hunting tree-squirrels from the other end of Roubeau Island, had stopped to ask for matches and to yarn a while in the warm sunshine of the clearing. St Vincent and Borg were accommodating them, the latter for the most part in meditative mono-syllables. Just to the rear, by the cabin-door, Bella was washing clothes. The tub was a cumbersome home-made affair, and, half-full of water, was more than a fair match for an ordinary woman. The correspondent noticed her struggling with it, and stepped back quickly to her aid.

With the tub between them, they proceeded to carry it to one side in order to dump it where the ground drained from the cabin. St Vincent slipped in the thawing snow and the soapy water splashed up. Then Bella slipped, and then they both slipped. Bella giggled and laughed, and St Vincent laughed back. The spring was in the air and in their blood, and it was very good to be alive. Only a wintry heart could deny a smile on such a day. Bella slipped again, tried to recover, slipped with the other foot, and sat down abruptly. Laughing gleefully, both of them, the corres-pondent caught her hands to pull her to her feet. With a bound and a bellow, Borg was upon them. Their hands were torn apart and St Vincent thrust heavily backward.

He staggered for a couple of yards and almost fell. Then the scene of the cabin was repeated. Bella cowered and grovelled in the muck, and her lord towered wrathfully over her.

'Look you,' he said in stifled gutturals, turning to St Vincent. 'You sleep in my cabin and you cook. That is enough. Let my woman alone.'

Things went on after that as though nothing had happened; St Vincent gave Bella a wide berth and seemed to have forgotten her existence. But the Swedes went back to their end of the island, laughing at the trivial happening which was destined to be significant.

CHAPTER XXIII

Spring, smiting with soft, warm hands, had come like a miracle, and now lingered for a dreamy spell before bursting into full-blown summer. The snow had left the bottoms and valleys and nestled only on the north slopes of the ice-scarred ridges. The glacial drip was already in evidence, and every creek in roaring spate. Each day the sun rose earlier and stayed later. It was now chill day by three o'clock and mellow twilight at nine. Soon a golden circle would be drawn around the sky, and deep midnight become bright as high noon. The willows and aspens had long since budded, and were now decking themselves in liveries of fresh young green, and the sap was rising in the pines.

Mother nature had heaved her waking sigh and gone about her brief business. Crickets sang of nights in the stilly cabins, and in the sunshine mosquitoes crept from out hollow logs and snug crevices among the rocks—big, noisy, harmless fellows, that had procreated the year gone, lain frozen through the winter, and were now rejuvenated to buzz through swift senility to second death. All sorts of creeping, crawling, fluttering life came forth from the warming earth and hastened to mature, reproduce, and cease. Just a breath of balmy air, and then the long cold frost again—ah! they knew it well and lost no time. Sand martins were driving their ancient tunnels into the soft clay banks, and robins singing on the spruce-garbed islands. Overhead the woodpecker knocked insistently, and in the forest depths the partridge boom-boomed and strutted in virile glory.

But in all this nervous haste the Yukon took no part. For many a thousand miles it lay cold, unsmiling, dead. Wild fowl, driving up from the south in wind-jamming wedges, halted, looked vainly for open water, and quested dauntlessly on into the north. From bank to bank stretched the savage ice. Here and there the water burst through and flooded over, but in the chill nights froze solidly as ever. Tradition has it that of old time the Yukon lay unbroken through three long summers, and on the face of it there be traditions less easy of belief.

So summer waited for open water, and the tardy Yukon took to stretching of days and cracking its stiff joints. Now an air-hole ate into the ice, and ate and ate; or a fissure formed, and grew, and failed to freeze again. Then the ice ripped from the shore and uprose bodily a yard. But still the river was loth to loose its grip. It was a slow travail, and man, used to nursing nature with pigmy skill, able to burst waterspouts and harness waterfalls, could avail nothing against the billions of frigid tons which refused to run down the hill to Bering Sea.

On Split-up Island all were ready for the break-up. Waterways have ever been first highways, and the Yukon was the sole highway in all the land. So those bound up-river pitched their poling-boats and shod their poles with iron, and those bound down caulked their scows and barges and shaped spare sweeps with axe and drawing-knife. Jacob Welse loafed and joyed in the utter cessation from work, and Frona joyed with him in that it was good. But Baron Courbertin was in a fever at the delay. His hot blood grew riotous after the long hibernation, and the warm sunshine dazzled him with warmer fancies.

'Oh! Oh! It will never break! Never!' And he stood gazing at the surly ice and raining politely phrased anathema upon it. 'It is a conspiracy, poor *La Bijou,* a conspiracy!' He caressed *La Bijou* like it were a horse, for so he had christened the glistening Peterborough canoe.

Frona and St Vincent laughed and preached him the gospel of patience, which he proceeded to tuck away into the deepest abysses of perdition till interrupted by Jacob Welse.

'Look, Courbertin! Over there, south of the bluff. Do you make out anything? Moving?'

'Yes; a dog.'

'It moves too slowly for a dog. Frona, get the glasses.

Courbertin and St Vincent sprang after them, but the latter knew their abiding-place and returned triumphant. Jacob Welse put the binoculars to his eyes and gazed steadily across the river. It was a sheer mile from the island to the farther bank, and the sun-glare on the ice was a sore task to the vision.

'It is a man.' He passed the glasses to the baron and strained absently with his naked eyes. 'And something is up.'

'He creeps!' the baron exclaimed. 'The man creeps, he crawls, on hand and knee! Look! See!' He thrust the glasses tremblingly into Frona's hands.

Looking across the void of shimmering white, it was difficut to discern a dark object of such size when dimly outlined against an equally dark background of brush and earth. But Frona could make the man out with fair distinctness; and as she grew accustomed to the strain she could distinguish each movement, and especially so when he came to a wind-thrown pine. She watched painfully. Twice, after tortuous effort, squirming and twisting, he failed in breasting the big trunk, and on the third attempt, after infinite exertion, he cleared it only to topple helplessly forward and fall on his face in the tangled undergrowth.

'It *is* a man.' She turned the glasses over to St Vincent. 'And he is crawling feebly. He fell just then this side of the log.'

'Does he move?' Jacob Welse asked, and, on a shake of St Vincent's head, brought his rifle from the tent.

He fired six shots skyward in rapid succession.

'He moves!' The correspondent followed him closely. 'He is crawling to the bank. Ah! . . . No; one moment . . . Yes! He lies on the ground and raises his hat, or something, on a stick. He is waving it.' (Jacob Welse fired six more shots.) 'He waves again. Now he has dropped it and lies quite still.'

All three looked inquiringly to Jacob Welse.

He shrugged his shoulders. 'How should I know? A white man or an Indian; starvation most likely, or else he is injured.'

'But he may be dying,' Frona pleaded, as though her father, who had done most things, could do all things.

'We can do nothing.'

'Ah! Terrible! terrible!' The baron wrung his hands. 'Before our very eyes, and we can do nothing! No!' he exclaimed, with swift resolution, 'it shall not be! I will cross the ice!'

He would have started precipitately down the bank had not Jacob Welse caught his arm.

'Not such a rush, baron. Keep your head.'

'But—'

'But nothing. Does the man want food, or medicine, or what? Wait a moment. We will try it together.'

'Count me in,' St Vincent volunteered promptly, and Frona's eyes sparkled.

While she made up a bundle of food in the tent, the men provided and rigged themselves with sixty or seventy feet of light rope. Jacob Welse and St Vincent made themselves fast to it at either end, and the baron in the middle. He claimed the food as his portion, and strapped it to his broad shoulders. Frona watched their progress from the bank. The first hundred yards were easy going, but she noticed at once the change when they had passed the limit of the fairly solid shore-ice. Her father led sturdily, feeling ahead and to the side with his staff and changing direction continually.

St Vincent, at the rear of the extended line, was the first to go through, but he fell with the pole thrust deftly across the opening and resting on the ice. His head did not go under, though the current sucked powerfully, and the two men dragged him out after a sharp pull. Frona saw them consult together for a minute, with much pointing and gesticulating on the part of the baron, and then St Vincent detach himself and turn shoreward.

'Br-r-r-r,' he shivered, coming up the bank to her. 'It's impossible.'

'But why didn't they come in?' she asked, a slight note of displeasure manifest in her voice.

'Said they were going to make one more try, first. That Courbertin is hot-headed, you know.'

'And my father just as bull-headed,' she smiled. 'But hadn't you better change? There are spare things in the tent.'

'Oh, no.' He threw himself down beside her. 'It's warm in the sun.'

For an hour they watched the two men, who had become

183

mere specks of black in the distance; for they had managed to gain the middle of the river and at the same time had worked nearly a mile up-stream. Frona followed them closely with the glasses, though often they were lost to sight behind the ice-ridges.

'It was unfair of them,' she heard St Vincent complain, 'to say they were only going to have one more try. Otherwise I should not have turned back. Yet they can't make it—absolutely impossible.'

'Yes . . . No . . . Yes! They're turning back,' she announced. 'But, listen! What is that?'

A hoarse rumble, like distant thunder, rose from the midst of the ice. She sprang to her feet. 'Gregory, the river can't be breaking!'

'No, no; surely not. See, it is gone.' The noise which had come from above had died away downstream.

'But there! There!'

Another rumble, hoarser and more ominous than before, lifted itself and hushed the robins and the squirrels. When abreast of them, it sounded like a railroad train on a distant trestle. A third rumble, which approached a roar and was of greater duration, began from above and passed by.

'Oh, why don't they hurry!'

The two specks had stopped, evidently in conversation. She ran the glasses hastily up and down the river. Though another roar had risen, she could make out no commotion. The ice lay still and motionless. The robins resumed their singing, and the squirrels were chattering with spiteful glee.

'Don't fear, Frona.' St Vincent put his arm about her protectingly. 'If there is any danger, they know it better than we, and they are taking their time.'

'I never saw a big river break up,' she confessed, and resigned herself to the waiting.

The roars rose and fell sporadically, but there were no other signs of disruption, and gradually the two men, with frequent duckings, worked inshore. The water was streaming from them and they were shivering severely as they came up the bank.

'At last!' Frona had both her father's hands in hers. 'I thought you would never come back.'

'There, there. Run and get dinner,' Jacob Welse laughed. 'There was no danger.'

'But what was it?'

'Stewart River's broken and sending its ice down under the Yukon ice. We could hear the grinding plainly out there.'

'Ah! And it was terrible! terrible!' cried the baron. 'And that poor, poor man, we cannot save him!'

'Yes, we can. We'll have a try with the dogs after dinner. Hurry, Frona.'

But the dogs were a failure. Jacob Welse picked out the leaders as the more intelligent, and with grub-packs on them drove them out from the bank. They could not grasp what was demanded of them. Whenever they tried to return they were driven back with sticks and clods and imprecations. This only bewildered them, and they retreated out of range, whence they raised their wet, cold paws and whined pitifully to the shore.

'If they could only make it once, they would understand, and then it would go like clock-work. Ah! Would you? Go on! Chook, Miriam! Chook! The thing is to get the first one across.'

Jacob Welse finally succeeded in getting Miriam, lead-dog to Frona's team, to take the trail left by him and the baron. The dog went on bravely, scrambling over, floundering through, and sometimes swimming; but when she had gained the farthest point reached by them, she sat down helplessly. Later on, she cut back to the shore at a tangent, landing on the deserted island above; and an hour afterwards trotted into camp minus the grub-pack. Then the two dogs, hovering just out of range, compromised matters by devouring each other's burdens; after which the attempt was given over and they were called in.

During the afternoon the noise increased in frequency, and by nightfall was continuous, but by morning it had ceased utterly. The river had risen eight feet, and in many places was running over its crust. Much crackling and splitting were going on, and fissures leaping into life and multiplying in all directions.

'The under-tow ice has jammed below among the islands,' Jacob Welse explained. 'That's what caused the rise. Then, again, it has jammed at the mouth of the Stewart and is backing up. When that breaks through, it will go down underneath and stick on the lower jam.'

'And then? and then?' The baron exulted.

'*La Bijou* will swim again.'

As the light grew stronger, they searched for the man across the river. He had not moved, but in response to their rifle-shots waved feebly.

'Nothing for it till the river breaks, baron, and then a dash with *La Bijou*. St Vincent, you had better bring your blankets up and sleep here tonight. We'll need three paddles, and I think we can get McPherson.'

'No need,' the correspondent hastened to reply. 'The back-channel is like adamant, and I'll be up by daybreak.'

'But I? Why not?' Baron Courbertin demanded.

Frona laughed. 'Remember, we haven't given you your first lessons yet.'

'And there'll hardly be time tomorrow,' Jacob Welse added. 'When she goes, she goes with a rush. St Vincent, McPherson, and I will have to make the crew, I'm afraid. Sorry, baron. Stay with us another year and you'll be fit.'

But Baron Courbertin was inconsolable, and sulked for a full half-hour.

CHAPTER XXIV

'A WAKE! You dreamers, wake!'

Frona was out of her sleeping-furs at Del Bishop's first call; but ere she had slipped a skirt on and bare feet into moccasins, her father, beyond the blanket-curtain, had thrown back the flaps of the tent and stumbled out.

The river was up. In the chill grey light she could see the ice rubbing softly against the very crest of the bank; it even topped it in places, and the huge cakes worked inshore many feet. A hundred yards out the white field merged into the dim dawn and the grey sky. Subdued splits and splutters whispered from out the obscureness, and a gentle grinding could be heard.

'When will it go?' she asked of Del.

'Not a bit too lively for us. See there!' He pointed with his toe to the water lapping out from under the ice and creeping greedily towards them. 'A foot rise every ten minutes.'

'Danger?' he scoffed. 'Not on your life. It's got to go. Them islands'—waving his hand indefinitely down river—'can't hold up under more pressure. If they don't let go the ice, the ice'll scour them clean out of the bed of the Yukon. Sure! But I've got to be chasin' back. Lower ground down our way. Fifteen inches on the cabin floor, and McPherson and Corliss hustlin' perishables into the bunks.'

'Tell McPherson to be ready for a call,' Jacob Welse shouted after him. And then to Frona, 'Now's the time for St Vincent to cross the back-channel.'

The baron, shivering barefooted, pulled out his watch. 'Ten minutes to three,' he chattered.

'Hadn't you better go back and get your moccasins?' Frona asked. 'There will be time.'

'And miss the magnificence? Hark!'

From nowhere in particular a brisk crackling arose, then died away. The ice was in motion. Slowly, very slowly, it proceeded down stream. There was no commotion, no ear-splitting thunder, no splendid display of force; simply a

187

silent flood of white, an orderly procession of tight-packed ice—packed so closely that not a drop of water was in evidence. It was there, somewhere, down underneath; but it had to be taken on faith. There was a dull hum or muffled grating, but so low in pitch that the ear strained to catch it.

'Ah! Where is the magnificence? It is a fake!'

The baron shook his fists angrily at the river, and Jacob Welse's thick brows seemed to draw down in order to hide the grim smile in his eyes.

'Ha! ha! I laugh! I snap my fingers! See! I defy!'

As the challenge left his lips, Baron Courbertin stepped upon a cake which rubbed lightly past at his feet. So unexpected was it, that when Jacob Welse reached after him he was gone.

The ice was picking up in momentum, and the hum growing louder and more threatening. Balancing gracefully, like a circus-rider, the Frenchman whirled away along the rim of the bank. Fifty precarious feet he rode, his mount becoming more unstable every instant, and he leaped neatly to the shore. He came back laughing, and received for his pains two or three of the choicest phrases Jacob Welse could select from the essentially masculine portion of his vocabulary.

'And for why?' Courbertin demanded, stung to the quick.

'For why?' Jacob Welse mimicked wrathfully, pointing into the sleek stream sliding by.

A great cake had driven its nose into the bed of the river thirty feet below and was struggling to up-end. All the frigid flood behind crinkled and bent back like so much paper. Then the stalled cake turned completely over and thrust its muddy nose skyward. But the squeeze caught it, while cake mounted cake at its back, and its fifty feet of muck and gouge were hurled into the air. It crashed upon the moving mass beneath, and flying fragments landed at the feet of those that watched. Caught broadside in a chaos of pressures, it crumbled into scattered pieces and disappeared.

'God!' The baron spoke the word reverently and with awe.

Frona caught his hand on the one side and her father's on the other. The ice was now leaping past in feverish haste. Somewhere below a heavy cake butted into the bank, and the ground swayed under their feet. Another followed it, nearer the surface, and as they sprang back, upreared mightily, and, with a ton or so of soil on its broad back, bowled insolently onward. And yet another, reaching in-shore like a huge hand, ripped three careless pines out by the roots and bore them away.

Day had broken, and the driving white gorged the Yukon from shore to shore. What of the pressure of pent water behind, the speed of the flood had become dizzying. Down all its length the bank was being gashed and gouged, and the island was jarring and shaking to its foundations.

'Oh, great! Great!' Frona sprang up and down between the men. 'Where is your fake, baron?'

'Ah!' He shook his head. 'Ah! I was wrong. I am miserable. But the magnificence! Look!'

He pointed down to the bunch of islands which obstructed the bend. There the mile-wide stream divided and subdivided again—which was well for water, but not so well for packed ice. The islands drove their wedged heads into the frozen flood and tossed the cakes high into the air. But cake pressed upon cake and shelved out of the water, out and up, sliding, and grinding and climbing, and still more cakes from behind, till hillocks and mountains of ice upreared and crashed among the trees.

'A likely place for a jam,' Jacob Welse said. 'Get the glasses, Frona.' He gazed through them long and steadily. 'It's growing, spreading out. A cake at the right time and the right place . . .'

'But the river is falling!' Frona cried.

The ice had dropped six feet below the top of the bank, and the Baron Courbertin marked it with a stick.

'Our man's still there, but he doesn't move.'

It was clear day, and the sun was breaking forth in the north-east. They took turn about with the glasses in gazing across the river.

'Look! Is it not marvellous?' Courbertin pointed to the mark he had made. The water had dropped another foot. 'Ah! Too bad! too bad! The jam; there will be none!'

Jacob Welse regarded him gravely.

'Ah! There will be?' he asked, picking up hope.

Frona looked inquiringly at her father.

'Jams are not always nice,' he said, with a short laugh. 'It all depends where they take place and where you happen to be.'

'But the river! Look! It falls; I can see it before my eyes.'

'It is not too late.' He swept the island-studded bend and saw the ice-mountains larger and reaching out one to the other. 'Go into the tent, Courbertin, and put on the pair of moccasins you'll find by the stove. Go on. You won't miss anything. And you, Frona, start the fire and get the coffee under way.'

Half an hour after, though the river had fallen twenty feet, they found the ice still pounding along.

'Now the fun begins. Here, take a squint, you hot-headed Gaul. The left-hand channel, man. Now she takes it!'

Courbertin saw the left-hand channel close, and then a great white barrier heave up and travel from island to island. The ice before them slowed down and came to rest. Then followed the instant rise of the river. Up it came in a swift rush, as though nothing short of the sky could stop it. As when they were first awakened, the cakes rubbed and slid inshore over the crest of the bank, the muddy water creeping in advance and marking the way.

'*Mon Dieu!* But this is not nice!'

'But magnificent, baron,' Frona teased. 'In the meanwhile you are getting your feet wet.'

He retreated out of the water, and in time, for a small avalanche of cakes rattled down upon the place he had just left. The rising water had forced the ice up till it stood breast-high above the island like a wall.

'But it will go down soon when the jam breaks. See, even now it comes up not so swift. It has broken.'

Frona was watching the barrier. 'No, it hasn't,' she denied.

'But the water no longer rises like a racehorse.'

'Nor does it stop rising.'

He was puzzled for the nonce. Then his face brightened.

'Ah, I have it! Above, somewhere, there is another jam. Most excellent, is it not?'

She caught his excited hand in hers and detained him. 'But, listen. Suppose the upper jam breaks and the lower jam holds?'

He looked at her steadily till he grasped the full import. His face flushed, and with a quick intake of the breath he straightened up and threw back his head. He made a sweeping gesture as though to include the island. 'Then you, and I, the tent, the boats, cabins, trees, everything, and *La Bijou*! Pouf! and all are gone, to the devil!'

Frona shook her head. 'It is too bad.'

'Bad? Pardon. Magnificent!'

'No, no, baron; not that. But that you are not an Anglo-Saxon. The race could well be proud of you.'

'And you, Frona, would you not glorify the French!'

'At it again, eh? Throwing bouquets at yourselves.' Del Bishop grinned at them, and made to depart as quickly as he had come. 'But twist yourselves. Some sick men in a cabin down here. Got to get 'em out. You're needed. And don't be all day about it,' he shouted over his shoulder as he disappeared among the trees.

The river was still rising, though more slowly, and as soon as they left the high ground they were splashing along ankle-deep in the water. Winding in and out among the trees, they came upon a boat which had been hauled out the previous fall. And three *chechaquos*, who had managed to get into the country thus far over the ice, had piled themselves into it, also their tent, sleds, and dogs. But the boat was perilously near the ice-gorge, which growled and wrestled and over-topped it a bare dozen feet away.

'Come! Get out of this, you fools!' Jacob Welse shouted as he went past.

Del Bishop had told them to 'get the hell out of there' when he ran by, and they could not understand. One of them turned up an unheeding, terrified face. Another lay prone and listless across the thwarts as though bereft of strength; while the third, with the face of a clerk, rocked back and forth and moaned monotonously. 'My God! My God!'

The baron stopped long enough to shake him. 'Damn!'

he cried. 'Your legs, man!—not God, but your legs! Ah! ah—hump yourself! Yes, hump! Get a move on! Twist! Get back from the bank! The woods, the trees, anywhere!'

He tried to drag him out, but the man struck at him savagely and held back.

'How one collects the vernacular,' he confided proudly to Frona as they hurried on. 'Twist! It is a strong word, and suitable.'

'You should travel with Del,' she laughed. 'He'd increase your stock in no time.'

'You don't say so.'

'Yes, but I do.'

'Ah! Your idioms. I shall never learn.' And he shook his head despairingly with both his hands.

They came out in a clearing, where a cabin stood close to the river. On its flat earth-roof two sick men, swathed in blankets, were lying, while Bishop, Corliss, and Jacob Welse were splashing about inside the cabin after the clothes-bags and general outfit. The mean depth of the flood was a couple of feet, but the floor of the cabin had been dug out for purposes of warmth, and there the water was to the waist.

'Keep the tobacco dry,' one of the sick men said feebly from the roof.

'Tobacco, hell!' his companion advised. 'Look out for the flour. And the sugar,' he added, as an afterthought.

'That's 'cause Bill he don't smoke, miss,' the first man explained. 'But keep an eye on it, won't you?' he pleaded.

'Here. Now shut up.' Del tossed the canister beside him, and the man clutched it as though it were a sack of nuggets.

'Can I be of any use?' she asked, looking up at them.

'Nope. Scurvy. Nothing'll do 'em any good but God's country and raw potatoes.' The pocket-miner regarded her for a moment. 'What are you doing here, anyway? Go on back to high ground.'

But with a groan and a crash, the ice-wall bulged in. A fifty-ton cake ended over, splashing them with muddy water, and settled down before the door. A smaller cake drove against the out-jutting corner-logs and the cabin reeled. Courbertin and Jacob Welse were inside.

'After you,' Frona heard the baron, and then her father's

short amused laugh; and the gallant Frenchman came out last, squeezing his way between the cake and the logs.

'Say, Bill, if that there lower jam holds, we're goners,' the man with the canister called to his partner.

'Aye, that it will,' came the answer. 'Below Nulato I saw Bixbie Island swept clean as my old mother's kitchen floor.'

The men came hastily together about Frona.

'This won't do. We've got to carry them over to your shack, Corliss.' As he spoke, Jacob Welse clambered nimbly up the cabin and gazed down at the big barrier. 'Where's McPherson?' he asked.

'Petrified astride the ridge-pole this last hour.'

Jacob Welse waved his arm. 'It's breaking! There she goes!'

'No kitchen floor this time, Bill, with my respects to your old woman,' called he of the tobacco.

'Aye,' answered the imperturbable Bill.

The whole river seemed to pick itself up and start down the stream. With the increasing motion the ice-wall broke in a hundred places, and from up and down the shore came the rending and crashing of uprooted trees.

Corliss and Bishop laid hold of Bill and started off to McPherson's, and Jacob Welse and the baron were just sliding his mate over the eaves, when a huge block of ice rammed in and smote the cabin squarely. Frona saw it, and cried a warning, but the tiered logs were overthrown like a house of cards. She saw Courbertin and the sick man hurled clear of the wreckage, and her father go down with it. She sprang to the spot, but he did not rise. She pulled at him to get his mouth above water, but at full stretch his head barely showed. Then she let go and felt about with her hands till she found his right arm jammed between the logs. These she could not move, but she thrust between them one of the roof-poles which had underlaid the dirt and moss. It was a rude handspike and hardly equal to the work, for when she threw her weight upon the free end it bent and crackled. Heedful of the warning, she came in a couple of feet and swung upon it tentatively and carefully till something gave and Jacob Welse shoved his muddy face into the air.

He drew half a dozen great breaths, and burst out, 'But that tastes good!' And then, throwing a quick glance about him, 'Frona, Del Bishop is a most veracious man.'

'Why?' she asked, perplexedly.

'Because he said you'd do, you know.'

He kissed her, and they both spat the mud from their lips, laughing. Courbertin floundered round a corner of the wreckage.

'Never was there such a man!' he cried, gleefully. 'He is mad, crazy! There is no appeasement. His skull is cracked by the fall, and his tobacco is gone. It is chiefly the tobacco which is lamentable.'

But his skull was not cracked, for it was merely a slit of the scalp of five inches or so.

'You'll have to wait till the others come back. I can't carry.' Jacob Welse pointed to his right arm, which hung dead. 'Only wrenched,' he explained. 'No bones broken.'

The baron struck an extravagant attitude and pointed down at Frona's foot. 'Ah! the water, it is gone, and there, a jewel of the flood, a pearl of price!'

Her well-worn moccasins had gone rotten from the soaking, and a little white toe peeped out at the world of slime.

'Then I am indeed wealthy, baron; for I have nine others.'

'And who shall deny? who shall deny?' he cried, fervently.

'What a ridiculous, foolish, lovable fellow it is!'

'I kiss your hand.' And he knelt gallantly in the muck. She jerked her hand away, and, burying it with its mate in his curly mop, shook his head back and forth. 'What shall I do with him, father?'

Jacob Welse shrugged his shoulders and laughed; and she turned Courbertin's face up and kissed him on the lips. And Jacob Welse knew that his was the larger share in that manifest joy.

The river, fallen to its winter level, was pounding its ice-glut steadily along. But in falling it had rimmed the shore with a twenty-foot wall of stranded floes. The great blocks were spilled inland among the thrown and standing trees and the slime-coated flowers and grasses like the titanic vomit of some Northland monster. The sun was not idle, and the steaming thaw washed the mud and foulness from the bergs till they blazed like heaped diamonds in the brightness, or shimmered opalescent blue. Yet they were reared hazardously one on another, and ever and anon flashing towers and rainbow minarets crumbled thunderously into the flood. By one of the gaps so made lay *La Bijou,* and about it saving *chechaquos* and sick men, were grouped the denizens of Split-up.

'Na, na, lad; twa men'll be a plenty.' Tommy McPherson sought about him with his eyes for corroboration. 'Gin ye gat three i' the canoe 'twill be ower comfortable.'

'It must be a dash or nothing,' Corliss spoke up. 'We need three men, Tommy, and you know it.'

'Na, na; twa's a plenty, I'm tellin' ye.'

'But I'm afraid we'll have to do with two.'

The Scotch-Canadian evinced his satisfaction openly. 'Mair'd be a bother; an' I doot not ye'll mak' it all richt, lad.'

'And you'll make one of those two, Tommy,' Corliss went on, inexorably.

'Na, there's ithers a plenty wi'oout coontin' me.'

'No, there's not. Courbertin doesn't know the first thing. St Vincent evidently cannot cross the slough. Mr Welse's arm puts him out of it. So it's only you and I, Tommy.'

'I'll not be inqueesitive, but yon son of Anak's a likely mon. He maun pit oop a guid stroke.' While the Scot did not lose much love for the truculent pocket-miner, he was well aware of his grit, and seized the chance to save himself by shoving the other into the breach.

Del Bishop stepped into the centre of the little circle, paused, and looked every man in the eyes before he spoke.

'Is there a man here'll say I'm a coward?' he demanded without preface. Again he looked each one in the eyes. 'Or is there a man who'll even hint that I ever did a cur-like act?' And yet again he searched the circle. 'Well and good. I hate the water, but I've never been afraid of it. I don't know how to swim, yet I've been over the side more times than it's good to remember. I can't pull an oar without batting my back on the bottom of the boat. As for steering

—well, authorities say there's thirty-two points to the compass, but there's at least thirty more when I get started. And as sure as God made little apples, I don't know my elbow from my knee about a paddle. I've capsized damn near every canoe I ever set foot in. I've gone right through the bottom of two. I've turned turtle in the Canyon and been pulled out below the White Horse. I can only keep stroke with one man, and that man's yours truly. But, gentlemen, if the call comes, I'll take my place in *La Bijou* and take her to hell if she don't turn over on the way.'

Baron Courbertin threw his arms about him, crying, ' As sure as God made little apples, thou art a man !'

Tommy's face was white, and he sought refuge in speech from the silence which settled down. ' I'll no deny I lift a guid paddle, nor that my wind is fair; but gin ye gang a tithe the way the next jam'll be on us. For my pairt I conseeder it ay rash. Bide a wee till the river's clear, say I.'

' It's no go, Tommy,' Jacob Welse admonished. ' You can't cash excuses here.'

' But, mon ! It doesna need discreemeenation— '

' That'll do !' from Corliss. ' You're coming.'

' I'll naething o' the sort. I'll— "

'Shut up !' Del had come into the world with lungs of leather and larynx of brass, and when he thus jerked out the stops the Scotsman quailed and shrank down.

' Oyez ! Oyez !' In contrast to Del's siren tones, Frona's were purest silver as they rippled down-island through the trees. ' Oyez ! Oyez ! Open water ! Open water ! And wait a minute. I'll be with you.'

Three miles up-stream, where the Yukon curved grandly in from the west, a bit of water appeared. It seemed too marvellous for belief, after the granite winter; but McPherson, untouched of imagination, began a crafty retreat.

' Bide a wee, bide a wee,' he protested, when collared by the pocket-miner. ' A've forgot my pipe.'

' Then you'll bide with us, Tommy,' Del sneered. ' And I'd let you have a draw of mine if your own wasn't sticking out of your pocket.'

' 'Twas the baccy I'd in mind.'

' Then dig into this.' He shoved his pouch into McPherson's shaking hands. ' You'd better shed your coat. Here !

I'll help you. And private, Tommy, if you don't act the man, I won't do a thing to you. Sure.'

Corliss had stripped his heavy flannel shirt for freedom; and it was plain, when Frona joined them, that she also had been shedding. Jacket and skirt were gone, and her underskirt of dark cloth ceased midway below the knee.

'You'll do,' Del commended.

Jacob Welse looked at her anxiously, and went over to where she was testing the grips of the several paddles. 'You're not—?' he began.

She nodded.

'You're a guid girl,' McPherson broke in. 'Now a've a wumman to home, to say naething o' three bairns—'

'All ready!' Corliss lifted the bow of *La Bijou* and looked back.

The turbid water lashed by on the heels of the ice-run. Courbertin took the stern in the steep descent, and Del marshalled Tommy's reluctant rear. A flat floe, dipping into the water at a slight incline, served as the embarking-stage.

'Into the bow with you, Tommy!'

The Scotsman groaned, felt Bishop breathe heavily at his back, and obeyed; Frona meeting his weight by slipping into the stern.

'I can steer,' she assured Corliss, who for the first time was aware that she was coming.

He glanced up to Jacob Welse, as though for consent, and received it.

'Hit 'er up! Hit 'er up!' Del urged impatiently. 'You're burnin' daylight!'

CHAPTER XXV

La Bijou was a perfect expression of all that was dainty and delicate in the boat-builder's soul. Light as an egg-shell, and as fragile, her three-eighths-inch skin offered no protection from a driving chunk of ice as small as a man's head. Nor, though the water was open, did she find a clear way, for the river was full of scattered floes which had crumbled down from the rim-ice. And here, at once, through skilful handling, Corliss took to himself confidence in Frona.

It was a great picture : the river rushing blackly between its crystalline walls; beyond, the green woods stretching upward to touch the cloud-flecked summer sky; and over all, like a furnace blast, the hot sun beating down. A great picture, but somehow Corliss's mind turned to his mother and her perennial tea, the soft carpets, the prim New-England maid-servants, the canaries singing in the wide windows, and he wondered if she could understand. And when he thought of the woman behind him, and felt the dip and lift, dip and lift, of her paddle, his mother's women came back to him, one by one, and passed in long review —pale, glimmering ghosts, he thought, caricatures of the stock which had replenished the earth, and which would continue to replenish the earth.

La Bijou skirted a pivoting floe, darted into a nipping channel, and shot out into the open with the walls grinding together behind. Tommy groaned.

' Well done !' Corliss encouraged.

' The fule wumman !' came the backward snarl. ' Why couldna she bide a bit?'

Frona caught his words and flung a laugh defiantly. Vance darted a glance over his shoulder to her, and her smile was witchery. Her cap, perched precariously, was sliding off, while her flying hair, aglint in the sunshine, framed her face as he had seen it framed on the Dyea Trail.

' How I should like to sing, if it weren't for saving one's

breath. Say the "Song of the Sword", or the "Anchor Chanty".'

' Or the "First Chanty",' Corliss answered. ' " Mine was the woman, darkling I found her," ' he hummed, significantly.

She flashed her paddle into the water on the opposite side in order to go wide of a jagged cake, and seemed not to hear. ' I could go on this way for ever.'

' And I,' Corliss affirmed, warmly.

But she refused to take notice, saying, instead, ' Vance, do you know I'm glad we're friends?'

' No fault of mine we're not more.'

' You're losing your stroke, sir,' she reprimanded; and he bent silently to the work.

La Bijou was driving against the current at an angle of forty-five degrees, and her resultant course was a line at right angles to the river. Thus, she would tap the western bank directly opposite the starting-point, where she could work up-stream in the slacker flood. But a mile of indented shore, and then a hundred yards of bluffs rising precipitously from out a stiff current, would still lie between them and the man to be rescued.

' Now let us ease up,' Corliss advised, as they slipped into an eddy and drifted with the back-tide under the great wall of rim-ice.

' Who would think it mid-May?' She glanced up at the carelessly poised cakes. ' Does it seem real to you, Vance?'

He shook his head.

' Nor to me. I know that I, Frona, in the flesh, am here, in a Peterborough, paddling for dear life with two men; year of our Lord eighteen hundred and ninety-eight, Alaska, Yukon River; this is water, that is ice; my arms are tired, my heart up a few beats, and I am sweating—and yet it seems all a dream. Just think! A year ago I was in Paris!' She drew a deep breath and looked out over the water to the further shore, where Jacob Welse's tent, like a snowy handkerchief, sprawled against the deep green of the forest. ' I do not believe there is such a place,' she added. ' There is no Paris.'

' And I was in London a twelve-month past,' Corliss meditated. ' But I have undergone a new incarnation.

London? There is no London now. It is impossible. How could there be so many people in the world? This is the world, and we know of fact that there are very few people in it, else there could not be so much ice and sea and sky. Tommy, here, I know, thinks fondly of a place he calls Toronto. He mistakes. It exists only in his mind—a memory of a former life he knew. Of course, he does not think so. That is but natural; for he is no philosopher, nor does he bother—'

'Wheest, will ye!' Tommy fiercely whispered. 'Your gabble'll bring it doon aboot oor heads.'

Life is brief in the Northland, and fulfilment ever clutters the heels of prophecy. A premonitory tremor sighed down the air, and the rainbow wall swayed above them. The three paddles gripped the water with common accord. *La Bijou* leaped out from under. Broadside after broadside flared and crashed, and a thousand frigid tons thundered down behind them. The displaced water surged outward in a foamy, upstanding circle, and *La Bijou,* striving wildly to rise, ducked through the stiff overhang of the crest and wallowed, half-full, in the trough.

'Didna I tell ye, ye gabbling fules!'

'Sit still, and bail!' Corliss checked him sharply. 'Or you'll not have the comfort of telling us anything.'

He shook his head at Frona, and she winked back; then they both chuckled, much like children over an escapade which looks disastrous but turns out well.

Creeping timidly under the shadow of the impending avalanches, *La Bijou* slipped noiselessly up the last eddy. A corner of the bluff rose savagely from the river—a monstrous mass of naked rock, scarred and battered of the centuries; hating the river that gnawed it ever; hating the rain that graved its grim face with unsightly seams; hating the sun that refused to mate with it, whereof green life might come forth and hide its hideousness. The whole force of the river hurled in against it, waged furious war along its battlements, and caromed off into mid-stream again. Down all its length the stiff waves stood in serried rows, and its crevices and water-worn caverns were a-bellow with unseen strife.

'Now! Bend to it! Your best!'

It was the last order Corliss could give, for in the din they were about to enter a man's voice were like a cricket's chirp amid the growling of an earthquake. *La Bijou* sprang forward, cleared the eddy with a bound, and plunged into the thick. *Dip and lift, dip and lift,* the paddles worked with rhythmic strength. The water rippled and tore, and pulled all ways at once; and the fragile shell, unable to go all ways at once, shook and quivered with the shock of resistance. It veered nervously to the right and left, but Frona held it with a hand of steel. A yard away a fissure in the rock grinned at them. *La Bijou* leaped and shot ahead, and the water, slipping away underneath, kept her always in one place. Now they surged out from the fissure, now in; ahead for half a yard, then back again; and the fissure mocked their toil.

Five minutes, each of which sounded a separate eternity, and the fissure was past. Ten minutes, and it was a hundred feet astern. *Dip and lift, dip and lift,* till sky and earth and river were blotted out, and consciousness dwindled to a thin line—a streak of foam, fringed on the one hand with sneering rock, on the other with snarling water. That thin line summed up all. Somewhere below was the beginning of things; somewhere above, beyond the roar and traffic, was the end of things; and for that end they strove.

And still Frona held the egg-shell with a hand of steel. What they gained they held, and fought for more, inch by inch, *dip and lift;* and all would have been well but for the flutter of Tommy's soul. A cake of ice, sucked beneath by the current, rose under his paddle with a flurry of foam, turned over its toothed edge, and was dragged back into the depths. And in that sight he saw himself, hair streaming upward and drowned hands clutching emptiness, going feet first, down and down. He stared, wide-eyed, at the portent, and his poised paddle refused to strike. On the instant the fissure grinned in their faces, and the next they were below the bluffs, drifting gently in the eddy.

Frona lay, head thrown back, sobbing at the sun; amidships Corliss sprawled panting; and forward, choking and gasping and nerveless, the Scotsman drooped his head upon his knees. *La Bijou* rubbed softly against the rim-ice and came to rest. The rainbow-wall hung above like a fairy pile; the sun, flung backward from innumerable facets, clothed it in jewelled splendour. Silvery streams tinkled down its crystal slopes; and in its clear depths seemed to unfold, veil on veil, the secrets of life and death and mortal striving—vistas of pale-shimmering azure opening like dream-visions, and promising, down there in the great cool heart, infinite rest, infinite cessation and rest.

The topmost tower, delicately massive, a score of feet above them, swayed to and fro, gently, like the ripple of wheat in light summer airs. But Corliss gazed at it unheeding. Just to lie there, on the marge of the mystery, just to lie there and drink the air in great gulps, and do nothing! —he asked no more. A dervish, whirling on heel till all things blur, may grasp the essence of the universe and prove the Godhead indivisible; and so a man, plying a paddle, and plying and plying, may shake off his limitations and rise above time and space. And so Corliss.

But gradually his blood ceased its mad pounding, and the air was no longer nectar-sweet, and a sense of things real and pressing came back to him.

'We've got to get out of this,' he said. His voice sounded like a man's whose throat has been scorched by many and long potations. It frightened him, but he limply lifted a shaking paddle and shoved off.

'Yes; let us start, by all means,' Frona said in a dim voice, which seemed to come to him from a far distance.

Tommy lifted his head and gazed about. 'A doot we'll juist hae to gie it oop.'

'Bend to it!'

'Ye'll no try it anither?'

'Bend to it!' Corliss repeated.

'Till your heart bursts, Tommy,' Frona added.

Once again they fought up the thin line, and all the world vanished, save the streak of foam, and the snarling water, and the grinning fissure. But they passed it, inch by inch, and the broad bend welcomed them from above, and only a rocky buttress of implacable hate, around whose base howled the tides of an equal hate, stood between. Then *La Bijou* leaped and throbbed and shook again, and the current slid out from under, and they remained ever in one place. *Dip and lift, dip and lift,* through an infinity of time and torture and travail, till even the line dimmed and faded and the struggle lost its meaning. Their souls became merged in the rhythm of the toil. Ever lifting, ever falling, they seemed to have become great pendulums of time. And before and behind glimmered the eternities, and between the eternities, ever lifting, ever falling, they pulsed in vast rhythmical movement. They were no longer humans, but rhythms. They surged in till their paddles touched the bitter rock, but they did not know; surged out, where chance piloted them unscathed through the lashing ice, but they did not see. Nor did they feel the shock of the smitten waves, nor the driving spray that cooled their faces.

La Bijou veered out into the stream, and their paddles, flashing mechanically in the sunshine, held her to the return angle across the river. As time and matter came back to them, and Split-up Island dawned upon their eyes like the foreshore of a new world, they settled down to the long easy stroke wherein breath and strength may be recovered.

'A third attempt would have been useless,' Corliss said, in a dry, cracked whisper.

And Frona answered, 'Yes; our hearts would have surely broken.'

Life, and the pleasant camp-fire, and the quiet rest in the noonday shade, came back to Tommy as the shore drew near, and more than all, blessed Toronto, its houses that never moved, and its jostling streets. Each time his head sank forward and he reached out and clutched the water with his paddle, the streets enlarged, as though gazing through a telescope and adjusting to a nearer focus. And each time the paddle drove clear and his head was raised, the island bounded forward. His head sank, and the streets were of the size of life; it raised, and Jacob Welse and the two men stood on the bank three lengths away.

'Didna I tell ye!' he shouted to them, triumphantly.

But Frona jerked the canoe parallel with the bank, and he found himself gazing at the long up-stream stretch. He arrested a stroke midway, and his paddle clattered in the bottom.

'Pick it up!' Corliss's voice was sharp and relentless.

'I'll do naething o' the kind.' He turned a rebellious

face on his tormentor, and ground his teeth in anger and disappointment.

The canoe was drifting down with the current, and Frona merely held it in place. Corliss crawled forward on his knees.

'I don't want to hurt you, Tommy,' he said in a low, tense voice, 'so . . . well, just pick it up, that's a good fellow.'

'I'll no.'

'Then I shall kill you,' Corliss went on, in the same calm, passionless way, at the same time drawing his hunting-knife from its sheath.

'And if I dinna?' the Scotsman queried stoutly, though cowering away.

Corliss pressed gently with the knife. The point of the steel entered Tommy's back just where the heart should be, passed slowly through the shirt, and bit into the skin. Nor did it stop there; neither did it quicken, but just as slowly held on its way. He shrank back, quivering.

'There! there! man! Pit it oop!' he shrieked. 'I maun gie in!'

Frona's face was quite pale, but her eyes were hard, brilliantly hard, and she nodded approval.

'We're going to try this side, and shoot across from above,' she called to her father. 'What? I can't hear. Tommy? Oh, his heart's weak. Nothing serious.' She saluted with her paddle. 'We'll be back in no time, father mine. In no time.'

Stewart River was wide open, and they ascended it a quarter of a mile before they shot its mouth and continued up the Yukon. But when they were well abreast of the man on the opposite bank a new obstacle faced them. A mile above, a wreck of an island clung desperately to the river bed. Its tail dwindled to a sand-spit which bisected the river as far down as the impassable bluffs. Further, a few hundred thousand tons of ice had grounded upon the spit and upreared a glittering ridge.

'We'll have to portage,' Corliss said, as Frona turned the canoe from the bank.

La Bijou darted across the narrower channel to the sand-spit and slipped up a little ice ravine, where the walls were less precipitous. They landed on an outjutting cake, which, without support, overhung the water for sheer thirty feet. How far its other end could be buried in the mass was matter for conjecture. They climbed to the summit, dragging the canoe after them, and looked out over the dazzle. Floe was piled on floe in titanic confusion. Huge blocks topped and overtopped one another, only to serve as pedestals for great white masses, which blazed and scintillated in the sun like monstrous jewels.

'A bonny place for a bit walk,' Tommy sneered, 'wi' the next jam fair to come ony time.' He sat down resolutely. 'No, thank ye kindly, I'll no try it.'

Frona and Corliss clambered on, the canoe between them.

'The Persians lashed their slaves into battle,' she remarked, looking back. 'I never understood before. Hadn't you better go back after him?'

Corliss kicked him up, whimpering, and forced him to go on in advance. The canoe was an affair of little weight, but its bulk, on the steep rises and sharp turns, taxed their strength. The sun burned down upon them. Its white glare hurt their eyes, the sweat oozed out from every pore, and they panted for breath.

'Oh, Vance, do you know . . .'

'What?' He swept the perspiration from his forehead and flung it from him with a quick flirt of the hand.

'I wish I had eaten more breakfast.'

He grunted sympathetically. They had reached the midmost ridge and could see the open river, and beyond, quite clearly, the man and his signal of distress. Below, pastoral in its green quiet, lay Split-up Island. They looked up to the broad bend of the Yukon, smiling lazily, as though it were not capable at any moment of spewing forth a flood of death. At their feet the ice sloped down into a miniature gorge, across which the sun cast a broad shadow.

'Go on, Tommy,' Frona bade. 'We're half-way over, and there's water down there.'

'It's water ye'd be thinkin' on, is it?' he snarled, 'and yo a-leadin' a buddie to his death!'

'I fear you have done some great sin, Tommy,' she said, with a reproving shake of the head, 'or else you would not be so afraid of death.' She sighed and picked up her end of the canoe. 'Well, I suppose it is natural. You do not know how to die—'

'No more do I want to die,' he broke in fiercely.

'But there come times for all men to die—times when to die is the only thing to do. Perhaps this is such a time.'

Tommy slid carefully over a glistening ledge and dropped his height to a broad foothold. 'It's a' vera guid,' he grinned up; 'but dinna ye think a've suffeecient discreemeenation to judge for mysel'? Why should I no sing my ain sang?'

'Because you do not know how. The strong have ever pitched the key for such as you. It is they that have taught your kind when and how to die, and led you to die, and lashed you to die.'

'Ye pit it fair,' he rejoined. 'And ye do it weel. It doesna behoove me to complain, sic a michty fine job ye're makin' on it.'

'You *are* doing well,' Corliss chuckled, as Tommy dropped out of sight and landed into the bed of the gorge. 'The cantankerous brute! he'd argue on the trail to Judgment.'

'Where did you learn to paddle?' she asked.

'College—exercise,' he answered, shortly. 'But isn't that fine? Look!'

The melting ice had formed a pool in the bottom of the gorge. Frona stretched out full length, and dipped her hot mouth in its coolness. And lying as she did, the soles of her dilapidated moccasins, or rather the soles of her feet (for moccasins and stockings had gone in shreds), were turned upward. They were very white, and from contact with the ice were bruised and cut. Here and there the blood oozed out, and from one of the toes it streamed steadily.

'So wee, and pretty, and saft-like,' Tommy gibed. 'One wouldna think they could lead a strong man to hell.'

'By the way you grumble, they're leading you fast enough,' Corliss answered angrily.

'Forty mile an hour,' Tommy retorted, as he walked away, gloating over having the last word.

'One moment. You've two shirts. Lend me one.'

The Scotsman's face lighted inquisitively, till he comprehended. Then he shook his head and started on again.

Frona scrambled to her feet. 'What's the matter?'

'Nothing, Sit down.'

'But what is the matter?'

Corliss put his hands on her shoulders and pressed her back. 'Your feet. You can't go on in such shape, They're in ribbons. See!' He brushed the sole of one of them and held up a blood-dripping palm. 'Why didn't you tell me?'

'Oh, they didn't bother—much.'

'Give me one of your skirts,' he demanded.

'I . . .' She faltered. 'I only have one.'

He looked about him. Tommy had disappeared among the ice-floes.

'We must be getting on,' Frona said, attempting to rise.

But he held her back. 'Not another step till I fix you. Here goes, so shut your eyes.'

She obeyed, and when she opened them he was naked to the waist, and his undershirt, torn in strips, was being bound about her feet.

'You were in the rear, and I did not know—'

'Don't apologise, pray,' she interrupted. 'I could have spoken.'

'I'm not; I'm reproaching you. Now, the other one. Put it up!'

The nearness to her bred a madness, and he touched his lips lightly to the same white little toe that had won the Baron Courbertin a kiss.

Though she did not draw back, her face flushed, and she thrilled as she had thrilled once before in her life. 'You take advantage of your own goodness,' she rebuked him.

'Then I will doubly advantage myself.'

'Please don't,' she begged.

'And why not? It is a custom of the sea to broach the spirits as the ship prepares to sink. And since this is a sort of a forlorn hope, you know, why not?'

'But . . .'

'But what, Miss Prim?'

'Oh! Of all things, you know I do not deserve that! If there were nobody else to be considered, why, under the circumstances . . .'

He drew the last knot tight and dropped her foot. 'Damn St Vincent, anyway! Come on!'

'So would I, were I you,' she laughed, taking up her end of the canoe. 'But how you have changed, Vance. You are not the same man I met on the Dyea Trail. You hadn't learned to swear, then, among other things.'

'No, I'm not the same; for which I thank God and you. Only I think I am honester than you. I always live up to my philosophy.'

'Now confess that's unfair. You ask too much under the circumstances—'

'Only a little toe.'

'Or else, I suppose, you just care for me in a kind, big-brotherly way. In which case, if you really wish it, you may—'

'Do keep quiet,' he broke in, roughly, 'or I'll be making a gorgeous fool of myself.'

'Kiss all my toes,' she finished.

He grunted, but did not deign a reply. The work quickly took their breath, and they went on in silence till they descended the last steep to where McPherson waited by the open river.

'Del hates St Vincent,' she said boldly. 'Why?'

'Yes, it seems that way.' He glanced back at her curiously. 'And wherever he goes, Del lugs an old Russian book, which he can't read but which he nevertheless regards, in some sort of way, as St Vincent's Nemesis. And do you know, Frona, he has such faith in it that I can't help catching a little myself. I don't know whether you'll come to me, or whether I'll go to you, but—'

She dropped her end of the canoe and broke out in laughter. He was annoyed, and a hurt spread of blood ruddied his face.

'If I have—' he began.

'Stupid!' she laughed. 'Don't be silly! And above all don't be dignified. It doesn't exactly become you at the present moment—your hair all tangled, a murderous knife in your belt, and naked to the waist like a pirate stripped for battle. Be fierce, frown, swear, anything, but please don't be dignified. I do wish I had my camera. In after years I could say: "This, my friends, is Corliss, the great

Arctic explorer, just as he looked at the conclusion of his world-famous trip *Through Darkest Alaska*.'

He pointed an ominous finger at her and said sternly, 'Where is your skirt?'

She involuntarily looked down. But its tatterdemalion presence relieved her, and her face jerked up scarlet.

'You should be ashamed!'

'Please, please do not be dignified,' he laughed. 'Very true, it doesn't exactly become you at the present moment. Now, if I had my camera—'

'Do be quiet and go on,' she said. 'Tommy is waiting. I hope the sun takes the skin all off your back,' she panted vindictively, as they slid the canoe down the last shelf and dropped it into the water.

Ten minutes later they climbed the ice-wall, and on and up the bank, which was partly a hillside, to where the signal of distress still fluttered. Beneath it, on the ground, lay stretched the man. He lay very quietly, and the fear that they were too late was upon them, when he moved his head slightly and moaned. His rough clothes were in rags, and the black, bruised flesh of his feet showed through the remnants of his moccasins. His body was thin and gaunt, without flesh-pads or muscles, while the bones seemed ready to break through the tight-stretched skin. As Corliss felt his pulse, his eyes fluttered open and stared glassily. Frona shuddered.

'Man, it's fair gruesome,' McPherson muttered, running his hand up a shrunken arm.

'You go on to the canoe, Frona,' Corliss said, 'Tommy and I will carry him down.'

But her lips set firmly. Though the descent was made easier by her aid, the man was well shaken by the time they laid him in the bottom of the canoe—so well shaken that some last shreds of consciousness were aroused. He opened his eyes and whispered hoarsely, 'Jacob Welse . . . despatches . . . from the Outside.' He plucked feebly at his open shirt, and across his emaciated chest they saw the leather strap to which, doubtless, the despatch-pouch was slung.

At either end of the canoe there was room to spare, but amidships Corliss was forced to paddle with the man between his knees. *La Bijou* swung out blithely from the bank. It was down-stream at last, and there was little need for exertion.

Vance's arms and shoulders and back, a bright scarlet, caught Frona's attention. 'My hopes are realised,' she exulted, reaching out and softly stroking a burning arm. 'We shall have to put cold cream on it when we get back.'

'Go ahead,' he encouraged. 'That feels awfully good.'

She splashed his hot back with a handful of the ice-cold water from over-side. He caught his breath with a gasp, and shivered. Tommy turned about to look at them.

'It's a guid deed we'll 'a doon this day,' he remarked, pleasantly. 'To gie a hand in distress is guid i' the sight of God.'

'Who's afeared?' Frona laughed.

'Weel,' he deliberated, 'I was a bit fashed, no doot, but—'

His utterance ceased, and he seemed suddenly to petrify. His eyes fixed themselves in a terrible stare over Frona's shoulder. And then, slowly and dreamily, with the solemnity fitting an invocation of Deity, he murmured, 'Guid Gawd Almichty!'

They whirled their heads about. A wall of ice was sweeping round the bend, and even as they looked the right-hand flank, unable to compass the curve, struck the further shore and flung up a ridge of heaving mountains.

'Guid Gawd! Guid Gawd! Like rats i' the trap!' Tommy jabbed his paddle futilely in the water.

'Get the stroke!' Corliss hissed in his ear, and *La Bijou* sprang away.

Frona steered straight across the current, at almost right angles, for Split-up; but when the sand-spit, over which they had portaged, crashed at the impact of a million tons, Corliss glanced at her anxiously. She smiled and shook her head, at the same time slacking off the course.

'We can't make it,' she whispered, looking back at the ice a couple of hundred feet away. 'Our only chance is to run before it and work in slowly.'

She cherished every inward inch jealously, holding the canoe up as sharply as she dared and at the same time maintaining a constant distance ahead of the ice-run.

'I canna stand the pace,' Tommy whimpered once; but the silence of Corliss and Frona seemed ominous, and he kept his paddle going.

At the very fore of the ice was a floe five or six feet thick and a couple of acres in extent. Reaching out in advance of the pack, it clove through the water till on either side there formed a bore like that of a quick flood-tide in an inland passage. Tommy caught sight of it, and would have collapsed had not Corliss prodded him, between strikes, with the point of his paddle.

'We can keep ahead,' Frona panted; 'but we must get time to make the landing!'

'When the chance comes, drive her in, bow on,' Corliss counselled; 'and when she strikes, jump and run for it.'

'Climb, rather. I'm glad my skirt is short.'

Repulsed by the bluffs of the left bank, the ice was forced towards the right. The big floe, in advance, drove in upon the precise point of Split-up Island.

'If you look back, I'll brain you with the paddle,' Corliss threatened.

'Aye,' Tommy groaned.

But Corliss looked back, and so did Frona. The great berg struck the land with an earthquake shock. For fifty feet the soft island was demolished. A score of pines swayed frantically and went down, and where they went down rose up a mountain of ice, which rose, and fell, and rose again. Below, and but a few feet away, Del Bishop ran out to the bank, and above the roar they could hear faintly his 'Hit 'er up! Hit 'er up!' Then the ice-rim wrinkled up and he sprang back to escape it.

'The first opening,' Corliss gasped.

Frona's lips spread apart; she tried to speak but failed, then nodded her head that she had heard. They swung along in rapid rhythm under the rainbow-wall, looking for a place where it might be quickly cleared. And down all the length of Split-up Island they raced vainly, the shore crashing behind them as they fled.

As they darted across the mouth of the back-channel to Roubeau Island they found themselves heading directly for an opening in the rim-ice. *La Bijou* drove into it full tilt, and went half her length out of water on a shelving cake.

The three leaped together, but while the two of them gripped the canoe to run it up, Tommy, in the lead, strove only to save himself. And he would have succeeded had he not slipped and fallen midway in the climb. He half arose, slipped, and fell again. Corliss, hauling on the bow of the canoe, trampled over him. He reached up and clutched the gunwale. They did not have the strength, and this clog brought them at once to a standstill. Corliss looked back and yelled for him to leave go, but he only turned upward a piteous face, like that of a drowning man, and clutched more tightly. Behind them the ice was thundering. The first flurry of coming destruction was upon them. They endeavoured desperately to drag up the canoe, but the added burden was too much, and they fell on their knees. The sick man sat up suddenly and laughed wildly. 'Blood of my soul!' he ejaculated, and laughed again.

Roubeau Island swayed to the first shock, and the ice was rocking under their feet. Frona seized a paddle and smashed the Scotsman's knuckles; and the instant he loosed his grip, Corliss carried the canoe up in a mad rush, Frona clinging on and helping from behind. The rainbow-wall curled up like a scroll, and in the convolutions of the scroll, like a bee in the many folds of a magnificent orchid, Tommy disappeared.

They fell, breathless, on the earth. But a monstrous cake shoved up from the jam and balanced above them. Frona tried to struggle to her feet, but sank on her knees; and it remained for Corliss to snatch her and the canoe out from underneath. Again they fell, this time under the trees, the sun sifting down upon them through the green pine needles, the robins singing overhead, and a colony of crickets chirping in the warmth.

CHAPTER XXVI

FRONA woke, slowly, as though from a long dream. She was lying where she had fallen, across Corliss's legs, while he, on his back, faced the hot sun without concern. She crawled up to him. He was breathing regularly, with closed eyes, which opened to meet hers. He smiled, and she sank down again. Then he rolled over on his side, and they looked at each other.

'Vance.'

'Yes.'

She reached out her hand; his closed upon it, and their eyelids fluttered and drooped down. The river still rumbled on, somewhere in the infinite distance, but it came to them like the murmur of a world forgotten. A soft languor encompassed them. The golden sunshine dripped down upon them through the living green, and all the life of the warm earth seemed singing. And quiet was very good. Fifteen long minutes they drowsed, and woke again.

Frona sat up. 'I—I was afraid,' she said.

'Not you.'

'Afraid that I might be afraid,' she amended, fumbling with her hair.

'Leave it down. The day merits it.'

She complied, with a toss of the head which circled it with a nimbus of rippling yellow.

'Tommy's gone,' Corliss mused, the race with the ice coming slowly back.

'Yes,' she answered. 'I rapped him on the knuckles. It was terrible. But the chance is we've a better man in the canoe, and we must care for him at once. Hello! Look there!' Through the trees, not a score of feet away, she saw the wall of a large cabin. 'Nobody in sight. It must be deserted, or else they're visiting, whoever they are. You look to our man, Vance—I'm more presentable—and I'll go and see.'

She skirted the cabin, which was a large one for the Yukon country, and came around to where it fronted on

213

the river. The door stood open, and, as she paused to knock, the whole interior flashed upon her in an astounding picture —a cumulative picture, or series of pictures, as it were. For first she was aware of a crowd of men, and of some great common purpose upon which all were seriously bent. At her knock they instinctively divided, so that a lane opened up, flanked by their pressed bodies, to the far end of the room. And there, in the long bunks on either side, sat two grave rows of men. And mid-way between, against the wall, was a table. This table seemed the centre of interest. Fresh from the sun-dazzle, the light within was dim and murky, but she managed to make out a bearded American sitting by the table and hammering it with a heavy caulking-mallet. And on the opposite side sat St Vincent. She had time to note his worn and haggard face, before a man of Scandinavian appearance slouched up to the table.

The man with the mallet raised his right hand and said glibly, 'You do most solemnly swear that what you are about to give before the court—' He abruptly stopped and glowered at the man before him. 'Take off your hat!' he roared, and a snicker went up from the crowd as the man obeyed.

Then he of the mallet began again. 'You do most solemnly swear that what you are about to give before the court shall be the truth, the whole truth, and nothing but the truth, so help you God?'

The Scandinavian nodded and dropped his hand.

'One moment, gentlemen.' Frona advanced up the lane, which closed behind her.

St Vincent sprang to his feet and stretched out his arms to her. 'Frona,' he cried, 'oh, Frona, I am innocent!'

It struck her like a blow, the unexpectedness of it, and for the instant, in the sickly light, she was conscious only of the ring of white faces, each face set with eyes that burned. Innocent of what? she thought, and as she looked at St Vincent, arms still extended, she was aware, in a vague troubled way, of something distasteful. Innocent of what? He might have had more reserve. He might have waited till he was charged. She did not know that he was charged with anything.

'Friend of the prisoner,' the man with the mallet said

authoritatively. 'Bring a stool for'ard, some of you.'

'One moment . . .' She staggered against the table and rested a hand on it. 'I do not understand. This is all new . . .' But her eyes happened to come to rest on her feet, wrapped in dirty rags, and she knew that she was clad in a short and tattered skirt, that her arm peeped forth through a rent in her sleeve, and that her hair was down and flying. Her cheek and neck on one side seemed coated with some curious substance. She brushed it with her hand, and caked mud rattled to the floor.

'That will do,' the man said, not unkindly. 'Sit down. We're in the same box. We do not understand. But take my word for it, we're here to find out. So sit down.'

She raised her hand. 'One moment—'

'Sit down!' he thundered. 'The court cannot be disturbed.'

A hum went up from the crowd, words of dissent, and the man pounded the table for silence. But Frona resolutely kept her feet.

When the noise had subsided, she addressed the man in the chair. 'Mr Chairman : I take it that this is a miners' meeting.' (The man nodded.) 'Then, having an equal voice in the managing of this community's affairs, I demand to be heard. It is important that I should be heard.'

'But you are out of order, Miss—er—'

'Welse!' half a dozen voices prompted.

'Miss Welse,' he went on, an added respect marking his demeanour, 'it grieves me to inform you that you are out of order. You had best sit down.'

'I will not,' she answered. 'I rise to a question of privilege, and if I am not heard, I shall appeal to the meeting.'

She swept the crowd with her eyes, and cries went up that she be given a fair show. The chairman yielded and motioned her to go on.

'Mr Chairman and men : I do not know the business you have at present before you, but I do know that I have more important business to place before you. Just outside this cabin is a man probably dying from starvation. We have brought him from across the river. We should not have bothered you, but we were unable to make our own island. This man I speak of needs immediate attention.'

215

'A couple of you nearest the door go out and look after him,' the chairman ordered. 'And you, Doc Holiday, go along and see what you can do.'

'Ask for a recess,' St Vincent whispered.

Frona nodded her head. 'And, Mr Chairman, I make a motion for a recess until the man is cared for.'

Cries of 'No recess!' and 'Go on with the business!' greeted the putting of it, and the motion was lost.

'Now, Gregory,' with a smile and salutation as she took the stool beside him, 'what is it?'

He gripped her hand tightly. 'Don't believe them, Frona. They are trying to'—with a gulping swallow—'to kill me.'

'Why? Do be calm. Tell me.'

'Why, last night,' he began hurriedly, but broke off to listen to the Scandinavian previously sworn, who was speaking with ponderous slowness.

'I wake wide open quick,' he was saying. 'I coom to the door. I there hear one shot more.'

He was interrupted by a warm-complexioned man clad in faded mackinaws. 'What did you think?' he asked.

'Eh?' the witness queried, his face dark and troubled with perplexity.

'When you came to the door, what was your first thought?'

'A-w-w,' the man sighed, his face clearing and infinite comprehension sounding in his voice. 'I have no moccasins. I t'ink pretty damn cold.' His satisfied expression changed to naïve surprise when an outburst of laughter greeted his statement, but he went on stolidly. 'One more shot I hear, and I run down the trail.'

Then Corliss pressed in through the crowd to Frona, and she lost what the man was saying.

'What's up?' the engineer was asking. 'Anything serious? Can I be of any use?'

'Yes, yes.' She caught his hand gratefully. 'Get over the back-channel somehow and tell my father to come. Tell him that Gregory St Vincent is in trouble; that he is charged with— What are you charged with, Gregory?' she asked, turning to him.

'Murder.'

216

'Murder?' from Corliss.

'Yes, yes. Say that he is charged with murder; that I am here; and that I need him. And tell him to bring me some clothes. And, Vance,'—with a pressure of the hand and swift upward look—'don't take any . . . any big chances, but do try to make it.'

'Oh, I'll make it all right.' He tossed his head confidently and proceeded to elbow his way towards the door.

'Who is helping you in your defence?' she asked St Vincent.

He shook his head. 'No. They wanted to appoint someone—a renegade lawyer from the States, Bill Brown—but I declined him. He's taken the other side, now. It's lynch law, you know, and their minds are made up. They're bound to get me.'

'I wish there were time to hear your side.'

'But, Frona, I am innocent. I—'

'S-sh!' She laid her hand on his arm to hush him, and turned her attention to the witness.

'So the noospaper feller, he fight like anything; but Pierre and me, we pull him into the shack. He cry and stand in one place—'

'Who cried?' interrupted the prosecuting lawyer.

'Him. That feller there.' The Scandinavian pointed directly at St Vincent. 'And I make a light. The slush-lamp I find spilt over most everything, but I have a candle in my pocket. It is good practice to carry a candle in the pocket,' he affirmed gravely. 'And Borg he lay on the floor dead. And the squaw say he did it, and then she die, too.'

'Said who did it?'

Again his accusing finger singled out St Vincent. 'Him. That feller there.'

'Did she?' Frona whispered.

'Yes,' St Vincent whispered back, 'she did. But I cannot imagine what prompted her. She must have been out of her head.'

The warm-faced man in the faded mackinaws then put the witness through a searching examination, which Frona followed closely, but which elicited little new.

'You have the right to cross-examine the witness,' the

217

chairman informed St Vincent. 'Any questions you want to ask?'

The correspondent shook his head.

'Go on,' Frona urged.

'What's the use?' he asked, hopelessly. 'I'm foredoomed. The verdict was reached before the trial began.'

'One moment, please.' Frona's sharp command arrested the retiring witness. 'You do not know of your own knowledge who committed this murder?'

The Scandinavian gazed at her with a bovine expression on his leaden features, as though waiting for her question to percolate to his understanding.

'You did not see who did it?' she asked again.

'Aw, yes. That feller there,' accusative finger to the fore. 'She say he did.'

There was a general smile at this.

'But you did not see it?'

'I hear some shooting.'

'But you did not see who did the shooting?'

'Aw, no; but she said—'

'That will do, thank you,' she said sweetly, and the man retired.

The prosecution consulted its notes. 'Pierre La Flitche!' was called out.

A slender, swart-skinned man, lithe of figure and graceful, stepped forward to the open space before the table. He was darkly handsome, with a quick, eloquent eye which roved frankly everywhere. It rested for a moment on Frona, open and honest in its admiration, and she smiled and half-nodded, for she liked him at first glance, and it seemed as though they had met of old time. He smiled pleasantly back, the smooth upper lip curling brightly and showing beautiful teeth, immaculately white.

In answer to the stereotyped preliminaries he stated that his name was that of his father's a descendant of the *coureurs du bois*. His mother—with a shrug of the shoulders and flash of teeth—was a *breed*. He was born somewhere in the Barrens, on a hunting trip, he did not know where. Ah, *oui*, men called him an old-timer. He had come into the country in the days of Jack McQuestion, across the Rockies from the Great Slave.

On being told to go ahead with what he knew of the matter in hand, he deliberated a moment, as though casting about for the best departure.

'In the spring it is good to sleep with the open door,' he began, his words sounding clear and flute-like and marked by haunting memories of the accents his forbears put into the tongue. 'And so I sleep last night. But I sleep like the cat. The fall of the leaf, the breath of the wind, and my ears whisper to me, whisper, whisper, all the night long. So, the first shot,' with a quick snap of the fingers, 'and I am awake, just like that, and I am at the door.'

St Vincent leaned forward to Frona. 'It was not the first shot.'

She nodded, with her eyes still bent on La Flitche, who gallantly waited.

'Then two more shot,' he went on, 'quick, together, boom-boom, just like that. "Borg's shack," I say to myself, and run down the trail. I think Borg kill Bella, which was bad. Bella very fine girl,' he confided with one of his irresistible smiles. 'I like Bella. So I run. And John he run from his cabin like a fat cow, with great noise. "What the matter?" he say; and I say, "I don't know." And then something come, wheugh! out of the dark, just like that, and knock John down, and knock me down. We grab everywhere all at once. It is a man. He is in undress. He fight. He cry, "Oh! Oh! Oh!" just like that. We hold him tight, and bime-by, pretty quick, he stop. Then we get up, and I say, "Come along back."'

'Who was the man?'

La Flitche turned partly, and rested his eyes on St Vincent.

'Go on.'

'So? The man he will not go back; but John and I say yes, and he go.'

'Did he say anything?'

'I ask him what the matter; but he cry, he . . . he sob, *huh-tsch, huh-tsch,* just like that.'

'Did you see anything peculiar about him?'

La Flitche's brows drew up interrogatively.

'Anything uncommon, out of the ordinary?'

'Ah, *oui;* blood on the hands.' Disregarding the murmur in the room, he went on, his facile play of feature and gesture giving dramatic value to the recital. 'John make a light, and Bella groan, like the hair-seal when you shoot him in the body, just like that, when you shoot him in the body under the flipper. And Borg lay over in the corner. I look. He no breathe 'tall.

'Then Bella open her eyes, and I look in her eyes, and I know she know me, La Flitche. "Who did it, Bella?" I ask. And she roll her head on the floor and whisper, so low, so slow, "Him dead?" I know she mean Borg, and I say yes. Then she lift up on one elbow, and look about quick, in big hurry, and when she see Vincent she look no more, only she look at Vincent all the time. Then she point at him, just like that.' Suiting the action to the word, La Flitche turned and thrust a wavering finger at the prisoner. 'And she say, "Him, him, him." And I say, "Bella, who did it?" And she say, "Him, him, him. St Vincha, him do it." And then '—La Flitche's head fell limply forward on his chest, and came back naturally erect, as he finished, with a flash of teeth, 'Dead.'

The warm-faced man, Bill Brown, put the quarter-breed through the customary direct examination, which served to strengthen his testimony and to bring out the fact that a terrible struggle must have taken place in the killing of Borg. The heavy table was smashed, the stool and the bunk-board splintered, and the stove overthrown. 'Never did I see anything like it,' La Flitche concluded his description of the wreck. 'No, never.'

Brown turned him over to Frona with a bow, which a smile of hers paid for in full. She did not deem it unwise to cultivate cordiality with the lawyer. What she was working for was time—time for her father to come, time to be closeted with St Vincent and learn all the details of what really had occurred. So she put questions, questions, interminable questions, to La Flitche. Twice only did anything of moment crop up.

'You spoke of the first shot, Mr La Flitche. Now, the walls of a log cabin are quite thick. Had your door been closed, do you think you could have heard that first shot?'

He shook his head, though his dark eyes told her he

220

divined the point she was endeavouring to establish.

'And had the door of Borg's cabin been closed, would you have heard?'

Again he shook his head.

'Then, Mr La Filtche, when you say the first shot, you do not mean necessarily the first shot fired, but rather the first shot you heard fired?'

He nodded, and though she had scored her point she could not see that it had any material bearing after all.

Again she worked up craftily to another and stronger climax, though she felt all the time that La Flitche fathomed her.

'You say it was very dark, Mr La Flitche?'

'Ah, *oui*, quite dark.'

'How dark? How did you know it was John you met?'

'John make much noise when he run. I know that kind of noise.'

'Could you see him so as to know that it was he?'

'Ah, no.'

'Then, Mr La Flitche,' she demanded triumphantly, 'will you please state how you knew there was blood on the hands of Mr St Vincent?'

His lip lifted in a dazzling smile, and he paused a moment. 'How? I feel it warm on his hands. And my nose —ah, the smoke of the hunter camp long way off, the hole where the rabbit hide, the track of the moose which has gone before, does not my nose tell me?' He flung his head back, and with tense face, eyes closed, nostrils quivering and dilated, he simulated the quiescence of all the senses save one and the concentration of his whole being upon that one. Then his eyes fluttered partly open and he regarded her dreamily. 'I smell the blood on his hands, the warm blood, the hot blood on his hands.'

'And by gad he can do it!' some man exclaimed.

And so convinced was Frona that she glanced involuntarily at St Vincent's hands, and saw there the rusty-brown stains on the cuffs of his flannel shirt.

As La Flitche left the stand, Bill Brown came over to her and shook hands. 'No more than proper I should know the lawyer for the defence,' he said, good-naturedly, running over his notes for the next witness.

'But don't you think it is rather unfair to me?' she asked, brightly. 'I have not had time to prepare my case. I know nothing about it except what I have gleaned from your two witnesses. Don't you think, Mr Brown,' her voice rippling along in persuasive little notes, 'don't you think it would be advisable to adjourn the meeting until tomorrow?'

'Hum,' he deliberated, looking at his watch. 'Wouldn't be a bad idea. It's five o'clock, anyway, and the men ought to be cooking their suppers.'

She thanked him, as some women can, without speech; yet, as he looked down into her face and eyes, he experienced a subtler and greater satisfaction than if she had spoken.

He stepped to his old position and addressed the room. 'On consultation of the defence and the prosecution, and upon consideration of the lateness of the hour and the impossibility of finishing the trial within a reasonable limit, I—hum—I take the liberty of moving an adjournment until eight o'clock tomorrow morning.'

'The ayes have it,' the chairman proclaimed, coming down from his place and proceeding to build the fire, for he was a part-owner of the cabin and cook for his crowd.

CHAPTER XXVII

FRONA turned to St Vincent as the last of the crowd filed out. He clutched her hands spasmodically, like a drowning man.

'Do believe me, Frona. Promise me.'

Her face flushed. 'You are excited,' she said, 'or you would not say such things. Not that I blame you,' she relented. 'I hardly imagine the situation can be anything else but exciting.'

'Yes, and well I know it,' he answered, bitterly. 'I am acting like a fool, and I can't help it. The strain has been terrible. And as though the horror of Borg's end were not enough, to be considered the murderer, and haled up for mob justice! Forgive me, Frona. I am beside myself. Of course, I know that you will believe me.'

'Then tell me, Gregory.'

'In the first place, the woman, Bella, lied. She must have been crazed to make that dying statement when I fought as I did for her and Borg. That is the only explanation—'

'Begin at the beginning,' she interrupted. 'Remember, I know nothing.'

He settled himself more comfortably on the stool, and rolled a cigarette as he took up the history of the previous night.

'It must have been about one in the morning when I was awakened by the lighting of the slush-lamp. I thought it was Borg; wondered what he was prowling about for, and was on the verge of dropping off to sleep, when, though I do not know what prompted me, I opened my eyes. Two strange men were in the cabin. Both wore masks and fur caps with the flaps pulled down, so that I could see nothing of their faces save the glistening of the eyes through the eye-slits.

'I had no first thought, unless it was that danger threatened. I lay quietly for a second and deliberated. Borg had borrowed my pistol, and I was actually unarmed. My rifle was by the door. I decided to make a rush for it. But no

223

sooner had I struck the floor than one of the men turned on me, at the same time firing his revolver. That was the first shot, and the one La Flitche did not hear. It was in the struggle afterwards that the door was burst open, which enabled him to hear the last three.

'Well, I was so close to the man, and my leap out of the bunk was so unexpected, that he missed me. The next moment we grappled and rolled on the floor. Of course Borg was aroused, and the second man turned his attention to him and Bella. It was this second man who did the killing, for my man, naturally, had his hands full. You heard the testimony. From the way the cabin was wrecked, you can picture the struggle. We rolled and tossed about and fought till stools, table, shelves—everything was smashed.

'Oh, Frona, it was terrible! Borg fighting for life, Bella helping him, though wounded and groaning, and I unable to aid. But finally, in a very short while, I began to conquer the man with whom I was struggling. I had got him down on his back, pinioned his arms with my knees, and was slowly throttling him, when the other man finished his work and turned on me also. What could I do? Two to one, and winded! So I was thrown into the corner, and they made their escape. I confess that I must have been badly rattled by that time, for as soon as I caught my breath I took out after them, and without a weapon. Then I collided with La Flitche and John, and—and you know the rest. Only,' he knit his brows in puzzlement, 'only, I cannot understand why Bella should accuse me.'

He looked at her appealingly, and, though she pressed his hand sympathetically, she remained silent, weighing pro and con what she had heard.

She shook her head slowly. 'It's a bad case, and the thing is to convince them—'

'But, my God, Frona, I am innocent! I have not been a saint, perhaps, but my hands are clean from blood.'

'But remember, Gregory,' she said, gently, 'I am not to judge you. Unhappily, it rests with the men of this miners' meeting, and the problem is: how are they to be convinced of your innocence? The two main points are against you—Bella's dying words and the blood on your sleeve.'

'The place was areek with blood,' St Vincent cried passionately, springing to his feet. 'I tell you it was areek! How could I avoid floundering in it, fighting as I was for life? Can you not take my word—'

'There, there, Gregory. Sit down. You are truly beside yourself. If your case rested with me, you know you would go free and clean. But these men—you know what mob rule is—how are we to persuade them to let you go? Don't you see? You have no witnesses. A dying woman's words are more sacred than a living man's. Can you show cause for the woman to die with a lie on her lips? Had she any reason to hate you? Had you done her or her husband an injury?'

He shook his head.

'Certainly, to us the thing is inexplicable; but the miners need no explanation. To them it is obvious. It rests with us to disprove the obvious. Can we do it?'

The correspondent sank down despondently, with a collapsing of the chest and a drooping forward of the shoulders. 'Then am I indeed lost.'

'No, it's not so bad as that. You shall not be hanged. Trust me for that.'

'But what can you do?' he asked, despairingly. 'They have usurped the law, have made themselves the law.'

'In the first place, the river has broken. That means everything. The Governor and the territorial judges may be expected in at any moment with a detachment of police at their backs. And they're certain to stop here. And, furthermore, we may be able to do something ourselves. The river is open, and if it comes to the worst, escape would be another way out; and escape is the last thing they would dream of.'

'No, no; impossible. What are you and I against the many?'

'But there's my father and Baron Courbertin. Four determined people, acting together, may perform miracles, Gregory, dear. Trust me, it shall come out well.'

She kissed him and ran her hand through his hair, but the worried look did not depart.

Jacob Welse crossed over the back-channel long before dark, and with him came Del, the baron, and Corliss. While

Frona retired to change her clothes in one of the smaller cabins, which the masculine owners readily turned over to her, her father saw to the welfare of the mail-carrier. The despatches were of serious import, so serious that long after Jacob Welse had read and re-read them his face was dark and clouded; but he put the anxiety from him when he returned to Frona. St Vincent, who was confined in an adjoining cabin, was permitted to see them.

'It looks bad,' Jacob Welse said, on parting for the night. 'But rest assured, St Vincent, bad or not, you'll not be stretched up so long as I've a hand to play in the rumpus. I am certain you did not kill Borg, and there's my fist on it.'

'A long day,' Corliss remarked, as he walked back with Frona to her cabin.

'And a longer tomorrow,' she answered, wearily. 'And I'm so sleepy.'

'You're a brave little woman, and I'm proud of you.' It was ten o'clock, and he looked out through the dim twilight to the ghostly ice drifting steadily by. 'And in this trouble,' he went on, 'depend upon me in any way.'

'In any way?' she queried, with a catch in her voice.

'If I were a hero of the melodrama I'd say, "To the death!" but as I'm not, I'll just repeat, in any way.'

'You are good to me, Vance. I can never repay—'

'Tut! tut! I do not put myself on sale. Love is service, I believe.'

She looked at him for a long time; but while her face betrayed soft wonder, at heart she was troubled, she knew not why, and the events of the day, and of all the days since she had known him, came fluttering through her mind.

'Do you believe in a white friendship?' she asked at last. 'For I do hope that such a bond may hold us always. A bright, white friendship, a comradeship, as it were?' And as she asked, she was aware that the phrase did not quite express what she felt and would desire. And when he shook his head, she experienced a glad little inexplicable thrill.

'A comradeship?' he questioned. 'When you know I love you?'

'Yes,' she affirmed in a low voice.

'I am afraid, after all, that your knowledge of man is very limited. Believe me, we are not made of such clay. A comradeship? A coming in out of the cold to sit by your fire? Good. But a coming in when another man sits with you by your fire? No. Comradeship would demand that I delight in your delights, and yet, do you think for a moment that I could see you with another man's child in your arms, a child which might have been mine; with that other man looking out at me through the child's eyes, laughing at me through its mouth? I say, do you think I could delight in your delights? No, no; love cannot shackle itself with white friendships.'

She put her hand on his arm.

'Do you think I am wrong?' he asked, bewildered by the strange look in her face.

She was sobbing quietly.

'You are tired and overwrought. So there, good night. You must get to bed.'

'No, don't go, not yet.' And she arrested him. 'No, no; I am foolish. As you say, I am tired. But listen, Vance. There is much to be done. We must plan tomorrow's work. Come inside. Father and Baron Courbertin are together, and if the worst comes, we four must do big things.'

'Spectacular,' Jacob Welse commented, when Frona had briefly outlined the course of action and assigned them their parts. 'But its very unexpectedness ought to carry it through.'

'A *coup d'état!*' was the baron's verdict. 'Magnificent! Ah! I feel warm all over at the thought. "Hands up!" I cry, thus, and very fierce.'

'And if they do not hold up their hands?' he appealed to Jacob Welse.

'Then shoot. Never bluff when you're behind a gun, Courbertin. It's held by good authorities to be unhealthy.'

'And you are to take charge of *La Bijou*, Vance,' Frona said. 'Father thinks there will be little ice tomorrow if it doesn't jam tonight. All you've to do is to have the canoe by the bank just before the door. Of course, you won't know what is happening until St Vincent comes running. Then in with him, and away you go—Dawson! So I'll say good night and good-bye now, for I may not have the opportunity in the morning.'

'And keep the left-hand channel till you're past the bend,' Jacob Welse counselled him; 'then take the cut-offs to the right and follow the swiftest water. Now off with you and into your blankets. It's seventy miles to Dawson, and you'll have to make it at one clip.'

CHAPTER XXVIII

JACOB WELSE was given due respect when he rose at the convening of the miners' meeting and denounced the proceedings. While such meetings had performed a legitimate function in the past, he contended, when there was no law in the land, that time was now beyond recall; for law was now established, and it was just law. The Queen's government had shown itself fit to cope with the situation, and for them to usurp its powers was to step backward into the night out of which they had come. Further, no lighter word than 'criminal' could characterise such conduct. And yet further, he promised them, in set, sober terms, if anything serious were the outcome, to take an active part in the prosecution of every one of them. At the conclusion of his speech he made a motion to hold the prisoner for the territorial court and to adjourn, but was voted down without discussion.

'Don't you see,' St Vincent said to Frona, 'there is no hope?'

'But there is. Listen!' And she swiftly outlined the plot of the night before.

He followed her in a half-hearted way, too crushed to partake of her enthusiasm. 'It's madness to attempt it,' he objected, when she had done.

'And it looks very much like hanging not to attempt it,' she answered a little spiritedly. 'Surely you will make a fight?"

'Surely,' he replied hollowly.

The first witnesses were two Swedes, who told of the wash-tub incident, when Borg had given way to one of his fits of anger. Trivial as the incident was, in the light of subsequent events it at once became serious. It opened the way for the imagination into a vast familiar field. It was not so much what was said as what was left unsaid. Men born of women, the rudest of them, knew life well enough to be aware of its significance—a vulgar common happening, capable of but one interpretation. Heads were wagged knowingly in the course of the testimony, and whispered comments went the rounds.

Half a dozen witnesses followed in rapid succession, all of whom had closely examined the scene of the crime and gone over the island carefully, and all of whom were agreed that there was not the slightest trace to be found of the two men mentioned by the prisoner in his preliminary statement.

To Frona's surprise, Del Bishop went upon the stand. She knew he disliked St Vincent, but could not imagine any evidence he could possess which would bear upon the case.

Being sworn, and age and nationality ascertained, Bill Brown asked him his business.

'Pocket-miner,' he challenged back, sweeping the assemblage with an aggressive glance.

Now, it happens that a very small class of men follow pocketing, and that a very large class of men, miners, too, disbelieve utterly in any such method of obtaining gold.

'Pocket-miner!' sneered a red-shirted, patriarchal-looking man, a man who had washed his first pan in the Californian diggings in the early fifties.

'Yep,' Del affirmed.

'Now, look here, young feller,' his interlocutor continued, 'd'ye mean to tell me you ever struck it in such-fangled way?'

'Yep.'

'Don't believe it,' with a contemptuous shrug.

Del swallowed fast and raised his head with a jerk.

'Mr Chairman, I rise to make a statement. I won't interfere with the dignity of the court, but I just wish to simply and distinctly state that after the meeting's over I'm going to punch the head of every man that gets gay. Understand?'

'You're out of order,' the chairman replied, rapping the table with the caulking-mallet.

'And your head, too,' Del cried, turning upon him. 'Damn poor order you preserve. Pocketing's got nothing to do with this here trial, and why don't you shut such fool questions out? I'll take care of you afterwards, you pot-wolloper!'

'You will, will you?' The chairman grew red in the face, dropped the mallet, and sprang to his feet.

Del stepped forward to meet him, but Bill Brown sprang in between and held them apart.

'Order, gentlemen, order,' he begged. 'This is no time for unseemly exhibitions. And remember there are ladies present.'

The two men grunted and subsided, and Bill Brown asked, 'Mr Bishop, we understand that you are well acquainted with the prisoner. Will you please tell the court what you know of his general character?'

Del broadened into a smile. 'Well, in the first place, he's an extremely quarrelsome disposition—'

'Hold! I won't have it!' The prisoner was on his feet, trembling with anger. 'You shall not swear my life away in such fashion! To bring a madman, whom I have only met once in my life, to testify as to my character!'

The pocket-miner turned to him. 'So you don't know me, eh, Gregory St Vincent?'

'No,' St Vincent replied, coldly, 'I do not know you, my man.'

'Don't you man me!' Del shouted, hotly.

But St Vincent ignored him, turning to the crowd. 'I never saw the fellow but once before, and then for a few brief moments in Dawson.'

'You'll remember before I'm done,' Del sneered; 'so hold your hush and let me say my little say. I come into the country with him way back in '84.'

St Vincent regarded him with sudden interest.

'Yep, Mr Gregory St Vincent. I see you begin to recollect. I sported whiskers and my name was Brown, Joe Brown, in them days.'

He grinned vindictively, and the correspondent seemed to lose all interest.

'Is it true, Gregory?' Frona whispered.

'I begin to recognise,' he muttered, slowly. 'I don't know ... no, folly! The man must have died.'

'You say in '84, Mr Bishop?' Bill Brown prompted.

'Yep, in '84. He was a newspaper-man, bound round the world by way of Alaska and Siberia. I'd run away from a whaler at Sitka—that squares it with Brown—and I engaged with him for forty a month and found. Well, he quarrelled with me—'

A snicker, beginning from nowhere in particular, but passing on from man to man and swelling in volume, greeted this statement. Even Frona and Del himself were forced to smile, and the only sober face was the prisoner's.

'But he quarrelled with Old Andy at Dyea, and with Chief George of the Chilcoots, and the Factor at Pelly, and so on down the line. He got us into no end of trouble, and 'specially woman-trouble. He was always monkeying around—'

'Mr Chairman, I object.' Frona stood up, her face quite calm and blood under control. 'There is no necessity for bringing in the amours of Mr St Vincent. They have no bearing whatsoever upon the case; and, further, none of the men of this meeting are clean enough to be prompted by the right motive in conducting such an inquiry. So I demand that the prosecution at least confine itself to relevant testimony.'

Bill Brown came up smugly complacent and smiling. Mr Chairman, we willingly accede to the request made by the defence. Whatever we have brought out has been relevant and material. Whatever we intend to bring out shall be relevant and material. Mr Bishop is our star witness, and his testimony is to the point. It must be taken into consideration that we have no direct evidence as to the murder of John Borg. We can bring no eye-witnesses into court. Whatever we have is circumstantial. It is incumbent upon us to show cause. To show cause it is necessary to go into the character of the accused. This we intend to do. We intend to show his adulterous and lustful nature, which has culminated in a dastardly deed and jeopardised his neck. We intend to show that the truth is not in him; that he is a liar beyond price; that no word he may speak upon the stand need be accepted by a jury of his peers. We intend to show all this, and to weave it together, thread by thread, till we have a rope long enough and strong enough to hang him with before the day is done. So I respectfully submit, Mr Chairman, that the witness be allowed to proceed.'

The chairman decided against Frona, and her appeal to

the meeting was voted down. Bill Brown nodded to Del to resume.

'As I was saying, he got us into no end of trouble. Now, I've been mixed up with water all my life—never can get away from it, it seems—and the more I'm mixed the less I know about it. St Vincent knew this, too, and him a clever hand at the paddle; yet he left me to run the Box Canyon alone while he walked around. Result: I was turned over, lost half the outfit and all the tobacco, and then he put the blame on me besides. Right after that he got tangled up with the Lake Le Barge Sticks, and both of us came near croaking.'

'And why was that?' Bill Brown interjected.

'All along of a pretty squaw that looked too kindly at him. After we got clear, I lectured him on women in general and squaws in particular, and he promised to behave. Then we had a hot time with the Little Salmons. He was cuter this time, and I didn't know for keeps, but I guessed. He said it was the medicine man who got horstile; but nothing'll stir up a medicine man quicker'n women, and the facts pointed that way. When I talked it over with him in a fatherly way he got wrathy, and I had to take him out on the bank and give him a threshing. Then he got sulky, and didn't brighten up till we ran into the mouth of the Reindeer River, where a camp of Siwashes were fishing salmon. But he had it in for me all the time, only I didn't know it—was ready any time to give me the double cross.

'Now, there's no denying he's got a taking way with women. All he has to do is to whistle 'em up like dogs. Most remarkable faculty, that. There was the wickedest, prettiest squaw among the Reindeers. Never saw her beat, excepting Bella. Well, I guess he whistled her up, for he delayed in the camp longer than was necessary. Being partial to women—'

'That will do, Mr Bishop,' interrupted the chairman, who, from profitless watching of Frona's immobile face, had turned to her hand, the nervous twitching and clinching of which revealed what her face had hidden. 'That will do, Mr Bishop. I think we have had enough of squaws.'

'Pray do not temper the testimony,' Frona chirruped, sweetly. 'It seems very important.'

'Do you know what I am going to say next?' Del demanded hotly of the chairman. 'You don't, eh? Then shut up. I'm running this particular sideshow.'

Bill Brown sprang in to avert hostilities, but the chairman restrained himself, and Bishop went on.

'I'd been done with the whole shooting-match, squaws and all, if you hadn't broke me off. Well, as I said, he had it in for me, and the first thing I didn't know, he'd hit me on the head with a rifle-stock, bundled the squaw into the canoe, and pulled out. You all know what the Yukon country was in '84. And there I was, without an outfit, left alone, a thousand miles from anywhere. I got out all right, though there's no need of telling how, and so did he. You've all heard of his adventures in Siberia. Well,' with an impressive pause, 'I happen to know a thing or two myself.'

He shoved a hand into the big pocket of his mackinaw jacket and pulled out a dingy leather-bound volume of venerable appearance.

'I got this from Pete Whipple's old woman—Whipple of Eldorado. It concerns her grand-uncle or great-grand-uncle, I don't know which; and if there's anybody here can read Russian, why, it'll go into the details of that Siberian trip. But as there's no one here that can—'

'Courbertin! He can read it!' someone called in the crowd.

A way was made for the Frenchman forthwith, and he was pushed and shoved, protestingly, to the front.

'Savve the lingo?' Del demanded.

'Yes; but so poorly, so miserable,' Courbertin demurred. 'It is a long time. I forget.'

'Go ahead. We won't criticise.'

'No, but—'

'Go ahead!' the chairman commanded.

Del thrust the book into his hands, opened at the yellow title-page. 'I've been itching to get my paws on some buck like you for months and months,' he assured him, gleefully. 'And now I've got you, you can't shake me, Charley. So fire away.'

Courbertin began hesitatingly : ' " *The Journal of Father Yakontsk, Comprising an Account in Brief of his Life in the Benedictine Monastery at Obidorsky, and in full of his*

234

Marvellous Adventures in East Siberia among the Deer Men."'

The baron looked up for instructions.

'Tell us when it was printed,' Del ordered him.

'In Warsaw, 1807.'

The pocket-miner turned triumphantly to the room. 'Did you hear that? Just keep track of it. 1807, remember!'

The baron took up the opening paragraph. '*"It was because of Tamerlane,"'* he commenced, unconsciously putting his translation into a construction with which he was already familiar.

At his first words Frona turned white, and she remained white throughout the reading. Once she stole a glance at her father, and was glad that he was looking straight before him, for she did not feel able to meet his gaze just then. On the other hand, though she knew St Vincent was eying her narrowly, she took no notice of him, and all he could see was a white face devoid of expression.

'*"When Tamerlane swept with fire and sword over Eastern Asia,"'* Courbertin read slowly, '*" states were disrupted, cities overthrown, and tribes scattered like— like star-dust. A vast people was hurled broadcast over the land. Fleeing before the conquerors,"*—no, no—*" before the mad lust of the conquerors, these refugees swung far into Siberia, circling, circling to the north and east and fringing the rim of the polar basin with a spray of Mongol tribes."'*

'Skip a few pages,' Bill Brown advised, 'and read here and there. We haven't got all night.'

Courbertin complied. '*"The coast people are Eskimo stock, merry of nature and not offensive. They call themselves the Oukilion, or the Sea Men. From them I bought dogs and food. But they are subject to the Chow Chuen, who live in the interior and are known as the Deer Men. The Chow Chuen are a fierce and savage race. When I left the coast they fell upon me, took from me my goods, and made me a slave."'* He ran over a few pages. '*" I worked my way to a seat among the head men, but I was no nearer my freedom. My wisdom was of too great value to them for me to depart ... Old Pi-Une was a great chief, and it was decreed that I should marry his daughter Ilswunga. Ilswunga was a filthy creature. She would not*

235

bathe, and her ways were not good. . . . I did marry Ilswunga, but she was a wife to me only in name. Then did she complain to her father, the old Pi-Une, and he was very wroth. And dissension was sown among the tribes; but in the end I became mightier than ever, what of my cunning and resource; and Ilswunga made no more complaint, for I taught her games with cards which she might play by herself, and other things." '

'Is that enough?' Courbertin asked.

'Yes, that will do,' Bill Brown answered. 'But one moment. Please state again the date of publication.'

'1807, in Warsaw.'

'Hold on, baron,' Del Bishop spoke up. 'Now that you're on the stand, I've got a question or so to slap into you.' He turned to the court-room. 'Gentlemen, you've all heard somewhat of the prisoner's experiences in Siberia. You've caught on to the remarkable sameness between them and those published by Father Yakontsk, nearly a hundred years ago. And you have concluded that there's been some wholesale cribbing somewhere. I propose to show you that it's more that cribbing. The prisoner gave me the shake on the Reindeer River in '88. Fall of '88 he was at St Michael's, on his way to Siberia. '89 and '90 he was, by his talk, cutting up antics in Siberia. '91 he came back to the world, working the conquering-hero graft in 'Frisco. Now let's see if the Frenchman can make us wise.

'You were in Japan?' he asked.

Courbertin, who had followed the dates, made a quick calculation, and could but illy conceal his surprise. He looked appealingly to Frona, but she did not help him. 'Yes,' he said, finally.

'And you met the prisoner there?'

'Yes.'

'What year was it?'

There was a general craning forward to catch the answer. '1889,' and it came unwillingly.

'Now, how can that be, baron?' Del asked in a wheedling tone. 'The prisoner was in Siberia at that time.'

Courbertin shrugged his shoulders that it was no concern of his, and came off the stand. An impromptu recess was taken by the court-room for several minutes, wherein

236

there was much whispering and shaking of heads.

'It is all a lie.' St Vincent leaned close to Frona's ear, but she did not hear.

'Appearances are against me, but I can explain it all.'

But she did not move a muscle, and he was called to the stand by the chairman. She turned to her father, and the tears rushed up into her eyes when he rested his hand on hers.

'Do you care to pull out?' he asked after a momentary hesitation.

She shook her head, and St Vincent began to speak. It was the same story he had told her, though told now a little more fully, and in nowise did it conflict with the evidence of La Flitche and John. He acknowledged the wash-tub incident, caused, he explained, by an act of simple courtesy on his part and by John Borg's unreasoning anger. He acknowledged that Bella had been killed by his own pistol, but stated that the pistol had been borrowed by Borg several days previously and not returned. Concerning Bella's accusation he could say nothing. He could not see why she should die with a lie on her lips. He had never in the slightest way incurred her displeasure, so even revenge could not be advanced. It was inexplicable. As for the testimony of Bishop, he did not care to discuss it. It was a tissue of falsehood cunningly interwoven with truth. It was true the man had gone into Alaska with him in 1888, but his version of the things which happened there was maliciously untrue. Regarding the baron, there was a slight mistake in the dates, that was all.

In questioning him, Bill Brown brought out one little surprise. From the prisoner's story, he had made a hard fight against the two mysterious men. 'If,' Brown asked, 'such were the case, how can you explain away the fact that you came out of the struggle unmarked? On examination of the body of John Borg, many bruises and contusions were noticeable. How is it, if you put up such a stiff fight, that you escaped being battered?'

St Vincent did not know, though he confessed to feeling stiff and sore all over. And it did not matter, anyway. He had killed neither Borg nor his wife, that much he did know.

Frona prefaced her argument to the meeting with a pity discourse on the sacredness of human life, the weaknesses and dangers of circumstantial evidence, and the rights of the accused wherever doubt arose. Then she plunged into the evidence, stripping off the superfluous and striving to confine herself to facts. In the first place, she denied that a motive for the deed had been shown. As it was, the introduction of such evidence was an insult to their intelligence, and she had sufficient faith in their manhood and perspicacity to know that such puerility would not sway them in the verdict they were to give.

And, on the other hand, in dealing with the particular points at issue, she denied that any intimacy had been shown to have existed between Bella and St Vincent; and she denied, further, that it had been shown that any intimacy had been attempted on the part of St Vincent. Viewed honestly, the wash-tub incident—the only evidence brought forward—was a laughable little affair, portraying how the simple courtesy of a gentleman might be misunderstood by a mad boor of a husband. She left it to their common sense; they were not fools.

They had striven to prove the prisoner bad-tempered. She did not need to prove anything of the sort concerning John Borg. They all knew his terrible fits of anger; they all knew that his temper was proverbial in the community; that it had prevented him having friends and had made him many enemies. Was it not very probable, therefore, that the masked men were two such enemies? As to what particular motive actuated these two men, she could not say; but it rested with them, the judges, to know whether in all Alaska there were or were not two men whom John Borg could have given cause sufficient for them to take his life.

Witness had testified that no traces had been found of these two men; but the witness had not testified that no traces had been found of St Vincent, Pierre La Flitche, or John the Swede. And there was no need for them so to testify. Everybody knew that no foot-marks were left when St Vincent ran up the trail, and when he came back with La Flitche and the other man. Everybody knew the condition of the trail, that it was a hard-packed groove in the ground, on which a soft moccasin could leave no impression; and that had the ice not gone down the river, no traces would have been left by the murderers in passing from and to the mainland.

At this juncture La Flitche nodded his head in approbation, and she went on.

Capital had been made out of the blood on St Vincent's hands. If they chose to examine the moccasins at that moment on the feet of Mr La Flitche, they would also find blood. That did not argue that Mr La Flitche had been a party to the shedding of the blood.

Mr Brown had drawn attention to the fact that the prisoner had not been bruised or marked in the savage encounter which had taken place. She thanked him for having done so. John Borg's body showed that it had been roughly used. He was a larger, stronger, heavier man than St Vincent. If, as charged, St Vincent had committed the murder, and necessarily, therefore, engaged in a struggle severe enough to bruise John Borg, how was it that he had come out unharmed? That was a point worthy of consideration.

Another one was, why did he run down the trail? It was inconceivable, if he had committed the murder, that he should, without dressing or preparation for escape, run towards the other cabins. It was, however, easily conceivable that he should take up the pursuit of the real murderers, and in the darkness—exhausted, breathless, and certainly somewhat excited—run blindly down the trail.

Her summing up was a strong piece of synthesis; and when she had done, the meeting applauded her roundly. But she was angry and hurt, for she knew the demonstration was for her sex rather than for her cause and the work she had done.

Bill Brown, somewhat of a shyster, and his ear ever cocked to the crowd, was not above taking advantage when opportunity offered, and when it did not offer, to dogmatise artfully. In this his native humour was a strong factor, and when he had finished with the mysterious masked men they were as exploded sun-myths—which phrase he promptly applied to them.

They could not have got off the island. The condition

239

of the ice for the three or four hours preceding the break-up would not have permitted it. The prisoner had implicated none of the residents of the island, while every one of them, with the exception of the prisoner, had been accounted for elsewhere. Possibly the prisoner was excited when he ran down the trail into the arms of La Flitche and John the Swede. One should have thought, however, that he had grown used to such things in Siberia. But that was immaterial; the facts were that he was undoubtedly in an abnormal state of excitement, that he was hysterically excited, and that a murderer under such circumstances would take little account of where he ran. Such things had happened before. Many a man had butted into his own retribution.

In the matter of the relations of Borg, Bella, and St Vincent, he made a strong appeal to the instinctive prejudices of his listeners, and for the time being abandoned matter-of-fact reasoning for all-potent sentimental platitudes. He granted that circumstantial evidence never proved anything absolutely. It was not necessary it should. Beyond the shadow of a reasonable doubt was all that was required. That this had been done, he went on to review his testimony.

'And, finally,' he said, 'you can't get around Bella's last words. We know nothing of our own direct knowledge. We've been feeling around in the dark, clutching at little things, and trying to figure it all out. But, gentlemen,' he paused, to search the faces of his listeners, 'Bella knew the truth. Hers is no circumstantial evidence. With quick, anguished breath, and life-blood ebbing from her, and eye-balls glazing, she spoke the truth. With dark night coming on, and the death-rattle in her throat, she raised herself weakly and pointed a shaking finger at the accused, thus, and she said, "Him, him, him. St Vincha, him do it." '

With Bill Brown's finger still boring into him, St Vincent struggled to his feet. His face looked old and grey, and he looked about him speechlessly. 'Funk! Funk!' was whispered back and forth, and not so softly but what he heard. He moistened his lips repeatedly, and his tongue fought for articulation. 'It is as I have said,' he succeeded, finally. 'I did not do it. Before God, I did not do it!' He stared fixedly at John the Swede, waiting the while on his laggard thought. 'I . . . I did not do it . . . I did not . . . I . . . I did not.'

He seemed to have become lost in some supreme meditation wherein John the Swede figured largely, and as Frona caught him by the hand and pulled him gently down, some man cried out, 'Secret ballot!'

But Bill Brown was on his feet at once. 'No! I say no! An open ballot! We are men, and as men are not afraid to put ourselves on record.'

A chorus of approval greeted him, and the open ballot began. Man after man, called upon by name, spoke the one word, 'Guilty.'

Baron Courbertin came forward and whispered to Frona. She nodded her head and smiled, and he edged his way back, taking up a position by the door. He voted 'Not guilty' when his turn came, as did Frona and Jacob Welse. Pierre La Flitche wavered a moment, looking keenly at Frona and St Vincent, then spoke up, clear and flute-like, 'Guilty.'

As the chairman arose, Jacob Welse casually walked over to the opposite side of the table and stood with his back to the stove. Courbertin, who had missed nothing, pulled a pickle-keg out from the wall and stepped upon it.

The chairman cleared his throat and rapped for order. 'Gentlemen,' he announced, 'the prisoner——'

'Hands up!' Jacob Welse commanded peremptorily, and a fraction of a second after him came the shrill 'Hands up, gentlemen!' of Courbertin.

Front and rear they commanded the crowd with their revolvers. Every hand was in the air, the chairman's having gone up still grasping the mallet. There was no disturbance. Each stood or sat in the same posture as when the command went forth. Their eyes, playing here and there among the central figure, always returned to Jacob Welse.

St Vincent sat as one dumbfounded. Frona thrust a revolver into his hand, but his limp fingers refused to close on it.

'Come, Gregory,' she entreated. 'Quick! Corliss is waiting with the canoe. Come!'

She shook him, and he managed to grip the weapon.

241

Then she pulled and tugged, as when awakening a heavy sleeper, till he was on his feet. But his face was livid, his eyes like a somnambulist's, and he was afflicted as with a palsy. Still holding him, she took a step backward for him to come on. He ventured it with a shaking knee. There was no sound save the heavy breathing of many men. A man coughed slightly and cleared his throat. It was disquieting, and all eyes centred upon him rebukingly. The man became embarrassed, and shifted his weight uneasily to the other leg. Then the heavy breathing settled down again.

St Vincent took another step, but his fingers relaxed, and the revolver fell with a loud noise to the floor. He made no effort to recover it. Frona stooped hurriedly, but Pierre La Flitche had set his foot upon it. She looked up and saw his hands above his head and his eyes fixed absently on Jacob Welse. She pushed at his leg, and the muscles were tense and hard, giving the lie to the indifference on his face. St Vincent looked down helplessly, as though he could not understand.

But this delay drew the attention of Jacob Welse, and, as he tried to make out the cause, the chairman found his chance. Without crooking, his right arm swept out and down, the heavy caulking-mallet leaping from his hand. It spanned the short distance and smote Jacob Welse below the ear. His revolver went off as he fell, and John the Swede grunted and clapped a hand to his thigh.

Simultaneous with this the baron was overcome. Del Bishop, with hands still above his head and eyes fixed innocently before him, had simply kicked the pickle-keg out from under the Frenchman and brought him to the floor. His bullet, however, sped harmlessly through the roof. La Flitche seized Frona in his arms. St Vincent, suddenly awakening, sprang for the door, but was tripped up by the breed's ready foot.

The chairman pounded the table with his fist and concluded his broken sentence, 'Gentlemen, the prisoner is found guilty as charged.'

CHAPTER XXIX

FRONA had gone at once to her father's side, but he was already recovering. Courbertin was brought forward with a scratched face, sprained wrist, and an insubordinate tongue. To prevent discussion and to save time, Bill Brown claimed the floor.

'Mr Chairman, while we condemn the attempt on the part of Jacob Welse, Frona Welse, and Baron Courbertin to rescue the prisoner and thwart justice, we cannot, under the circumstances, but sympathise with them. There is no need that I should go further into this matter. You all know, and doubtless, under a like situation, would have done the same. And so, in order that we may expeditiously finish the business, I make a motion to disarm the three prisoners and let them go.'

The motion was carried, and the two men searched for weapons. Frona was saved this by giving her word that she was no longer armed. The meeting then resolved itself into a hanging committee, and began to file out of the cabin.

'Sorry I had to do it,' the chairman said, half-apologetically, half-defiantly.

Jacob Welse smiled. 'You took your chance,' he answered, 'and I can't blame you. I only wish I'd got you, though.'

Excited voices arose from across the cabin. 'Here, you! Leggo!' 'Step on his fingers, Tim!' 'Break that grip!' 'Ouch! Ow!' 'Pry his mouth open!'

Frona saw a knot of struggling men about St Vincent, and ran over. He had thrown himself down on the floor and, tooth and nail, was fighting like a madman. Tim Dugan, a stalwart Celt, had come to close quarters with him, and St Vincent's teeth were sunk in the man's arm.

'Smash 'm, Tim! Smash 'm!'

'How can I, ye fule? Get a pry on his mouth, will ye?'

'One moment, please.' The men made way for her, drawing back and leaving St Vincent and Tim.

Frona knelt down by him. 'Leave go, Gregory. Do leave go.'

He looked up at her, and his eyes did not seem human. He breathed stertorously, and in his throat were the queer little gasping noises of one over-wrought.

'It is I, Gregory.' She brushed her hand soothingly across his brow. 'Don't you understand? It is I, Frona. Do leave go.'

His whole body slowly relaxed, and a peaceful expression grew upon his face. His jaw dropped, and the man's arm was withdrawn.

'Now listen, Gregory. Though you are to die—'

'But I cannot! I cannot!' he groaned. 'You said that I could trust to you, that all would come well.'

She thought of the chance which had been given, but said nothing.

'Oh, Frona! Frona!' He sobbed and buried his face in her lap.

'At least you can be a man. It is all that remains.'

'Come on!' Tim Dugan commanded. 'Sorry to bother ye, miss, but we've got to fetch 'm along. Drag 'm out, you fellys! Catch 'm by the legs, Blackey, and you, too, Johnson.'

St Vincent's body stiffened at the words, the rational gleam went out of his eyes, and his fingers closed spasmodically on Frona's. She looked entreaty at the men, and they hesitated.

'Give me a minute with him,' she begged, 'just a minute.'

'He ain't worth it,' Dugan sneered, after they had drawn apart. 'Look at 'm.'

'It's a damned shame,' corroborated Blackey, squinting sidewise at Frona whispering in St Vincent's ear, the while her hand wandered caressingly through his hair.

What she said they did not hear, but she got him on his feet and led him forward. He walked as a dead man might walk, and when he entered the open air gazed forth wonderingly upon the muddy sweep of the Yukon. The crowd had formed by the bank, about a pine tree. A boy, engaged in running a rope over one of the branches, finished his task and slid down the trunk to the ground. He looked quickly at the palms of his hands and blew upon them, and a laugh went up. A couple of wolf-dogs, on the outskirts, bristled up to each other and bared their fangs. Men encouraged them. They closed in and rolled over, but were kicked aside to make room for St Vincent.

Corliss came up the bank to Frona. 'What's up?' he whispered. 'Is it off?'

She tried to speak, but swallowed and nodded her head.

'This way, Gregory.' She touched his arm and guided him to the box beneath the rope.

Corliss, keeping step with them, looked over the crowd speculatively and felt into his jacket-pocket. 'Can I do anything?' he asked, gnawing his under lip impatiently. 'Whatever you say goes, Frona. I can stand them off.'

She looked at him, aware of pleasure in the sight. She knew he would dare it, but she knew also that it would be unfair. St Vincent had had his chance, and it was not right that further sacrifice should be made. 'No, Vance. It is too late. Nothing can be done.'

'At least let me try,' he persisted.

'No; it is not our fault that our plan failed, and . . . and . . .' Her eyes filled. 'Please do not ask it of me.'

'Then let me take you away. You cannot remain here.'

'I must,' she answered, simply, and turned to St Vincent, who seemed dreaming.

Blackey was tying the hangman's knot in the rope's end, preparatory to slipping the noose over St Vincent's head.

'Kiss me, Gregory,' she said, her hand on his arm.

He started at the touch, and saw all eager eyes centred upon him, and the yellow noose, just shaped, in the hands of the hangman. He threw up his arms, as though to ward it off, and cried loudly, 'No! no! Let me confess! Let me tell the truth, then you'll believe me!'

Bill Brown and the chairman shoved Blackey back, and the crowd gathered in. Cries and protestations rose from its midst. 'No, you don't,' a boy's shrill voice made itself heard. 'I'm not going to go. I climbed the tree and made the rope fast, and I've got a right to stay.' 'You're only a kid,' replied a man's voice, 'and it ain't good for you.' 'I don't care, and I'm not a kid. I'm—I'm used to such things. And, anyway, I climbed the tree. Look at my hands.'

245

'Of course he can stay,' other voices took up the trouble. 'Leave him alone, Curley.' 'You ain't the whole thing.' A laugh greeted this, and things quieted down.

'Silence!' the chairman called, and then to St Vincent, 'Go ahead, you, and don't take all day about it.'

'Give us a chance to hear!' the crowd broke out again. 'Put 'm on the box! Put 'm on the box!' St Vincent was helped up, and began with eager volubility.

'I didn't do it, but I saw it done. There weren't two men—only one. He did it, and Bella helped him.'

A wave of laughter drowned him out.

'Not so fast,' Bill Brown cautioned him. 'Kindly explain how Bella helped this man kill herself. Begin at the beginning.'

'That night, before he turned in, Borg set his burglar-alarm—'

'Burglar alarm?'

'That's what I called it—a tin bread-pan attached to the latch so the door couldn't open without tumbling it down. He set it every night, as though he were afraid of what might happen—the very thing which did happen, for that matter. On the night of the murder I awoke with the feeling that someone was moving around. The slush-lamp was burning low, and I saw Bella at the door. Borg was snoring; I could hear him plainly. Bella was taking down the bread-pan, and she exercised great care about it. Then she opened the door, and an Indian came in softly. He had no mask, and I should know him if ever I see him again, for a scar ran along the forehead and down over one eye.'

'I suppose you sprang out of bed and gave the alarm?'

'No, I didn't,' St Vincent answered, with a defiant toss of the head, as though he might as well get the worst over with. 'I just lay there and waited.'

'What did you think?'

'That Bella was in collusion with the Indian, and that Borg was to be murdered. It came to me at once.'

'And you did nothing?'

'Nothing.' His voice sank, and his eyes dropped to Frona, leaning against the box beneath him and steadying it. She did not seem to be affected. 'Bella came over to me, but I closed my eyes and breathed regularly. She held the slush-

246

lamp to me, but I played sleep naturally enough to fool her. Then I heard a snort of sudden awakening and alarm and a cry, and I looked out. The Indian was hacking at Borg with a knife, and Borg was warding off with his arms and trying to grapple him. When they did grapple, Bella crept up from behind and threw her arm in a stranglehold about her husband's neck. She put her knee into the small of his back, and bent him backward and, with the Indian helping, threw him to the floor.'

'And what did you do?'

'I watched.'

'Had you a revolver?'

'Yes.'

'The one you previously said John Borg had borrowed?'

'Yes! but I watched.'

'Did John Borg call for help?'

'Yes.'

'Can you give his words?'

'He called, "St Vincent! Oh, St Vincent! Oh, my God! Oh, St Vincent, help me!"' He shuddered at the recollection, and added, 'It was terrible.'

'I should say so,' Brown grunted. 'And you?'

'I watched,' was the dogged reply, while a groan went up from the crowd. 'Borg shook clear of them, however, and got on his legs. He hurled Bella across the cabin with a back-sweep of the arm and turned upon the Indian. Then they fought. The Indian had dropped the knife, and the sound of Borg's blows was sickening. I thought he would surely beat the Indian to death. That was when the furniture was smashed. They rolled and snarled and struggled like wild beasts. I wondered the Indian's chest did not cave in under some of Borg's blows. But Bella got the knife and stabbed her husband repeatedly about the body. The Indian had clinched with him, and his arms were not free; so he kicked out at her sideways. He must have broken her legs, for she cried out and fell down, and though she tried, she never stood up again. Then he went down, with the Indian under him, across the stove.'

'Did he call any more for help?'

'He begged me to come to him.'

'And?'

'I watched. He managed to get clear of the Indian and staggered over to me. He was streaming blood, and I could see he was very weak. "Give me your gun," he said; "quick, give me it." He felt around blindly. Then his mind seemed to clear a bit, and he reached across me to the holster hanging on the wall and took the pistol. The Indian came at him with the knife again, but he did not try to defend himself. Instead, he went on towards Bella, with the Indian still hanging to him and hacking at him. The Indian seemed to bother and irritate him, and he shoved him away. He knelt down and turned Bella's face up to the light; but his own face was covered with blood, and he could not see. So he stopped long enough to brush the blood from his eyes. He appeared to look in order to make sure. Then he put the revolver to her breast and fired.

'The Indian went wild at this, and rushed at him with the knife, at the same time knocking the pistol out of his hand. It was then the shelf with the slush-lamp was knocked down. They continued to fight in the darkness, and there were more shots fired, though I do not know by whom. I crawled out of the bunk, but they struck against me in their struggles, and I fell over Bella. That's when the blood got on my hands. As I ran out the door, more shots were fired. Then I met La Flitche and John, and . . . and you know the rest. This is the truth I have told you, I swear it!'

He looked down at Frona. She was steadying the box, and her face was composed. He looked out over the crowd and saw unbelief. Many were laughing.

'Why did you not tell this story at first?' Bill Brown demanded.

'Because . . . because . . .'

'Well?'

'Because I might have helped.'

There was more laughter at this, and Bill Brown turned away from him. 'Gentlemen, you have heard this pipe dream. It is a wilder fairy story than his first. At the beginning of the trial we promised to show that the truth was not in him. That we succeeded, your verdict is ample testimony. But that he should likewise succeed, and more brilliantly, we did not expect. That he has, you cannot doubt. What do you think of him? Lie upon lie he has

248

given us; he has been proven a chronic liar; are you to believe this last and fearfully impossible lie? Gentlemen, I can only ask that you reaffirm your judgment. And to those who may doubt his mendacity—surely there are but few—let me state, that if his story is true; if he broke salt with this man, John Borg, and lay in his blankets while murder was done; if he did hear, unmoved, the voice of the man calling to him for help; if he did lie there and watch that carnival of butchery without his manhood prompting him—let me state, gentlemen, I say, let me state that he is none the less deserveful of hanging. We cannot make a mistake. What shall it be?'

'Death!' 'String him up!' 'Stretch 'm!' were the cries.

But the crowd suddenly turned its attention to the river, and even Blackey refrained from his official task. A large raft, worked by a sweep at either end, was slipping past the tail of Split-up Island, close to the shore. When it was at their feet, its nose was slewed into the bank, and while its free end swung into the stream to make the consequent circle, a snubbing-rope was flung ashore and several turns taken about the tree under which St Vincent stood. A cargo of moose-meat, red and raw, cut into quarters, peeped from beneath a cool covering of spruce boughs. And because of this, the two men on the raft looked up to those on the bank with pride in their eyes.

'Tryin' to make Dawson with it,' one of them explained, 'and the sun's all-fired hot.'

'Nope,' said his comrade, in reply to a query, 'don't care to stop and trade. It's worth a dollar and a half a pound below, and we're hustlin' to get there. But we've got some pieces of a man we want to leave with you.' He turned and pointed to a loose heap of blankets which slightly disclosed the form of a man beneath. 'We gathered him in this mornin', 'bout thirty mile up the Stewart, I should judge.'

'Stands in need of doctorin',' the other man spoke up, 'and the meat's spoilin', and we ain't got time for nothin'.'

'Beggar don't have anythin' to say. Don't savve the burro.'

'Looks as he might have been mixin' things with a grizzly or something',—all battered and gouged. Injured internally, from the looks of it. Where'll you have him?'

Frona, standing by St Vincent, saw the injured man borne over the crest of the bank and through the crowd. A bronzed hand drooped down and a bronzed face showed from out the blankets. The bearers halted near them while a decision could be reached as to where he should be carried. Frona felt a sudden fierce grip on her arm.

'Look! look!' St Vincent was leaning forward and pointing wildly at the injured man. 'Look! That scar!'

The Indian opened his eyes, and a grin of recognition distorted his face.

'It is he! It is he!' St Vincent, trembling with eagerness, turned upon the crowd. 'I call you all to witness! That is the man who killed John Borg!'

No laughter greeted this, for there was a terrible earnestness in his manner. Bill Brown and the chairman tried to make the Indian talk, but could not. A miner from British Columbia was pressed into service, but his Chinook made no impression. Then La Flitche was called. The handsome breed bent over the man and talked in gutturals which only his mother's heredity made possible. It sounded all one, yet it was apparent that he was trying many tongues. But no response did he draw, and he paused disheartened. As though with sudden recollection, he made another attempt. At once a gleam of intelligence shot across the Indian's face, and his larynx vibrated to similar sounds.

'It is the Stick talk of the Upper White,' La Flitche stopped long enough to explain.

Then, with knit brows and stumbling moments when he sought dim-remembered words, he plied the man with questions. To the rest it was like a pantomime—the meaningless grunts and waving arms and facial expressions of puzzlement, surprise, and understanding. At times a passion wrote itself on the face of the Indian, and a sympathy on the face of La Flitche. Again, by look and gesture, St Vincent was referred to, and once a sober, mirthless laugh shaped the mouths of them.

'So? It is good,' La Flitche said, when the Indian's head dropped back. 'This man make true talk. He come from White River, way up. He cannot understand. He surprised very much, so many white men. He never think so many white men in the world. He die soon. His name Gow.

'Long time ago, three year, this man John Borg go to this man Gow's country. He hunt, he bring plenty meat to the camp, wherefore White River Sticks like him. Gow have one squaw, Pisk-ku. Bime-by John Borg make preparation to go 'way. He go to Gow, and he say, "Give me your squaw. We trade. For her I give you many things." But Gow say no. Pisk-ku good squaw. No woman sew moccasin like she. She tan moose-skin the best, and make the softest leather. He like Pisk-ku. Then John Borg say he don't care; he want Pisk-ku. Then they have a *skookum* big fight, and Pisk-ku go 'way with John Borg. She no want to go 'way, but she go anyway. Borg call her "Bella," and give her plenty good things, but she like Gow all the time.' La Flitche pointed to the scar which ran down the forehead and past the eye of the Indian. 'John Borg he do that.

'Long time Gow pretty near die. Then he get well, but his head sick. He don't know nobody. Don't know his father, his mother, or anything. Just like a little baby, just like that. Then one day, quick, click! something snap, and his head get well all at once. He know his father and mother, he remember Pisk-ku, he remember everything. His father say John Borg go down river. Then Gow go down river. Springtime, ice very bad. He very much afraid, so many white men, and when he come to this place he travel by night. Nobody see him 'tall, but he see everybody. He like a cat, see in the dark. Somehow, he come straight to John Borg's cabin. He do not know how this was, except that the work he had to do was good work.'

St Vincent pressed Frona's hand, but she shook her fingers clear and withdrew a step.

'He see Pisk-ku feed the dogs, and he have talk with her. That night he come and she open the door. Then you know that which was done. St Vincent do nothing. Borg kill Bella. Gow kill Borg. Borg kill Gow, for Gow die pretty quick. Borg have strong arm. Gow sick inside, all smashed up. Gow no care; Pisk-ku dead.

'After that he go 'cross ice to the land. I tell him all you people say it cannot be; no man can cross the ice at that time. He laugh, and say that it is, and what is, must be. Anyway, he have very hard time, but he get 'cross all right. He very sick inside. Bime-by he cannot walk; he

251

crawl. Long time he come to Stewart River. Can go no more, so he lay down to die. Two white men find him and bring him to this place. He don't care. He die anyway.'

La Flitche finished abruptly, but nobody spoke. Then he added, 'I think Gow damn good man.'

Frona came up to Jacob Welse. 'Take me away, father,' she said. 'I am so tired.'

CHAPTER XXX

NEXT morning, Jacob Welse, for all of the Company and his millions in mines, chopped up the day's supply of firewood, lighted a cigar, and went down the island in search of Baron Courbertin. Frona finished the breakfast dishes, hung out the robes to air, and fed the dogs. Then she took a worn Wordsworth from her clothes-bag, and, out by the bank settled herself comfortably in a seat formed by two uprooted pines. But she did no more than open the book; for her eyes strayed out and over the Yukon to the eddy below the bluffs, and the bend above, and the tail of the spit which lay in the midst of the river. The rescue and the race were still fresh with her, though there were strange lapses, here and there, of which she remembered little.

The struggle by the fissure was immeasurable; she knew not how long it lasted; and the race down Split-up to Roubeau Island was a thing of which her reason convinced her, but of which she recollected nothing.

The whim seized her, and she followed Corliss through the three days' events, but she tacitly avoided the figure of another man whom she would not name. Something terrible was connected therewith, she knew, which must be faced sooner or later; but she preferred to put that moment away from her. She was stiff and sore of mind as well as of body, and will and action were for the time being distasteful. It was more pleasant, even, to dwell on Tommy, on Tommy of the bitter tongue and craven heart; and she made a note that the wife and children in Toronto should not be forgotten when the Northland paid its dividends to the Welse.

The crackle of a foot on a dead willow-twig roused her, and her eyes met St Vincent's.

'You have not congratulated me upon my escape,' he began, breezily. 'But you must have been dead-tired last night. I know I was. And you had that hard pull on the river besides.'

He watched her furtively, trying to catch some cue as to her attitude and mood.

'You're a heroine, that's what you are, Frona,' he began again, with exuberance. 'And not only did you save the mail-man, but by the delay you wrought in the trial you saved me. If one more witness had gone on the stand that first day, I should have been duly hanged before Gow put in an appearance. Fine chap, Gow. Too bad he's going to die.'

'I am glad that I could be of help,' she replied, wondering the while what she could say.

'And of course I am to be congratulated—'

'Your trial is hardly a thing for congratulation,' she spoke up quickly, looking him straight in the eyes for the moment. 'I am glad that it came out as it did, but surely you cannot expect me to congratulate you.'

'O-o-o,' with long-drawn inflection. 'So that's where it pinches.' He smiled good-humouredly, and moved as though to sit down, but she made no room for him, and he remained standing. 'I can certainly explain. If there have been women—'

Frona had been clinching her hand nervously, but at the word burst out in laughter.

'Women?' she queried. 'Women?' she repeated. 'Do not be ridiculous, Gregory.'

'After the way you stood by me through the trial,' he began, reproachfully, 'I thought—'

'Oh, you do not understand,' she said, hopelessly. 'You do not understand. Look at me, Gregory, and see if I can make you understand. Your presence is painful to me. Your kisses hurt me. The memory of them still burns my cheek, and my lips feel unclean. And why? Because of women, which you may explain away? How little do you understand! But shall I tell you?'

Voices of men came to her from down the river bank, and the splashing of water. She glanced quickly and saw Del Bishop guiding a poling-boat against the current, and Corliss on the bank, bending to the tow-rope.

'Shall I tell you why, Gregory St Vincent?' she said again. 'Tell you why your kisses have cheapened me? Because you broke the faith of food and blanket. Because

254

you broke salt with a man, and then watched that man fight unequally for life without lifting your hand. Why, I had rather you had died in defending him; the memory of you would have been good. Yes, I had rather you had killed him yourself. At least, it would have shown there was blood in your body.'

'So this is what you would call love?' he began, scornfully, his fretting, fuming devil beginning to rouse. 'A fair-weather love, truly. But, Lord, how we men learn!'

'I had thought you were well lessoned,' she retorted; 'what of the other women?'

'But what do you intend to do?' he demanded, taking no notice. 'I am not an easy man to cross. You cannot throw me over with impunity. I shall not stand for it, I warn you. You have dared do things in this country which would blacken you were they known. I have ears. I have not been asleep. You will find it no child's play to explain away things which you may declare most innocent.'

She looked at him with a smile which carried pity in its cold mirth, and it goaded him.

'I am down, a thing to make a jest upon, a thing to pity, but I promise you that I can drag you with me. My kisses have cheapened you, eh? Then how must you have felt at Happy Camp on the Dyea Trail?'

As though in answer, Corliss swung down upon them with the tow-rope.

Frona beckoned a greeting to him. 'Vance,' she said, 'the mail-carrier has brought important news to father, so important that he must go outside. He starts this afternoon with Baron Courbertin in *La Bijou*. Will you take me down to Dawson? I should like to go at once, today.

'He . . . he suggested you,' she added shyly, indicating St Vincent.